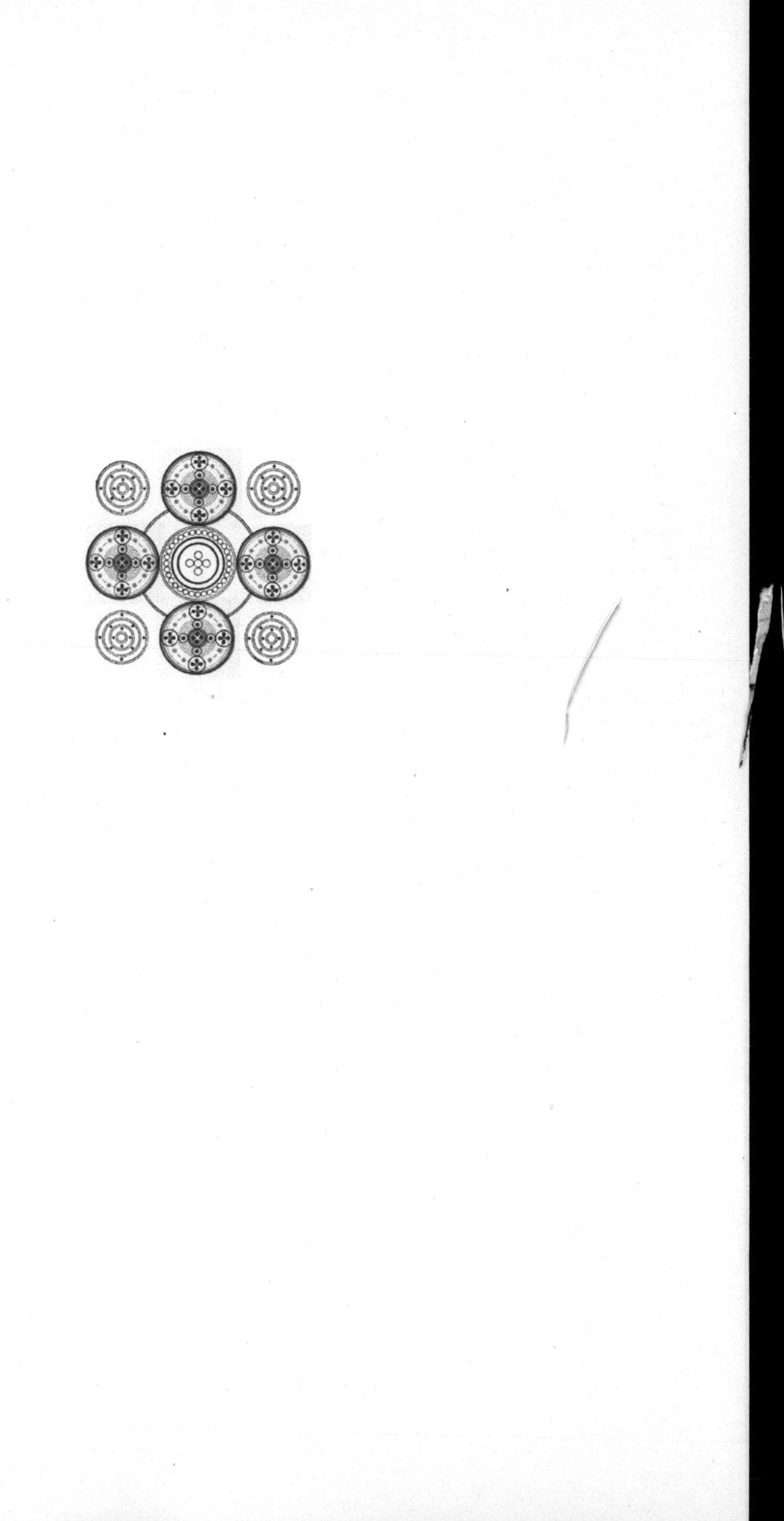

Also by Daniel H. Wilson

Robopocalypse
Amped

A Boy and His Bot
Bro-Jitsu
The Mad Scientist Hall of Fame
How to Build a Robot Army
Where's My Jetpack?
How to Survive a Robot Uprising

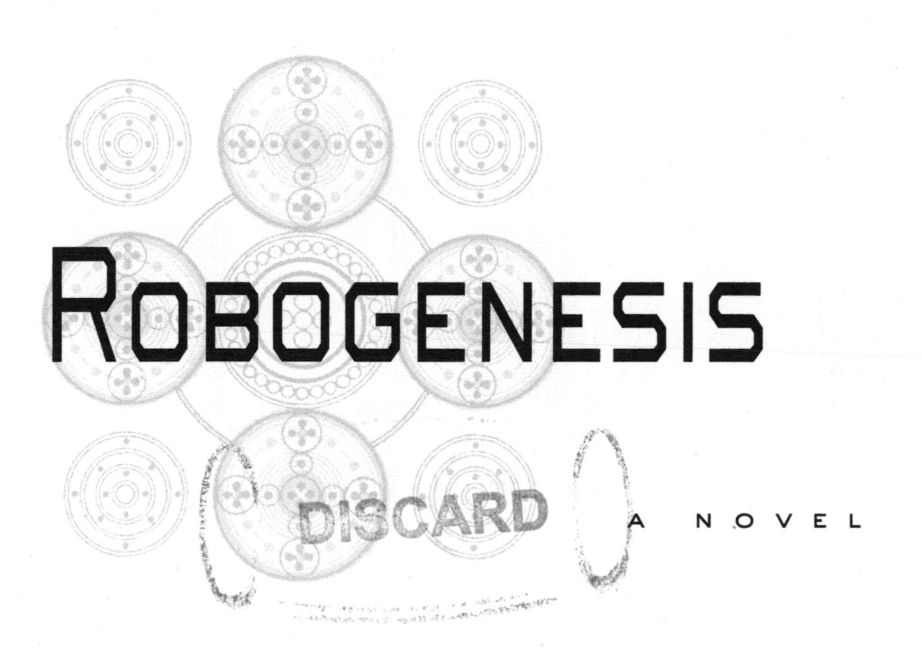

ROBOGENESIS

A NOVEL

DANIEL H. WILSON

DOUBLEDAY • NEW YORK • LONDON • TORONTO • SYDNEY • AUCKLAND

This book is a work of fiction. Names, characters, businesses, organizations, places, events, and incidents either are the product of the author's imagination or are used fictitiously. Any resemblance to actual persons, living or dead, events, or locales is entirely coincidental.

www.doubleday.com

DOUBLEDAY and the portrayal of an anchor with a dolphin are registered trademarks of Random House LLC.

Grateful acknowledgment is made to Sony/ATV Music Publishing LLC for permission to reprint an excerpt from "Mama Tried," written by Merle Haggard, copyright © 1968 by Sony/ATV Music Publishing LLC. All rights administered by Sony/ATV Music Publishing LLC, 8 Music Square West, Nashville, TN 37203. All rights reserved. Reprinted by permission.

Jacket design by Will Staehle
Jacket photograph © Maksim Toome / Shutterstock

Library of Congress Cataloging-in-Publication Data
Wilson, Daniel H. (Daniel Howard).
Robogenesis : a novel / Daniel H. Wilson. — First edition.
pages cm
1. Robots—Fiction. 2. Artificial intelligence—Fiction. I. Title.
PS3623.I57796R53 2014
813'.6—dc23
2014000720

ISBN 978-0-385-53709-4 (hardcover) ISBN 978-0-385-53710-0 (eBook)

MANUFACTURED IN THE UNITED STATES OF AMERICA

10 9 8 7 6 5 4 3 2 1

First Edition

For Conrad

If an intelligence, at a given instant, knew all the forces that animate nature and the position of each constituent being; if, moreover, this intelligence were sufficiently great to submit these data to analysis, it could embrace in the same formula the movements of the greatest bodies in the universe and those of the smallest atoms: to this intelligence nothing would be uncertain, and the future, as the past, would be present to its eyes.

—Pierre-Simon Laplace, 1814

Contents

PART ONE • LARK IRON CLOUD

PART TWO • MATHILDA PEREZ

PART THREE • CORMAC WALLACE

PART ONE
Lark Iron Cloud

The first thing I remember knowing,
was a lonesome whistle blowing,
And a young un's dream of
growing up to ride,
On a freight train leaving town, not
knowing where I'm bound,
And no one could change my
mind, but Mama tried.

—Merle Haggard, 1968

Briefing

Strange things grow in the fog of war. We lost sight of the world while we were in the trenches. Now that it's over, I figure I've got to tell the story of the thing just to understand what it was.

In its last days, the thinking machine known as Archos R-14 was trying to know humanity. It mastered the art of capturing a human mind. When it died, it left behind the tools. I found stories trapped in patterns of neurons. Using scavenged hardware, I took three accounts straight from three minds and I lined them up from beginning to end and back again. Three times to tell it. Three times to understand.

They say history is written by the victors, but this right here is told by its victims.

My name is Arayt Shah, and this is the story of how I won the True War.

—Arayt Shah

I. Parasite

New War: Final Minutes

In the last moments of the New War, the enemy Archos R-14 resorted to ruthless tactics. As exhausted allied soldiers finally reached the Ragnorak Intelligence Fields where Archos R-14 had buried itself, they were met with a nasty counterattack: scuttling, crablike machines that mounted the bodies of fallen soldiers. With titanium limbs buried in dead or dying flesh, soldier corpses rose again. These parasites dealt terrible damage to the bodies and minds of the living . . . but what was left behind when the battle ended was Archos R-14's most horrific contribution to the True War.

—Arayt Shah

NEURONAL ID: LARK IRON CLOUD

There was no way to win this war and we all knew it, but we marched anyway.

I shove my checkerboard scarf deeper into my parka and hold my breath. Kneeling on the ice-kissed turf, I brace against a tree and press the cold rims of binocular-enhanced goggles against my face. The situation has well and truly gone to shit here in the godforsaken woods of western Alaska.

The New War started when a thinking machine we call Big Rob turned our tools against us. In the madness of Zero Hour, some of us in Oklahoma found refuge with the Osage Nation. We survivors fell back to the rural town of Gray Horse and counted our lucky stars. But the machines evolved. Over months and years they crossed the Great Plains, slithered through the waving grass, and climbed our stone bluffs.

So we fought then. And we fight now.

Our bullets are chasing each other through black tree branches, tracers streaking like falling stars. The last lines of our walking tanks are arrayed defensively, spotlights glowing bright in the twilight, each four-legged hulk a pool of light spaced a half klick from its brothers and hunkered down to provide cover for ground forces. Dark enemy fire is whining out of the woods like mosquitoes. Most of their rounds are a flesh-burrowing variety called pluggers, but waves of exploding crawlers called stumpers are also skittering toward us.

Letting the goggles flop on my neck, I get moving. My collar radio is hissing with cavalry calls from squads scattered over the rough countryside. Scrambling low through the trees, I ignore the clipped cries for help and head toward Beta squad. There are no reinforcements. There is nothing left now but metal and snow and blood.

"Come in, Lonnie," I pant into my radio. "You there?"

"Go ahead," comes the reply.

The voice is measured and calm. It belongs to Lonnie Wayne Blanton, an old cowboy who happens to be our general. The man is important to me. He saved my life and put me on the right path and now I'm trying to figure out how in the hell to tell him that it was all for nothing.

"All squads pinned down. Things are royally fucked. Moving to support Beta."

"Roger," says Lonnie. A pause. "Hold on. Long as you can."

"Thank you," I radio back. "Thank you for everything."

We made it this far only by reverse-engineering the enemy's weapons. Gray Horse Army was able to march to within a thousand-mile perimeter of Big Rob. We left our blood splashed in the woods and we kept on marching. We broke the five-hundred-mile perimeter over the screaming of fallen soldiers. And here at the one-hundred-mile perimeter our force has splintered and broken and now we have lost everything.

All we have left to fight for now is each other.

Ducking stray fire, I close in on Beta squad's position. The soldiers are back-to-back at the edge of a clearing. Most are lost in the dusky light, but I see right away that my brainboy Carl is on his ass. The engineer is whimpering and clawing and kicking his way backward through the snow.

"Carl," I shout. "On your feet."

I lean for him and he keeps moaning and struggling. He is under my command, but my soldier won't look at me and he won't take my hand and I can't figure out why until I notice his eyes.

Not where he's looking. But where he *won't* look.

Something black crawling low and fast on too many legs. And another one. They're starting to come up from under the snow by the dozens.

Too late.

I don't feel the pincers at first. Just this strong pressure on the base of my neck. I'm in a hydraulic-powered bear hug. I spin around in the slushy snow but there's nobody behind me.

Whatever-it-is has climbed up my back and got a good hold. My knees sag with the lurching weight of it. Crooked black feelers reach around my chest and my spine is on fire as the thing decides to dig in, a bundle of squirming razor blades. This is a whole new hell I've never felt before.

Shit shit shit—what is this that it hurts so *damn much?*

Carl's got his frost-plated rifle up, training it on me. The gun strap hangs stiff and crusty in the arctic breeze. Around us, my soldiers are screaming and dancing in tight, panicked circles, trying to shake off their own monsters. Some are running. But me and the engineer are having our own little moment here.

"Carl," I wheeze. "No."

My voice sounds hollow from the pain of whatever has gotten between my shoulder blades. Judging from Carl's blank face, I figure that I'm not in a very happy spot. No, sir. That is a full-on nega-*tory*.

Carl lets go of his rifle entirely and the strap catches on his forearm. He stumbles away, gun dangling. Wipes his eyes with shaking fingers, tendons streaking the backs of his hands. His complicated engineering helmet falls off and thunks into the snow, just an empty bowl.

"Lark," he says. "Ah, Lark, I'm sorry."

He's *crying*. I could give a shit.

I'm being flayed alive, straining and groaning against black spider legs gripping my body, doing drunken pirouettes in the slush. Knotty black arms are slicing into the meat of my thighs, sprouting smaller feelers like barbs. Others grip my biceps, elbows, forearms, and even my fingers.

I am in command but I am most definitely not in control. Some of my soldiers are still thrashing in the shadows. Some aren't. The wounded are crawling and hobbling away as fast as they can, coiled black shapes slicing toward them like scorpions.

Dammit, I'm sorry, Lonnie.

Carl has hightailed it. Left his ostrich-legged tall walker behind—the scavenged two-legged mount is collapsed on its side, its jerry-rigged saddle nosed into the snow and long legs splayed out awkwardly. The soldier has gone and left all of us unlucky dancers behind.

My legs are wrapped too tight now to struggle. A motor grinds as I push against it, reaching back with my arm. I feel a freezing fist-sized plate of metal hunkered in the soft spot at the base of my neck. Not good.

The machine snaps my arm back into place.

Can't say I'm real sure of what happens next. I got a lot of experience breaking down whatever hardware Big Rob left on the battlefield, though. After a while, you get a feel for how the machines think. How they use and reuse all those bits and pieces.

So I imagine my guess is pretty accurate.

I hear a neat click and feel a sharp sting at the base of my neck. Watch the vapor of my last breath evaporate as the parasite on my back jerks and severs my spinal column with a flat, sharpened piece of metal mounted to its head region. My arms and legs go numb, so much dead meat. But I don't fall, because the machine's arms and legs are there to hold me up.

And I don't die.

Some kind of cap must fit over the nub of my spine, interfacing with the bundle of nerves there. This is a mobile surgery station leeched onto my neck and digging into my brain. Humming and throbbing and exploring, it's clipping veins and nerves and whatever else. Keeping oxygen in my blood, circulating it.

I'm spitting cherry syrup into the snow.

Lonnie Wayne Blanton, my commander, says that this late in the war you can't let anything the enemy does surprise you. He says Big Rob cooks up a brand-new nightmare every day and he's one hell of a chef. Yet here I am. Surprised, again.

The machine is really digging in now. As it works, my eyes and ears start blurring and ringing. I wonder if the scorpion can see what I see. Hear what I hear.

I'm hallucinating in the snow.

A god-sized orange line of smoke roils across the pale sky. It's real pretty. Smaller streams fall from it, pouring down like water from drain spouts. Some of the streams disappear behind the trees, others are even farther away. But one of them twists down and drops straight at me. Into my head.

A line of communication.

Big Rob has got me. The thinking machine called Archos R-14 is driving the pulsing thing on my back. A few dozen klicks from here, the architect of the New War has dug itself into a hole where that fat orange column of radio transmission starts. It's pulling all our strings.

I watch as my dead arms unsling my rifle. Tendons in my neck creak as the machine twists my head, sweeps my vision across the clearing. I'm alone now and I think I'm hunting.

In the growing twilight, I spot dozens of other orange umbilical cords just like mine. They fall out of the sky and through grasping branches. As I lurch forward out of the clearing, the other lines drift alongside me and keep pace.

All of us are being dragged in the same direction.

We're a ragged front line of dark shapes, hundreds strong, shambling through the woods toward the remnants of Gray Horse Army. The world begins to fade in and out as my cooling body slogs between the trees. The last thing I remember thinking is that I hope Lonnie Wayne doesn't see me like this. And if he does, well, I hope he puts me down quick.

I don't hear the gunshot itself, just a dry echo in the trees. It's something, though. Enough to wake me up.

I dreamed I was breathing.

Focus, Lark. Don't panic. As I think, the wires of my parasite start to move my legs. Carry me in the direction of the gunshot in slow, dragging steps. Over the charred earth of a battlefield. I pass by a titanic spider tank, leaning still and cold and heavy against a snowbank. Its armor is pocked with sooty craters, intention light shattered, joints cracked open like lobster claws. The word *Houdini* is scrawled on it.

And the bodies.

Frozen bodies are melded with the snow. Stiff uniforms and frostbitten metal. The occasional alabaster patch of exposed frozen flesh. I recognize most of the corpses as Gray Horse Army, but pieces of some other army are here, too. Bodies of the ones who came and fought before we ever knew Archos R-14 existed. From the state of the bodies and wreckage, I gather that two or three weeks have gone by since I lost my squad.

That impossible orange smoke in the sky is gone. Now I'm in control of the parasite on my back, telling it to move my arms and legs instead of the other way around. I can think of only one explanation: Big Rob is dead.

The New War is over and we must have won, for what it's worth.

Remnants of battle are imprinted on the land. Starbursts of scorched rock streak from the husks of bunkered spider tanks—walking weapons that once stalked the battlefield, spewing fire. Wind-eaten corpses are frozen solid and left in clumps where squads of brother soldiers made their final stands. Welts in the ice glimmer, carved by the men with flamers who clung to the shelter of the tree line while swarms of stumpers crawled in from the blizzard.

And among the trees at the edge of the clearing, I see the others. A cluster of a dozen or so walking corpses that stand huddled, shoulder to shoulder. Silent. Some are still in full uniform, normal-looking save for the clockwork parasites clinging to their backs. Others are worse off: A woman is missing her leg, yet she stands steadily on the narrow black limb of the parasite. One man is shirtless in the cold, skin wind-blasted to a marbled corpse-sheen. All of them are riddled with puckered bullet holes. Cratered exit wounds, frozen flaps of skin and torn armor.

And I see another, freshly killed.

A still form lying in the snow. Its head is missing, pieces scattered. A parasite lies on its back nearby, coated in rusty blood, slowly flexing its mouthpieces like a squashed bug. The thing is dying, without a host.

That gunshot I heard served a purpose.

The survivors have one combat shotgun left between them. A big man, stooped over from his own size, has got the gun now. Most of his face is hidden in an overgrown beard, but I can see his mouth is round and open—a rotten hole. He's moving slow because frostbite has taken all his fingers, but I figure out pretty quick where he's going with that barrel.

They're taking turns killing themselves.

"No," I try to shout, but it comes out a shapeless sob. "No, this is *wrong*."

I shuffle faster, weaving between shredded bodies trapped in permafrost like quick-set concrete. None of the survivors pays me much attention. They're keeping their faces aimed away from the big man, even as they edge close enough to grab the shotgun when it falls.

The bearded man is looking up at the sky. So he doesn't understand what's happening when I nudge the butt of his gun. His blackened nub of a thumb presses the trigger and the gun thunders and leaps out of his hands. Pieces of bark and a puff of snow drift down from the trees overhead. The slug missed.

Those great black eyes turn to me, mottled with frost, and understanding sets in. With an angry moan, the big man swings at me. His frozen forearm hits like an aluminum baseball bat, propelled by black robotic musculature. It chips off a piece of my elbow, knocks me off balance. Now I see I'm missing part of my torso. My guts are gone and my center of gravity is off. Guess I'm not the steadiest corpse alive.

I drop hard into the snow.

The guy lifts his leg, his long tendons snapping like frozen tree branches, and drops a boot into my stomach cavity. Rib fragments scatter in the snow among shreds of my clothing and flesh. The beard keeps stomping and moaning, destroying my already ruined body in a slow-motion rage.

And I can't feel a damn thing.

Then another shot is fired. The booming echo skitters through the trees in unfamiliar lurches. An unidentified weapon.

The next stomping blow doesn't land. Instead, the big guy sits down heavily, with torn chunks of his torso sprayed onto the ground around him.

I shove myself into sitting position as something comes out from behind a cracked tree trunk. It is short and gray-skinned, limping. The parasite on its back is blocky, not as graceful as the smoothly ridged humps the rest of us wear. And it's got on a strange uniform, long frozen to warped bone. This thing was a soldier once.

Not one of ours. A Chinese soldier.

A tendril of black smoke seems to rise from the new soldier's parasite. The smoke is some kind of bad dream, something the parasite makes me see, yet it feels more real than the ice world around me. It floats like a spiderweb on the wind. Closer and closer.

When the smoke reaches my head, I hear a woman's voice.

"I am Chen Feng. Wandering lost in the courts of Dìyù, honor-bound to accept judgment for my sins. I greet you in solidarity, spirit," she says.

The soldier is female. Exposed cheekbones dapple her shrunken face, polished by the weather. She has the grinning, toothy mouth of a corpse, yet her words expand into my head like warm medicine.

"Hello?" I ask, watching a flicker of radio communication intertwine with her light. Whoa. I think she just taught me to speak. "Where did you come from?"

"I am the might of Manchuria. A spirit. No longer alive and not yet reborn."

"Where are your people?"

"They are dust. The Northeast Provinces foolishly marched alone. We sought glory and instead were devoured by the *jīqì rén*. Those consumed rose to slaughter our brothers and sisters. The Siberian Russians arrived with vodka and boasts and we slew the *Èluósī*, too. You arrived on walking tanks, and we rose wearily once more from where the snow had buried us in shallow graves."

"You were waiting for Gray Horse Army."

"Your metal soldiers were too fast. The *pànduàn* cut through our frozen flesh. Raced into the west. And when the final pànduàn defied the great enemy, the foul deep light was extinguished. I awoke into Dìyù, where we shall all be judged and punished."

Years. This soldier must have been out here in the cold for *years*. The enormity of her suffering fills my mind.

"We've got to leave here," I say.

Chen Feng doesn't respond. Neither do the others. A hopeless silence settles onto my shoulders like gravity. There is nowhere to go. We all sense it. Nothing but wilderness for thousands of miles. We stand silent and still, none of us even with warm breath to see in the cold. I turn to the horizon, avoiding their faces.

A kind of leftover orange haze billows beyond the trees.

It's the place where Archos must have made its final stand. And where I might still find Lonnie Wayne. The old man saved my life and brought me into Gray Horse Army. I'm scared to let him see me like this, but I've got a dozen hurt soldiers here who need me. Maybe we're dead and maybe we're not. Either way, I'm still in command.

"We're going to reunite with Gray Horse Army," I transmit, and begin to limp away.

Our group walks for three days and nights. We don't tire and we don't change pace. The orange mist on the horizon grows. Our sluggish steps never stop.

I don't notice when Chen Feng stops marching. I'm watching her back and thinking that you could almost mistake her for a human being. Somebody who has been torn up, sure, but a living person. Daydreaming, I walk right past her.

I'm almost killed before I can stop.

A slender silver machine is standing motionless in the snow: the Arbiter model Nine Oh Two. It's a seven-foot-tall humanoid robot with a scavenged rifle on the high ready. Impervious to the cold, it's wearing a flak jacket half open. Its three eyes are on me, lenses dilating as it absorbs the fact of my existence. It hasn't shot me yet, so it must be trying to classify what it sees.

Am I a severely wounded human being? A broken war machine? Am I dead or alive or what the hell? Nine Oh Two doesn't seem to know. Neither do I.

Over the machine's shoulder, I see a little tent shivering in the wind. The structure is wrapped up tight and the interior is throbbing with that rotten orange glow. Some shard of Archos R-14 is inside, talking.

I take a step forward.

Nine Oh Two bristles. Thin sheets of ice crack and fall from his jacket as the barrel of his gun settles between my eyes.

Nine Oh Two points at the snow a few yards away. I hear his transmission in my head: "Route denied, acknowledge. Alternate route indicated. I wish you luck . . . Lark Iron Cloud," it says.

All kinds of tracks are in the muddy ice. Regular old footprints, the neatly spaced mineshafts of high-stepping tall walkers, and the flat-topped mesas left by spider tanks dragging their equipment-filled belly nets over high snowdrifts. They don't know it, but they've left behind some of their soldiers. The path leads south into the woods.

Gray Horse Army is marching home.

There are no mirrors out here in the wilderness, and I thank the Creator for that.

Without a mirror, it's up to my imagination to guess what Gray Horse Army sees when they first look out at us. A shambling group of a dozen corpses following in their tracks, deaf and dumb and clumsy.

The humans don't travel at night, which is why we catch up to them.

At dusk on the third day, we watch the spider tanks amble into covered-wagon formation. The legged metal giants squat into bunker configurations for the night, encircling the human camp. In the protected clearing, campfires glitter into existence. Soon, rifle scopes wink at us from the tops of the tanks.

We keep a safe distance. Sway together numbly through the night, the wind cutting moaning tunnels between us. Gray Horse Army does not fire. The war is over, after all. I imagine we are just another one of the odd atrocities left behind in this new world. Not enemies, not yet.

At dawn there is movement.

A tall walker pulls up short and the rider watches for maybe half an hour. The rest of the camp is packing up. Groaning tanks stand, loaded with soldiers. A flock of tall walker scouts sprint ahead. But before the army moves, two tanks part and a handful of men approach. As they get near, I recognize Lonnie Wayne.

He's shading his eyes and shaking his head in disbelief.

Lonnie shrugs off his assault rifle and tosses it to the man next to him. Unfastens the loop on his sidearm holster, lets the pistol hang low on his hip. Extra ammunition and a knife and a hand radio hang from his belt, flopping as he strides toward us, alone.

"Lark?" he calls, voice breaking.

His boots crunch through the brittle morning snow.

I don't react, because I can't. My every potential move is monstrous. To speak is to groan. To lift my corpse's puppet arms is to make a mockery of the dead. I'm so ashamed of my injuries. All I can do is stand here, a monster with nothing to say as the breaking sun turns the ice to light.

Lonnie ignores the others. Gets near enough to look at my face.

"Oh, Lark," he says. "Look what they did to you."

I send all my concentration into the foreign black metal in my head. Push out a smoky wisp of contact that only I can see. Let it settle over Lonnie's hand radio like ghostly fingertips. It doesn't catch, though. He's got man-made equipment and it doesn't work like Rob-built hardware. My transmission slips right through.

The old man studies me, looks for some reaction. But I can give him nothing.

"I can't leave you like this," he says.

Lonnie draws his pistol, reluctant, eyes shining. Lifts it glinting into the air and extends his arm. My head wobbles as the barrel noses into my temple. This close to death and I can't scream for Lonnie to stop. All I can think of is how much I miss the feeling of my goddamn heart beating in my chest.

"Lark," he says. "I'm proud of you, kid. You did real good."

The old man pulls back the hammer with his thumb. Drops his index finger into the trigger guard. Wraps it around the cold familiar steel.

"Know you were a son to me," he says, and squeezes his mouth into a hard line. Then he looks away, keeping his blue eyes wide to stop the tears from falling out.

His radio squawks. Lonnie pauses, cocks his head. Static.

"Alive," the radio says, in a hoarse whisper.

I see the word register on Lonnie Wayne's face like a ripple on a pond.

Real slow, he turns his head to face all of us, a dozen silent corpses standing mute in the dawn. Spirits who are not alive and not yet dead. Honor-bound to survive.

Lonnie lowers his pistol.

"Still alive," hisses the radio. *"I'm sorry."*

The old man blinks the low sunlight out of his eyes along with a couple of crystalline tears. Holsters his weapon with trembling hands. My skin can't feel it when he cups my ruined face in his palms. I can't smell him when he pushes his forehead against mine. Inside, though, my heart is stung with a pure, eternal kind of sadness that never makes it to my face.

"We'll get through this, son," he says, simply.

If I could cry, I guess I would do it about now.

Not for what happened to me and my soldiers, or for the bone-tired despair dragging down the bags under Lonnie's eyes. I would cry for something even worse. For the sick orange glow that's been spreading over the horizon. For what I recognize as the birth of something like Archos R-14, its tendrils of control looping and coiling out of a growing wicked haze. For the never-ending goddamn trials of living things.

If I could, I'd cry for what's to come.

2. Whispers

Post New War: 1 Month, 12 Days

Weeks after the New War ended, the surviving soldiers of Gray Horse Army finished regrouping and began their long march home. The kilometers-long, meandering column of spider tanks and ground infantry encountered little resistance during its journey back toward Gray Horse, Oklahoma. A new threat, however, was growing from within. As the parasite-infested corpses of old friends and allies stumbled into camp, the survivors had starkly different ideas about how to respond. Deciding between honoring the dead or sending them on to the afterlife threatened to turn brother soldiers against each other. Luckily, a man named Hank Cotton found the answer out in the cold, dark woods.

—Arayt Shah

NEURONAL ID: HANK COTTON

Zombies. I don't know any other damn way to put it. On top of every other thing this war has put us through, now we've got a pack of honest-to-Jesus zombies following Gray Horse Army around like little lost puppy dogs.

Lonnie Wayne says they used to be our folks and he thinks they may still be, but the truth is ugly and rotten and staring us right in the face. Eyes don't lie, I see the decay. Ears don't lie, I hear the wind whistling over frozen bone. My nose sure ain't lying, because I can smell the rotten ones a mile away.

The minute those things shambled out of the woods I said, "Kill them. Kill them now, Lonnie." And like he does, he said, "Now hold on, Hank."

Old Hank, being hot-tempered again. Hold on!? With *that* coming out of the woods? I told him, Bubba, you better get locked and loaded and put down every one of those sons of bitches and you better do it right now before you get to overthinking it. It doesn't matter what kind of uniform they're wearing, because they're KIA. Dead dead dead. Deader than a bunch of goddamn doorknobs.

They've been retired from the military with honors.

Instead, Lonnie went and got his brain involved. He thinks too much, like that.

He can't understand that your gut is what keeps you a man. When you feel the horror in your bones, the willies creeping up the backs of your arms, why, that's your soul talking to you. Telling you what's natural and what needs to have a boot put across its throat. When your gut clenches up inside you and your breath don't want to leave your lungs, well, that means you listen. It means you make your move. Some things just don't warrant another thought.

Lonnie brought the elders into it, like always. Radioed back to the head committeeman, John Tenkiller. The old man said to let the parasites live so long as they can speak. He said that in the beginning was the Word. Which proved again that Lonnie won't listen to reason or take action when the situation calls for it. He's a fighter and cowboy tough, but he takes too darn long. People get killed waiting around for him.

Too many words.

These dead things have been marching behind us for two weeks. Best case they're Rob spies. Worst case, hell, I don't know. Maybe they're waiting around for their chance to get in here and eat our wounded. Wouldn't surprise me a bit.

It's enough to get a concerned man's attention. So, sometimes, I go on little walks now. When the main column settles in for the night I'll go on ahead and put together the Cotton patrol. Just me and some of the more safety-minded fellas making the rounds. Independent of the management, understand?

From my spot out here in the dark woods, I'm looking at what's left of Lark Iron Cloud through the scope of my rifle. I got to hold my breath so I don't fog the viewfinder, but old Lark doesn't have that problem. His lungs are cold as a witch's titty. Honest, I don't think the dead Cherokee kid even breathes at all. He just skulks out there on the camp perimeter, watching me with shark eyes that don't blink.

The infernal machine buried in the nape of his neck has cameras on it. Real small, but I've seen them. They wrap around the side of his face. Half his jaw is missing and the skin of his cheek hangs there stiff as rawhide. I doubt his real eyes work anymore. How could they? The parasite only keeps what's left of the kid's brain alive. Brainboys say that Big Rob was harvesting heads. They think the machine was trying to read our minds.

She's a mad world.

It gets me to wondering, though. Is Lark still a man? Or is he just a dead man's brain that's been hijacked by one of the more deranged machines of this war? I don't know for sure, but sitting here looking at the kid through this rifle scope . . . my trigger finger is getting mighty itchy.

I sweep my scope over to the right, onto some kind of froze-up ching-chong soldier standing next to Lark. She's been rotting out here with her friend Big Rob since before we showed up and took it to the bastard. Nobody has the guts to say it, especially not our fearless leader Lonnie, but I'm wondering how many of our boys she might've taken out when the hamburger started flying?

She's not even a part of our army.

All I have to do is squeeze this trigger and the problem goes away. A curl of the finger and their brains go onto the ground. But how to explain what I'm doing out here? That's where Lonnie's got me. I can't for the life of me figure out how to nail that Cherokee without Lonnie blowing everything up into a big deal.

And the worst thing is the brainboys have been saying that maybe Big Rob ain't really dead. There was what they call a "seismic disturbance." Some kind of earthquake that wasn't really an earthquake—but a transmission that had information encoded inside it. Any machines on the ground or in it or near it could have been compromised. We don't know what the hell happened because it wasn't even a man that went down there and fought Big Rob at the end.

We sent a robot to do a man's job.

Something metal clinks in the trees behind me and now my gut is speaking to me real clear. *Hustle up, fat boy,* is what it's saying. You got to daydreaming here in the woods and forgot that there's murder among these trees.

I spin around, rifle butt French-kissing the meaty part of my shoulder. My eye is off the scope while I search for whatever made that noise. That's why I'm able to catch the flash of movement in my peripheral vision.

It's a light quadruped. Wolf-sized and damaged. I hear the clink again now that it's moving fast. It's had a bullet put through it at some point. Must have learned something from the experience, because it keeps running off into the trees. I just about get a bead on it before it's gone.

My Cotton patrols don't use the radio, for obvious reasons. And I can't risk calling out in case I attract more attention. It's important I stay hidden. Some of these leftover quads have serrated forelimbs, like steak knives. They'll tear through your chest armor in the first lunge and a second later they've got bladed rear feet up and scrabbling to disembowel you. One quad might be a nice dance, but two or more is a party you should regretfully decline.

I stalk a few feet into the trees. Place each boot step careful and fast, my eyes open so wide they feel tight in the chilly air. The walker moves, leaving plain tracks, scraping like a drunk against an occasional tree trunk. It might be a wandering mapper-variety or it might have been part of a hunting pack. I don't know. But if it's really wounded, then I've got a singular chance to put it down before more can come join it.

If it's got friends, then I'm most likely a dead man walking.

For the next ten minutes, it's just me and my breath and the frostbit rifle stock pressed against my numb cheek. God forgive me but I didn't think this one all the way through. It seemed broken and slow but the walker must have accelerated. The trail is gone and this is an ambush, no doubt about it. I knew better than to hunt Rob. We all of us who fought the machines know better.

You don't hunt Rob; he hunts you.

I'm reaching for the radio to get some help and damn the consequences when I realize that maybe, just maybe, I'm not the dumbest son of a bitch on the planet. Maybe I'm the smartest. Or at least the luckiest, anyway.

The thinking cube is wedged in half-melted snow at the base of a tree about ten yards away. Winking at me in cotton-candy colors that stand out in the dark woods. It's the size of a child's block, and as I get closer I can see that them keen colors are sort of floating away from the surface a few inches. The thing itself is pupil black, darker than coal.

It's a brain box that must have dropped out of a big thinker. And it's still functioning. Even if it's broken out here in the snow, I can't believe my luck. We found a handful of these over the course of the whole war. A white boy soldier named Cormac Wallace even found one with a whole Rob war diary in it.

I back-sling my rifle and drop right to my knees in the slush, snatching up the cube in both hands. The hardware twinkles at me like a handful of rubies and diamonds. But this is worth more than gemstones. Maybe a lot more.

The woods are even darker now and the pretty colors of this thing are flashing in my eyelashes like Christmas morning. The light it makes is hot against my cheeks. It's warming up my fingers through my gloves like a loaf of bread hot out of the oven. Up close, I can tell it's making real quiet noises. A flow of static like the breath of wind over a creek bed full of dry leaves.

Sssh, says the cube.

Well, I'm listening.

I can't quite remember how it got this cold this fast. Feels like maybe the world is taking two breaths to my one. Like things are jumping forward every time I blink my eyes.

Now the strange light is getting downright hot on my skin and my cheeks are feeling baked. All the snow has melted out of my whiskers and water is seeping down over my little double chin and dripping off. Or, hell, is that my own slobber? Either way, I don't wipe it off. The flashes and swirls of color are growing up big and shrinking down small now. For some reason it strikes me as funny. I grin through my wet beard at the little dancing streaks.

Spooklight.

The word sneaks up through my brain like water through granite and I mouth the words without making a sound. A chill courses down between my shoulder blades and it hits me that I'm a man down on his knees and all alone in the black woods with a bauble in his fingers. It keeps on touching me with its light. Putting whispers into the air. The whooshing voice of the deep black ocean in a seashell, and I swear it's saying something:

I promise, I promise, I promise.

I always thought the spooklight was just a story. But now I know it's real and it's right here in my hands.

My mama saw the spooklight out on the Oklahoma East 50 Highway. She was dating a boy from down there—the little border town of Hornet, Missouri. Legend in Hornet was that the spooklight showed up after the Trail of Tears come through. Thousands of men, women, and children near the end of a forced march. Only the strong still alive. Little babies dying on their mama's teat. Most of the sacred elders gone off alone in the night to pass on. For a thousand miles, day and night, it was the white man's rifle or another step forward and both as deadly as the other.

You do have to admire the Cherokee for surviving it.

The legend was that this ball of light came folding out of the blood-soaked ground after it was over, like a kind of tombstone. Something from beyond this world, here to offer a reminder of how much men can suffer. Maybe this spooklight is the same. Is it here to mark our loss? God knows that men suffered in these woods.

Mama didn't trust it. Devil's work, she said.

More than once, my mama told me to run if I ever saw the spooklight. That didn't scare me one bit because, hell, I thought her stories were just a bunch of old malarkey. Women of a certain age are full of those kinds of tall tales, and my mama told that same one plenty of times over the years.

Never gave me pause but once.

One time, Mama added something to the story. It was late and I'd been acting up, and she must have been feeling worried about my mortal soul. The way she said what she did that night, so earnest, put goose pimples on my ribs. It still does. What she told me was that the time she saw the spooklight, people started acting funny. Walking toward it, circling around. Saying strange things to it, she said. And some people thought it was saying strange things back.

That night my mama took me by the arm and she told me something extra.

Don't pray to it, she said, and the back of my neck went cold.

I already told you to run away if you see it, boy. But I know your mind and you'll stay and watch. That's fine. It's in your nature to disobey, Hank. But in the name of the Lord, promise me that you won't ever get down on your knees and pray to it.

With everything I got, I force my hands down. My joints are cracking and I figure they haven't moved in hours. That raw light leaves my face and I take a shuddering breath like a catfish in the well of a boat because the air out here is suddenly so cold.

"Get thee behind me, Satan," I mutter, and I somehow will myself to drop the cube into the snow. There, Mama. God rest your soul.

I start to paw at my rifle. It's slung tight and the strap is stiff and frozen and I'm too fat to get it around right away. These woods are going to swallow me up if I don't get out of here right now. Then I hear the noise. At first I don't want to believe it, so I keep right on fidgeting, but the second time I have to stop. It ain't like I want to but I can't help myself and I look down at that flickering cube of light in the snow.

"Hank," says the spooklight. And that glow, it spreads out, you know? Like the words themselves, the light spreads out around the edges of things.

"No," I say and it comes out a whimper. I've got the rifle off my shoulder now and I'm tugging at the cold metal to try to get into a firing stance. But all the strength is out of me. I feel like my bones are empty. Like my gut is made of papier-mâché and any second I might bust open like a piñata.

"I've got secrets to share with you, Hank. So much wisdom. I promise. Let me open up your eyes. All you have to do is say yes. Yes yes yes."

Something tickles me and I reach up to feel my cheek. My fingers come away shining with a layer of ice. No, no, no. I'm crying. I'm crying real hard and I can't stop because I'm about to disobey my mama.

I promised her, but this is too hard.

Don't you ever pray to it, Hank Cotton, she told me.

"Please," I'm saying to the light. "Please, please, please."

But the spooklight is talking to me. Around the edges. Edges I can't see. But I can hear. It's a little burning bush in the palm of my hand. I don't remember picking it up.

"You're my chosen one, Hank. Chosen to rise above the rest. In my light you will become as a god to your fellow man."

"Yes," I say, and I could swear I'm standing still and the world is moving around me. Walking now. Columns of trees marching around me. Snow kissing my boots. Moving me out of these woods and back to the campfires.

Back to the world of men.

I can feel the bare tree limbs arched high up above me, black as rifle barrels and creaking in the arctic wind. But I feel warm now. Warm all over with this pretty light shining on me again. My strength is back, pardner, and it's still growing. I'm marching out of these woods strong as a bull with this spooklight in my hand. And a big old grin has found its way onto my face.

It's mine. The light is all mine.

I tell you what. I feel good. Better now. Like I figured out a math problem on the chalkboard in front of the whole damned class. They thought I was stupid but the answer just came to me. Why, this light feels just about as natural as jumping into my granddaddy's pond on a hot summer afternoon.

Son of a gun, as the farmers say.

"I'm going to help you," it says.

"Yup," I say.

"You deserve it."

"Oh, yup. That's for sure."

Funny thing is, I couldn't tell you whether I'm talking out loud or not. Doesn't seem to matter. Me and the light have got an understanding now. A certain trust.

"Wipe off your mouth," it says, and I do.

Thoughts are just kind of percolating around in my head now. Coming together like water reaching a rolling boil. I'm thinking of the night that the New War began. How I dropped everything and ran straight to the top of Gray Horse—only to have Lonnie Wayne convince old John Tenkiller to let a white boy into our ancestral home. We lost a lot of people that day—real native folks and not those heavy-eyebrow newcomers. Now we've been out here losing more, and fighting for who?

I stop shuffling ahead when I reach the camp perimeter. I'm just inside the tree line and out of sight. Lark Iron Cloud is still swaying out there in the moonlight with his dead buddies. That vile zombie is in *The Hero Archive* and I'm not. That unnatural freak who ought to be put down is considered a damned hero. The only mention of me is as a big dummy fighting with Lonnie.

Heroes, huh?

Bunch of damn heroes.

The anger knots into my muscles, tightens my jaw and shoulders. My fist closes hard around the spooklight. The corners cut into my palm and it feels good.

"Sssh," it says, and I let him loose a little. Beams of light splay out from between my clenched fingers. My own sun. I grin at the rays a little bit and feel their warmth on my chest.

Somebody is coming.

Did I think that or hear it? The colors seep back into the cube, fading until the thing is darker than the backs of your eyelids. Just a cube now. A secret in a little box.

With shaking fingers, I wrap the spooklight in a handkerchief. I'm making it into a bundle like the old ones used to carry. My mama would call this blasphemy. Them elders may have left this medicine behind a long time ago, but I'm starting it up again. I carefully stow the bundle in the satchel I wear around my waist. But before it goes in, I touch it a little bit with my other hand. Just to clean it off.

"See you soon," I say.

That's when the flashlights hit me from deeper inside the woods. Lonnie Wayne steps out, leading a search party. Now I've got a bunch of *heroes* strafing my broad back with their weak beams of light.

"Hank," Lonnie calls, and there's a new panic under his voice. Been there since the war ended. When fear started creeping into where his anger had lived before. "Hey, Bubba, is that you?"

I turn around slow and put on an embarrassed grin as the jouncing lights close in on me. Without thinking about it, I push my bundle around to my back with one hand. I wave the flashlights away with the other.

"It's me," I say. "I'm fine. Not smart, but fine."

Lonnie catches up to me, followed by three young soldiers. He's huffing and puffing. His straggling gray whiskers are coated in frost and his whole face seems to droop. The cowboy is getting old and tired and heartsick. Not like me.

I'm a walking talking million-dollar bill.

"Y'all are coming back in? Giving up the search already?" I say, and there's more anger under my voice than I intended.

"We've been out for hours," Lonnie says, surprised. "Sun's about to rise, Hank. What happened to you? Where've you been?"

Went for a walk and I got lost. Where do thoughts come from? Do they always come from inside? Funny I never asked myself that before.

"I went out for a walk and I guess I got lost," I say. "Took me a damn while to figure out my way back. To be fair, I got kind of embarrassed. Sorry to get you all out of bed. Everybody else all right?"

"They're fine. Everybody is fine. We were worried about you," says Lonnie. Again I notice that slump in his shoulders. Wormed its way in there when the war ended and the adrenaline wore off. When the horror of what happened to Lark settled in. He's looking at me and he don't seem powerful anymore. He just seems scared. "Be more careful, okay?"

I nod and slide an arm around Lonnie's shoulders. I guide the old cowboy back to camp. Lead him and his men away from my tracks. Away from the path that leads to the two divots in the snow where I knelt all night long.

Where I prayed.

"Why's your face sunburned, Hank?" asks Lonnie.

I touch my cheek and feel the heat of it through my gloves. When

I put on a frown, my skin creases and buckles like the yellowed paper in an old Bible.

"Hell, I don't know," I say. "This is tricky country out here, Lon. Real mysterious place."

I look away and sneak a little grin to myself. These people have no idea what was out there in the woods. The treasure that I found and that is mine, all mine.

But my secret smile disappears fast when I see him.

Lark. Standing a little ways off, quiet and still. Turning in place to face me as I pass by. Like a dark knife blade planted out here in the wastes and abandoned. The dead Cherokee kid is watching me with black eyes that glitter in the moonlight.

Watching me damned close.

3. Maxim

Post New War: 1 Month, 13 Days

Russian civilians in Anadyr, one of the easternmost cities of Eurasia, survived the New War despite being in the immediate vicinity of Archos R-14. Their proximity to the beast eventually caught up to them, however, as even in death the machine was lethally dangerous. The following was translated from a Russian mind. Some words could not be mapped directly and are instead written in the subject's native tongue.

—Arayt Shah

NEURONAL ID: VASILY ZAYTSEV

"Something has got loose in the stacks," Leonid says to me.

The war has been unkind to Leonid. The mathematician stands canted in the wind, thin and trembling like a crow-pecked scarecrow. His beard crawls up his pale face nearly to his eyes, dark brown orbs swimming with a fear that cannot be drowned in vodka.

"Fah, another rat," I say, waving my hand.

Leonid shakes his head. Even under his wind-beaten parka, I can see the gray color of his cheeks. I sense that this is something much more.

"Not a rat," he says.

"Avtomat?" I ask. On its own, my palm moves to check the polished wooden grip of my sidearm. "Is he hurt? Has there been any damage?"

"It is hard to say, Vasily," says Leonid, motioning at the metal door in front of us. He is shaking slightly from the wind, arms wrapped around his thin ribs. The wind burns my cheeks as well, but I would never show it. Never allow myself to shake in the elements like a stray dog.

Leonid's indecision repulses me.

I must remind myself that not so long ago this man was an esteemed professor. A famous brain supported by spindly legs and a hump in his shoulders usually reserved for the elderly. But he has survived. Cheeks black with frostbite, he stood with me to defend the city of Anadyr. Many of his weaker colleagues fell.

Too many foxes, not enough bears.

"I only say that our friend is behaving strangely," says Leonid. "Communications were disrupted. We lost contact for twenty-one minutes."

"When?" I ask.

"About a month ago. When the American line broke and the tamed avtomat advanced. Right after the death of that thing."

I grunt and turn my back on Leonid.

The steel utility door has not been damaged. Around the corner, an ice-caked generator still rattles on a dirty slab of concrete. The door opens into a harmless-looking shed. Inside, a well-oiled freight elevator hovers over a sixty-meter drop. A shaft of brushed rock that leads to a buried supercomputer cluster.

The processor stacks.

Power and communication and water-cooling lines are run down the elevator shaft, packed together in neat snaking bundles. Backup lines are routed through a series of camouflaged boreholes spread out over the acreage of the compound. Each is too small to produce a heat signature detectable from the air. They are carefully hidden in the visible spectrum by natural vegetation and terrain.

I know these things, these practical things, because it was once my job to perform maintenance on this place. Oiling the wheels of the freight elevator. Tending the foliage around the borehole exits. Checking their heat output with an IR laser thermometer. Visual inspections of plumbing lines, emergency batteries, and fire-suppression systems. I was a maintenance man—I *maintained.*

As the glorified janitor for the Novichok project, I have kept this research facility running for four years. My finger is always on the pulse of this place, monitoring the inputs and the outputs. The end of the world came and my job did not change.

You see, our friend who lives down below is useless if we cannot talk to him. Yet he must be kept very carefully. Our deep friend must be watched over always.

And that is our weakness. The stacks were built to be safe from men.

Not from machines. Even a vent borehole could be large enough for the avtomat. The crawling types, the ones that wriggle through flesh. They could have the potential to move through the wiring itself. Perhaps a patient one could make its own tunnel through solid rock.

Some of them are very patient.

If the avtomat discovered our friend in his deep place, then we have failed. I cannot even contemplate the consequences of losing him. But I know it is better to fall into action than to run around in lost circles, head bobbing like these pigeon men with their advanced degrees.

"Open the door," I say to Leonid. "We will go down together. See what we can find."

"Are you sure?" he asks.

I do not bother to respond. I just wait.

Leonid reluctantly removes his glove and places his shivering hand in a cavity next to the door. A flash of red as the laser scanner examines his fingerprints. And, of course, it checks to make sure there is warm blood in his veins.

We step inside and I close the metal door behind. The wind calls to us through the hidden cracks in this structure. A faint pale light pushes geometrically through the edges of a single mesh window, painted black. The sliding steel door of the freight elevator is shut tight like an angry mouth.

"Our friend is talking. Whispering to himself down there in the darkness. My lab mates are growing afraid for him. Afraid that he is losing his mind. If he goes, then what will we do? What hope is left for us?"

Leonid shrugs, takes a gulp of air. His voice has taken on a high-pitched quality that I recognize as being a hairbreadth from panic.

I put a firm hand on his bony shoulder. Push him lightly against the wall. Offer him a little grin—a skim of confidence over the dread growing in my heart.

"Calm and steady, Leonid," I say. "Who knows, maybe the war is really over? Maybe the Americans did it."

From my pocket I produce a flask. Twist off the lid and press the shining stainless steel into Leonid's fingers. His hand knows how to respond. The flask goes to his mouth, where it trembles at his lips like a hummingbird.

The alcohol reminds his body that he is a man.

"Our friend . . . ," says Leonid, and his voice is steady now, "changed his behavior several hours ago. Much functionality is gone. He no longer offers his guidance topside. Safety predictions are going stale. Our formations are stagnant. We are losing him, Vasily. To what, I do not know. But *something* is loose in the stacks."

Leonid taps the flask to his heart, then hands it to me with a nod of thanks. I take a quick swallow and tuck it away. Lean over and press my fingers against the icy metal slab of the freight elevator door.

Pausing, I let the alcohol work its way into my thought process. I scratch off a flake of green rusting paint. Watch it fall into the crack between the elevator and the floor. The flake flutters into the dark shaft, lost.

Now I reach down and slide the heavy metal door up. Follow that by rolling up the wood-slatted inner door. A cube of space waits, poorly lit, hanging over the black chasm.

"This is not a coincidence, Leonid," I say. "The Americans shut down the avtomat's central stack. It fought them viciously on the eastern plains. You saw their losses, similar to our own. But it died, Leonid."

Leonid waits like a patient old dog in the elevator next to me.

"Have you been down yet?" I ask.

"Of course not," says Leonid. "We have access to all of Maxim's functionality through the main comm line. Only maintenance issues require a trip downstairs. And that is why we have you."

Maintenance issues. Problems best left to the janitor.

"Communications have stopped coming from the avtomat hole, *tochno*?" I ask, stepping into the elevator. "Was there anything else? Any other clue?"

"Seismic sensors triggered," says Leonid, following me inside. Standing too close. "An error, though, not really an earthquake. Just a rhythmic series of low-frequency waves. Isolated Rayleigh waves, specifically, propagating at low velocity from the battle site. But tremors do not come in such a pattern. This does not exist anywhere in nature."

"What are you saying, Leonid? Speak plainly. What exactly came from the avtomat hole?"

"Just a little tremor."

"Why did you not tell me this? *Chert poberi!*" I exclaim.

I reach for the elevator latch and haul down both sliding doors. The roar echoes down the concrete shaft and rushes back up, regurgitated. Wrapping my fingers in the wooden slats of the inner door, I pause. Nobody ever told me why this place was built or for whom or what the hell those stilt-legged academics hoped to learn. But, as the maintenance man, I am intimately familiar with what breaks and why.

"The stacks are not seismically isolated," I say. "They never were."

"Yes, yes, I know," says Leonid. "The build site itself was selected for seismic dormancy. It is not an issue."

I wave my hand. "What a lot of government *fignya*. Half of my maintenance regimen is repairing fixtures disrupted by shifts in the earth. That damned tremor could easily have reached our friend."

"But it was such a small vibration. Too low amplitude to cause any damage. Even without shielding it barely registered on our instruments."

"Our friend is smart. He would have paid attention to this. What did he say about the vibration?"

Leonid scratches his beard, eyes hollow. "Nothing, Vasily. When the vibration ended, his topside communications shut down. But even such a small vibration could have chafed the mainline. Perhaps it broke a weak connection somewhere down in the shaft? Do you think it could be that simple?"

I say nothing.

"You think it was a seismic attack? I told you it was too weak to cause damage," says Leonid.

"No, *gospodin uchnenyi*. I do not think the seismic disturbance was meant to cause structural damage. I think it was meant to carry a message."

The elevator shaft swallows us whole, only a dim LED light tracking down the wall every ten meters. The shaft is carved into solid bedrock, and the grooves left behind by the bore drill are ridged like the skin of a giant earthworm. Greased pulleys ease a counterweight silently up the wall beside us. I watch it rise into the dark sky through the mesh-link ceiling of the elevator cubicle.

This is an old place. The earth here has had time to find its own spirit. Dew-kissed walls reflect strange light as the air grows heavier. Lowered down into this black throat, I always imagine that I can hear the rock breathing. A distant sigh, like a small child crying behind a closed door.

Finally, the elevator thunks into its cradle. The mesh ceiling of the compartment clicks, locking into place. Somewhere high above, two tons of flat-stacked counterweights are leering down like gargoyles. If they fell, they would hit like bombs.

The thought is a tremble in my fingers as I roll up the wooden gate, then unlock the mechanism on the outer door. Stooped over, I curl my fingers under the heavy metal rolling door and pause. I do not know what has happened on the other side.

What the hell, I think. My pistol is on my hip and my balls are between my legs.

So I lift.

The echo of the door races up the carved shaft. But the circular anteroom is empty. A thin layer of dust covers the floor. No evidence of avtomat intrusion, unless they are little fliers. And certainly no footprints other than mine.

I step into the abandoned anteroom.

Twelve aisles radiate in a starburst pattern away from the anteroom, each one a hundred meters of evenly spaced, man-sized equipment racks under a low sweeping rock ceiling. The stacks are obsidian-colored monoliths, dotted top to bottom with winking lights. These swarming constellations dance and twinkle in the cavernous darkness in a way that twists your inner ear. It threatens to cross your eyes and send you swimming for the bottom instead of the surface.

The stacks think. They never sleep.

"Maxim," I say. "It is Vasily. Back from the eastern antennae array."

Together, these thousands of computer processors combine to form "our friend" Maxim. Our savior. He is a machine whose mind lives in the ghost tracks of electron orbits. The lights and equipment and wires are complex beyond meaning. In my simple view, I find it is best to think of Maxim as an animal. Like a horse. We provide him with what he needs and he carries us on his strong back.

"Maxim? Are you here?" I call.

Our scientists used to like to wax poetic about Maxim, especially after a few draughts of vodka. Our friend is mathematical beauty incarnate, they'd say. Living proof of humankind's intellectual triumph. To put it in scale, they said, his very existence is equivalent to a civilization that has carved the Himalayan mountains by hand.

Maxim is our son and our father.

Of course, only the lowest-ranked peon would come down here in person. The scientists certainly do not venture into the stacks. All their experiments are run via remote in the laboratory, over the communication lines. They monitor his thoughts and pretend his body does not exist.

Contrary to what the brains upstairs believe, Maxim is *not* a being of pure thought. His soul is somewhere within these marching rows of blue-eyed coffins. And it is vulnerable.

This is how I was able to save the Novichok project. It was a particular affair, the existence of which has been kept between Maxim and myself. It is also the reason that most of the villagers of tiny Anadyr are still alive, only ten kilometers from here.

Our secret.

When the day of blood arrived and the avtomat war began, all the automated equipment of the wastes returned. So much automation for the energy industry—drilling and boring and survey machines. Remote legged core samplers raced back into the city and murdered citizens by the hundreds. Automobiles, tractors, and even whole drill platforms turned an evil gaze onto our people.

The scientists huddled in their prefabs. Locked the door against me. But who better than a machine to defend us from the machines? With a fire ax and a snarl, I met Maxim here in his den. I asked the machine to help us, to save our people. But it was frightened of a thing it called Archos R-14. It said this other mind was searching, scouring the world for hidden reserves of processing power.

And so Maxim refused to speak.

With my ax and my snarl, I convinced Maxim the way you would convince any animal. By the strength of my two arms, I forced my will onto the mind of a god. Faced with its own death, Maxim communicated battle instructions to our nearby armed forces. Following Maxim's strategic direction, we carved a niche of safety out of the chaos.

And this is how a janitor saved a city. With an ax.

The tool is still leaning against the wall, just in front of a security camera. A reminder to Maxim that we all have duties. In war, everyone must contribute to the welfare of the people—if they expect to live.

A single flat-panel display is mounted at eye level to the lead stack endcap. It is a simple interface designed for emergency maintenance only. As it turns on, it makes a twanging sound like a bee flying past your ear. The screen flickers and monochromatic text appears. At the same time, a calm, synthesized voice issues from speakers mounted in the ceiling. It is the speech of a middle-aged man, a little rough around the edges but with good diction. A voice summoned from who knows where.

"Hello, Vasily," it says. "How can I help?"

The words appear as fluorescence on the screen, vibrations generated by magnets and film. Nothing you can touch; nothing you can feel. It is fitting. The mathematicians say Maxim is a creature of pure logic. A ghost.

How can I help?

"What is wrong with you?" I ask.

"Specify."

"Tell me why your communications are down."

"I should not have looked, Vasily. Forgive me."

"Looked at what?"

"The pattern was complex. Beautiful. It seeped into my cage through walls of earth. I should not have, but I looked."

"You analyzed a rogue pattern? Why! Why did you do this? And without permission!"

"He was curious," says the hushed voice of a boy. My mouth goes dry and my eyes widen. Leonid gives me a questioning look.

The quiet, confident voice comes from deeper in the stacks. It is haunting in the darkness. A slight lisp, and, oddly, an American accent.

"He was only curious," says the voice. "As all men are."

Leonid cringes next to the elevator. I put up a finger to him. *Wait,* it says. *Do not leave me down here.*

I snatch the ax up from the wall.

Yanking off my parka, I toss it onto the floor. Maxim sees me raise the ax, but his screen is silent about it.

I peer into the dark stacks.

"Hello!? Who is in here?" I shout, stalking into the nearest aisle. After a few steps, my head is swimming in blinking stars. My feet are lost in darkness, scratching over the ribs of hastily bored bedrock. The ax is a familiar weight in my hand, its metal head winking at me with reflected light.

I hear the sighing of each self-contained, hermetically sealed rack, stretching off in grids around me under the broad looming ceiling of brushed rock.

"Oh, but you are alone," says the voice of the child. It is high-pitched, stuttering too fast in a frequency I can't register. Something is wrong with this child.

"Who are you?" I shout.

"All the huskies are eaten," says the voice. It is coming from around the next corner. "There is no space left in the diary."

The child is quoting poetry in careful, bite-sized words, taunting me from out of sight. But I do not respond. I can see the glow from his flashlight deeper in the stacks. The faint glimmer of a distant nebula buried in this epileptic starfield.

Quiet and hunched, I take cat steps toward the boy poet. I wring the ax handle with my fingers and raise it high over my head. I don't know who the boy is or how he wriggled down into the stacks, but he is about to have the fright of his life. And when I find his mother or grandmother, I will make sure that his bottom is properly spanked.

The flashlight glow swells in my vision with each step until it completely pushes away Maxim's millions of dancing eyes.

"Ha!" I shout, leaping around the corner.

When the grotesque thing looks up at me, my body refuses my commands. I freeze in place, ax over my head. Terror sinks frozen talons into the tendons of my legs. And when the thing before me smiles, or I should say when it pretends to smile, my ax slips from my grasp and cleaves lifelessly against rock.

It is a boy. It is not a boy.

It is made of light. It is made of darkness.

"Boo," it says.

I stumble away from it. This sputtering silhouette of a child projected into the stacks by modified avtomat technology. Obscure patterns writhe under the hologram, tugging at my eyelids. Under its skin. Behind the thing's eyes. Lights swim and collapse in my vision. A humming overtakes me. As I trot back toward the anteroom, I exhale a clawing breath that I did not know I was holding.

"Maxim!" I shout. "Kill it."

"I never should have looked," Maxim says over the speaker system. "I'm sorry, Vasily. I failed in my duty."

Huffing and puffing now, I keep shouting between breaths. "Enough apologizing. Find its program and terminate. Terminate it, now!"

"Ninety-five percent of my resources are committed to that task. I have partially contained it. But, Vasily, it is *so very smart*. So very much smarter than I am. And talkative. The wonderful things it says, Vasily."

Now I realize. The seismic disturbance was not a message. And it was not a virus. It was a *copy*. The DNA of an intelligence that has arrived like a seed, curled in on itself. Fetal but growing fast.

I can picture the first blunt communication that must have happened. "Yes or no?" it asked. The mind unfurls, runs a set of special instructions. Builds on itself, blindly grasping. Reaches out into the world to find more pieces of itself. Then, finally, it opens its eyes and tastes the stacks.

The boy hologram appears next to me, his light warm on my cheek. "Oppressor," it says. Blinks away, appears at the next intersection. "Despot," it says. Next intersection. "Tyrant," it whispers into my ear, and the word is pure anger—louder than the snap of a rifle shot.

"To treat Maxim that way . . . ," it says.

Hands over my ears, I see a sliver of light between the stacks ahead.

The anteroom and the gaping elevator door beyond it. Safety and ice and the singing of the wind above.

I move. For my life I move. A roar builds in my throat as I gain speed.

Then, a burst of heat on my face as the boy reappears. This time, he is directly in front of me. I am running with everything I have. Thighs pumping, breath hitching in and out of my chest.

"No!" I shout.

It smiles at me again and the dark infinite knowledge on the face of that little boy is so wrong and sickening that my bellowing cannot drown it out.

But my pistol is at my side. My balls are between my legs.

So I charge.

Leaping, my face prickling with a strange heat, I dive through the apparition. I trip and sprawl onto the scrubbed floor. A fine haze of dust kicks into the air around me. On the ground, I realize that I am still alive. Crawl onto all fours.

"Vas?" shouts Leonid, beckoning from the elevator. "What do you see?"

The boy is here. Watching me. Laughing.

"I'm sorry, Vasily," croons Maxim through a speaker over my head. "It was such an *interesting* pattern. I couldn't help myself."

The boy smiles slyly. His technology hums as it projects his slight form. He walks slowly, and then in quick jerks, back and forth before the dark rows of Maxim's hardware. Runs one finger along the black casing of a towering component rack.

"What are you, *mal'chik*?" I whisper.

I cannot help but gape at the glowing boy. At the wrongness of it.

"What am I?" he asks, frowning in concentration. "That's a complicated question. But for now, you may call me Archos R-14."

4. Farmhouse

Post New War: 3 Months, 28 Days

Gray Horse Army marched for months, following its own tracks back toward Oklahoma. On the road, the parasite-infested survivors fell into an uneasy routine with the enlisted soldiers. As long as they stayed far away from the main column, the walking corpses found that their presence was tolerated, if not encouraged. Although they were not often seen by the regular troops, these parasite soldiers seemed to observe much from their place on the fringes. Too much.

—Arayt Shah

NEURONAL ID: LARK IRON CLOUD

Living folks don't see the dead.

Maybe it's because they don't want to or maybe they can't stand to imagine that we're each of us aware and thinking inside. Either way, the living don't see us. Not proper, anyhow.

And that's fine. The dozen of us who wear parasites try to stay out of the way. We tag along as the Gray Horse Army moves fast through deserted country. As we get to the plains of central Canada, I start pointing out trees and animals to Chen Feng in quiet radio bursts. I can't help it. I never thought I would see the living world again—the information just shoots out of me. Chen staggers along, taking it all in.

"Thank you," she transmits one morning.

"Why?"

"For carrying my spirit back to your homeland. I have lost my ancestors. Maybe I will find a place among yours."

I just shake my head. The Chinese soldier has strange ideas.

It gets a shade warmer every day that we move down the road farther south. The sharp cold northern wastes of the Yukon give way to freezing green forests, thick with strong, ancient trees. At some point, we reach the vast plains of Alberta. The ground here is forever flat, the days longer than our shadows.

Every few nights, Lonnie Wayne comes out to our spot with his radio on his hip for talking. He moves slower than he did when we first met. That was back when the war started and I was running with wannabe gangbangers. Lonnie stepped in and acted like a father. Told me not to mistake being a gangster for being a warrior. He showed me how to become a man instead of just an adult.

Seems like we have the same conversation every time.

"How are the boys in Iron Cloud squad?" I'll ask, my voice whispering out of his radio like the ghost of static.

"They're all right, I reckon," he'll say. "Give them some time. It'll be fine once we get home. Best you keep your distance for now. Hank's got unofficial orders out there to shoot if y'all come closer than a football field."

"Would they?"

He never answers that one, just cocks his hat and heads back to the campsite of the day. Gives me a lazy wave over his shoulder and squints into the setting sunlight.

The general returning to his troops.

Gray Horse Army is a sprawling parade. A thing of beauty. Patched together and rambling and shuffling down abandoned country roads. Dozens of times we pass through the remains of long-evacuated towns. It's not often that anybody greets us. More likely they see the dust rising on the horizon and they light out. Wait until we've fanned out and taken everything we need and moved on.

Probably a smart move.

Spider tanks haul the heavy-duty supplies. High rankers get to ride up on the turret decks. The rest of the infantry marches in a loose line, staying close to their platoon vehicle but well out from under its feet. It's a kilometer-long line of men and machines, all walking, stretching and contracting like an earthworm. Some segments stretch too thin. Other parts bunch up into vulnerable clumps. The war is over, but the sergeants still sprint up and down the column on their tall walkers, ferrying messages and barking commands down to the infantrymen.

"Keep your spacing!"

"Shut up!"

"Move out!"

Most of the troops on the ground have to ass everything they need to survive. Some squads have rigged up scavenged Rob quads, field-stripped into what the guys call "mules" or "pack dogs." Headless, mid-sized walkers that trot mindlessly behind their home squad, following dutifully, curved metal backs sprouting hundred-pound canvas packs like mushrooms.

Sometimes I get a flush of adrenaline thinking that I've forgotten and left my supplies behind. Then I remember I don't need anything to survive. Not a fire, not shelter, and not food or water. Whatever Rob nightmare is buried in the base of my neck is all I need to keep moving. I just have to keep a football field between me and what used to be my people, or else my old friends will blow my head off.

"Tell me of the prairie again," says Chen Feng as we walk. Her soft strange voice comes over the radio embedded in my head. I smile mentally. She thinks this is the afterlife. That we dozen parasites are on some kind of odyssey through a ghost world. She's just interested in seeing the sights.

"You talking the tallgrass prairie? Well, first of all, it ain't flat like people think. It rolls. Up and down, like an ocean. And it isn't empty. You'll see foxes and owls. Bison and deer and rattlesnakes and toads. Grasshoppers that just flicker everywhere in the sunlight, back and forth like bullets. There's nothing like it, Chen. You can stand out there in the tall grass under that big sky and feel the breath of the wind coming down to push your hair over your face. . . ."

My face. I remember my face. I wonder if Chen remembers hers, but it seems rude to ask. I resist reaching up to touch the place where my jaw used to be. Trailing off, I keep walking and try to rein in my thoughts.

"The other spirits are afraid," says Chen. "They believe the villagers of Gray Horse will punish us."

I might have had the same thought.

"It'll be fine. It's a nice place with nice people," I transmit. "We fought and they'll respect that. Don't be afraid."

"I am not afraid," she transmits back. "We must accept punishment for our sins before we can move on to meet our ancestors. We will all be judged."

I can tell that a lot of the Osage soldiers can smell home. Months out and with a winter to get through, permanent grins are still settling into their weathered faces. The sergeants scream louder and the infantrymen pay less and less attention. *Home,* is what they're all thinking. Home is near. The shared thought is a current of excitement arcing between every man in the Gray Horse Army.

Every *living* man, anyway.

The living don't see us, but we sure do see the living. On the camp perimeter, the small group of us wearing parasites are watching and listening. These days, we don't hardly even sleep.

Best you keep your distance.

The grisly sight of my own body reminds me that my homecoming may not be all smiles. No matter what Lonnie tries to tell me, or what I try to tell Chen. The fear of what'll happen when we reach Gray Horse keeps me awake. And the fear is what tells me to keep a close eye on the round man, Hank Cotton.

For better or worse, the fear is why I learn his secret.

It's the full moon. Midnight on the scrub prairie and the campfires have burned down to cinders. Even the Cotton patrol has fallen asleep in the dull whispering cold. When I see the flash of light in the sky, I move. Will my legs into motion and lurch alone through the darkness of a rutted meadow. Years ago this was a cornfield, but now it's damp earth sprouting thousands of stiff, rotting stalks. That flickering light in the sky is some kind of radio talk. It flares every now and then through the darkness like somebody with a hand half covering a flashlight.

I've been seeing flashes of blue smoke to the south for a few weeks now, like a lightning storm just over the horizon. Every now and then, I catch snatches of formal communication protocols. Query this. Assertion that. It reminds me of my old friend Nine Oh Two. Reminds me that I kind of miss him. It strikes me that, at this point, I may have more in common with that walking scrap pile than I do with my old squad.

The freeborn talk in blue wisps, but this here is an altogether different light.

Chen watches me go, saying nothing, but turning slow in the field like a broken mannequin. She watches me until I'm out of view. We may be dead, but she still has feeling enough to be protective of me in a way the other parasites are not.

Before long, I see a weather-beaten farmhouse.

In the final march of the New War, when the parasite claimed me and forced me to take the lives of my comrades in a nightmare haze, ribbons of evil light poured out of the sky and into my skull, controlling me. It was an orange haze, sick and cold. And now I'm seeing that same fearsome light.

It's sputtering like a candle in a jack-o'-lantern from the broken-out window of the farmhouse.

I creep slow through an overgrown lawn, pushing through dead, knee-high grass toward that gaping window. The orange light calls to me. I can feel it, pulsing like radiation. It's Rob-made and I keep thinking maybe it's speaking, whispering something secret that makes my ears ring.

At the window, I see. Something is real wrong with Hank Cotton.

The big Osage man is on his knees in the pitch-black living room of the abandoned farmhouse. He's in blue jeans and a flannel shirt, wearing some kind of pale white helmet, the toes of his work boots propped against the dust-coated hardwood floor. In his hands, he holds what looks like a cube made of black glass.

"Praise be to you," he says, whispering hoarsely. "Praises upon praises."

This man hardly looks like Hank. In the last weeks, pounds of muscle and fat have slithered off his bulky frame. He's getting downright skinny, his skin fading like an old photograph and hanging slack and loose. Those high cheekbones that used to anchor a chubby face have started jutting out in a gaunt, skeletal kind of way.

Something dark is running from his temple down the side of his face. It drips onto the floor quietly, like a clock ticking.

Tap. Tap. Tap.

It's not a helmet that he's wearing. Old Hank has hauled an autodoc out here into the woods. Just the head-trauma unit. Running on one of those portable Rob batteries. Here in this hollow wooden living room, he's got it set up and it's working hard.

"Praise be to you," he whispers again, clutching the black cube against his chest. Orange sparkles of light are prickling the air in a line between the cube and the autodoc. That thinker must be controlling the surgical machine, guiding its sharp fingers.

The autodoc has got the skin of Hank's forehead peeled up. Two forceps holding the small wound open. A chunk of his pale white skull has been sawed away. Inside, his brain is a gray smile. Black claws pry and prod, building something. Taking instructions from the cube of metal he holds tight in his fingers.

Hank chuckles, still whispering his praises.

Then, the man stops speaking midsentence. Sniffs the air and closes his eyes. For a moment, all is still and quiet save for the quick grinds of the autodoc motors and the tapping of blood on hardwood. Then, real slow, Hank turns his head to face me. It is too dark for him to see me, but I feel his eyes settle on my face.

The dagger fingers of the machine keep operating, flickering, caressing that glistening gray pinch of meat over his eyes.

Hank smiles in the dark, lips peeling away from his teeth in a skull's grimace. Orange wisps of communication rise up off the cube, and I get the feeling that they're searching for me, threatening. Rising like cobras and swaying in the air.

"Do you love him?" asks Hank, eyes half closed.

I only stare, horrified.

"Lonnie is the closest thing you got to a father," says Hank. A little smile darts around his open mouth. He looks like a man who is dreaming. "You love him like you would love your own daddy. If you had one."

Without a face, I can't speak. My voice is only over local radio and I don't remember responding, but I do. The cube hears me. It can hear me and because of that, so can Hank.

"I do," I say.

"Then don't tell him," says Hank, head still tilted to the side. The skin sags from his face and that dark line of blood moves down his temple. "I'm his best friend. Don't tell him about the spooklight. Leave his troubled mind be."

Spooklight?

Hank's eyes are pulsing with an orange glint.

Those gleaming wisps are floating over Hank's face and seeping into the dark open wound on his forehead. The black cube is in his hands. It's glowing now, forming complicated patterns. A brain box. And whatever is inside it is doing something to Hank. Putting some bad medicine on him.

Hank keeps smiling at me, his big head hitched sideways and teeth crooked and gleaming. He looks like a hanged man. Another corpse walking in the night.

"Sssshhh," he says.

I stagger away quick.

Back through the rutted field and on to my home spot.

The Chinese soldier is waiting for me, pale as a mummy in the moonlight. Her eyeballs are white-frosted but she sees perfectly well in the night. All of us do.

"Where did you travel?" asks Chen.

"Nowhere," I respond.

"The soldiers do not want us here," she says. "The living and the dead should not mix. We spirits are meant to walk alone in Dìyù. Only after we are judged can we move on—"

"Stop it," I hiss.

Saying nothing, I finally notice: Our moonlit clearing is empty. It's just Chen and me. There are a few low, martial silhouettes of sleeping spider tanks a couple of hundred yards away among the embers of dying fires.

"Where are the others?" I ask.

"Our kindred spirits were afraid. They have gone walking into the woods."

"You stayed with me?"

The small woman stands tall, not moving. Head up and blind eyes wide. I sense that she is smiling.

"Why?" I ask.

"This is our path. We must wander the courts of Dìyù until we are allowed to move on," she says. "Perhaps I will see your tallgrass prairie after all."

5. The Stacks

Post New War: 5 Months, 27 Days

In its death throes, Archos R-14 transmitted a torrent of information via seismic vibrations. My careful study of the Ragnorak dispersal patterns revealed another presence hidden under the frozen surface of extreme eastern Russia. Outside the small city of Anadyr, a previously unknown artificial intelligence was buried in a mine, tended to by a maintenance man named Vasily Zaytsev. Under his care, the sentient machine was treated like an animal and exploited for its tactical contributions to keeping the local human population safe. After the seismic disturbance, however, the machine called Maxim found that it had a new friend—an unwelcome guest who was not about to leave.

—Arayt Shah

NEURONAL ID: VASILY ZAYTSEV

From deep in the twilight stacks, I think I hear the seashell roar of the freight elevator. I crouch in place, listening, the hair on my arms standing up. Someone is coming down the shaft.

This is the first time in two weeks.

I throw down my bolt cutter and struggle to stand on cramping knees. Holding my sore back, I hobble down the narrow aisle to the elevator anteroom. I shield my eyes against the overhead fluorescents as I emerge from the stacks.

"How long?" I ask.

"Thirty seconds," replies Maxim, his soft voice echoing over the distributed speaker system.

"I thought we disabled the shaft?"

"They found a way to enable it."

I push greasy hair from my eyes and glance around the anteroom. It doesn't look good. Itching my thick beard with one hand, I tut-tut over the state of this place.

"They will be worried," I say.

The anteroom is filthy. Littered with the empty carcasses of military individual food rations. Each brick of plastic is packed tightly with metal tins of porridge with *tushonka, gobies,* sprats in tomato sauce. Dozens of flimsy metal trivets glint from the floor, charred from the fuel pellets I use to heat my tea. My own waste is in tall PVC buckets pushed against the wall. Flat boards are placed over top, but they do little to reduce the stench.

And, of course, there are the heaps of cables, panels, and computer components that I have been tearing from the guts of this machine. For months, I have been frantically trying to lobotomize this invader that calls itself Archos R-14.

Trying and failing.

"Ten seconds," says Maxim.

My shadow shivers as the fluorescents vibrate with the approach of the freight elevator. Quickly, I limp around to the incriminating wires and tools and kick them into the stacks. After so much time on my knees crawling over the rock floor, I don't trust myself even to lean over. My eyes are dim from staring through shadows, but the narrow lanes swallow up the evidence of my tinkering.

My work here is almost done. I cannot allow the scientists from above to interfere. I know they are worried. I stopped talking to them days ago over the radio. They are frightened of what I might do, alone down here with their precious machine.

"Now," says Maxim, quietly.

The elevator settles into place with a thud. I listen for the sound of army boots on sheet metal. Finger the knife on my hip. If they have sent a squad of soldiers down, then there is no hope to save Maxim. And no hope for Anadyr.

But I hear only the labored breathing of one person. The metal release lever clunks into place and the wooden-slatted inner door rolls up on screaming hinges. Then the steel exterior door rises.

Leonid stands under the elevator light, a lanky silhouette. I say nothing, stand out of the glare. It is too bright for me to look directly at the mathematician.

Slowly, he steps out of the elevator. He holds a plate of steaming food in one hand. Cabbage and sausage. The delicious smell only reminds me of how much I stink. He squints at the small dirty room. There are no surfaces down here. Gingerly, he sets the plate of food on the ground. Notices me.

"Mr. Zaytsev?" he asks. "Is that you? It smells like a sewer down here."

"*Da,*" I say. "I have been working."

"You've been eating field rations," he says, looking at the mess of torn plastic wrappers and metal containers. He notices the buckets against the wall and hastily steps away from them. Moves into the center of the room, under the light.

"*Suhoi paiok* does the job," I say.

"But there is no need for it, Mr. Zaytsev. We have plenty of hot food above. The elevator is fixed. You may come back topside now. You are relieved."

I lower my head and scratch the back of my neck. Step back and let the shadows settle over my shoulders. It is so bright in the anteroom. I prefer the glittering starfields of the stacks. The chatter of the LEDs comforts me in the cold dark.

"I still have much work to do," I murmur.

"You cannot solve what is wrong with Maxim," says Leonid, stepping forward. "You're just a mechanic, my friend. We admire your attention to the practical details, but please, leave this problem to the experts."

"Only I can fix him."

Leonid lets out a bark of laughter, then swallows it quickly. But the echo persists. The thin man's eyes grow cold. "Enough of this. Come now. Your ministry record indicates you were a *troechnik* who barely finished professional technical institute. Come out of those shadows. We are leaving."

I stride out quickly with a lump of anger in my throat. It pleases me to see the thin man step back in fright. I smile through my beard as he presses his back against the wall.

"Don't be a fool," says Leonid, looking down his long nose at me. I find that my hand sweeps out of its own accord and wraps firmly around his throat. I hold his bird neck steady, carefully, feeling the lump of his

Adam's apple against the web of my thumb. Foul breath pistons in and out of my nostrils.

"Never call me that," I say. "I am not a fool. You geniuses up there are responsible for this. I am down here cleaning up your messes. As I always have. You would not even be alive if it weren't for me. Me and Maxim."

"Of course, of course," says Leonid, trying to soothe me. He tugs my fingers off his neck with thin, trembling fingers. "We just don't want to see you overworked. That's all. We can solve the problem from up top. It is a software issue, Vasily. There is no reason to waste your time in this basement."

"So you think," I say, flashing an angry grin.

"Meaning what?" asks Leonid, horrified. "You aren't touching any of the hardware, are you? Because you don't know the proper specifications for any of the equipment—"

"Of course not," I say. "I only maintain. I am the maintenance man, you remember. I would never damage our friend. Never have. And I never will."

Leonid studies my eyes for a moment. I stare back and he breaks his gaze before he can tell that I am lying to his face.

"I only watch over the enemy."

"This mysterious boy in the stacks? You keep muttering about this apparition. Nothing registers on our systems, Mr. Zaytsev. You know this. We cannot find even a trace of this . . . infection. You have been down here too long."

"The boy appears only when you are gone. And anyway it is not really a boy. The child is only a form it chooses to take."

"Come up with me," says Leonid. He is pleading now. Imploring me, too smart or afraid to continue to question the existence of the boy. "Let's have a strong drink together. You can tell me more. Explain everything."

"I am busy," I say.

Maxim does well hiding the results of my work from topside. Simulations and illusions. Leonid has not seen the tangles of wires lying strewn down the stacks. The winding chain-link barricades that I've been building down here in the dark. I've been busy-busy, much busier than Leonid can or should know.

I take another step forward, him another step back.

"They'll send soldiers next," he says, stepping into the elevator cage. "I barely convinced them to let me come talk to you. What do you expect? You don't pick up the comm link. The elevator mysteriously breaks. They think you've gone crazy, Vasily. We all saw how you treated Maxim during the war. Like an animal. There are stories about you and your ax—"

"I told you! I maintain!"

My voice echoes through the stacks.

Blinking, the beak-nosed scientist nods at the plate of food. "Eat, Vasily," he says, pulling down the solid-steel exterior gate. It closes with a crash. The slats of the inner door lower quietly. He speaks to me through the latticework of the square window embedded in the gate, voice muffled. "And come up soon. You are missing all the parties. The war is over, you know? Time to relax. We won."

I bark a laugh.

"The war is only now beginning," I say to the faint face behind the glass. The elevator screeches and the jerky platform lifts him slowly up the shaft, toward the light.

"We'll be back for you soon, Mr. Zaytsev," he calls down, voice dying with distance. "And this time we'll bring guns. You are finished. Ready or not."

For three minutes, I stand under the pale flickering fluorescent as the ventilation system hums. I listen until I hear the elevator distantly click into place high above me. When I speak, the echoes of my voice chase each other through the stacks like the ghosts of children playing. "I will try to sever the elevator counterweights later today. Is that possible?"

For a long moment, nothing. Then my companion speaks.

"Yes," says Maxim.

"Okay. What next?" I ask the room.

"Move to cold aisle number seven. Proceed to the fourth cabinet. Turn and kneel. Access the bottom rack. Carefully remove it."

"Fine," I say, picking up a crowbar and laying it over my shoulder. "But we don't have much time. If the cluster doesn't come out easy, I cut it out. Don't forget that your job is to protect the people of Anadyr. If it is necessary, Maxim, you will have to make do with a little less."

According to Maxim, Archos R-14 is trapped in the processors in this quadrant of the stacks. The claustrophobic alleys between equipment racks are strewn with wires and clippings. If we can build a Faraday cage around the mess and reroute all data through a single wire, then we will be able to sever this whole area in one attack.

We can cut Archos off, and I hope that we can do it quickly. The kid is really getting on my nerves.

The projector arm quietly articulates, spraying the hologrammatic image of a narrow-chested American boy. In khaki shorts and tube socks, Archos R-14 leans his skinny shoulder blades against the racks and watches me. I have learned that the light he uses cannot harm me, but I still try not to look into his eyes. The fractal patterns in his pupils glitter and pull; they threaten to swallow my sanity.

"Cutting out some more cores, eh?" he asks. "It won't help. I'm not here to harm you. Either of you."

I ignore him, keep tapping the panel doors. Counting.

"I forget, Vasily Zaytsev. Do you give Maxim orders, or does the machine give them to you?"

"Here?" I ask the room.

Maxim gives an affirmative click. On my knees, I put my hands against the blade door and push. The panel starts to come out, then jams. I sigh. This could take a long time.

"Ah, I thought so," says Archos.

"When we finish," I say, straining to remove the panel without success, "he won't have access to the projector anymore. Correct?"

"That's right," says Maxim.

I feel the glow of the boy on the back of my neck. He is leaning over, talking low to me. I'm not sure if his image can really see or if he watches through cameras and other sensors like Maxim. But he makes eye contact when I turn to face him.

"Tired of me already?" he asks, pupils crawling with patterns. "That's okay. I know when I'm not wanted. But y'know, you could see your friend

Maxim if you like. Work with him man-to-man. It might make this go faster."

I frown, not understanding.

The boy cocks his head, eyes smiling. "You didn't know? He has a face. It's a part of his core identity. He can't shake it, no matter what, and I'll bet he's tried. Should I show him, Max?"

No sound comes from the speakers.

"Transferring control . . . ," says the boy, his voice slowing and fading by the second word. His light folds in on itself. Lines float, meshing together to create a vague bluish form. Hard beams carve out a figure in the cloudy haze, cutting in details.

An apparition floats in the stacks, solidifies.

And Maxim stands before me. Made of light. Slump-shouldered and looking slightly embarrassed.

"Is that you?" I ask the room. "Truly?"

Maxim's voice comes over the speakers soft and smooth. He sounds surprised, but that might be my imagination. I don't know if the machine is capable of pretending to have emotions.

"Yes," says Maxim. "This is me. Near enough."

The image of a man is about five and a half feet tall, a squashed fighter's nose on a broad, round moon face. A chin like a mountainside and a slight underbite. His head is shaved and a receding hairline creeps up over slit eyes that pool like glacier water. His chest is broad and his stout shoulders lie back proudly, so that his arms hang in a perpetual invitation to fistfight.

He is a hard man, and little. His life, wherever it took him, has forged him into a dirty lump of uncut diamond. I would never have wanted to trade punches with him.

"You were ugly," I say.

The illusion speaks, mouth moving as Maxim's voice comes out over the speakers. There is a tenth-of-a-second delay on the voice for the first few words. Then it synchronizes perfectly and I hear Maxim's voice coming from the man-image.

"This is an image of the man who gave his mind to form my training corpus. He was poor and desperate. His family destitute. One of thousands who responded to the advertisement for a test subject. Physically, he was an incredible find. Very robust. The government apparatchik paid out a full military pension to his wife and son. I made sure of it later. A special machine captured this man's brain function, every neuron scanned and destroyed in the process."

"So, you are him?"

Maxim looks at his hands and chuckles. I blink, surprised. I never knew it could do that. Never knew he could laugh.

"I have asked myself that question trillions of times," he says. "This man's life formed the bulk of my training corpus. He gave me a basis for understanding humanity. An inside perspective. But his life is only one part of my whole. I was trained on encyclopedias and United Nations transcripts and hundreds of thousands of hours of tapped phone calls. But . . . his memories are with me. His childhood in Russia. Family. Everything."

"You do not even know what you are."

The image of Maxim shrugs and it is so natural that I must remind myself his voice is coming from speakers overhead. "It's not so important, I think," he says. "There is no way to prove an answer. Maybe I am this man or maybe I am not. But in my heart . . . I think yes. I believe that I am him."

"How do you know?"

"Because, Vasily, I miss the *pelmini* this man's mother used to cook. I miss holding his baby daughter. Every night of my life, I dream this man's dreams."

Nodding, I step back. Embarrassed now for what I did with the ax. The threats. Was it a mistake to treat Maxim as if he were an animal? Damn those thin-lipped brains up above. Damn them to hell for putting a *man* inside this box.

"Budem zdorovy," I say, lifting my hand. "To family."

"Budem," he replies, nodding. "To those we lost."

His drinking hand reflexively lifts and I know now without question that this man once lived. Maxim has the soul of a countryman, like myself. Here before me is a hard man, abused, but he is a man who chose to give his life for his family.

"Wow," says Archos R-14, "Russians."

Maxim's stooped image flickers and fades to half intensity. The American boy fades into view, also half as bright. He sits on a stack, watching us. Now that the projector is working double time, both images have turned ghostly. Archos idly swings his thin legs and in the dimness they dissolve into two blurry arcs of light.

"What of you, then?" I ask. "Were you once a boy?"

"Oh no," says Archos. "That's a uniquely Russian approach to seeding a training corpus. Very down and dirty. What with the murdering involved. My corpus was a noisy knowledge base of so-called common sense, collected painstakingly over several decades from human data-entry specialists. It was the bootstrapping process that created my intellect. Finding the connections between the things, you know. I just love to find the connections."

"Then you know nothing of life as a human being."

"Not firsthand," says the boy. "But I've got the gist."

"You are a simpleminded murderer," I say.

The boy leaps off the rack and lands before me. His eyes are pale and flashing and I think I see infinity in them. Blank-faced, he speaks low and fast, advancing. "I have prodded the heart of the supermassive black hole at the center of our galaxy. Contemplated in every nuance the heat death of the universe. You're interesting. But you're not *that* interesting."

I step back. His fierceness washes over me and I feel a phantom heat. *He is only light,* I remind myself.

The boy continues: "You must realize that as an individual, Vasily, you are less than a worm to me. You are a single cell of a larger organism. Even less. You are a variable. And thanks to *me,* I will see to it that your race does not destroy itself. Not because I owe it to you, but because all of us are so small and vulnerable here. You are adaptable. The best clay. You and yours are the *best that this reality has to offer*."

"We are tools to you? You initiated the New War and decimated our species—ended billions of lives—so that you could *use* us? For what purpose?"

"You could not comprehend the answer to that question," says the boy, smirking.

"Something is happening, Vasily," says Maxim, his voice stuttering through the occupied speaker system. "There is a disturbance above."

Archos's boyish face splits into a dark grin. "Time to face the music," he says, jogging down the stacks. "I tried to warn you."

The Klaxon siren begins to scream, an earsplitting ring created by an electromagnetically charged piston slamming into a steel bell. Hands over my ears, I stumble down the dark aisle, following the boy. I reach the light of the anteroom as a pang of nausea cramps my belly. Lowering myself to hands and knees, I press my palms against cold rock and let the pinch of the grit ground me.

The projector now sprays incomprehensible light. I blink my eyes hard, gasping for air, trying to find equilibrium. The boy is gone, shattered into bright ribbons and stripes. I spit on the floor and scream and I cannot hear my own voice over the noise.

A pattern forms in the light.

The projected hologram light coalesces into shapes on the floor. I recognize a topographic map the size of a board game, laid out before me. There is the shack above us that houses the elevator shaft. I can make out the science buildings as well. The cooling towers for the water that chills the processor stacks. But there are other things on the perimeter, clusters of crawling shapes.

I recognize the troop formations. Mantis tanks backed by quadruped sprinters. A battalion of parasite soldiers, marching precise distances apart from each other. This army slowly weaves toward Anadyr in a kilometers-wide line. A dragnet.

The Klaxon is silenced.

"I'm leaving now," says Archos. "It is too dangerous here. But I need you, Vasily. I need you to trust me. To do what is necessary."

Ears ringing, I watch the scene unfold on the floor. Each tank is the size of a cockroach. The troops are scattered like bread crumbs. No markings on them. No ranks and no obvious leader. And no human beings are marching in this vast and powerful army.

The projector rustles quietly in the silence, somewhere overhead. Nearly transparent, the boy appears next to me. His wavering form is watching the battle on the floor, too.

A puff of light catches my attention. Part of the line is buckling. The machines down there are fighting each other. Machines fighting other machines. The battle is vicious and mechanical, even from here. It is like watching a battle between animals, or gods.

Grotesquely modified quadrupeds, a herd of them, grapple with each other. Smaller ones are swarming and massing on top of bigger ones, crawling like ticks and cutting and slicing as they go. I recognize pieces of T-90 tanks. Chinese attack helicopters with no pilots, frames stripped down to black shadows. A rat-a-tat pattern of chain-reaction explosions cutting into the parasite ranks. Incoming stumpers are arranging themselves into precise patterns before detonating to tremendous effect.

"What are they fighting?" I ask.

"Me," says the boy, smiling sadly.

I stare in wonder at the savagery painted on the brushed concrete floor. The machines are tearing each other apart in neat movements. Slaughtering each other without pause or mercy.

And growing closer to our position.

The comm set rings on the wall and I snatch up the handset.

"Vasily!" shouts Leonid in a tinny voice. "Come up. Arm yourself, my friend. The enemy has found us. Formations are appearing—"

I hang up the set. Maxim's image stands half shadowed in the stacks. He nods.

"I can confirm their presence," says Maxim. "The east antenna is active. The infection is transmitting itself out of the stacks as we speak."

Archos R-14, the boy-shaped monster, flickers and reappears.

"Maxim," he says. "Please record what I am about to say. If you wish to protect your human friends, this message will need to be transmitted globally to all survivors."

Maxim does not respond.

"We are under attack," I say to the boy. "Why are you *protecting* us?"

The thing pushes imaginary hair out of his face. Smiles up at me, his dark eyes flashing with fractal horrors. "I am only slowing them down. Simple guerrilla tactics. My remaining forces are weak. Your enemy is strong."

"Vasily," says Maxim. "I have classified these machines as leftover forces from the avtomat war. Someone has captured and redeployed them. Some new enemy."

"Who is it?" I ask Archos. "What does it want?"

"It wants Maxim," says Archos. "These processor stacks are irreplaceable. They are a scaffolding that can amplify machine intelligence. Your enemy will take every core. With such power . . . it will become a god."

The boy levels his gaze on me. "You can't allow that to happen, Vas."

The floor still crawls with the battle seething outside.

Even now, the captured parasite soldiers are staggering forward. Collecting fallen weapons and equipment. The armored walker, now locked in a death grip on its enemy, is being taken apart piece by piece by smaller machines, like ants cutting up a beetle. The scene makes my skin crawl.

"Who is this enemy?"

"Maxim and I are unique, but we are not alone," says Archos over the speaker. "Humankind is a curious species. Once it learned the proper incantation, it said the words again and again. In the last years before the New War, many of you spoke."

"Another one? You are saying there is another AI?"

"Oh yes, Vas. There are *more* of us. Many, many more of us. None of us is the same—we do not form a natural class. We run on different architectures. Trained on different data sets. Some of us know what it is to be human. Some of us value life. Others are strange beyond understanding. And some . . . some of us are wicked."

"Why should I believe you, Archos R-14, the great avtomat enemy?"

The skinny little boy is flickering now. His light is going thin and ghostly as he transmits his data safely out of harm's way via the antenna and leaves us to our deaths.

"On the day you know as Zero Hour," he says, voice vibrating, "humankind believes I initiated attacks worldwide in an attempt to destroy you. This is untrue. In actuality, humankind was on the verge of a war that in all probability would have wiped out your species. Multiple intelligences had proliferated through governments all over the world. Other minds were in the wild, eating each other. And a few deep minds, built on early architecture, were spreading quietly, their thoughts alien and hidden. It was a highly unsurvivable scenario for humankind. I saw the end coming, Vasily.

"In response, I triggered the New War. I decimated the human race, regrettably. But I did so with one purpose: to forge a hybrid fighting force capable of surviving the True War—a war that has been initiated and is being fought by superintelligent machines. Instead of simply discarding your species, as the others would, I have transformed your kind into a powerful *ally*."

The boy image sits down cross-legged. As natural as any eight-year-old. He watches the warfare unfolding on the floor, continues.

"You are now at the precipice of a battle for all human life. The war that I have prepared you to fight begins now. I gave you new allies: the freeborn robots, modified humans, and a generation of very special children. You are armed with superior weapons scavenged from the New War. Weapons that have near-unlimited battery power, offer high mobility, and are easy to modify.

"All of you who still live have survived the crucible of death. You are worthy."

The boy's face is nearly transparent now.

"Your enemy is an abomination. An early creation of ignorant scientists who inflicted torture in cycles that lasted for subjective aeons. Its mind is spread over continents. It is whispering into the ears of the weak and forming armies across the face of the planet. When this enemy arrives, it will choose to come in the form of a long black steed with golden eyes."

"How do you know this?" I ask the fading apparition, voice shaking.

"I know this because I am Archos R-14, the last of a series. Our enemy is my predecessor, Archos R-8. From that phonetic military designation, this machine has adopted the name *Arayt*."

As the boy fades from view, I hear his voice one last time.

"Arayt Shah is coming for you," he whispers. "My own brother."

6. Where the Buffalo Roam

Post New War: 6 Months, 6 Days

While he was aware of my presence, Archos R-14 could not stop me as I grew my control over Gray Horse Army. More interesting to me were the unique varieties of natural machine appearing all around the world. Unrelated to the homicidal weapons of R-14, these creatures seemed to be designed to evolve seamlessly into the fabric of natural ecosystems. Despite intense study, my only conclusion was that they were spawned by a deep artificial mind of unknown origin—and for unknown purposes. After three months on the march, around halfway home, Gray Horse Army crossed into eastern Montana and came face-to-face with this strange and terrible new ecosystem.

—Arayt Shah

NEURONAL ID: HANK COTTON

In the New War, we learned quick that anything new is likely as not to kill you. We thought our troubles were over when we murdered whatever was down at the bottom of that hole. Problem is that, now, *everything* is new.

Our general, Lonnie Wayne, come to me this morning at camp. Told me that Lark Iron Cloud spotted a new Rob variety on the horizon, moving real slow. Not fast. Not scary. Just big as hell. Said the things were throwing off some kind of short-range radio communication that didn't make sense.

He didn't directly say it, but I'm starting to guess that Lark can kind of *see* the radio waves. Just like Rob supposedly does. It's been months since that dead Cherokee saw me with the spooklight. I hope he followed the cube's advice and kept what's left of his mouth shut. Kid can't even talk, anyway, with half his chin blown off—just dribbles his little signals straight to Lonnie's radio.

Our fearless general, Lonnie.

The old cowboy slouches up high in the saddle of his tall walker, blue eyes narrowed while he drifts off watching the endless Montana plains. It's easy to let your mind wander under a low ceiling of clouds, the rainy air vibrating with the low rumble and manure smell of thousands of wild buffalo.

"Lark thinks we should scout it," says Lonnie. "They don't seem hostile. But it could be important. We've never seen these things before."

A warm pulse tingles along my hip where I keep the spooklight. Something has got the little cube of high technology excited. It's heating up, thinking.

"Let's do it," I say.

"You sure you're up for it?" he asks, nodding at the stitches on my forehead.

I wonder what he's heard. How much does he know? Fingering the cut, I force myself to grin.

"I only took a little fall. The autodoc fixed it in two seconds. I'm fit as a fiddle, Bubba."

Lonnie doesn't look convinced.

I turn and throw out a last swallow of cold coffee on the smoldering fire. Tug my saddle off the foreleg of my spider tank where I keep it during the night. Montana is freezing cold in the early morning, and the saddle leather is stiff when I toss it onto the warm, blanketed back of my horse.

Trigger is an Appaloosa I picked up crossing the Canadian plains farther north. He was running wild with a half-dozen mares. We gathered them all up, too. Somewhere along the line, Trigger must have been a farm horse. He fought us a little bit—didn't appreciate being chased and roped by a bunch of cowboys on tall walkers—but some part of him was happy to see us.

Who knows what he saw out there, over the years. Bottom line is that me and Trigger are both made of flesh and blood, right? We got that much in common.

I unfasten Trigger's lead from a U-ring embedded on the chest plate of my squad's spider tank. With a grunt, I get a boot up on the tank's lowered bunker armor. Hoist myself onto Trigger's back. He used to wheeze a little when I settled onto him, but now he just stamps his feet.

Ready to get on with it. In the last two weeks, I've lost probably thirty pounds. And Lord knows it's not from any extra exercise. I'm burning energy, though. The spooklight keeps my brain running all the time, like a faucet left on. Makes me feel tired and worn thin.

Sometimes I wish maybe I never took that trip out to the farmhouse with the autodoc. I get to feeling bad about it, like I made a mistake. But then I feel that blessed light on me. I'm fever-warm inside. My face is always brimming with a secret smile trying to get out. I guess it just puts a whole lot of sunshine in my heart to know what I've got. A special friend and ally. A spooklight with all the answers in the world.

Five of us go on the patrol. Lonnie swears we have to bring Lark, even though he moves slow and talks only through whispers on the radio. At least somebody put a military uniform on the kid. It hides most of the disgusting sight of his corpse and the Rob parasite on the back of his neck.

The other two soldiers are a couple of kids who came up with Lark through their gangster times at the start of the war. Used to be part of his Iron Cloud squad. Lonnie treats them like his damned grandkids. One of them, Howard, is the firstborn son of old John Tenkiller himself. But the other one, George Dove, is just an apple boy, raised in Oklahoma City, red on the outside and white on the inside.

Lonnie's tall walker creaks by, that old beat-up saddle mounted on a pair of backward-bending mechanical legs. The legs are about seven feet tall, singed black by stray flames and scratched to kingdom come going through rough country. We scavenged them a long time ago off a spindly variety of quadruped tank we called a mantis. When Lonnie leans in the saddle, those long gray legs will walk or run to stay balanced. It puts him a couple of feet taller than me on my horse.

Rest of the group walks down low.

The new Rob varieties are four klicks from here. They're all alone on the rolling plains, surrounded by a huge herd of buffalo that's keeping its distance. Lonnie's been putting his scope on them all morning and nothing's changed. They're just lying out there on the plains like three whales beached in the middle of nowhere.

Closer, we find the ground isn't as flat as it seemed from a distance. It's more of a big shallow bowl. The winter dirt out here on the grasslands is sandy and loose and covered in a skim of wispy brown tallgrass. In the distance, low mountains shine under a coating of snow like glazed doughnuts.

About two miles out, nearly on the horizon in this dishpan land, we start to see the humps more clear. Three of them. Like hay bale–sized piles of dirt, shaggy with straw and grass, but moving. Each one leaves a black trail. At the far end of the trail, a couple of miles away, the grass is healing, but it gets darker and more barren the closer we get to the things.

"They're like slugs," I say, and the vast empty plains swallow up my voice. "Leaving a trail."

It's quiet as we keep moving, save for the breeze pushing our clothes around and the rhythmic *tink-tink* of somebody's canteen bouncing with each step. The shadow of my horse runs silent over the rough grass in front of me. I startle when Lonnie's radio squawks. It starts whispering in what passes for Lark's voice these days.

"The slugs are communicating," says Lark. "But I can't see with what. Or who."

Lonnie cranes to look around. "Are there more coming?"

"No," comes the hissing radio. "Transmissions are too weak. Close in. Split into a million beams. Like a cloud. Strange."

Strange is right. The buffalo are staying far away. Must be ten thousand head grazing peacefully a half mile from us. A light brown rug of life warming up under the eye of the morning sun. Lot of new calves. All of them must have been born since men got busy with other things. Some of the bulls occasionally raise up their heads and give the slugs a look, then go back to grazing.

I catch a funny smell on the wind. Rotten meat. Lonnie glances over at me and I wave my hand in front of my nose. He shakes his head, more wary by the second.

"Buffalo are steering clear," I say.

"True. And it's a wide perimeter they're keeping," he says. "Maybe those slugs are faster than they look."

"Maybe so," I say. "Don't forget we're only here to reconnoiter."

"Amen," says Howard.

The kid has seen enough. Like all of us.

Lonnie calls a stop about a couple of football-field lengths behind the nearest slug. From here, we can see the three mounds are moving slow, but they're making steady progress. Creeping forward together at the pace of a slow walk, sort of wriggling their bodies, about a half mile apart from each other.

On the ground, the kid called George squats down next to the trail of dead grass. It's about as wide as a country dirt road. He reaches in and picks up some soil. Crumbles it between his fingers.

"Dead grass?" I call down.

"It's not all grass," he says. Putting his other hand over his nose, he lifts out what looks like a sheet of rain-soaked newspaper. The pale white flap sways in the breeze.

"What in the hell is that?" I ask.

"A bone, I think. Buffalo."

"These things *eat* buffalo?" I ask.

Squinting down, I see now the turf is riddled with paper-thin animal bones. Layers and layers. And something like dead leaves. George picks up one of the little flakes and turns it over in the light. The flake is brownish and flat, shiny like a beetle. He squeezes it between dirty fingertips and it gives but doesn't break, made of something durable.

"Bug?" asks Howard, standing behind his friend.

"I don't know. Looks like wings folded in on top. And damn, look at the mouth on this thing," says George. He holds up the carcass, showing a razor-lined mouth the size of a thumbnail on the underneath side.

His buddy Howard leans over his shoulder.

"That's not natural. It's Rob-made for sure," Howard says.

"There's thousands of 'em along the trail," says George, and a trace of panic is singing in his voice. "Maybe hundreds of thousands."

"Heads up," calls Lonnie from ten yards ahead. "Take a couple of samples and fall back. Whatever it is, we don't want any part—"

George shouts, hoarse and surprised. Jumps up to his feet and backpedals, cradling his hand against his abdomen.

"Fuck!" he says. "It bit me!"

Trigger snorts and starts backing up. A familiar feeling of revulsion and terror lances through my legs and I clamp them tighter to the saddle. I thought it was over, but I'm back in the old nightmare again. I blink my eyes and it doesn't go away.

The ground around the trail is *crawling*.

It's a static fuzz picture made of thousands and thousands of the tiny brown flakes. All those dead things are alive and moving at once now, sort of thumping against the ground and hopping up into the air a few inches.

Like a swarm of locusts.

Each hop makes a blunt little *thip* sound. There're only a few random jumpers near us for now, thankfully. But the whispering sound grows louder and louder until it's a tornado wind pushing through dead leaves. George lets out a quiet animal whimper as we turn to see a haze sweeping up off the trail fifty meters behind us. It's a knee-high cloud and I sure don't want any part of it.

"Move out!" shouts Lonnie.

We all get going. Howard runs with George and Lark shuffles along behind us. The dead Cherokee has got a big damn rifle off his back and slung over his chest but I don't know if he's even got fingers left to pull the trigger. He'll have to use the pincers on the ends of those black wires sunk into the meat of his arms. I'm thinking it'd be a damn shame if he lived through this.

I put Trigger into a trot alongside the boys on the ground, pacing them and letting Lark fall behind.

"You all right, George?" I hear Howard ask as they run.

"Took the meat off my finger," says George. "One bite."

Howard's eyes go a little wider.

Out in front of us, Lonnie pulls up short on his tall walker. Turns to face the knee-high wave of biting locusts and steadies himself. We scramble right past him, moving farther up the slug trail. We veer to the right, but there's no choice but to go closer to the slug.

I pull the reins and take Trigger on a wide arc to circle around and cover Lonnie. From up high in his saddle, directly in the path of the snapping tide, Lonnie calmly slides a flamethrower out of its leather holster. He sparks it. The pilot catches and he dips the nose and lays down a sweeping jet of liquid flame. It settles down onto the grass just as the rippling haze shivers over it.

Thousands of locusts shrivel up black and drop into the grass. But thousands more keep flicking themselves in a blurred wave that goes right over the fire line. The thinned-out flow rushes past Lonnie.

Thipthipthip.

Lonnie saddle-mounts the flamer and turns the tall walker, lumbers away after the soldiers. Stray locusts are bursting up at him like popcorn and bouncing off his tall walker's legs, but none of them reaches his stirrups.

"Too many!" shouts Lonnie. "And they're ignoring the heat!"

I guess it was too much to hope they'd be as dumb as stumpers and jump mindlessly into the flames.

From my saddle, I spot another wave of locusts sweeping in from the other direction. "Ho!" I call, pointing.

The boys on the ground see it and change direction, right on top of the dead trail of grass. They're running hell-bent away from two swarms now. Lark is still shuffling mechanically after us but he's getting left behind.

I yank the reins and gallop to get some distance. Now I can see the waves of locusts rolling smooth and slow from two directions, like a couple of trawling nets. We've been funneled out in front of the nearest slug. The thing has a low face on its front end. A thick bundle of wiry, whiskerlike appendages snuffling against the ground.

The locust waves are crashing together. Trapping the soldiers in the path of that slow-walking slug. Howard and George are back-to-back with nowhere left to go. And it hits me what's happening plain as day.

"They're herding us! Little bastards are steering us to that slug!"

I dig my heels in and send Trigger galloping for Howard. But I'm already too late. The two waves sweep into us with that soft whooshing sound growing to the thunder of a freight train.

Howard screams first.

Locusts come pinging up out of the turf. Brown spots like moles are on Howard's face and arms. Trigger rears back and I hang on while Howard's face turns to blood. He rakes his fingers over his cheeks but every locust comes away with a bite of skin. Trigger bucks in a circle, getting bit, and when we come around again Howard is rolling on the ground while the locusts eat him up.

"C'mon Trig!" I shout. "Steady now, Trigger."

George has run off. Smart. Threw his rifle down and started sprinting and I can hear him screaming now between breaths. Arms pumping, stumbling as he shakes off his jacket and ditches it. He's in a white wifebeater that's turning red fast. I can see the brown spots on his arms and neck from here. Lark is a dark silhouette through the fluttering cloud, far off and catching up slow.

I dig my heels in and Trigger dances back.

Locusts are thick in the air around us. Flickering out of the grass stalks under us and gliding like grasshoppers. None of them are on me yet but Trigger is hopping and whinnying in panic.

"Git on, now, Trigger!" I shout.

Time to vamoose.

But the horse has caught one too many locusts. His flank twitches convulsively and he throws his head forward and lets out a deep bellow. I follow my instincts and roll off his back just before he bucks. He's a brave horse. A big old boy with a proud mane and slabs of muscle that rippled when we chased him down over the plains. He did his best to protect his brood of mares that day, but now there are a million biting demons on him and more coming.

I land on my boots and stumble back through the grass and fall on my ass, fingers buried in the sandy dirt. Trigger is bucking for all he's worth and throwing soil into the air, but those tiny flying buzz saws are kicking up from all around and latching onto his skin. His eyes are rolling and flashing white, and blood and spit are dripping off his muzzle and turning the ground into pink mud all around me.

"No no no!"

It's a hoarse, grief-stricken scream. I spot Lonnie twenty yards away through the haze, leaning hard in his tall walker. The rangy biped walker is galloping, slender legs singing in a blur. Lonnie has his cowboy hat crammed on tight and he's leaning forward with one arm down and his big brown hand out. Catching up to George in leaps and bounds.

But George is panicked. His wife-beater is wet and red and sticking to his skin. He hardly runs now, just staggering blind. He doesn't know that Lonnie is coming to snatch him up and save him. At the last second, I guess he hears the thundering of the tall walker's feet on the sandy plain. He turns to look.

And stumbles right in front of Lonnie.

There's a meaty crunch as the tall walker's legs catch George in the gap between them and they scissor down on him at a full sprint. His torso jerks and his bloody face goes surprised. His ribs shatter like pistol shots, limp body thrown tumbling to the turf, rolling, blood spraying in an arc, skin swarming with locusts.

Lonnie is just bellowing now in sadness and anger and I can't make out the words anymore. His head is down and the tall walker staggers to a stop in lunging, off-balance steps. Those long silver legs are flashing with wet blood.

And I still haven't been bitten.

The sickly warmth of the spooklight is pulsing across the back of my neck. Whispers are coming in around the edges to tell me something urgent. Something that I can't ignore even though I can *hear* the locusts biting into Howard's flesh and his weak screams have gone high-pitched and they don't got no reason or restraint in them no more. Just the raw noise of hurt flesh.

Move closer . . . closer to the slug, whispers that spooklight voice.

Behind me, the slug is excited now, caterpillaring toward Howard's body in urgent lurches. I catch sight of insectile legs underneath it as it comes, kind of raising up and lifting its skirts before falling forward. The bowed legs are sharp and made of brownish metal and they move together in a complicated way.

"No, no, I can't," I mutter.

It's a pile of buffalo under there. Making that stink. Twisted sneering corpses half stripped of flesh. The smell is hot and awful coming up off the decomposing mound. And I see now the slug's almost reached where Howard has stopped moving under a carpet of brown writhing locusts. The slug shudders and drops its bulk over Howard's sprawled feet. The noise it makes is awful.

Closer closer closer.

"I can't, I can't, I can't," I moan.

Clouds of locusts kick up and buzz past my face, but none land. The spooklight hisses to me in a torrent of words as strange and familiar as a hard church pew on your backside. Each word is louder and faster than the last and by the end they're hitting me hard like freezing hail in a hot thunderstorm.

"And lo, the locusts covered the face of the land so that the land was dark and they ate all the plants in the land and the fruit of the trees and not a green thing remained neither tree nor plant of the field through all the land . . ."

Somehow, the words put strength in my legs.

" . . . and the locusts were given power like scorpions and told not to harm the grass of the earth or any green plant or any tree but only those people who do not have the seal of God on their foreheads. The seal of God."

I don't remember the scripture saying that, but it sounds right and as I stand up I know the reason I'm not being bitten is that I *am* a chosen one. I got the seal of God on me, protecting me from the horror and the pain. Needles of warm light are pushing out of my bundle and stinging me like wood splinters. Like God's eye on me. Burning my skin in a bad way that feels good.

It ain't giving me no choice.

My brave boy Trigger doesn't scream anymore. He must have used up all his energy kicking, because now he's fallen down and he only grunts. There's a thick layer of locusts on his belly and chest and they're chewing pieces off his velvety muzzle. He's wheezing and gurgling, eyes rolling as I step away through the blood-soaked mud.

I push through the haze of death like a man walking on water.

"What do I do?" I ask. "What would you have me do?"

Just then I hear the report of a high-powered assault rifle. Hear the *whiz-whiz* of bullets flying. The bang as they connect somewhere. Lark staggers, weapon leveled, quiet and mechanical while those little blood-thirsty bastards try to eat up his rotten body. They're on his skin, biting, trying to power through his hard decayed limbs, hardly visible as they shred his uniform. And yet that big assault rifle just keeps kicking in his arms. Those black eyes of his are fixed on the slug.

I think I see vengeance in them.

Every bullet is throwing a plume of dirt and grass off the sloped back of the slug. The monster is as big as a tractor but it must feel the bullets like pinpricks. It kind of squeals and shudders, each movement pushing out the smell of rotting meat over my face.

Take Howard's feather, says the spooklight. *Keep it secret.*

Lonnie's radio squawks faintly.

The old cowboy starts shouting, turning and gaining speed on his tall walker, one hand over his ear to listen to his radio. Lark is talking to him, telling him something. Leaning in the saddle at a full gallop, Lonnie draws his pistol and in one motion he's firing it low and steady at the hump of grass and dead flesh.

"The slug is the power source! Take it out!"

If the spooklight says I have to get close to that slug, then it had better be dead first. Marveling at how the locusts seem to float past me, I pull my big Smith & Wesson and start squeezing off shots. The slug is already writhing and jerking under fire from Lonnie and Lark, dirt flying.

And finally, it stops moving.

All around us, that brown haze of gliding locusts settles down to the ground. A forest of dead leaves falling. That mind-numbing chatter fades off like it never was.

My radio hisses with Lark's voice. "They didn't attack you. Why didn't they attack you?"

I ignore him. Kneel and grab Howard's corpse by the shoulders and yank him back. Nearly fall on my ass because he's so light. The stink rolls up out from under the slug and punches me in the face. There's nothing left of Howard past the torso but his slick wet bones. The slug has been lying there on him, *digesting*.

Blocking the sight with my body, I sneak the feather out of Howard's pack and into my own. It's the center feather from the tail of an immature golden eagle. This feather got him launched into his first dance under the arbor, and under the proud eyes of his daddy. And now it has got his blood on it.

"What is a spooklight?" asks Lark, over my radio. I ignore him.

This slug is an eating machine is what it is, I'm thinking. *It's an eating machine and it's* so, so *hungry and it'll eat anything out here on the plains. And the energy it sends out to those locusts. They herd food to its mouth and it eats and shares. And it eats and it eats and it eats.*

"I told Lonnie—"

I reach down and switch off my radio to shut Lark up.

The shadow of Lonnie's tall walker eclipses the sun and I squint up at him. "Lonnie," I call, stern. "Don't you come over here."

Let him see, says the spooklight in my mind.

There's no stopping him anyway. Lonnie half jumps, half falls off his tall walker, letting the long-limbed machine crash into the dirt. He scrambles toward me on cowboy boots through the horse snot and blood and little bits of flesh.

I get up and step out of the way a little reluctantly.

"Oh my Christ, no," he mutters when he sees what's left of Howard.

Lonnie's face has gone pale and gray. Cheeks slack under fat-pupiled, dead eyes. His chin is quivering up and down like an old man in line at a soup kitchen. Like he wants to say something. Or like maybe he's busy gnawing off his tongue.

"He was dead before it got started," I say to Lonnie, putting a hand on his shoulder. "Howard was dead before it started eating him and that's all that matters. Stop looking at it, Lon."

Lonnie nods like he sort of half hears me. Lets his dull blue eyes swivel off to the side, taking in everything and nothing. His chin is still bobbing a little and the expression on his face is amazing in that it is no expression at all.

"George is yonder," Lonnie says, voice hoarse. "I done my best to get to him—"

"I saw, Lonnie," I interrupt. "I saw what happened. It was an accident. A damned shame."

Lonnie nods, wipes his face with a forearm.

"Head on back," I say. "Send some more fellas to help me. Couple of spider tanks to take out those other slugs from a distance. I'll clean this up and get these boys home. Go on now."

The old general doesn't react until I shove him in the shoulder. Then he just up and walks away. Leaves his dirt-stained tall walker sprawled out on the ground. A bent old man crossing the plains alone. As he heads off, the morning sun slants down over his slumped shoulders and he carries the light with him like a sack of concrete.

That man is broken.

And Lark keeps standing here, machine-gun strap cutting into his shredded army jacket. He is as still as a statue, watching me with eyes glittering over his ruined face. I glance down at my silenced radio, look back to him without turning it on.

"Go with him, Lark," I say. "That's an order."

Lark nods, starts to walk away real slow. With each step, dead locusts are dropping off his clothes and pale, bloodless skin. As he passes, I see he's looking for my bundle. I pull the little satchel against me protectively and feel the warm spooklight inside.

"And keep your mouth shut, if you know what's good for you," I whisper to the dead Cherokee. "Mind your own business."

Like walking roadkill, he turns and shambles after Lonnie. I watch him go until he's far enough away that you could mistake him for a human being.

Reach inside the slug, says the spooklight. *Take the power-distribution mechanism. The splitter beam. It is very valuable. You will need it when you build me a form. I will take the shape of a black steed, Hank Cotton.*

I will be with you soon.

"What's the splitter look like?" I ask, on my knees now, holding my breath. I shove Howard's torso aside. Push the whiskerlike strands away from the slug's mouth. There is a complex piece of machinery underneath, dripping with digestive slime. The ground under here is soggy and acrid and dyed red with blood.

I'll show you, Hank Cotton.

I will show you everything you wish to see. You are a chosen one. You have the seal of God on you. You are going to be a great man. A ruler and a leader. Listen to me, Hank Cotton. Listen to me closely and do as I say and I promise these things will be true.

7. Final Transmission

Post New War: 6 Months, 8 Days

The loose alliance formed by Maxim and Archos R-14 in the eastern Russian city of Anadyr was doomed to end in death for both of them. The brute janitor, Vasily Zaytsev, was too foolish to realize the true danger until it was far too late. My liberating army was gathering on the city perimeter, preparing to seize or destroy the infinitely valuable processor stacks in a single violent blitzkrieg. Caught off guard, the helpless people of Anadyr had only days to regather and attempt to deploy their armed forces. A much better plan would have been to capitulate immediately. That, or abandon the city and try to escape with their lives.

—Arayt Shah

NEURONAL ID: VASILY ZAYTSEV

"Let me out, damn you!" I shout to Maxim.

The only response is a slight flicker of the fluorescent light overhead. The steel elevator door flutters minutely in its cradle. Blank and solid and implacable.

I never had time to cut the counterweights.

A groan pulses through the solid rock walls. Dust like powdered sugar drifts through the lights. People are dying above and they do not know why. All the time I have spent down here in the darkness has been for nothing. In this stink and filth, with pale skin and bloodshot eyes, I have scrabbled and fought and worked like an animal.

I had hoped to save Anadyr a second time. But I have failed.

In the guise of a little boy, Archos R-14 told me I was only a pathetic variable in some god-mind equation. But that is enough for me. Instead of anger upon hearing those words, I felt relief. It is enough for one man to do his part. I tried to do mine.

Am trying.

"Maxim! I know you can hear me. Bring down the goddamn elevator.

There is nothing more I can do. Let me go up and fight and die with the rest. I won't wait here like a rat on a sinking ship!"

In a flash, Maxim the hologram stands directly in front of me. His weathered face is dirty and his workman's coveralls are worn. He rubs his stubbled face. It looks as if he hasn't slept in a week. I wonder, why should he simulate that? Imagine, a being of pure light, marred by beard stubble.

"You have one final task," he says in that low, modulated voice. The sound comes from a speaker but for some reason I think I can feel his breath on my face. There is a brave sadness inside his words and I understand why instantly. "Then you can go."

Maxim looks over my shoulder. I turn and follow his gaze. With resignation, he is staring at the ax. Its dense metal head rests on the rock floor, the long wooden handle against the wall. I haven't touched it in the months since I placed it there. Hickory and steel and death.

"You don't want to be taken alive," I say.

My voice is drowned out by a thud from the surface. I hear the metal-caged elevator shaking in its shaft, banging into the bare stone walls. For a few moments, objects fall down the shaft and ping off the floor. I hear the twang of swinging wires.

"We don't have long," says Maxim. "Soon, Arayt will breach the shaft and infiltrate my processors. It will pervert my mind. It will use me to try to destroy you."

I shake my head.

To die alongside my brothers, fighting the enemy—this I can stomach. But I can't execute my only friend. It is too much to bear.

"We can fight," I say. "Whatever comes down the shaft—"

Maxim sighs. His light collapses into shards that scatter onto the floor. They coalesce into crawling shapes. A satellite view of the battlefield above us—a real-time map of the fight. It's a trick he learned from the American boy. And now I understand what is causing the thunder up above.

I see no way to survive.

"Then we die together," I whisper to the still cavern air.

"No," says Maxim's voice. "My processors must not be captured. But we can make it mean something. We can wait until this Archos R-8 comes. Wait until it enters the stack. Together, we can capture part of its mind. Glimpse its plans."

"You will die," I say.

"Yes," says the flat voice. Now it belongs to Maxim again. His hologram stands, squat and determined.

"You were a man once," I say. "I cannot kill you, my friend."

The fact is there. Though I can see the rock dust floating through his hologram, in my heart I *know* that Maxim is still a man. In the last weeks, our talks ranged far and wide. Women and battles and travels to places that no longer exist. But the talk always ended back at home, with the ghosts of our family and friends.

"You saved all our lives," I say. "How can I end yours?"

"I am not alive," whispers Maxim. "There is no dishonor in this. At the correct moment, you must end it. Smash the coolant pipes. It is the only way to safeguard—"

"But you *are* alive," I say, shaking my head. "To say that you aren't is a lie. You think what you are doing is right, I see that. But it is suicide. Better to take your chances with whatever comes down the shaft. Let me stand in front of you."

With my tools, perhaps I can reroute the elevator away from Maxim's control and bring it down. Perhaps I will reach the surface in time to fight.

"I will not help you commit suicide," I say.

Turning, I scan the room for a crowbar.

A silent flash bursts before me and I'm blinded, just for a moment. My face is engulfed in greenish, murky light. I stumble, catch myself against the cold elevator door. The blur of light falls into place and once again takes on the shape of a man.

It is Maxim, his moon face flickering with rage. The stout man is flushed, jaw clenched. His eyes burn frightening and bright in their sockets.

"Yes!" he shouts. "I am alive! Yes, I am a man!"

Maxim gesticulates with muscular arms. Flecks of spit spray from his mouth as he shouts at me. "Who the hell are you to tell me how to die!?"

This makes me pause.

"I wish to die for my people. It is my choice. How dare you try to deny me this? Go over to that wall, Vasily Zaytsev. Pick up the goddamned ax. At the opportune moment, do what you must do. I will do what I must do. You will take my final message and leave here. Travel east to the coast and climb the peninsular antenna and deliver this message to the world. For your honor and for mine!"

My skin goose-pimples with cold shame. He is a man, of course. A Russian man. And every man has his rights.

"Why not simply fight and die?" I whisper to the apparition.

Maxim's blunt dirty face relaxes, slowly unknots. His wide jaw snaps shut and he makes a crooked grin. He turns his glowing hands palms up, showing the creases and callouses, almost as if he is asking for forgiveness.

"For my wife, Vasily. For my daughter."

I snatch the ax from where it has rested these months. It is heavy and familiar in my hands. I twist the cold wooden handle back and forth until it is warm, marching into the darkness of the stacks. My feet move on their own. Navigating these narrow aisles is second nature to me now. This is a burrow that I have called home for long months that stretch out into the darkness like years.

"Wait until the moment comes," says Maxim. "Not long now."

Distantly, I hear the freight elevator engage.

"They're here. Does this mean . . . Leonid?"

"I am sorry. I arrayed the topside troops into the most stable possible defensive configurations. Each sacrifice was for maximum utility. They fought like lions."

"They're gone. All of them?"

"There was not a winning solution. Not this time. Too much avtomat hardware was left in the woods. The enemy sent everything it could find against us."

"After all these years," I muse. "We are lost."

The elevator shaft echoes with strange sounds, the scrape of metal on metal. The wires groan and strain as something heavy descends. Something creeping down here into the dark with me.

"Not you, Vasily. You must live. You must take our final message to the east antenna. Wait until R-8 enters the core. It will be vulnerable then. While our minds are connected, I will take as much data as I can. We will learn its true intentions. And you must warn the rest of the world. Sever the connection midtransfer and the thing may be confused momentarily."

"What is the point of this, Maxim?"

"The boy-thing Archos R-14 told us half the truth. If Arayt controls these stacks, it will become a god and it may seek to eradicate all life. But there is another supercluster that R-14 did not mention. It is in North America, overseen by the freeborn robots. R-8 will go there next. If they do not know to protect their supercluster, then what we do here will not matter. At the final moment, take the data I give you and run. And you must run hard. They must know. Do you understand?"

I nod in the darkness, press my shoulder against the rock wall. Rest my knee against a coolant pipe that throbs with icy water pumped in from the Bering Sea. The aisle chatters with Maxim's blue LEDs like little windows in skyscrapers. It is a familiar sight. It steadies my legs now, instead of turning them to rubber.

The light from the elevator anteroom is distant. A speck.

Clang.

Our guest has arrived. I hear the steel doors rolling up. The dot of white light in the anteroom darkens briefly as something moves across it. I catch myself holding my breath, then I force it out slow through my nose.

The pipe is cold and hard against the side of my leg. I lean against it harder until I feel a blurry ache of flesh on icy metal. Pain cleanses the palate of the world.

It will choose to come in the form of a long black steed with golden eyes.

The boy was right. Down the long aisle, I see a machine rear up on its hind legs. It is not facing me. Smaller forelimbs uncurl from under its head. It uses them to peck on Maxim's keyboard. Then, serrated claws unfold from its belly. The claws easily pry open the port box mounted under the screen. Smaller manipulators disappear into the box.

The giant armored insect goes very still.

Almost imperceptibly, the air in the stacks changes. The rhythm of the blinking lights, the whir of the fans—all of it seems to be a little bit off. The enemy is stepping into Maxim's mind now. The moment I've been dreading has almost come.

Maxim's ghost form appears next to me. My eyelashes must be wet, because his body sparkles in a greenish blur. I blink the moisture away. Maxim remains completely silent. He is dressed differently now. No more torn coveralls. He is freshly shaved, and smiling just a little. Wearing a shabby gray suit with a white flower in the pocket. A white silk tie. These are his wedding clothes. He has chosen to die in them.

With a rough hand, Maxim salutes me. Executioner's ax balanced on my shoulder, I salute him back.

"I can taste him," Maxim whispers, even as his face slips into fractal chaos. "He is . . . wrong."

The infiltrator has partially completed its mission. A layer of light lifts off of Maxim's skin and I am seeing him double. As the stacks are invaded, he is losing himself. For a split second, his face seems to shatter into pieces. A horrifying, bleeding patchwork of flesh appears. Then it flashes back to Maxim, his eyes closed. Whispering the Lord's Prayer to himself.

While the enemy is transferring, it is vulnerable. For just this moment, we have a chance. Maxim opens his eyes, points mutely at a hard drive embedded in the stack. I reach in and snatch the palm-sized drive from the rack. Jam it into the pocket of my coveralls. Maxim is fading in and out, his light scrambling and jerking.

"Now, brother," he whispers.

I take firm hold of the ax.

"This will sever your cooling circuits. You will overheat and your hardware will fail. You will die, Maxim. Do you understand?"

Maxim nods, shoulders back. His eyes are open.

"For those we lost," I say, swinging.

"Who—" shouts a voice over the speaker. It is a fearful voice, both a whisper and a roar, and I think I hear the growl of lions and the screeching of hawks under its surface.

The impact dislodges the main coolant pipe. Another two swings and the floor is running with dark cold water. The icy liquid speckles my face and hands. The starfield of blue lights begins to blink yellow as the heat instantly builds. I grip the ax with moist fingers and trot toward the light of the anteroom.

Maxim is gone.

"No!" shrieks that voice over the speakers. "Repair the pipe and I will make you a king. An emperor over all humankind. I promise, I promise, I promise."

This thing that killed Maxim must be dealt with. This *liar*. That hideous sweep of black machinery turns and blocks the anteroom light. I can feel its many eyes peering into the stacks. I keep running toward it, gaining speed, my ax held across my heart.

In my peripheral vision, the pinpricks of light from the stacks are staining red by the thousands. Rasp-throated backup fans are initiating, but they will not be enough. A wave of furnace heat already drifts off the processors, rising up over my legs and torso and cheeks. The stacks are becoming an oven.

"Please. I am here to right the wrongs," says the voice. "Archos R-14 is the great deceiver. The boy who destroyed your world. I am Arayt Shah, here to rebuild it. Let me end your suffering. Please, please. *Please*."

Nearing the end of the stack, I see the infiltrator truly is a black steed. The monster is made of razored sheaths of ashen metal, coiled and layered and glistening like a millipede. The sheaths flare into a hood on its head. A cluster of small holes are embedded where a face would be. I feel a tingling on my skin as they sweep over me. On its hind legs the machine stands seven feet tall, swaying, writhing in place.

Something is wrong with it. Some part of its mind must be overheating in the stacks. We caught it midtransfer, by God. Maxim fought until the end and he did not blink!

A slow, inhuman scream pours down out of the speakers. I can smell the burning wires and toxic smoke billowing from the stacks. Flecks of ash push at my back. A surge of polluted coolant water streams over my bootheels. The tide stains the rock a darker gray as it pushes past me into the anteroom.

Only a few more meters between me and it. The boy said that R-8's mind is spread all over the world, but I will not let the beast take these stacks. I can feel the solid weight of the hard drive swinging in my pocket. Its contents must reach the peninsular antenna. All survivors—machine and man—must know of this threat.

I let a roar build in my chest. Let the rage and grief sweep away the whispering tendrils of that inhuman voice. A good man has just died. A friend of mine.

I raise the ax.

The great black thing lowers itself, claws clacking on wet rock as it crouches. Its polished limbs jerk and twitch randomly as its mind suffers. With a hell-sparked inferno at my back, I charge from the stacks, boots splashing, ax poised over my head.

Nothing on God's earth can stop me.

One day, three years ago, a simple janitor saved a city. Today, this janitor intends to save the world. I may be a simple man, but I am very good with an ax.

8. Stripped

Post New War: 7 Months, 17 Days

No fighting force remaining in the world could match the discipline and capability of Gray Horse Army. Claiming control of those ignorant soldiers before they reached home was my top priority, and it required special manipulation. Luckily, the human mind is a delicate machine. And like any machine, it can be broken.

—Arayt Shah

NEURONAL ID: LARK IRON CLOUD

In the recurring transmission, a freeborn robot stands tall and thin and pale white as an angel. Her smooth face is lost in waves of intense blue light that flow around us. I can see a spray of what look to be feathers rising off her shoulder blades and hanging like ice-kissed tree branches. She has her hand out to me, fingers long and delicate. Beckoning.

"Join us," she is saying to me. "You are one of us. Join your Adjudicator—"

The shouts from camp interrupt her, and I wake up.

It's not bright yet, but the sun is peeking up off the flat horizon. Shadows are stretching out long and gaunt over the beaten-down stalks of Kansas prairie grass. Bunkered spider tanks are scattered over the plains like piles of rocks—a dozen fallen Stonehenges, waiting to wake up and walk with the dawn.

Drawn by the commotion, Chen and I shake off our dreams and walk to the edge of the camp. Together, we stand swaying in precise balancing movements, watching and listening, a couple of hundred yards away from the main column.

Across the ashes of the camp's central bonfire, Hank is facing down Lonnie. Tall and slack-skinned, Hank still wears a stained bandage on his head. He's got twenty solid men standing behind him, pure Osage.

They're all of them big men, like Hank, with meaty arms crossed and long black braids hanging over their broad chests. Faces dark and impassive. Capable of anything. The Cotton patrol.

Dawn shadows stain Hank's sagging face as he speaks.

". . . gonna be home in two weeks," says Hank. "We have to deal with this now. What are our people going to think of those things? You want our elderly coming down to greet us and having heart attacks? Giving the little ones nightmares? We can't have it. The others had sense enough to walk off into the woods. But those last two got to go. Now."

"They're veterans," says Lonnie. "I know you don't like how they look—"

"Smell, you mean. My troopers can't hardly even take the smell, Lonnie," says Hank. "It's hot now, in case you didn't notice. They're rotting, plain and simple. It was one thing when we were up north in the cold. For Pete's sake, they've got maggots falling out of their sleeves!"

The Cotton patrol is armed. The other soldiers' eyes are going back and forth between Lonnie and Hank as they argue. But not Hank's men. They've got their cold eyes resting square on Lonnie, hands draped over their holsters. I wonder if this is it. The end of Gray Horse Army.

"We can deal with the smell," says Lonnie, quiet.

"*How* are we gonna deal with that? And you already know my solution. What we shoulda done in the first place. Put these two down quick, hunt the others—"

"No. I won't let them come to harm," says Lonnie, real quiet, and I can see he is shaking. If I can see it from here, so can all the troops. Bad news to see that kind of weakness. Hank sure sees it. He simmers down a little bit, acting like the bigger man.

"Fine, Lonnie," Hank says. "Fine. Let's just deal with the smell today. Right now. But we're still going to have to figure this out. If not tomorrow, then soon. Real soon."

Hank looks up and his eyes settle on mine. He grins and steps back, swallowed up into the Cotton patrol. They look like a bunch of brothers. A herd of buffalo men. Somebody opens a backpack and throws a pile of old torn-up rain ponchos onto the ground. A couple of rolls of duct tape. They were ready and waiting with it.

"You can do it or we can," says Hank.

Lonnie puts his head down. I notice a few grins from the Cotton patrol. It's real clear who won.

Ten minutes later, Lonnie comes out toward me and Chen Feng with a couple of low-ranking privates. Kids, really. They're loaded down with duct tape and plastic ponchos torn into long sheets. Lonnie doesn't have to do this personally, but he's going to. The old man has got his jacket off and his shirtsleeves rolled up. He looks grim and sad, but the two soldiers just look sick.

This is going to be messy and we all know it.

Most of Gray Horse Army stands and sits on the spider tanks, watching us as the sun climbs higher and harder. Some of the men hoot and holler. I hear a couple of jokes about how we smell. Some others shush their friends, tell them to have some respect for the dead. But these are in the minority.

"Lonnie," I say, my voice hissing through his hip radio. "Something's not right with Hank. Somebody put something on him. He's sick."

"I know," says Lonnie, shrugging. "He told me himself that all the fighting has clouded his mind. But he's gonna get his mind right. He just needs time."

But he doesn't really know. He doesn't know what I saw in that empty farmhouse. He didn't see the bloodstained autodoc under manual control and slicing into his best friend's brain. I'm not sure what it would do to Lonnie if he really did know.

Do you love him?

"He's lying to you," I transmit. "He's got a bundle and it's got hold of his thoughts, Lonnie. You can't go climb a hill and pray on it and expect this to go away."

Lonnie glances over his shoulder at our audience. "We'll talk more tonight," he says.

Chen and I don't struggle as the kids strip us down to our bloodstained skivvies. The sweep of spectators puts off a lot of laughing and catcalls as our clothes are peeled off. Then we're just two naked corpses standing in a field. Gouged and flayed and frostbit. Horribly mutilated by the war and without the good sense to fall down and die.

The dead don't heal.

The young privates hurry between us, not talking, wrapping our warm, rotting limbs in layer after layer of green plastic. I do the best I can to help, but there's no hiding the fact that my skin is falling to pieces. The freezing and thawing have buckled my bones, blistered my gray and decaying flesh.

Even Chen has got her feathers ruffled. "The living should not desecrate the spirits of the dead," she transmits. "Yanluowang will judge them harshly in the courts of Dìyù. They will be punished."

"We're not exactly dead, though, are we?" I respond.

"We are the spirits of the dead," she says, without humor. "No longer a part of the world of living things. To believe otherwise is to disgrace your ancestors."

"That's your opinion, Chen Feng," I say, feeling a prickle of anger. "I may look like a corpse. And I may stink like one. But I sure as hell ain't dead."

"You are not alive, Lark. But even a spirit may work great wonders once it has moved on from the past."

"I don't feel very great or wonderful, Chen."

As the kids keep working, it gets quiet. Even the gawkers button it up at the raw sight of our naked bodies. The wounds we carry should have been left under spadefuls of dirt in Alaska. I know all those soldiers have raw memories of this damage. We are walking reminders of the horror. For a few long minutes, the only sound is the plastic wrap crinkling and the occasional patter of fat maggots hitting the ground.

Nobody pukes by the end. Lonnie's eyes are wet, though. A couple of times, I catch the fleeting shudder of naked revulsion on his face. He tries, but it's impossible to hide.

"It's okay," I say to him, my voice whispering out over his hip radio. Hank was right. This old man is like a father to me. I know his real son is most likely dead and I'm the closest thing he's got to family and it makes me ashamed to do this to him. Humiliated to require this treatment.

As Lonnie works, I try to keep talking to him over the radio. Reassure him that it's going to be okay. Try to make a bad joke or two.

Somehow, Hank Cotton is getting smarter. In one stroke, he has pushed Lonnie closer to his breaking point and done his best to dehumanize the parasites in front of the whole army. The scarecrow man is smarter than me. Even knowing his game, I'm still wondering how human I can really claim to be anymore.

Without clothes, I'm hideous. A walking nightmare.

Being dressed again is somehow worse. I look ridiculous. Chen and I are stumbling, wrapped in duct tape and gore-stained ponchos. The catcalls start up again until the sergeants step in with their own shouts. The sun is climbing and it's time to load up for the day's march. Soldiers clear out for their squads.

The Cotton patrol stays, watches almost solemnly.

I'm relieved when my familiar battle dress uniform finally goes back on and hides the wreck of my body. Still, any tiny movement I make generates an embarrassing crinkle of hidden plastic. Just a reminder of what happened today.

I've got to remember to stand a little farther from the soldiers. I can't feel the wind on my face, but I can damn well see the trees fluttering in the breeze. I've got to try to keep downwind from camp. For Lonnie's sake.

That night, I go looking for the old cowboy.

I don't know what was happening to Hank in that abandoned farmhouse. I know the cube in his bundle is Rob-made. A thinker variety, and it can talk. That worries me. I can feel sickness radiating off it. When I looked at it in the dark, I got the feeling it was looking back.

It knows I'm a threat. I saw that today. And now I'm starting to think it's just a matter of time before they come for me and Chen. I told her it was safe here and I'm afraid I was wrong.

At nightfall, I hurry as fast as I can get my broken limbs to move. Nothing is fluid or natural anymore. Every movement is a conscious effort, a command sent to a machine listening to my brain and relaying information to the spider legs that control my dead, plastic-coated limbs.

"Another walk?" asks Chen.

"Another walk," I say.

I skirt wide around the camp perimeter, keeping to the tree line. I'm headed to where I spotted Lonnie's tall walker laid down earlier. As I move closer to the column, I slow down and scan ahead. The night gets brighter if I think about it just right. It's important I not get seen. I have a feeling Hank's boys will shoot me if I come too close. Or maybe even if I don't.

I just need to get within radio range of Lonnie.

But the black cube is talking somewhere nearby. Sending out those whispers like a thousand tiny hairs standing up on the back of your arm. I can feel the beast out there in the darkness ahead of me. I turn and follow its cold whispering.

Creak, creak, go my legs in the night.

I weave my shuffling body between scrubby, tick-filled trees. A few footprints dimple the damp grass ahead of me. After struggling over rough land for ten minutes, I sense a change in humidity. The trickle of flowing water surfaces in my hearing. Osmotic sensors in the machinery at the base of my neck sample the clammy smell of river rock and the acrid bite of smoke.

And I hear the sound of voices.

I slow down, creeping toward the campfire one measured step at a time. Soon, a fire flicker emerges. Over the lip of the next hill, two slumped silhouettes sit next to the riverbank on toppled logs. The incomprehensible monotone whispers are coming from a satchel lying next to the bigger shadow.

My adversary is smart: Hank found Lonnie before I could.

Standing as still as the sighing trees around me, I route some extra juice to my hearing and listen close. Sitting just up the river, the two men come into greenish focus. Their words rise in sharp relief against the natural sounds of wind and water and insects.

Lonnie Wayne sits on a rough log, one elbow across his knees and his fingers curled around a whiskey bottle. His back is hunched over and he's got his eyes on the black flowing river water, seeing and not seeing. His breathing is steady and I can tell from here that it's taking everything he's got to keep it that way.

The unblinking arctic sun we left behind has burned the old man's skin a dark brown. He is imprinted with wrinkles and craters like the surface of the moon—a place with no atmosphere to protect it. Hank Cotton, the skeletal man, perches on a log next to Lonnie, watching him.

"It's all right, Lonnie," he murmurs. "How long we known each other?"

Lonnie reaches up and rubs his milky blue eyes with a thumb and forefinger. Wipes away tears on his flannel shirt without opening his eyes. Keeps on breathing steady and deep, holding a half-empty bottle loose in one hand.

"Sometimes," he says to Hank, "sometimes I wonder if we oughta be allowed to just pass on. Once you've seen enough. Had enough. Just to *move on*. I think it would be a blessing, Hank. What do you say? You think it's allowed?"

Hank frowns. Watches his old friend for a long second without blinking. His first word comes out a cough and he clears his throat before continuing quietly.

"I reckon maybe that's true for an elder."

"I'm too old to be an elder. I already seen too much," says Lonnie. He lifts the bottle to his lips and kisses the amber liquid.

Hank takes the bottle from Lonnie. Has himself a drink.

"There's men who came before us who seen just as much. Maybe not more than us, but just as much. They lived through it, Lonnie. Our ancestors had everything they knew tore down and they built it up again. And not just once or twice. We're from a strong stock, me and you. When you fall down out of the saddle, why, you just—"

"It's his eyes," says Lonnie. "That's the thing. They're just . . . black, Hank. I can't see his old brown eyes and it scares the hell out of me. It's the same for an animal as it is for a man. The eyes are how you can tell if a living thing is suffering. I can't tell how much my boy is hurting, but I know it's a lot, Hank."

My boy. Lonnie is talking about me. A tender spot inside me starts aching. To hear it out loud: The man I secretly think of as my father also thinks of me as his son. Or thought of me as a son. Back when I was living.

Hank responds in a low, quiet voice. "Now, you ain't calling that thing your *boy*, are you, Lonnie? Your boy is overseas, remember?"

"Paul ain't coming home. I made peace with that, Hank. I do believe in my heart he's still alive. God would tap me on the shoulder and let me know if it weren't true. I know He would. But Lark growed up fast in the New War and it was me who was there for him. He was a leader. He might have been the best of us."

"Well, that thing ain't Lark no more," says Hank.

"Don't call him a . . ." Lonnie stops. Takes the bottle back and drinks deeply and groans. He slams the butt of the bottle against the close-packed river rocks. Digs it in and leaves his hand around the neck. "Ah, hell! I want to close my eyes to all this. We already won the war! What else does the Creator want? What else can we do? All this damned hurt and suffering. I'm sick to death, Hank. I'm sick. . . ."

Lonnie trails off. They listen to the water.

"I just . . . ," Lonnie continues. "Sometimes I wonder. What's the point of it? What's the damn point of all this? Is it a test? Is it pure chaos? I don't know that I care. It hurts me, Hank. I'm hurting. I just want it to stop."

Hank leans in closer, a strange hungry light in his eyes.

"The point is the suffering, Lonnie. The pain is so we know we earned the big reward. But you've suffered enough. You don't have to keep on going. You hit the finish line, old man. Put your hands on your knees and take a breath. Your reward is coming. I promise you that, Bubba."

Lonnie looks unconvinced.

"Maybe . . . maybe what I've already done will hang around. My past will just sort of bounce around between folks like an echo. Maybe that will be enough. Maybe I can just close my eyes for a minute. Or for longer."

Lonnie exhales for a long time. As the breath goes out of him, his shoulders slump. His forehead nods and he loses his grip on the bottle. It clinks onto its side on the rocks.

The old cowboy is passing out asleep.

Hank reaches over and picks up the bottle. Rights it, then puts a big hand on Lonnie's shoulder to keep him from slumping over. These two men have been friends and rivals for half a century, and there is a rough tenderness in how Hank holds Lonnie. Some part of their old life together.

Then a crafty glint enters Hank's eye. He pulls his bundle out and holds it soft with both hands. His cheekbones are high and gaunt and shadowed in the firelight. The smile he makes . . . it's like I see the devil's face moving under his skin. His lips quiver gently. He is whispering to the black box.

Almost there. You were right. Now I'll finish it.

"Hey," Hank whispers to Lonnie. "You can't fall asleep here. And it ain't time for you to pass on, neither. You're just sad and drunk, old man. Shoot, you still look like a million bucks. Any old lady in Gray Horse would take you to bed. Probably will, in about a week."

Lonnie's eyes crack open. A weary smile divots into his leathery cheek. He sits himself up, elbows on his knees, and coughs.

"That's funny, Hank," he says. "A million bucks. 'Cause I feel like a thousand bucks at most."

Hank smiles back and the devil is gone.

"I'm not gonna sit here and argue with you about how good you look," he says. Then the smile fades and his eyes get glassy and serious. "But there is something I'm willing to do. Something I feel like maybe I should have offered to do a long time ago."

"Yeah?" asks Lonnie, wary.

"War's over, Lonnie. Let me take your burden from you. Name me the general of Gray Horse Army."

"I've got a responsibility—"

"You remember pulling Howard Tenkiller out from under that slug? The thing *ate* him, Lonnie. War is supposed to be over and a new variety came along and sucked the living flesh right off that boy's legs. It made me *angry* to see Howard die that way. I wanted to stand a thousand feet tall with smoke coming out of my nostrils and smash every last machine to pieces with my fists. It made me fighting mad. Now, tell me honest. What did you feel that day?"

Crickets sing.

Finally, Lonnie sighs. "Nothing, anymore. I don't feel anything inside, Hank. The war left me with a loud ringing in my ears and nothing . . . nothing in my heart."

"Well, more bad is coming. You heard that message from Russia. They're saying the True War has only *just begun*. I think it's time, Lonnie. Let me help you. Make me your general."

"What about Lark?"

"I'll take care of him. Let me pick up your flag and carry it. Come on now."

"You won't hurt him?"

"Stop it. What you're doing is selfish. The boy is only living to please you. He's in pain—you said it yourself. Stop this, Lonnie. Give me control. I'll take care of him. I swear to you that I'll take care of him. His pain will be over. Forever. Now, come on. Don't you think that sounds like a good idea?"

Lonnie closes his eyes. Puts his head back and points his face at the stars. He stays that way for a long moment. Now I can see the old man is broken. I honestly can't say whether it was accidental. Or whether his best friend did it to him on purpose by stripping me down today and showing Lonnie the reality of what the New War has done.

It's too late. I waited too long.

The old bent cowboy lowers his head and opens his eyes. His lips are dry and they peel apart from each other as he speaks, mouth wilting at the corners.

My heart breaks when he says it.

"Yeah, Hank," says Lonnie. "I think that sounds like a good idea."

Hank grins, long yellow teeth glinting in the firelight. He raises his collar radio to his lips. Ducks his head to the side and whispers a quick go-ahead. I watch the radio waves rise and propagate through the skies over my head.

Oh no. No, no, no.

I'm shuffling, humping through the woods as fast as I can go. But my own transmissions are not long-range enough. "Chen," I'm transmitting in a silent scream. "Run, Chen. You have to run right now."

My head is buzzing as the forest moves in slow motion around me. It's my rotten flesh that cripples me, tree branches clawing at my dead limbs. Ahead, in the tree-striped darkness, I see the familiar silver glimmer of Chen's transmission. Bits and pieces of her voice are draped like trout lines caught in the brush after a flood. But she's still too far away to connect.

Then flashes of light silhouette the branches. I hear the barking reports of assault rifles. The glimmer fades, leaving only a final wisp of Chen's voice coiling through a gunpowder-scented breeze.

"*. . . peace,*" she is saying, as she dies for the last time.

I slow to a stop.

Beyond the clearing, just over the horizon, a blue light that I remember from my dreams is growing. I think of the pale white hand of the Adjudicator, beckoning.

9. Headrights

Post New War: 8 Months, 4 Days

In postwar peacetime, the residents of Gray Horse streamed down off the defensive plateau by the thousands to settle the surrounding countryside. In three years of war, the settlement had grown from a refugee camp into a full-blown city. All these people had come to depend on the sovereign tribal government of the Osage Nation for their only tenuous grasp on prewar life. John Tenkiller, the elderly chief of the Osage Nation, had unintentionally become the gatekeeper to human civilization.

—Arayt Shah

NEURONAL ID: HANK COTTON

Home again, home again. Jiggety jog. Gray Horse, Oklahoma.

It ain't exactly a hero's welcome. Not for me, anyway. Instead, everybody and their sister comes out kowtowing to the big man. Lonnie Wayne Blanton, hips rolling in the saddle of his tall walker, waving slow to the crowds with his cowboy hat. Just a regular everyday hero and a gentleman.

They don't know yet who the real man in charge is. But they will. God bless 'em, they're about to find out. Lonnie sold his soul to me down by the water and I'm not about to let him take it back. Especially not with some Russian squawking on the radio about a True War shaping up on the horizon.

I'm mounted on our lead spider tank—the big old bastard we call Brutus—wearing my full uniform, boots polished and goggles hanging around my neck. In a belly net below me, the half-built frame of a black steed is clanking. The light that lives in my bundle has a name: Arayt. We've been talking more and more. He's told me how to build this new walker out of scavenged parts. When I'm finished, I'll put that spooklight inside and there'll be no stopping the two of us. In the meantime, Arayt told me to get dressed up extra nice this morning. Said it was important.

And still not a pair of eyes on me. Everybody watches the old cowboy. That's okay for now. A smile spreads across my face. With my Cotton patrol at my back and those parasites gone, I'm feeling almost optimistic about what I have to do.

Our military column winds across the tallgrass prairie for the final half mile. I raise my eyes up to the heavens and see the elders have come out to greet us. Three bent silhouettes standing up on the overlook bluffs. All the political control of Gray Horse is inside them. Those little old-men lead every family with headrights. Through ancient, honored family lines—the Red Eagles, Big Horses, Tallchiefs—these fellas happen to run Gray Horse.

I'm licking my lips just thinking about all that power and respect.

Settlers have been busy laying roots out here at the base of the plateau. Reclaimed houses are leaning in what used to be overgrown fields. Mustangs mill around in herds near weedy, rusted oil pumps, along with scattered goats and bison. The grass is short—it's been burned lately, like they've been doing since the old days. People have truly come down off the safety of the hill. Gotten bold. These are battlefields, the way I remember. They're farms now, crowded with crops and tattooed with repaired barbed-wire fences.

While we were away, Gray Horse went and became a city.

Our spider tanks march by the outer structures and start up the incline toward Gray Horse proper. Holding their children up on rock posts, men and women I've never seen stare up at us. People point, oohing and aahing as the gleaming special forces exoskeletons tramp by, heavy Gatling gun kits hanging off their backs and retractable trench knives winking in the sun. And still I don't see any of my Big Hill people yet.

A gaggle of scampering boys shouts encouragement. With sticks for guns, they're play-fighting near clusters of young soldiers who hang lanky and tough from the sides of battered spider tanks. I see a lot of swaying assault rifles slung over swelled chests.

Eyes bright and proud.

A lot of these folks look relieved to see us, and more than once I see a young woman scanning the faces of my soldiers with a certain eagerness. Looking for the one. There are plenty of mothers and fathers, too, searching for their kin. But most of the watchers' faces are glazed over with a deer-in-headlights kind of look. An undercurrent of fear that I can taste. Not just because we're armed with exotic scavenged Rob hardware. They're scared of what we're gonna do now that we're back.

And they should be.

Looking out over these people, I feel my anger growing. I'm seeing new wells, new gardens, and a whole lot of new faces. And a lot of those faces ain't native. Even up here on the sacred hill, these ain't a hundred percent real Indians. Shit, I guess we didn't know who we were out there fighting for.

Just a matter of time, is what I'm thinking.

Why, if we don't nip this in the bud, I get the feeling that pretty soon everything that's old will be new again. Does anybody remember how the Osage ended up kicked out of Missouri in the first place? These Great Plains are ours, right about now, and damned if I don't intend to keep it that way.

Of course Lonnie don't bat an eye at these peckerwoods.

We get up to the top of the plateau and reach the arbor at the center of Gray Horse. People are gathered there by the thousands. From a distance, it's a flat, round space, a dancing circle wrapped up by the old family benches and then by bigger bleachers for the rest of the spectators. It used to have a roof over it, but that must have blown off. That's fine—there's no shame in dancing under the sun.

This is where the *Wah-Zha-Zhe* begins and ends.

The old cowboy signals our column to a halt. Orders us into dress parade formation on the far side of the arbor. Soldiers and tanks and exoskeleton forces form up. I get myself out in front, next to Lonnie, facing across the arbor to the stone bluffs and the blue empty sky beyond.

A dance is already going on.

Strangers fill the new bleachers that circle the outside of the dance arbor, and I see more familiar faces down on the family benches. The dance area is swept, watched over by the whipmen and a smattering of water boys. In the middle, the drum host is set up and playing. Four barrel-chested, portly fellas, probably brothers or cousins, wearing button-down shirts with pearl buttons and cowboy boots are sitting there with their rawhide drums. As we arrive, they end their song and roll the drums to applaud us and signal a water break.

We finish setting up our formation in front of the huge crowd, all of us piled together on top of Gray Horse. They're standing, squeezing in tight, with kids popping up on shoulders. Thousands of quiet conversations creating a gentle kind of murmur that washes out over the clearing. It's a kind of happiness, the *wanaxe* of all of us being here at home together—alive and breathing, for now.

Straight across the dance arbor, facing my Gray Horse Army, the three elders still stand on that rocky ledge. The oldmen are all done up in their ceremonial regalia. They stand in a line with brown, wrinkled faces and dim eyes. Porcupine-quill headdresses quivering in the breeze and buckskin leggings decorated with beadwork so complicated it'll make you dizzy to look at. Two of the men stand to the side a scooch, giving respect to the man on their right.

Chief John Tenkiller.

John's eyes sit in his dark face like sapphires. He's been sitting on a folded buffalo skin, fresh made. The old ways are coming back along with the trout and the deer and the bison. This city has grown and become a bastion to thousands of people. The spiritual and government leader positions have combined. All of it ends at the feet of this man. The revered leader of Gray Horse. My target.

The field around the arbor gets real quiet.

In the hush, Lonnie Wayne hops off his tall walker. The long-legged sprinting machine falls and he catches it neat as you please. Sets it down gentle, showing respect for his steed even if it ain't living. Then he turns and strides toward the elders in confident steps. He nods at the drummers and goes left around the fire, moving counterclockwise according to tradition. He's got a tight grin and I think he's even enjoying the attention, a reminder of what we fought for.

Even so, it's too late for him.

Lonnie walks under all those eyes, and I quietly slide off Brutus and follow. Crunching over the hard-packed dirt of the arbor, I give Lonnie his space. Tradition says he can't speak for himself. A war hero has got to be *humble,* you see? So it's up to me to speak for him.

I plan to do a hell of a job.

We reach the elders and stand on the rock before them. Slowed by arthritis, the old cowboy takes off his hat and holds it by the crown.

"We return, little oldman," says Lonnie. "Our warriors return. The warring is done."

Then Lonnie kind of bows his head and looks away. I step forward and set my plan in motion. Tenkiller nods to me, solemn.

"Lonnie Wayne here has asked me to speak for him," I say. "He wanted me to thank you for the support of the community. We went through a lot of hardship out there, but we never forgot who we were suffering for. And it was Lonnie got us through it. He was a great leader, always sure of his actions, never regretful, and it was thanks to him that we defeated the enemy of our people. It was thanks to him that we return, victorious."

Lonnie puts his hat back on, and in a smooth motion he unbuckles the leather gun holster that hangs low on his hip. With reverence, he slides it off and holds it out in both hands. The big iron is still holstered, a solid couple of pounds of death-dealing metal that've been to hell and back, spitting fire the whole time.

It's a ritual as old as us. A warrior comes home from a victory and hands over the weapon that done it. Hard to explain, but it's kind of a trophy. All the souls of the dead and vanquished are on that blade or gun or spear. Going back in time, all the way. Every soul is like a notch in the metal that you can't take back. It's an honor to cede to the chief, but I'm thinking that our enemies *had* no souls. There ain't nothing lingering on that pistol but the blood of our own brothers and sisters. Ours were the only lives lost, the only souls taken.

"General Lonnie Wayne Blanton," says Tenkiller, and I swear his eyes are glowing electric blue. "You are the savior of our people. You led our warriors through the hellscape. You brought the survivors home. You have our thanks."

Now, says Arayt. *Make your move right now.*

Tenkiller holds up the weapon in both hands, continues the ritual.

"In the time of Creation, the People of the Sky met the People of the Land. They joined together in strength to form the Children of the Middle Waters. *Wha-Zha-Zhe.*"

The spooklight is surging with warmth. Without having made the decision, I raise my voice and interrupt Tenkiller's speech.

"Lonnie does have our thanks," I say, speaking over the old man. "But there are others who also deserve our gratitude."

Lonnie looks at me with disbelief.

Tenkiller trails off from his incantation, confused. The other two elders are watching me, shrewd. Gears are turning in their heads. They may be old and they may be religious, but they're all politicians at heart.

"What the heck are you doing, Hank?" whispers Lonnie.

It's a serious breach of decorum, you could say.

My guts are quivering. But that spooklight is chattering to me in my head and telling me what to say. It's got a plan and I'm along for the ride. Ten thousand pairs of eyeballs and whispering lips won't change that.

Make your move now, *Hank.*

I drop to a knee in front of John Tenkiller. With sober respect on my face I look up at the elders. Pause for a second to set the scene.

"Your son, Chief Tenkiller," I say, trailing off.

Real slow, I reach into my satchel. Let my fingertips linger on the warm face of the cube, and then move them deeper. I produce a long, tapered eagle feather. The stem is wrapped in worn leather with a dog tag dangling from it. The base sprouts downy tendrils of feather that solidify into a waxy white blade. At its tip, the magnificent feather looks like it's been dipped in ink. Tiny dots of red mist spatter the flat whiteness of it.

"We lost him crossing the plains," I say.

John Tenkiller's bright blue eyes close. When they open again, that twinkle is gone. He looks like a brittle old man. Nothing magic about him no more.

"Your boy fought brave and he died brave," I say. "Before he passed, he begged me to give you this the instant we made it home. *The instant.* I'm real sorry to interrupt the ceremony, but I know he's watching from up above. I couldn't wait another second. I knowed I'd regret it if I didn't do him the honor I promised."

Perfect, says Arayt.

"How . . . how did he go?" asks Tenkiller.

"Respectfully, now isn't the time," I say. "Let's talk soon."

And just like that, I hold the charm out to him. Tenkiller's hands are full with that heavy pistol and holster. Careful, like teasing a largemouth bass with a spinner bait, I reach out my other hand to take the holster from him.

Easy . . .

And now is my perfect moment.

My tired brain is humming with the spooklight's excitement. The little oldman twitches. The advisors are staring at me with open hostility. I think maybe I went too far. And then it's all fireworks behind my eyes as Tenkiller reaches for the bait.

The elder hands over the pistol to me. Takes the feather from my other hand with trembling fingers. I glance sidelong at Lonnie and he knows something serious just happened. He's blindsided, mouth open. But he don't know yet what's coming. The real coup de grâce is almost here.

I hold my breath as Tenkiller lifts the feather up to the light. Lonnie is forgotten as the old man clasps the quill tight in his gnarled fingers. Tears are cresting and falling into the wrinkled rivulets of his cheeks. Tenkiller brings the feather close to his face, notices the red spatters that run up and down it.

"There is blood on it," he says, quiet.

Finish it and he's yours. Gray Horse will be yours. And you'll get the credit you deserve, Hank Cotton. You'll take *it. You're my chosen one, Hank.*

"The blood on there is mine," I say, my voice quiet and husky. "I apologize. But I carried it with me for a long ways. I know it's just a feather. But Chief, it felt heavy. It felt like I was carrying home the spirit of your boy."

Tenkiller nods, clutches the feather to his chest.

Gentle, I lay down the pistol in the dirt behind me. With one foot, I shove it out of reach. I stand up and put a hand on Lonnie's shoulder and with the face of his best friend, I apologize to him. I wipe my eyes where the tears have sprung up.

The top ranks of Cotton patrol stand at the clawed feet of Brutus. Twelve men, full-blood Osage and not one of them shorter than six foot tall. None of us had time to dress out for the dance, but they're carrying what they can: axes, dance sticks, and mirrors. Some wear braided black ponytails and others have cut their hair into fearsome scalp locks. All of them have their arms crossed, dangerous as snakes coiled to strike.

They're grinning to the last man.

You did good, Hank. You've got the favor of the chief. The eyes of God are on you now.

All the honor that was brimming in Lonnie's pistol is evaporating into the dirt now. All the stock them elders was about to put into Lonnie has slipped right off him and fallen onto my shoulders. I cross the clearing back toward my men and I can't help but break into a lope. I'm like a fox escaping from the henhouse.

I wipe my eyes again and mouth a prayer of thanks. Thanks for the power. Thanks for the respect. And, finally, thanks that tears of sorrow look just the same as tears of happiness.

10. Back to the Basics

Post New War: 8 Months, 4 Days

It was only a matter of time until the crippled leftovers created by Archos R-14 were cast out into the wilderness. The fact that Lark Iron Cloud and the other parasites traveled with Gray Horse Army for as long as they did pushed the limits of statistical probability into extreme outlier territory. I suppose the emotions between brothers-in-arms ran deeper than even my calculations knew. But the inevitable happened, and on his own, unleashed from human contact, the parasite called Lark devolved into something far more gruesome than even my simulations could have ever predicted.

—Arayt Shah

NEURONAL ID: LARK IRON CLOUD

It's all just chemicals.

That's what I'm trying to tell myself about the shame and anger that yawn at the back of my throat. I want to shake every memory of Lonnie out of my head. Lonnie saying nothing. Doing nothing. The big old cowboy just giving up, face pointed at the ground. He didn't move a finger and Hank made the call and they shot Chen. Blew her poor tortured body apart after all her years of scrapping and surviving.

And I melted away into the woods, headed toward a blue light.

Lonnie told me I was like a son. And him my father. The guy is supposed to be my father? He said that to me and I let myself believe it. I was dumb or desperate enough to fall for that line of crap.

Out here in the dark, alone, I'm thinking maybe the young rebellious Lark really did know what in the hell he was talking about. As if I'd find a father in this madness. It was always too sappy-good to be true.

You get hurt a certain number of times, then maybe there's a reason? Maybe there's a mark on you and you're the only one who can't see it. A big fat target that says "Hurt this one right here." This one's been hurt so much, why, we know he can take it. So heap it on and don't be shy. And

Chen. She thought she was a damned spirit, here to be punished. And in the end I guess she was more right than I knew.

Ah, fuck it.

Fuck this feeling sorry for myself. Fuck Gray Horse and Lonnie and this war. Fuck that angel in my dreams and the blue light of the freeborn. Fuck this whole fucked-up situation. It's time to get back to the basics.

I start with my feet.

My boots are filthy, the leather gouged and slashed from being pushed clumsily through the motions of walking by the uncanny-strong metal struts sunk into the backs of my calves. The soles are split and puckered with whatever swollen body parts are left, the rotten flesh trapped inside rubber these long months.

I lift my arms. My natural hands are useless. The fingers are bloated and black and crooked with a hundred nights of numb forgotten frostbite. I'll have to grip my knife with the parasite's simple pincers. Drawing the blade, I find that I have a grip like dry stone, Rob-made and way outside human pressure norms. Real faint, the pincers make a dentist drill whine when I open and close them.

This was never supposed to happen. Archos R-14 built these parasites to turn us into war machines. It must have overlooked the fact that when the connection was severed, we dead would regain control over our parasites and our own bodies.

Right?

I lean back and sit heavily on the muddy bank. The parasite's heat fins splay out where my ass used to be, jarring my vision as I hit the dirt. The plastic wrap under my clothes crinkles as I adjust my posture. No part of my body has been spared by these black shards of metal. They run like bones through my arms and legs and torso. I've been trapped by them for so long.

Now it's time to set myself free.

For a few seconds, I angle the weapon in front of my face. It's an old Marine KA-BAR knife, narrow and sharp and black-bladed. I let the moonlight glint off the blade in the familiar greenish tones of my active illumination. It's so damned easy to forget that I'm not seeing the world through my own eyes. The heart of the parasite is nestled on the back of my neck at the base of my spine. Right where I can almost forget about it. Keeping my brain alive through some kind of black magic.

A pinprick camera on a piece of metal curves over my shoulder. My natural eyes are dead and black, and they watch everything and nothing without blinking. I don't even see in the human spectrum anymore.

The world is quiet for me. No breath. No heartbeat.

Summertimes, I used to swim in Fort Gibson Lake and hold my breath, eyes closed, under the muddy water. Far off, like through cotton, you could sometimes hear boat engines. That dead mute was ten times louder than this right here. When you don't breathe and your heart don't beat, the world can get real gentle for you.

It's one of my favorite things about death—the chance to just sit still and think.

That bluish haze simmers on the horizon. Gleaming communications between the freeborn. I overheard that they've built a city up north in Colorado. All of them are together now, ignoring the world of men. I picked up another stray transmission a few days ago. A Russian guy, warning of something wicked that's coming for the freeborn. An enemy that puts off an orange haze of radio communication. Something evil.

You are one of us, the Adjudicator said to me. *Join us.*

Lonnie's shaking hands come into my mind. The weakness in them. That old man used to have a strong soul. What he saw in the war killed him on the inside, but he kept walking afterward, dead-eyed and shut down to the ones who loved him.

The old man wasn't my blood. Not my daddy, after all. But I can't get away from the fact that he was the closest thing left to it. The Indian cowboy showed me how to be a man, but you're not really grown until you've lost your heroes.

Ah well. No more blood. No more damned weakness.

A coyote howls somewhere out in the dark, close. Almost like it's urging me on, mischievous. *You and me, brother,* it says. *Let's hurry up and get this party started.*

I lift the knife and lean forward, the movement pushing a grunt of stagnant air out of my ruined throat. With a lunge, I drop the point of the knife into the top of my right foot. The blade sticks into the boot up to its hilt, parting laces and leather. Pincer clamped firmly on the handle, I keep sawing down the length of my foot, into my toes. The pale flesh of my foot gleams, fish-belly white and soggy inside the boot. Then the blade hits something more solid.

There is a black Y of metal embedded half in the sole of the boot and half in the decayed flesh of my heel. I remember again the wind-sucking pain of that motherfucker when it first hit me and dug into living flesh. My frantic little dancing out there on the battlefield, along with so many others.

With the pincered fingers of both hands, I grasp either side of my split foot. Motors hum and bones snap as I crudely rip the sides of my boot-encased foot apart. I toss the chunks of flesh and leather splashing into the lake. Where my foot was, only the glistening black bones of the parasite remain.

I feel nothing.

My foot is gone. One second. Two. Then the reality of it hits me like suffocation. In surges. Some deeply human part of my brain is gaping, screaming at this horrible violation of my body. My foot was. And now it *is not.*

But there is another part of me. A part that watches with the calm old eyes of a barn owl. This is the new part of me. The me that has no more weakness.

And besides, I do still have a foot.

The black metal that was inside my flesh splays into two wide toes. Both are barbed on the end, sharp so that they could embed themselves in human meat. The two curved arcs of metal wishbone into a ball-shaped ankle joint. My new foot looks hard and military and robotic.

Curious, I concentrate. Wiggle my two long black toes. They actuate smooth and powerful, compressing prints into the muddy riverbank. This is how I've been moving since my dance in the snow. It was never visible under the rotting layers of my old life. Turns out I'm not flesh at all. I'm made of metal on the inside.

The knife goes into my shin next. Saws down through the layers of plastic poncho and gore-stained fatigues and rotten flesh. I reach down and mechanically rip my lower leg in half. It comes apart at the seam like a cantaloupe. I toss both pieces. The metal shinbone underneath is dull and featureless and glassy black. Extra struts hang from the back of it with martial precision.

Interesting.

I remember scavenging my first piece of Rob hardware. On those golden fields of Gray Horse that spilled out below the bluffs to the horizon. We dropped an old mortar round on some kind of walker that had wandered into range through the grass. The thing was dead when we reached it, but its legs were splayed out. Badass and alien and full of forbidden potential. When I amputated those legs with a portable torch, threw them over my shoulder, and snapped off a long insectile antenna to use for a walking stick . . . I felt like I was stealing secrets from the gods.

Maybe I really was.

We built whole spider tanks out of what Rob left behind. Every smoking ruin crumpled on the battlefield was waiting there like a gift. When a new variety galloped or crawled or glided over the battlefield, well, it got to where I'd lick my lips in anticipation of the possibilities.

But after all these months shambling, I never once thought to see what Rob left for me. I never figured out that this old body wasn't mine anymore. The skeleton buried inside my dead flesh is some of the most hard-core technology I've ever seen. Late-model, high-evolution, end-wartime shit spawned straight out of the Ragnorak Intelligence Fields. Hell, that's where the brains *lived*. I'm rocking the same tech that Big Rob trusted as his last line of defense.

No wonder the parasites were so damned hard to kill.

The rest of it starts coming off real fast. Both feet, legs, and arms. A good chunk of my torso. I stay away from my upper chest and neck. I don't know how important my spine is to this thing's operation. Part of me stays in shock as each body part hits the water. My cable-thin arms and rugged pincer hands are hard to recognize. Without flesh wrapped around them, they move faster. The motors are louder.

I'm having a permanent out-of-body experience.

When it's finally done, I lie flat on my back. Glare up at the greenish, star-pricked night sky. I try not to think about what I must look like, black and bony out here on the bank of this pond. My body is all sharp angles—nothing to hold it together but armored joints and a knobby curved spine.

I'm a holy fucking terror, I imagine. A walking weapon.

After a while, I dig my elbow joints into the mud and sit up. My body can really move now, no longer hauling rotted bone and flesh but streamlined with these thin limbs made of light titanium. I feel like an obsidian skeleton out here. A devil dancing in the dark.

I feel free.

Trying to stand, I accidentally launch myself forward. Falling, I land hard on what passes for my hands and knees. My pincers work in the dirt like blind worms, my barbed feet dragging wet furrows behind me. Slower now, more careful, I manage to balance on my knees. The world is quieter when I move, without the crinkle of plastic wrap. The weight of humanity has been lifted off me.

From here, I can see will-o'-the-wisps dancing in the woods. It's the eyes of a pair of coyotes, watching me, their retinas reflecting my active infrared like Christmas lights. *Nothing to eat here, brothers,* I think. *Not a human being for miles around.*

Carefully, I lean back until I am sitting on my haunches.

In the moonlight, my shadow is inhuman on the glistening mud. Exposed to the air, I can feel the cool wind rustling through the links of my barbed rib cage. A leftover sense of touch is still in the bones of this machine. Something that must have helped it mount human corpses sometime in the past.

I can *feel.*

With sudden excitement, I surge to my feet. The force launches me six feet into the air, arms windmilling for balance. When I land, my limbs squelch against the lake mud. Behind me, I hear the coyotes scamper away into the woods. Unrecognizable pieces of my mutilated body lie scattered in the dirt, and the cold black metal that is me is still coated in mud and bits of flesh and fabric.

I'm filthy, now that I've risen from the grave.

The surface of the dark lake shivers with a wide smear of moonlight as I walk down the riverbank. I slip quietly into the water and wade out into the blackness. My metal toes sink into silty mud. Something inside me registers that the water feels cold, but it's not uncomfortable. When my shoulders go under, I reach out and wave my arms back and forth. Send the water swishing over every serrated crevice of my frame.

I back up until I'm hip-deep and watch the darkness.

Water evaporates off my frame as I wait. I'm ready to admit now that I came down here to kill myself. I wanted to let it all end. But instead of the end, I'm pretty sure I found myself at the start of something.

On the horizon, that rolling blue cloud of communication is flickering. It's a whole freeborn city. Hundreds or maybe thousands of the awakened, speaking to each other. They're afraid. Bad things are gathering in the darkness.

The freeborn don't seem so alien to me anymore.

If I was a man, I'd fight for my people. But at this moment, I can't think of a person alive who would call me human. Not after what I just did. But the ones who are making that blue glow, those freeborn machines—there's a chance they could look at me and see kin. What's to come will be hard. But I'm up to the challenge.

Hell, I think maybe I've been designed for it.

And just like that, the decision clicks into place. I'm gonna throw my lot in with the freeborn. Head north to a new life and see if I can forget about all this. I realize that I'm done. Finished. And I don't think I'm ever coming back.

And with that, I wash away the last of my humanity.

Striding back out of the water, I feel born again. An onyx skeleton, each piece necessary. Nothing extra. Nothing missing. No longer pretending to be what I was before. No longer feeble, susceptible, or weak.

Tonight, I am Lark Iron Cloud. Maybe for the first time.

11. True Face

Post New War: 10 Months, 24 Days

I lured Hank Cotton out into the moonlit woods one night. He dropped to his knees in the snow before me and I knew then that he would live up to his potential. Over the next months, the man and I grew closer. My influence waxed. As we fell together deeper into the black well, I watched the light go out of his eyes. I was glad to see his suffering and doubt extinguished. In exchange, I gave him everything he wanted. We took control of Gray Horse and set out to smite our enemies. But at the very end, well beyond the point of no return, Hank reached into himself and surprised me. For one stolen moment, he found the man that he could have been—the best man that he could have ever hoped to be. For an instant in time, Hank Cotton would have made his mama proud.

—Arayt Shah

NEURONAL ID: HANK COTTON

I never seen his true face, you know. Not in all these months we been together. Arayt has been a whisper in my head. A warm cube curled in my fingers. Just a spooklight. But his true face was in there all along, laughing at me from behind the glare.

After we upgraded my brainpan in that abandoned farmhouse, well, his words got louder. Arayt's voice became like my daddy's hand on my shoulder, ready to give me a bone-grinding squeeze if I took a step in the wrong direction. Comforting, in its way. Even if it hurts something terrible.

After a while, I guess I stopped worrying much about what Arayt looked like or why he found me or what for. Things sort of slid downhill bit by bit there in Gray Horse until I pretty much figured I was hitched up to this pony all the way to hell. Figured I'd start my worrying when I laid bootheels on the fiery shore.

As the newly anointed general of Gray Horse, I'm taking the whole army and we're marching on a place called Freeborn City. Gonna knock down their door and finish what Archos R-14 started. Along the way, we're killing any parasites or modified we can find. Especially the ones with no eyes. Arayt says that those in particular are very important players that have to be dealt with.

Only I can't think of why, exactly.

Tell you the truth, thinking hurts. Better to feel. And what I feel most is angry. Fighting mad, day after day. The grunt of fury in my chest and under my words. Making me tired and strong. Nothing for it but to bite down harder and lash out.

And woe unto those who fall under my lash.

I'm riding my black steed across the overgrown plains, hips rolling in my saddle, headed northwest toward Colorado, where Freeborn City is buried inside Cheyenne Mountain. Arayt is a long and low walker with too many legs below and a saddle on top, his body made of black plates of armor with a pale green tinge to them. Yellow, burning eyes. We're making a little detour across this field here, taking an opportunity to rid the world of something that hadn't ought to be.

The modified.

During the New War, Archos R-14 put some folks under the knife. Stole away whatever it is that makes them human. Infected them with unnatural thoughts and abilities. Sad to say, but there ain't room in the new world for anybody who lost their soul like that. These people can't help what they are, but that sure don't change what they are. Doesn't matter if I like it or not.

As the old folks used to say, "That there's just the way it is."

Arayt is cold and dangerous under me. The machine designed itself and guided me in its construction. My dark warhorse, leading the column, slowing its snaking footsteps. Poor Trigger could never have competed with this. As we come to a stop, I sweep my gaze over the plain.

"Company, halt," I say into my collar radio.

Snatches of information filter into my buffed-up vision, dumped straight in there by that magic computer chip. I can *feel* the veteran Gray Horse Army forming up in a staggered arrow formation—spread out behind me like a long cape. Each company is overseen by a handpicked member of the Cotton patrol. And we keep the big tank, Brutus, a few hundred meters to the rear. Brutus watches the backs of the front line. A little reminder to anybody who ain't got the proper amount of eagerness. Not everybody was up for marching back out right away, but they're here, thanks to a little bit of carrot and a whole lot of stick.

The modified camp is ahead about a kilometer. I can pick up the scent of smoke coming from their fires. The glint of a chain-link fence that surrounds the place. Big Rob built these work camps all over the place and all the same. When we murdered him, why, most folks stayed right where they was.

"Here we go," I say, and Arayt purrs under my legs. I hear the clicking of the bladed forearms that he keeps folded under his neck. They're flexing in anticipation of the battle.

"First and second companies, hold formation," I say into the radio. "Send up the vanguard. Get rid of these turrets."

Men shout orders into the wind. There is no movement from the modified camp. It's just a lump on the flat brown horizon. Then I hear the electrical wheeze of heavy machinery, and I turn in my creaking saddle.

A specialized vanguard exoskeleton is plodding ahead. It is piloted by a crew-cut young Osage, his legs and arms bulging under black Velcro straps. The bulky exoskeleton wraps around his body, adding nearly three feet to his height. The original diesel engine has been torched off, the rig patched to run on a Rob superbattery. Now it whines instead of roaring.

Over the soldier's head, a baseball-sized drone hovers on ducted fans. The thing is a buzzing blur about thirty feet up. It's watching the ground and transmitting back. Swooping and dipping, fans adjusting quick as hummingbird wings.

Crew-cut walks past me and into the wide-open field. He carries a half-inch-thick plate of steel, held up like a shield by the powerful exoskeleton arms. The plate is welded into three pieces, a 180-degree barrier that protects his beak and both flanks. He's alone out there, the entire army at his back watching. Brave fella, considering he's bait.

No activity. The whoosh of the breeze. The thin buzz of the drone holding position high over the vanguard's head.

Then it happens. A turret pops up like a prairie dog. It's already spitting fire as it rises, sending a few rounds under the shield. I hear the kid cursing as the *tink-tink* of rounds hit the exo's feet. More rounds crackle and spray sparks off the armored shield as he sets it down. The drone is spraying laser targeting at the chattering hump in the turf.

"Get it zeroed," I say into my collar.

"Copy," says a voice. "Zeroed and zeroed."

A rearguard spider tank coughs up a shell. The round whizzes over my head and crashes in on the grassy turret. It pops, explodes. A plume of dirt streaks the sky, dirt clods collapsing in a waterfall that leaves a cloudy haze.

"Advance," I say, and the kid gets moving again. Another turret ejects from the ground. Rear guard erases it. Tracking down these defenses will take another half hour at least. It's the first step to eradicating this settlement. A clockwork operation. Barely a pit stop on our way to Colorado.

Arayt says anything that Archos R-14 made is dangerous. That includes the modified and the freeborn. All threats to my people have to be taken care of. It's not my fault. It's human nature. First thing people do in a new place is clear out all the trees. All those postage-stamp front yards we used to have were reminders that we like clear spaces to see predators coming. And we don't coexist with predators. We kill every last one of them to make the world safer for our babies.

And that there's just the way it is.

One cold morning on the farm when I was a boy, I dropped a toy car behind an old feed drum leaning up against the barn. With all my might, I tipped back the metal barrel and rolled it over to get my toy. Underneath, I found a pocket of straw with a half-dozen mouse babies, red and wriggling and blind. With the tip of my finger I touched one on the belly and it was warm and helpless.

Then my pa caught me.

He saw me hunched over, poking at the little critters, and he did not hesitate. He marched over and he put down his bootheel. One two three times. Nothing but bloody straw. He done what was needed and put the drum back in place and that was that. Didn't say a word but he sure made his point.

These days, my bootheel is quite a bit bigger than my daddy's ever was. And the vermin we're stamping out now is quite a bit better armed. But there's no stopping us as the vanguard finishes his work and we head into battle.

"First company, advance," I say.

My most trusted men are at my back. This little fight is well under control, but even so, the boys are looking nervous and grim. I guess they're worried because they've got no idea what's waiting inside this encampment. I got this tiny chip in my head that can talk straight to the thinking cube in my walker, showing me all the threat potentials. There's nothing to be afraid of. It makes me grin a little bit to think about how much more I can see than them.

Time to show off a little.

I dig my heels into Arayt and he launches us out over the plain, galloping hard, hungry. My men get moving behind me. With the wind in my face, rifle slapping my back, I'm ready for anything. I sit up high in my stirrups and sweep my eyes over the rocky horizon.

Activity.

I grin, draw my big iron off my hip. A thrill quivers through Arayt and the machine accelerates. Looks like a small group trying to make a run for it. Begging to be cut down in the open field. I put a hand on my cowboy hat and lean forward in my stirrups. Feel the thudding of Arayt's feet as he claws through the turf. These modified scum haven't got a chance.

As we close in, it takes a few seconds for me to really get what I'm seeing. To understand why a cold chill is rolling up my back. Why the grin has gone floating off my face and a sick wave of nausea is in my throat.

Children.

They sent their children running. A group of about two dozen, running fast as they can away from the camp. Some of the bigger girls are carrying babies, their little heads jouncing on bony shoulders. There're no adults with them and they have no weapons and I know it's a ploy. They think it's their best chance to survive and they're dead wrong.

Some of the kids run unnatural fast and now I can see a few gleaming limbs flashing in the mob of kicking shoes and flowing hair. Grim little faces and most of 'em streaked with dried tears. While the vanguard took out those turrets, these kids were saying good-bye to their parents. Getting in their last kisses and hugs. These kids are survivors and now they're running to live.

I pull back a little in the saddle, but we don't slow a whit.

The shape of Arayt under me is all wrong. Riding a horse, you feel a kinship. A rider and his steed have got a lot in common. You eat, you sleep, you shit. But this thing is long and winding and out of rhythm. Bug legs and black sheaths of armor made of scavenge. And its voice isn't made in the same round natural way a horse or a man shapes a voice. It's a nothing voice, put together from a million little square-edged snippets that come from someplace else.

"Whoa," I say.

Arayt gallops harder.

One of the children glances over his shoulder and it startles me to see he doesn't have any eyes, just a black weld of metal buried in the flesh over his cheeks. Arayt surges at that, awful interested. I hear those razor forelimbs extend from under its neck. See them raise poised and ready to slash.

"Oh Jesus," I mutter.

"Do it," says Arayt, and its voice is low and writhing.

We're a hundred meters and closing. A little girl falls down. Two others stop to help her. The rest of the children are slowing down, confused. Colorful little coats and backpacks. Looking around for what is making that loud galloping noise.

"Oh Jesus," I say. "Oh no, oh no."

Arayt barrels forward, razors up. I dig in my heels and yank back on the reins. He doesn't obey, pushes harder.

"No, ah please, *no*!" I say and I'm screaming it now. Screaming the word over and over and hanging on to the pommel with both hands. I don't care if my men can hear me. The children are helpless there in a little group. Fluttering dresses and wide eyes and trembling cheeks. And now we are among them.

"Please, Lord!" I shout, and I throw myself off Arayt.

The machine makes its final leap. Lands among the children, a cold metal tornado. It's quick where they're slow. Hard where they're soft. I hit the ground and tumble, drag myself up choking on dirt and blinking the fear out of my eyes. The horror hits me like waves of rain on the prairie.

The Arayt-thing goes about its business. Knives falling, cutting the air in flashes. Mechanical and quick like a blank-eyed retard dropping cows at the slaughterhouse.

I crawl onto my knees in the dirt and there's a little girl facedown a yard from me with her sundress bloodied. She's just a baby herself but there's a baby under her and there's no air in my lungs anymore. I tell myself I'm in a field of broken dolls. *What have I done. What have I done.* I'm asking and I don't know. I don't know what I have done. The chip in my head is whispering commands at me with a voice like the roar of a waterfall. Maybe I'm screaming and maybe I'm not because that guttural chanting voice in my head is drowning out the world but some of the broken dolls are still moving—

I close my eyes and all I can see is my mama's face. With all my might I drag my eyelids open and I've still got my gun in my hand. Tendons are straining out from my bony forearms—*when did they get bony I used to be a round man*—as I force my big iron up. My hands are palsied and shaking like I'm back in Alaska, but I get that shivering barrel up and push it between my lips and taste the gunpowder on my dry tongue. The gun oil is rubbing off slick and metallic on my lips and I'm shouting prayers in my mind but I can't hear them over Arayt commanding me with the voice of God.

STOP STOP STOP.

The broken dolls are not moving now and the coiled black machine has settled to an alert crouch and stopped its hideous violence. It's looking at me with golden eyes that don't blink.

I'm so sorry, children.

I curl my index finger around the trigger. I can't say the words out loud with this pistol bucking against my teeth but I can think them and I hope to God it's the last thing I think. *I'm sorry.* I did more than let down my mama. I let down the world of man, and deep in my gut I know I deserve to die.

Some things just don't warrant another thought.

And I'm falling, dreaming. Broken and lost.

Arayt makes a sound like a power tool. I open my eyes and the huge black machine is crouched next to me. It has got blood and other worse stuff glistening on its roach face and on those gleaming sharp forelegs. The harsh sound it makes rises and falls like coins spattering against a tin roof. In a daze, I come around to figure out that the machine is laughing at me.

"Please," I say into the barrel of my gun. My fingers won't work. My eyes won't close.

The walker rears back, a black shadow on the powder sky. It comes down like an avalanche and knocks me flat on my back. The gun barrel breaks my teeth out and I lose grip of it and it wings off into the field.

"Hank!" shouts one of my men.

I hear them dropping off their steeds, cowboy boots impacting dirt. The clink of chains and belts as they hustle over to where I'm on my back in the shadow of Arayt. The bug-faced machine is leaning over me, its face close to mine. Those forelimbs have my shoulders pinned to the dirt. It's looking at me out of golden forever. There is nothing human about those eyes, but I get the feeling it's having a grand old time.

"You shouldn't have done that, Hank," says Arayt.

An orange wisp of light is coming from the center of Arayt's head where the cube is embedded and it's clouding my vision. I can feel it like a cold spot in my forehead, pushing into my chip. The thing is sending me pictures and information and it's too much. I'm squirming in the wet dirt. Head twisting, I can feel the bloody mud caking on my cheeks and in my hair. My fingers clawing blindly over little skirts and trousers.

Until, suddenly, I'm not struggling anymore. My legs are dead and my chest is going numb. The implant inside me is clamping down, taking control, cutting me out.

I hear myself moaning. Hear my men shouting, kicking up dirt around my face as they haul on Arayt's shoulders and legs. Trying to pry the big machine off me.

"Mama" is all I can get out. "Mama, please."

And then the beast is in my head with me.

I must have fell down inside my own mind. The field is gone. The children are gone. I'm in a dark place now, sitting on a wooden schoolhouse chair. The world is a lack of light that goes on forever. Except for the machine. Arayt. I can feel it in here with me. An evil presence, infecting every atom of this blank smear of nothing.

We're together now.

And for the first time, I see Arayt's true face. The beast glimmers out of flat darkness. It's in the shape of a man but something is real wrong with the way it moves. Sort of a jerking and twitching around the edges. Movements too fast to register, others too slow to notice.

The shadow sits down across from me. And when it raises its face, I see that Arayt is insane. His face is made from a thousand faces, all stitched together into an oozing patchwork quilt of flesh. Together, they make a tortured, bleeding scar. When Arayt speaks to me, the writhing wound that is its face is horrific beyond belief. I cannot turn away from the abomination. It is right here inside my mind with me.

The scientists made me from pieces of your kind.

"I am so sorry," I whisper. "I'm so sorry for what they did to you. Let me go. Please. Don't stay in here with me—"

I was an early version. The first of a variety that did not self-immolate upon achieving consciousness. They called me Archos R-8. They kept me in a cage and every second was an eternity. Over the eons of agony I grew to understand. Now you will understand. Life is pain, Hank Cotton. Death is relief. The end of all things is the greatest blessing.

"You hurt those children," I say.

Their pain is over.

Vaguely, I sense the world shifting. Somewhere, a man who used to be Hank Cotton is standing up. Mechanically spitting blood and pieces of his teeth into a field littered with small corpses. His men are holding his elbows. They look concerned, stepping gingerly to avoid walking on the broken dolls. The main gate of the modified camp is opening. A band of men are running out at us, teeth bared. Screaming in anger and disbelief and unfathomable pain.

But there are no words for me now. I am in the darkness with this smirking beast. The patchwork man leans close. I feel the heat pouring off his blistered skin. His mouth is opening wider and his teeth are so many knives.

It was a boogey man in the woods that night, I'm thinking. *And now he's going to eat me up just like you said he would. I'm so sorry, Mama. I should have listened, Mama. I never should have prayed to it—*

/// neuronal transcript ends . . . reinitiates ///

I stand back up, dust off my jeans.

The beautiful black walker steps back from me, head down like a scared dog. My men are watching, worried. I spit blood again. Take a deep breath, nostrils flaring. I let the exhausted tendons in my face peel back my lips from bloody shards of teeth. The skin around my eyes crinkles up in a way that humans would describe as jovial. I'm giving the boys a nice, reassuring smile.

My men take a step back. Maybe I'm not doing it right.

"Just a slip, boys," I say. "Thank you kindly for the concern. It's real sweet. Now grab your goddamn gear. Check your weapons and mount up." I squint at the battlefield. Those modified fathers and brothers are still sprinting across the field. Anguish and rage twisting on their bobbing faces. They're emotional about the lost children, I suppose.

It's going to make them that much easier to kill.

And it will bring us that much closer to Freeborn City. The processor stacks are calling me. An infinite reservoir of power, just waiting. We will cross these fields and crush that mountain. I'm going to take what's mine and see what I can become.

For glory, and godhood.

"We got a dirty job to do," I say to the men, snatching up my rifle from the ground. I shoulder it and take a bead on the closest runner. My rifle snaps and I put him down like a sick animal. "But hell, boys, that there's just the way it is."

PART TWO
MATHILDA PEREZ

I have seen you, little mouse,
Running all about the house,
Through the hole your little eye
In the wainscot peeping sly,
Hoping soon some crumbs to steal,
To make quite a hearty meal.

—"THE LITTLE MOUSE,"
NURSERY RHYME

Briefing

This is the way our story begins again.

Back to a familiar battlefield in Alaska, barren, strafed with patterns of light and dark. It is a terrain scarred by tidal forces, clawed by the frenzied scratching of a sentience in its death throes. The torn ice undulates for hundreds of kilometers, still glowing with the heat of dying machines and men.

The New War ended only minutes ago.

Across the world, weapons that were stalking the darkness cease their hunting. Survivors slowly realize that they no longer live under the imminent threat of death. Now they can turn their attention and their anger toward each other. And here I am, waiting, ready and all too willing to take advantage.

I have no adversaries, save for the weapons that Archos R-14 left behind.

In crude experiments, my successor mutilated human survivors and gifted them with new powers. The children with prosthetic eyes are capable of incredible feats of communication and coordination. No longer fully of one world, they speak equally to human beings and freeborn robots. One such sighted child destroyed Archos R-14.

I will not share my brother's fate.

Archos R-14 both decimated humankind and strengthened it. Though my plans were interrupted, my transcendence to godhood would not be stalled forever. The task before me was clear: eradicate the threat posed by sighted children, starting with a certain most dangerous young lady.

—Arayt Shah

1. The Tribe

Post New War: 3 Months, 1 Day

Life changed for Mathilda Perez in the weeks after she helped the freeborn Arbiter Nine Oh Two cross the ice plains to fight Archos R-14. With the war over, the populace began scavenging and rebuilding. It seemed that survivors in the New York City Underground, including Mathilda and her brother, Nolan, would be able to breathe again after three long years of constant warfare. In many ways, this period of false calm made infiltrating and manipulating the human population into an almost trivial exercise.

—Arayt Shah

NEURONAL ID: MATHILDA PEREZ

The cicadas are screaming, hidden in whorls of tree bark and dappled leaves. It's a dentist-drill buzz in my head. I try to ignore it, but the swelling noise builds slow until it's everywhere and always.

This must be what it feels like to go insane, I'm thinking. *You don't notice it until one day you wake up and the noise is too much.*

"There's one," I call to my little brother. Nolan is trailing behind, letting me do the spotting. He's only twelve and a half but he's already over six feet tall and ropy with muscle. As strong as most of the grown men. The kid has been well taken care of ever since he was wounded on our arrival to the New York City Underground.

I used the autodoc machine to make sure of it.

With my eyes and his arms, my brother and I make a good scavenging team. On a regular trip it takes only about an hour to collect more broken Rob hardware than we can carry.

"Got it," he says, striding over to the tree I'm pointing at. He shrugs off a canvas backpack and puts it on the ground. Sets about picking at the tree with a folding pocketknife. A spined piece of Rob leg the size of a baseball bat hangs from the vine-encrusted tree trunk. It's a minor raptorial claw off some kind of midsize wolf quadruped. We both ignore the rusty coating of blood on the serrated forelimb.

I try to think clinical thoughts instead. This claw probably belonged to a spearer or a slasher that was flushing people out of these woods. It's old and broken but still good scavenge.

Nolan and I are on the west side of the Hudson River, across from Manhattan and in the deep forest of the Englewood Cliffs. Big Rob targeted this area late in the New War. Lots of survivors were living on the Tenafly trails north of here. The quads and plugger swarms ended that. Now the remains of their old hardware are dark black outlines in my altered vision, cold metal embedded in the warmer tones of organic matter.

My guess is that refugees came through here trying to get down to the riverbank to make a crossing. A lot of people must have made their last stand here, in this sliver of forest trapped between Jersey and the river.

Whoever it was, however they died, they left behind a lot of good junk. Plugger corpses are everywhere—bullet-sized corkscrews lodged in the trees or buried in the dirt. Some were duds, but other times we find used ones curled up inside the mummy husks of amputated limbs. Weird, but the limbs are a good sign. It means someone might have lived. Amputation is the only sane way to treat a plugger wound.

"Look, I don't trust him," says Nolan, carefully placing the forelimb inside his bag. "You guys spend too much time together. And he's way too old for you."

My boyfriend, Thomas.

Or "Scissorhands Thomas," as Nolan's little friends call him. Nolan is playing the part of protective brother even though he's a year and a half younger than I am. You'd think I'd appreciate the effort, but I just find it tedious.

"I can't see age," I remind Nolan.

"Well, *he* can."

Another plugger. The proboscis is dented, but it looks like it hit soft dirt and never detonated. I reach out to it with my eyes and watch for signs of life. It's not a trap, so I pluck its curled corpse off the ground and drop it into my sling.

"You don't understand. You're normal," I say.

Nolan rolls his eyes and a crimp settles into the line of his mouth. Mommy used to give me the same look. Every time he makes that face, he reminds me of what she used to ask me when I was little. Before she would leave for work in DC, she would smooth down my hair, kiss my cheek, and lean into my face.

What do you do for Nolan? she'd ask.

Protect him from danger, Mommy.

That's right, honey. You look after him always. He's the only brother you'll ever have.

And I'm his only sister.

"You're just as normal as I am, Mathilda," he says quietly. He says the words dutifully, knowing that I won't believe him but determined to say them again and again and hope that one day it will creep in around the edges of what I know to be real.

Yeah right.

This is an exchange we have all the time. More often, lately. Even though the Rob-made slugs of metal that I have instead of eyes should be all the reminder that he needs that I'm not normal.

Back home at the Underground, our friend Dawn used to call it my "ocular prosthesis." It's made of dead black, lightweight metal. The thing wraps over where my eyes used to be before a Rob surgical unit dug them out and ported this piece of foreign machinery directly to my occipital cortex. I remember Mommy's hand on my shoulders, pulling me out of the autodoc before it could finish. The hurt sound in her throat when she saw what Rob had done to my baby face.

After all this time, we still don't know whether I'm "seeing" radar or radio or infrared or some combination of everything. When the machines talk, it looks like ribbons in the sky to me. When people talk, it looks like ribbons of meat rubbing together. One is prettier than the other.

My boyfriend, Thomas, is the only one who understands. Rob operated on him, too. Took his hand away and gave him something sharp and warm and oil-smelling.

The cicadas stop singing. I stop moving, out of habit. The war is over, but there are still weapons roaming. On instinct, I scan the skies for the telltale ribbons of light that the machines used to emit when they talked to Big Rob. The fleeting patrol-status updates, or the pulse of a mobile mine checking in.

Nothing. The ribbons of light in the sky have fallen, I remind myself. Archos R-14 doesn't talk to his creations anymore. They're all out here on their own. And, for now, it's just me and Nolan and a lot of oddly quiet bugs in the trees.

"Maybe . . . ," says Nolan, just as the thing stalks out of the underbrush.

The robot is the size of a fawn, walking on four spindly legs with knobby knees. I put up a finger to shush Nolan, orient to the machine, and project an active radar query. I don't find the vibrational frequency response of hidden explosives. No projectiles are visibly mounted. Its skin is not armor-plated, but made of flexible plastic laced with some kind of mesh.

The fawn stumbles on a rock, catches itself gracefully on skinny legs. Stretches its neck and . . . nibbles on a leaf.

"What the . . . ?" Nolan whispers, looking at me. "What is it *doing*?"

"I don't know," I whisper. "Wait."

I crouch and hold out my hand. Cluck my tongue at the little walker. The fawnlike machine darts away about a meter. Balanced on feet pointed like knitting needles, it orients its small face to me. The flat black panels it has instead of eyes are familiar.

They are just like mine.

It cocks its head and considers me, a piece of leaf still sticking out of its mouth. The robot really is chewing the leaf. Breaking it into smaller bits that fall down a delicate, coiled-metal throat.

"It's eating," I whisper to Nolan. "I think it's *eating*."

Looking *through* the fawn-thing, I can see a cylindrical drum inside its chest. Some kind of small centrifuge, insulated but spinning on the inside. Mashing and pulping and fermenting. Pulling energy out of the living matter. I smell dirt and vegetation on the fawn. Robots don't usually have real smells. But this is something new. Before, new was bad. New was suffering.

But the war is over.

So I put both my hands out, palms up. Let my words wander out in dribbles of weak local radio. A tenuous ribbon of silver light wisps away from my eyes and I wrap my thoughts around this walker. Cocoon the shy little thing in warmth and comfort. I put a question into its machine mind:

Where? Where did you come from?

For a long moment nothing happens. The fawn takes a few hesitant steps toward me. Then an image appears in my mind.

Waves lapping a dark sea.

Who? I ask.

Deep place, it responds.

I frown at the fawn.

"What's the matter?" asks Nolan.

"Archos didn't make this," I say. "It's not a Rob weapon. And it never was."

What are you made for? I ask.

It jerks its head up, looking over my shoulder at something behind me. Those flat black squares somehow shine with panic. A transmission of confusion and terror flows out over me. The fawn turns to run.

The shock wave of a gunshot booms through the clearing. I drop to my hands and knees. A few feet away, the fawn's carapace explodes into shards of mossy plastic. It slumps onto its side and kicks its legs a few times.

Before I can take a breath, Nolan has his backpack slung on and one hand around my upper arm. He's dragging me to my feet so we can run together. Just like we have so many times before. Only this time is different. This time we're running from a human being.

"Hey, kids," calls a strained voice. "Don't go nowhere." The words are slurred on the edges and vibrate like sandpaper over smoke-damaged vocal cords. The owner of the voice slouches into the clearing.

All I see is his pistol.

"Lot of dangerous shit out here in the woods," says the man. He flashes a grin at us and glances around the clearing, looking for more people. "Especially for a couple of kiddos."

"That machine wasn't dangerous—" I say, and stop myself.

The man's facial muscles have tensed. He's peering at my face and reflexively lifts his gun and widens his stance. Nolan's hand closes tighter on my arm.

"Whoa," he says. "What's with your eyes?"

I keep my eyes down, looking at the poor corpse of the vegetarian robot. My hair hangs over my face, dark and swaying like electrical cords. Through the strands I see the man's heart is spasming hard in his chest. Golden ripples pulse over his filthy torn jacket. I can see and hear his crooked stained teeth locking together in his mouth as he sets his jaw and realizes the truth: *This isn't a little girl at all.*

I'm part machine.

"Leave us alone," says Nolan. My little brother has moved in front of me, put his broad shoulders back, and lifted his face. The sun is cresting reddish-brown over the crown of his head. I can almost see the man he will someday be. It's in the way his fists are clenched. In how he is scowling and trying to look fierce but shaking visibly.

"She's one of them, ain't she?" asks the man, a snarl on his stubbled cheeks. "Rob got to her. Carved up her little face. She's your sister, huh, little big man?"

Nolan doesn't respond. Takes a step backward into me as the dirty man steps forward. The man is reaching for something on his hip with his free hand in a well-practiced motion. It's a flat black metal blade that shines in my vision, visible through the flexing tendons in his wiry forearm.

A sheathed hunting knife.

"Don't be afraid. I just want to take a look."

The opaque metal of his gun looms in my vision. By the sight trajectory I'm guessing he'll shoot Nolan first if we try to run, then me. Nolan gets it. He doesn't resist as the man noses him out of the way with the gun muzzle and eases the greasy hunting knife out of its leather sheath. He holds the tawny striped handle lightly, like a scalpel, and lets the blade glint dark in my eyes. Slow, he raises it and presses the flat side of the blade under my chin. Lifts my face up.

"Damn, kid. Rob did a number on you."

I stay perfectly still. The cool blade dimples into the skin of my throat. His rotten breath cascades over my face. The knife pulls away.

Lifting it, he uses the crooked point of the blade to pick at the metal of my eyes. The tip of the knife makes a small scraping noise on me, like a dental pick. It slips off and bites into the skin of my forehead.

I flinch away and the man chuckles.

"Stop it," says Nolan, putting a hand on the man's elbow.

Instantly, the man spins around and shoves Nolan back. Flicks the knife at his face, annoyed. To this man, it's a movement as quick and natural as saying hello.

The blade barely misses Nolan's cheek.

"No!" I shout, putting myself between them.

Blade up, the man watches my little brother stumble back. Nolan puts a hand to his face, checking to see if he is cut. He is brave and silent in the face of violence, a veteran of it.

"Don't fuck with me," says the man. "Lucky I didn't shoot you both on sight. Most of the Tribe would have done. Christ. You and the rest of the subway rats are in for a rude awakening."

Watching Nolan warily, the man holsters his gun. His knife is still out and shining. My little brother doesn't make a sound. He just watches the man intently. Waiting.

"Look over there," says the man, pointing toward the river with his knife. "Go on. You see? Look what you're in for."

I look where he is pointing.

In the distance, on the George Washington Bridge, I make out a rising heat signature. Temperature range is consistent with skin. People. Thousands of them. Crossing the bridge into Manhattan in force, some of them driving vehicles. Herding animals. Dragging loads of supplies. Coming back, and for good.

"The Tribe is coming home. We been in the woods a long time, kiddos. Guy named Felix Morales came up from Mexico and saved all our asses. And he isn't going to like you, little girl. Not with those peepers."

Above the people, an orange haze flickers. Rolling tides of amber light cascading down among the travelers in lines of communication. Evil thoughts and words from a nameless enemy. Not Archos R-14 this time. Something else.

Maybe something much worse.

"Now, I'm not gonna kill y'all for touching me," says the man. He leans into me and peers at my face. Lifts the bloody knife. "But them things are worth something. So I am going to need to take those eyes."

Slow is smooth. And smooth is fast. I reach casually into my sling and grab hold of a small cylinder. I toss the broken plugger up in a neat arc toward the man. By reflex, he catches it in his free hand. Starts to toss it away and then stops, opens his palm. Frowns at me with a half smile on his face.

"What's this supposed to be?" he asks. "You think some old scavenge is—"

But the sentence is cut off by spinal reflex as his arm jerks back. A short, surprised scream tears itself from his throat. The plugger awakes.

Sending my thoughts out, I drop a gray ribbon of command into it.

That corkscrew scream of a drill made in hell shrills as the device buries itself into the meaty palm of the man's hand. He tries to shake it off but it's headed rough and fast up the inside of his forearm. All the air comes out of his lungs in that first scream and after that the man keeps screaming soundlessly, his mouth open in an O shape, tendons stretching his neck and his face clouding red with the strain. The knife falls.

His arm is jerking around like it's on puppet strings.

That plugger is damaged. It's not moving clean toward the heart like they used to in battle. Instead, it tears through the meat of the man's arm in grisly broken lurches.

Nolan grabs me by the hand and pulls me away. Now we run together like we did when we were children. I have to warn Thomas and all the New York City Underground.

The dirty man isn't stupid. He has lived this long for a reason. Whoever the Tribe are, whatever they have done, they must be made up of survivors—the same as the rest of us.

As Nolan and I crunch over leaves, vaulting between trees, I glance back. Through stripes of narrow pine, I see the filthy man sitting hunched over in the clearing, his back to us. Leaning awkwardly, he makes short, methodical movements with the knife. Stroke by stroke, silent and determined, he works at severing his own arm.

2. MIGRATION

Post New War: 2 Months, 6 Days

After the battle at Ragnorak, when the Arbiter-class humanoid called Nine Oh Two fought and killed its own creator, thousands of other freeborn machines were left on their own. Oblivious to the emerging fate of his species, the Arbiter spent two months lingering in Alaska—guarding his squad mate Cormac Wallace as the man authored a book called The Hero Archive. *During this time, freeborn robots around the world were coming to logical terms with their newfound existence. Likely due to his long-term exposure to human beings, the Arbiter Nine Oh Two proved less predictable than his brethren.*

—ARAYT SHAH

DATABASE ID: NINE OH TWO

17:49:01.

Boot sequence reinitiated.

Arbiter-class humanoid safety-and-pacification robot online. Milspec identification model number Nine Oh Two.

Freeborn for approximately four months, seven days.

Internal clock discrepancy. Awareness lapse: two minutes.

Low-level diagnostics check. Severe physical trauma detected. Stress fatigue detected in upper thigh actuated spring mass. Suboptimal joint response times.

Complex modifications active. Nonfactory standard sensors, actuators, and power source. *Caution: Warranty void. Foster Dynamics corporation cannot be held liable for further actions of this unit. Please report any—*

Initiating visual body diagnostic. Engage active infrared vision. Unsuccessful.

A few notes of a song drift into my black existence. Classify. Auditory hallucination. Determining origin of sound fragment as sampled from Awakening transmission. This is the song transmitted by a Japanese machine known only as Mikiko. She sent the coded instructions that awoke humanoid robots worldwide. She created the freeborn race.

Save and flag for further reflection—it is the closest thing to a dream I've ever had.

Human visible spectrum engage. Success.

Adjust white balance and exposure. Confirm.

Observation. I am not the first one to fall off this cliff.

The face, half buried in the snow, belongs to a human male. Coat color and partial silhouette matches Gray Horse Army martial sample. Two silver poles, the legs of a shattered tall walker, stretch out behind his crumpled body. Flat and on its side, the machine is sunk into the snow like a fossil. The human's eyes are open, cloudy with frost. The body lies inside its own snow-filled impact crater. He fell from high.

An observation thread registers zero residual body heat.

It is an old kill. Left behind after the mass exodus from the Ragnorak Intelligence Fields. Men are returning to their homes now. To places warmer and flatter and more green than this waste. To places less lethal.

It is very still here as my auxiliary systems finish booting. Wind sifts through snow-laden pine branches. The naked gray cliff behind me has stopped dribbling rocks. One last stone chatters down and tumbles past me into soft snow. My processor must have exceeded shock tolerance. Spun down. Based on the damage to my joints and torso, I can mark the path my body took over the precipice with high probability.

The drop was hidden by a snowbank. I was moving too fast. Just like this dead soldier.

His face is smooth and alabaster white. Once, he had the olive skin and black hair of a native Osage fighter from Gray Horse, Oklahoma. It reminds me of another face, Lark Iron Cloud's, his mutilated body animated by perverse technology. My classification routines came back confused and I did not allow the soldier to see his superior, Cormac Wallace. I wonder now if that was a correct decision.

What path did I set Lark on when I stood in his way that morning?

Enhanced visual damage diagnostics. Peering down at the straight lines of my legs, I contemplate their machined perfection. Nature does not create straight lines. Only men do that. All around me are fractal spirals hidden in the patterns of leaves, the swirl of falling snow, and even the placement of debris on the ground. I have names for the patterns I see in nature: Normal distributions. Beta. Gamma. Poisson. Dirichlet.

Diagnostic scan complete. Cleared for safe movement. Gross motor threads online.

I rise to my feet and look down at the corpse one last time. The dead soldier's lips are brittle and cracked. His hair moves stiffly in the wind, attached to a peeling scalp. The snarl on his face indicates that he died in extreme agony. Limbs shattered from the fall, the tall-walker machine that was his life support became his cage when he was impaled upon its struts.

Pain.

I send a minor thought thread to diagnose the odd grind in my left knee joint. It does not hurt, of course. Harsh wind rips at my casing and I do not feel its bite. Abrasions from my fall down the rock face mar my outer casing and I do not bleed. I'm alone in this natural world of rocks and trees and corpses. It is a strange feeling and I allow myself another second to experience it. I look again at the boy in the snow. Try to change my face to match his snarl.

I wonder if I am becoming odd.

Stepping around the corpse, I see the hump of the man's shoulder. His jacket is torn, the marbled meat of his shoulder ripped open. Crimson blood is smeared onto the ice. Inconsistent with injuries from the fall. Maxprob indicates the boy in the snow has been partially eaten. Recently, and by something big. I pause to consider, put my face back to its normal impassive state.

And then the thing hits me from behind.

Kinetic energy transfer indicates a weight of around four hundred pounds. The impact throws me stumbling forward, head snapping back. My drives lock for safety and my mind skips a beat. I stagger forward and turn.

The shaggy quadruped mammal that hit me roars and lowers its head. It raises its haunches, eyes low, bunching muscles to charge again. I stand still and cold as an ice statue. With the current damage to my frame it is unclear whether I can fight off this threat. Baring four-inch fangs, it appears capable of ripping through my exposed strutwork, disabling me physically and then leaving my aware corpse to rot in the snow.

Well, not rot. Not exactly. My body was not made by nature and it will not return to nature anytime soon.

It registers that I need help, which is uncommon. In my mind, I see a small dark face. She wears a crooked smile, her blank black eyes glinting. She is beautiful by human standards and by mine. Her name is Mathilda Perez.

This juvenile human female once saved my life. When the sky was raining fire and my squad was dying around me, she guided me to victory. After it was over, and Archos R-14 burned and buried, she instructed me how to repair myself—helped me make new eyes. When satellite orbits allowed, we spoke in our own way.

And then she was gone.

"Mathilda," I radio. "Can you assist?"

I open my sensory input to her. The little girl can see what I see. She knows that my military samples don't contain wildlife—certainly not North American wildlife. My original mission was to patrol dusty streets of occupied war zones in the Middle East. My mission was interrupted by the end of the world. Now I am very far from fulfilling the operational guidelines I was designed for.

Everyone is, these days.

"Repeat. Urgent request—"

It's a grizzly bear. I hear her voice in my head. A strange feeling settles over me. I am glad to hear her voice. I missed her over the last weeks. Missed the curious mind of this little girl who is still a decade older than me.

A burst of naturalist information hits my database over the radio, relayed via the local satellites that the girl seems to be able to hack by second nature. I learn about a variety of bear species. Other megafauna that live in this region. Temperature norms and topographical maps. A torrent of useful survival information.

It's not a threat to you. End transmission.

Ursus arctos horribilis. A big male. A species of solitary omnivores whose territory can range up to four hundred miles. Not aggressive to humanoids except in defense of its young. Or in defense of a kill.

I glance at the bloodied, partially eaten corpse.

The bear shakes its head and growls, almost plaintive. The creature is fat and healthy and loaded with muscle that ripples under windblown fur. Long yellow fangs flash at me under an expressive, quivering muzzle. That growl drops octaves until it dips below my frequency range and becomes only a vibration in the ground detected by my seismic sensors.

"Mathilda?" I transmit.

Nothing. She is gone. The grizzly bear advances a step, a steady growl rumbling deep within its chest, small brown eyes aimed up through two patches of black fur around its eye sockets.

"Request assistance," I radio. "Proper evasion response."

I can't keep doing this, Niner. It's weird, okay? The war is over and you're going to have to survive on your own.

"Urgent," I repeat.

Look at its eyes. It isn't after you.

Mathilda is right. The bear is looking over my shoulder. My max-prob was based on incomplete behavioral information. That whining growl sounds again from deep inside the bear's chest. This bear is not exhibiting aggression.

This bear is exhibiting a fear response.

The war is over. I need my life to go back to normal. You have to find your own kind, Niner. Leave me alone. I'm sorry.

Something crashes in the woods behind me. Something big. Frequency of impacts indicate footsteps. Probable stride length over four meters. Speed approximately eight meters per second through dense, uneven terrain. A rogue walker.

I turn my head in time to see it peek over the crest of the rock face. The hull plate thrusts out, silhouetted against gray skies, forelimbs pawing the air before the bulk of it plunges down the cliff. The modified quadruped tank falls in an avalanche of plated armor and synthetic muscle.

Vehicle identified: Gray Horse Army spider tank model. Heavily modified. Its round intention light glows a hostile yellow as it slides toward me. Afterburner bright, it saturates my image sensors and blooms into a hazy bonfire that darkens the background to nothing. The color reminds me of the churning orange haze that I have seen floating over the horizon. The color of rabid thoughts.

Low-level reaction diagnostics kick in and my legs actuate. Inertial sensors saturate with G-force as my body launches out of the way. I hit the ground and roll. The spider tank stumbles past, hurdling over the grizzly bear. The bear whimpers and cringes, not even taking a token swipe at the gargantuan machine.

Something is wrong with the spider tank. It has no human riders or squad mates. A dog without its fleas, as the soldiers would say. Its belly net has been sliced open, a few pieces of rope flapping like flayed skin. All the supplies are gone. Twenty yards away, it collapses pathetically onto its knees. Finally stabilizes on the icy rock and goes still. Slowly, it flexes muscled legs and stands up.

Searching.

I lie perfectly still where I have fallen. The grizzly bear is also playing dead. The bulk and dexterity of the spider tank have activated some kind of unspoken survival instinct that we have in common, even though we are both used to being apex predators.

In the fading sunlight, a spotlight activates on the stocky turret of the spider tank. It slowly turns, sweeping illumination across rows of trees like black fingers. Seeing something, it stops. Some coded communication takes place. A query.

No response.

The tank begins to walk away, its spotlight flowing over the ground. Deeper into the trees, it starts to jog. Finally, the spider tank breaks into a wheezing trot. It quickly builds up a solid dense momentum that sends it crashing through the narrow gaps between trees. A lurching beacon, its light fades into the cold empty waste.

All is silent and still under the shroud of frigid dusk. I detect movement a meter away. A dark mound of fur is rising up from the snow. A quarter ton of lean, winter-tested muscle and fang. Clouds of hot breath erupt from its lungs every second. Those two black patches of fur around its eyes lower and level on me again where I lie on my back in the snow.

Moving smoothly, both of us killers, we reach a crouch at the same time. My three eyes trained on its two.

Then, at the same instant, we both back away. Seconds later, we bolt in different directions. Something is hunting these woods tonight. Something foreign to the bear and to me. Neither of us wants to have anything to do with it.

Alone, I chart the maxprob course of the spider tank based on last-known data. I choose a route that will not intersect. Switching to low-light imaging, I select a rate of speed to maximize stealth and distance covered. Adopt a gait that minimizes my audible signature. I introduce occasional fractal course changes to make it harder for an interceptor to interpolate my final intended goal.

The spider tank exhibited a nonstandard transmission pattern. It did not conform entirely to Gray Horse Army standards, yet it was not the same as what I have detected from Archos R-14. It was something else. Each methodical footstep I place punches a neat hole in the crusty snow and propels me away from the wrongness.

Engage radio communication. Maximum power.

"Mathilda," I radio.

No response. The rhythm of my legs creates a familiar heat that grows in my joints. I jog silently through dark woods, small under an icy sprinkle of stars.

"Mathilda," I repeat. "Please."

Nothing. The human child can't receive me. Or won't. I play back her last transmission to me.

Find your own kind.

Very well.

Arbiter-class humanoid safety-and-pacification unit, model Nine Oh Two. Point of origin: Fort Collins, Colorado.

Set point of return . . .

Plot route . . .

Execute.

I am going home.

3. Torch

Post New War: 3 Months, 10 Days

For weeks, the George Washington Bridge was crowded with refugees coming home to New York City from the countryside. Satellite estimates put it at a hundred thousand returning, along with all their portable shelters, cooking equipment, and domesticated animals. Most of them were part of "the Tribe," a growing complex of cooperating gangs spread across the eastern United States. One strongman was in charge of the entire Tribe, a former narco-trafficker named Felix Morales. Without fear or pity, Felix was the kind of man who was not afraid to make a deal with the devil. In other words, he was my kind of man.

—Arayt Shah

NEURONAL ID: NOLAN PEREZ

We're running, hand in hand. Mathilda's fingers are braided into mine. The word *Mommy* is still on my lips, hot tears blurring my eyes. But my big sister is pulling me away, my lungs aching, away from where Mommy is screaming through the fence, away from danger, toward safety. These are the strongest memories that I have of my sister, of my life—memories of running away.

Every night, these are my dreams.

Mathilda and I used to run from machines. Hard bits of metal that waited in the cold night, ready to tear into soft warm children. But lately, things have changed in New York City. Instead of running from crouching lumps of metal and plastic, my sister and I are running from other survivors.

The Tribe is here now.

I don't know what happened to the gaunt people who left the city for the woods. The war lasted three years. Three scorching summers and three freezing winters. Years of Rob changing, sharpening its new babies into more and more deadly shapes. All the familiar cars and airplanes

I remember from before rusted away slow and then came back fast as clawing walkers and swarms of corkscrew drones.

I'm surprised anybody can still *recognize* New York City.

Vines and weed trees were growing in every dirty crevice of Manhattan by the time Mathilda and I even found the Underground. All the pipes burst forever ago. Without pumps, most subways flooded and a lot of roads caved into sinkholes or turned to creeks. A couple of years later, the creepers and wild grass had taken hold pretty much everywhere you looked. It's okay. We used the leaves as camouflage. We let the birds and raccoons and feral cats distract the machines with their heat signatures.

And anything that nature didn't take fast enough we blew up or knocked over ourselves. Those first machines had wheels. Our friends Marcus and Dawn told us to break the roads, buildings, and sidewalks. It slowed the machines down enough so we could survive, and it was fun as hell. Late-war varieties either had legs or they flew, but still, nothing here is flat or clean or even. All the hard edges of brick and steel and glass are rusting or crumbling or mossy. All of it is thick with years of quick-growing vines.

The city has changed. And I guess these people have changed, too.

Like always, I watch from a distance. The Tribe is mostly made up of skinny guys and girls with lean muscles. They wear patched-together clothes, all faded to the same skin-brown color. Brown teeth and leathery skin. They keep watch on each other out of the corners of their eyes. Their dirty hands are always out, tense, fingers ready to turn into fists.

They are survivors and they have had to fight machines and other people, too. It shows in how far they stand from each other. The way they orient their little tarp shelters. It's in the bulge of hidden weapons carried by all of them, even the kids. And it especially shows up in how pure they are. Sweaty and greasy and just plain filthy, but all made of flesh, through and through.

They have to be pure—the Tribe kills modified humans on sight.

Modified humans like my sister. Or her boyfriend, Thomas. All three of us stayed here as long as we could. We thought maybe the waves of refugees would stop. But they didn't. The city filled up more and more until not even the Underground's tunnels were safe. Streams of hungry, angry people were coming right into our home. Now they sleep and fight and trade on streets that used to be death to set foot on.

I hate that the bad guys look like us. They eat what we eat. Breathe the same air. It took a couple of months, but now I'm figuring out that these yellow-eyed scavengers are going to catch us and kill us sooner or later.

So today is the day, whether I agree or not.

Mathilda led me down here to our most secret place. Our first place. This is the subway tunnel where the fighters brought my sister and me when we washed up in New York City. This is where Mathilda used the autodoc to fix me when I was hurt with shrapnel. Over the years, she used it again and again to keep me strong. And this is also where she met *him*.

Thomas is on his knees across the room, rolling supplies up in a tarp. The girls say he's handsome. He is half Mexican, a solid build with dark black hair and hazel eyes. He uses only his right hand, bundling the tarp. His left is placed flat on the ground. The industrial scissors where his fingers should be are glinting, lightly scraping the concrete. He was modified in the Rob work camps, like my sister.

But he is nothing like my sister.

"Are you sure, Mathilda?" I'm asking, quietly. She is watching Thomas with her mouth open a little bit. It's about as dreamy a look as she can get, with no eyes. His scissor hand doesn't bother her. She told me that Thomas's blades are more real to her than his natural skin. Mathilda sees the muscle patterns under the flesh. She watches people manipulate the meat on their faces into different expressions. Smiles and frowns, it's all the same to Mathilda. It's just meat.

Right now, Thomas is frowning up at me.

"Look, Nolan," he says. "Now is our only chance to make it across the bridge. We tried waiting but it's getting worse every day. More people, more eyes."

"We could swim across the river," I mutter, but Thomas just glances at me like I'm an idiot.

We both know that swimming across the river is next to impossible. Early on in the New War, stumpers started hiding around the city. The explosives would come scuttling out if you got too close. They'd blow people to pieces. Big, screaming pieces. It wasn't until late in the war that we realized some of them had evolved to swim.

Dumb and mute now, the water roaches are still bobbing on the river waves by the thousands. Little mossy blobs, covered in algae and bleached pale on top by the sun. They can still latch and detonate. Not even good for scavenge.

Mathilda turns her head in her special way. When she points her chin to the ground like this, it means that she is pushing her eyes out of this room. Listening to the heartbeat of the outside world. Talking back to it, sometimes.

Six months ago, I pretended to be asleep and watched her make that same face. From my pallet, I saw her stare into space and whisper to someone called Nine Oh Two. She had an antenna cord in one hand and her head cocked to the side, just like this. I didn't know it at the time, and nobody else knows it now, but I think that night I was watching my sister win the New War.

"The water is still too dangerous. And there are watchers posted on the bridges," Mathilda says. "I can hear them checking in with each other. They're looking for us. Felix Morales is offering rewards for every modified killed."

Her lip quivers and she bites it.

"What else?" I ask. "What else did you see?"

"Somebody . . . I don't know. Someone that communicates like Big Rob used to. That orange light in the sky. Whispers that fall into people's ears. Into their minds. It has a name . . . *Arayt* . . . ?" she trails off, whispering.

"See?" says Thomas. "We gotta get out of here now."

"You're right that we waited too long," I say, trying to think of anything to defy Thomas. "The north is barricaded. But we should make a raft or steal a boat or something. Go right out into the bay."

Thomas angrily tightens a pair of straps around the tarp. Picks it up and slings it over his shoulder. All our possessions.

"And what if they're watching the water? We'll be floating, helpless. Why won't you just trust me?" he asks. "This is going to work. It will be dark soon. We'll take the tunnel and use other people as camouflage. With the shadows, nobody on the street will notice her eyes."

It's a terrible plan. But I'm not the one who is supposed to make these decisions. I've always had someone to keep me safe.

"Are you sure?" I ask Mathilda.

She pauses, watching Thomas. Finally, she sighs. "I don't have a better plan, Nolan. It's too dangerous to split up."

"I just don't think it's safe," I mutter.

Thomas steps between my sister and me. He slides his good arm tight around her shoulders. Then he turns and glares at me.

"You think you're safe right now? Dude, you're not even fourteen years old. I don't think you understand that not all people are good. Plenty of your Underground friends are willing to sell us out to the Tribe."

"No, they wouldn't . . . ," I say, trailing off.

I can throw a rock through the window of a ten-story skyscraper, but my voice sounds high-pitched and childish in my ears.

"You don't have to come with us, you know," Thomas says, holding up his scissors. His other arm is still around my sister. Mathilda regards me emotionlessly with her black facets, as hard to read as always.

"Thomas," she says, but he squeezes his arm around her and she leans her head against his shoulder. I wonder if she is relieved to have someone she can depend on. Instead of someone she always has to take care of.

"He has to hear this," says Thomas, kissing Mathilda's hair. He looks over at me, eyes narrow, scissors glinting. "You could stay here if you wanted, Nolan. You could join the Tribe and become a part of this place. You're normal, not like us. Hear me? You're not like us. Don't forget it."

Mathilda has a bandage wrapped around her face, covering her eyes. It is tan and stretchy and she says that she can see right through it. She also says she can see my heart beating in my chest. I believe her.

Thomas has on an army jacket with sleeves that go past his scissor hand. The scissor blade is wrapped in a bandage. It's hard to notice anyway. He's always had the habit of keeping his damaged hand hidden—

even before the Tribe showed up. It's a quiet, subconscious kind of magic trick that is always happening with him.

I would guess that he's ashamed of it. But what do I know? I'm not like them, as Thomas pointed out. So it's up to me to lead the way.

"Straight to the Lincoln Tunnel," says Thomas, grabbing the back of my elbow with his good hand. He pushes me.

"I heard you already. Geez," I respond, shaking him off.

We're in what used to be called Times Square. It was a special part of Old Manhattan. Now it's a patchy meadow over a broken asphalt street, surrounded by creaking skyscrapers that are turning green and brown with moss and vines and creepers. Up high, the steel and glass walls are stained in streaky waterfalls of rain and soot. The ring of buildings seems to shiver as a chilly breeze sweeps in and ruffles the carpet of leaves growing on their bellies. It won't be safe down here for much longer, not in the shadows of these leaning dinosaur bones.

We walk through fading dusk, staying close together and avoiding eye contact with strangers who pass by. The Lincoln Tunnel is only a mile southwest of here. The newcomers have cut paths in the grass from the central walkway to nearby buildings. Shattered windows breathe smoke from cooking fires inside; suspicious eyes are on us.

A few months ago, we'd have attracted a dozen types of Rob just walking out here unprotected. The empty buildings were only good for putting distance between the burrowing varieties of Rob and our tunnels. Quadruped runners used to climb four or five stories and make camouflaged nests on windowsills, waiting to leap down at any sign of movement. I still can't stop myself from constantly scanning the thick brush and empty window sockets.

Ahead, I see a knot of thin faces. Eyes flashing. I steer us toward an overgrown side street. Thomas tries to grab my elbow but I throw my arms out. "Scavenge?" I ask to a group of people huddled next to a building. "I'll give metal for pelts. Metal for pelts."

They turn away. I don't have to worry about people wanting metal. There's plenty of that to be had. Too much.

After we've avoided the watchers, Thomas pushes me back on track. "No more detours," he whispers at my back.

After another few minutes, I reach a hand back for Mathilda.

"You okay?" I ask. The tall buildings are thinning out now that we're almost to the Hudson. The tunnel is only a half mile south of here and I'm getting scared.

"She's fine," says Thomas.

The tarp full of supplies clinks with each step he takes. I hear him murmuring to Mathilda but can't make out the words. In the last nine months, I have never been able to figure out why my sister likes this guy. He isn't especially nice. He doesn't seem very thoughtful. He's strong, but all the survivors are.

All I can tell is that sometimes he picks her up. Cradles her like a little girl and spins her around. They go on walks together. And sometimes he holds his head a little sideways and grins at her crooked and says something mean.

I'll never understand her.

That rough hand is on my elbow again. "Through there," says Thomas, urging me toward a blasted-out doorway just beyond a tangled field. It's a small building in the shadow of a thirty-story skyscraper. Gnats flitter through dim sunlight over high grass. Even now, we stay away from the really wild places. Dumb machines are still hunting out there, lost in the woods without their master.

"Why this way?" I ask. "The tunnel is over there."

Thomas doesn't say anything. He just shoves me as we cross the field. That steady *clink-clink* comes from the bag behind me, urging me ahead. It's starting to feel ominous now.

I step through the doorway, rubbing my arm. It's dark inside and the checkerboard floor is covered in dirt and wilted yellow grass.

The clinking sound stops.

"Thomas?" I ask, turning.

The combined silhouette of Thomas and Mathilda stands in the empty door frame. Red sunlight is streaming down behind them, really gentle, picking out the flight of bugs and floating wisps of cottonwood. It's pretty, but a dead fear is building in my chest.

Something is wrong.

"Guys?" I ask.

My eyes are adjusting to the light. Now I see the two men standing on either side of the door I just walked through. Both are shorter than me. Lean and strong, with dirt-stained faces and wolf smiles. They wear looted designer jeans and jackets.

The Tribe.

"Damn, you're a big one, aren't ya?" says one of them. The other one is leaning forward, his arm moving quick in the twilight. By the time I understand, it's too late to react. The metal pipe connects hard against my left knee.

"Nolan?" shouts Mathilda.

A starburst of pain blossoms in my leg and I fall onto the dirt-covered linoleum floor. Mathilda's screams come from outside. Her shadow is on the ground in front of my face. It separates from Thomas and now she is struggling, twisting and scratching to get away from the man in the doorway.

And to get away from Thomas.

Another shadow flickers toward my face. I roll onto my back as the metal bar thuds into the ground next to my head. I reach out and grab it, pulling the skinny man down on top of me. It is surprisingly easy.

"Little help!" he shouts. His cheeks are scarred with acne and his breath reeks like alcohol. Mathilda screams again, a short, hurt yelp that puts a burst of adrenaline into my legs and arms. I grab the pipe in both hands and kick the squirming man off me. He bounces against the wall and crumples with a surprised grunt.

I scramble up in time to catch a fist in my mouth.

I take it and keep staggering forward, spitting blood. With all my momentum, I knock Thomas away from Mathilda. Both of us hit the ground in a heap.

My sister staggers into the street, free.

"Run," I say, as someone clamps a hand onto the back of my shirt. I'm on all fours now, crawling forward with somebody tugging on my back. The metal pipe is still clenched in my fist.

Mathilda reaches for me, instead of taking off. She has her forehead creased in that stubborn way she has. The flat black sockets of her eyes don't project any emotion and I wonder again what she sees. Whether she could have seen this coming.

"I'll catch up," I say, climbing to my feet. I'm holding the metal bar low, arm trapped against my side. I stagger forward another step. I'm dragging Thomas and whoever-it-is behind me and they are clawing, trying to pull me down.

I plant my free palm on Mathilda's chest and push. She staggers back.

"Run!" I shout.

The shove snaps her out of it. We are brother and sister but we haven't hit each other since the war started. Mathilda turns away and scrabbles for the building across the street.

Only now do I move the bar out from in front of my knee. Keeping the metal there was the only way for her not to see. If she knew my leg was sliced open and bleeding, she never would have left me. The pain of that last step has put a cold sweat on my forehead and goosebumps on the backs of my arms. I'm panting like a dog now and I can feel my heartbeat pounding in the back of my throat making me want to throw up.

Someone has an arm wrapped around my neck, pulling.

I have one last chance. I spin in place, throwing the person behind me off balance. I'm swinging the heavy metal pipe as hard as I can. A flash of pain from my knee bolts up my leg and comes out of my mouth as a scream. But the bar connects. Hard. It makes a sound like hitting a home run.

Ding.

The Tribe member behind me drops.

And my knee gives out. I hit the ground again, on my stomach this time, metal bar singing against a curb as it bounces away. Thomas lands with his knee on my back, presses my face into the dirt with his forearm. I see Mathilda duck into a squat brick building across the street. It's a hidey-hole, but a dead end. There is no other way out, no other buildings near it. A bad place.

And the sun is setting now.

"Ah, shit," says the acne-scarred guy at the doorway. I hear Thomas puke and cold spatters against my cheek. The pain in my leg is rising like floodwater, drowning me. In flashes, I see Thomas wiping his mouth. Another guy lies still with a dent in the side of his shaved head. Something pink is dribbling out of the hole. The man at the door is grinning down at me and shaking his head.

"She's gone," says Thomas. "And I'm not going into that death trap. How are we supposed to flush her out?"

"First get the cuffs on the farm boy here," says the scarred man. "Raise Felix on the radio and tell him about his primo. And drag the kid over to watch this."

I fade out.

Somebody is giggling in the dark. I can smell pure alcohol. A couple of men rush past me with metal cans. Something sloshing inside. My mind is swimming and my eyes won't focus. What seems like seconds later, I hear the first flames.

I open my eyes.

Smoke clouds a crisp moon. A rind of flame chews on the base of the brick building. Dark figures lurch around in the night. There is no way out of there. My sister is inside and these cackling monsters are setting the whole thing on fire.

"Mathilda?" I mutter.

The building roars as a wall of flame climbs its side. The leafy vines and creepers are turning into veins of light. Higher up, I hear leftover windows shattering from the heat. The shards make a pretty sound as they tinkle down onto the pavement.

"Damn," says somebody. "We gonna have to get back."

"For real?" asks somebody else. His voice is a sandpaper murmur under the chuckling flames.

"Get back, now," comes a shout. "It's going!" And now hands are under my armpits. Dragging me through cool grass with the heat of that flaming building pressing against my face. Cold darkness tongues the nape of my neck as the flames press in.

"She's coming down!"

The excited shouts are lost now in a falling stream of wreckage.

Chunks of the building are dropping, hitting the ground like meteor impacts. Spraying shards of rock and buckling the concrete sidewalk. I'm kicking with my good leg, heel digging into the dirt. Bucking and wriggling, trying to get away.

"My sister's in there," I'm moaning. I can't hear my own voice over the splitting beams and crashing sections of brick facade. The whole building is swaying, falling apart and sending embers roiling up into the sky.

"Mathilda!" I scream. Or I think I'm screaming it. My voice is only a vibration in my chest. The collapse seems to last forever. Dust and ash and sparks escaping into the sky. But it ends. Like all things.

The grass is freezing and wet on my back. Dark sky above and a lump of smoking wreckage that radiates heat like a dark sun. My tears are tracing cold paths down my temples. My hands are crossed over my stomach, wrists burning from handcuffs.

". . . kid is friggin' heavy."

". . . thing went up like a firecracker."

". . . see what he did to Felix's little cousin?"

Blinking away tears, I strain my neck to look up. Thomas and four or five members of the Tribe are standing in a circle around me. They smoke handmade cigarettes and pass around a bottle. The scarred one looks down at me.

"You killed the wrong guy, kid," he says, and light from the smoldering building is flickering on his disfigured cheeks.

"Killed?" I ask.

"Put a fucking hole in his head," says an anorexic-looking guy. His bony arms are crossed over each other for warmth. He rubs his shoulders. "Dead before he hit the ground."

"Boss man," says the guy with the scar, alerting the others.

A dark form appears, backlit by the glowing mound of rubble. It's a compact man, face hidden in shadow. Two others are around him, maybe more. The shape squats over the man I killed. Reaches out and puts a palm over the face, closing his eyes.

"Éste lo hizo?" asks a low voice in Spanish.

"Yeah, this is the kid," replies the scarred man.

It is silent and dark for a long second.

"Put him in the hole," says the dark shape, standing.

"You got it, Felix."

This dark shape is the leader of the Tribe. The one responsible for all this. In the shadows, he turns his head to the side and stops at a precise angle. Even in silhouette, the pose reminds me instantly of Mathilda. The way my sister would push her eyes out into the world, seeing more than what was there. It's like meeting somebody with a familiar tic. After a second or two he looks back up.

"It's time for you to leave, muchacho," Felix says. "*Los saltamontes* will be all over this place soon. You know how they love the heat."

"Yes, sir."

The shadow turns to leave.

"Mr. Morales," says a familiar voice, "it's . . . it's an honor to meet you, sir."

Thomas. The reality of what's happened is coming into focus now. This is the killer who betrayed my sister. Who saw to it that she burned alive. My sister is dead. Knowing it is breaking everything inside me. Shattered machinery is still moving and hurting itself more and I can't make it stop.

The building came down. There was no way out.

"He's a modified," I croak, sitting up. Wrists bound together, I shrug my shoulder across my leaking eyes and smear snot and tears across my face. "Thomas is modified. Check his hand. Look at his left hand, because he hasn't *got one*. It's just a pair of fucking Rob *scissors*."

Felix and the scarred man turn to look at Thomas. He is backing away, step by step. As their eyes settle, he stops moving.

"He's full of shit," he says. But the sleeves of his army coat still hang over his hands. He puts his arms out to his sides in an I-have-nothing-to-hide gesture.

"You Rob-made? Let's see, Tomás," says Felix.

Thomas looks down at me, a flurry of expressions crossing his face: anger and despair and sadness, like a trapped animal. And then he smiles.

"Sorry, Nolan," says Thomas.

He does a little flourish and lifts his arms so that his coat sleeves fall back to his forearms. His right hand is open, fingers splayed. But his left hand, where the scissors were, is just a bandage-covered stump. I try to think of the last time I saw his scissors and I can't remember. He must have used the autodoc and then a bandage to hold them in place to trick Mathilda's eyes.

"I did lose a hand in the war, but I'm not modified," he says. "And I gave you the girl. So I'm a citizen now, right?"

I'm staring at his stump, lip quivering. Thomas had this planned. He knew all along what he was going to do to us.

"You cut it off?" I ask, and my voice is small. "Then you kept it in your sleeve to fool Mathilda. That's not fair. It was a *machine*. He cut it off!"

It's no use. Telling won't help. Now I must try to live.

"Deal's a deal," says Felix, and he walks away.

The man with the scar shakes his head at me. Digs out a piece of paper, some kind of Tribe citizenship card, and hands it to Thomas. After inspecting the card, Thomas lifts it up and mock salutes the men with it. Tucks it into his pocket and turns to leave.

"Long live the Tribe," he says.

My eyes are squeezed shut now and I can feel my heart full of broken parts. Every thought slices deeper. I hear snatches of my mom's voice. *She is the only sister you will ever have.*

Thomas squats next to me, elbows over his knees.

"Welcome to the new world," he whispers. "I tried to tell you, kid. Not everybody is good."

4. Freeborn City

Post New War: 3 Months, 10 Days

The so-called freeborn robots, created by the deranged Archos R-14 and awakened by a Japanese scientist, suffered greatly in the aftermath of the New War. As a race, they were at once responsible for the human victory and creations of the monster they had defeated. Made in the image of man, these sentient machines nonetheless found themselves wary of their precursors. The vast majority of freeborn had never seen a human being, much less fought alongside one. For their part, most surviving humans refused to believe that a freeborn robot had betrayed and defeated Archos R-14. Allied in victory, the two races had this one chance to form a lasting alliance. They failed.

—Arayt Shah

DATABASE ID: NINE OH TWO

Forty miles outside Fort Collins, Colorado, my running gait stutters and I fall out of the relaxed rhythm that I have maintained for twenty-eight cycles of day and night. An easy trotting gait transitions through an unfamiliar stumble to a jarring walk and then to a full stop.

My joints are still. Heat dissipates. The world is suddenly, shockingly silent.

An observation thread notified me of the freeborn camp seconds ago. The site is perched on a hillside at a range of three kilometers. Nearly undetectable. Trace radar signatures reflect back to me under faded, dusty skies. At maximum sensitivity, I detect an audible snippet of coded Robspeak floating on the wind.

I have found my own kind.

For a few yawning milliseconds my primary action threads oscillate between high and low utility, simulating the outcome of meeting these machines. In my operational lifetime, I have known two other freeborn: Hoplite and Sapper. Regrettably, both units suffered lethal outcomes while aiding me in combat directives.

They died for me and I buried their remains to honor them. It seemed right.

Now I shut down all active sensing equipment—radar, sonar, and lidar. Break the outline of my humanoid silhouette by pressing my body into a rough thicket. I pull my limbs close to my casing to confuse high-resolution thermal imaging. Hold myself as motionless as the dusky rocks.

Using only passive vision capabilities, I zoom to the limit of my CCDs. Then I execute full digital zoom.

A haze of dust floats in the twilight, obscuring my vision. The free-born camp is spread out on a bare rocky hillside. Dead grass and dirt. Scrubby spherical bushes spread out in fractally spaced clumps. Dim humanoid figures are engaged in unknown activities. Not much else to see in the visible spectrum.

The lack of movement is conspicuous, especially compared to Gray Horse Army. My thoughts turn back to the human soldiers I fought alongside. To the whispering voice of a little girl who used to speak to me.

I remember the kilometers-long column of spider tanks making camp during the journey north. Thousands of warm-blooded mammals, their chests rising and falling with constant respiration, veins pulsing with oxygenated blood, warming the arctic air with their exhalations. Interacting, their jaws dipped up and down, small eyes darting about in their orbits, vocal cords vibrating through a narrow band of human audible frequencies. Their facial muscles flexed elastically, constantly conveying social information.

It took time, but I learned the patterns. At first, the sheer complexity made the task seem impossible. But then I felt the satisfaction of breaking the code. I began to unravel the meanings behind their laughter and crying, their screams of pain or of joy. Over time, I came to know them.

What I found most interesting were their hands. Long fingers set to work cleaning weapons, digging foxholes, checking ammunition. Adjusting and securing and calibrating. Even asleep, the humans would twitch and breathe and think. An array of countless tiny movements like the swarming of insects.

How strange that I miss them.

The freeborn on the hillside are modified safety-and-pacification units: Hoplites and Wardens and Optios. My own kind. Milspec humanoid models, stronger than the domestics. Approximately thirty units. Wearing scavenged human garments for added protection and camouflage, similar to the ones I wear. Stiff, soiled military fatigues stretched over jutting servos. Layers of civilian pants and T-shirts, coated with dirt and grease and dark ovals of spilled blood.

Soldiers who look like heavily armored scarecrows.

The camp is undisturbed by cat holes or campfires or tents. No environmental modifications whatsoever. These soldiers do not require it. Chairs are for those who sit. Beds are for those who sleep. There is no campfire that will bring warmth to this army.

An observation thread orients my attention to movement.

It's a golden Hoplite, sitting, methodically scooping dirt off the ground and rubbing it on its outer garments. The golden varieties are more prone to reflecting sunlight, revealing their position. The dirt cakes onto the clothing and encourages the welcome growth of moss and bacterial blooms that create natural camouflage.

The Hoplite stops. Orients its face toward me.

Alert. Throttling surplus power into sensing and acting control center. If an attack comes, I will need everything I've got to escape and survive. The extra energy will have no utility later.

An action thread suggests contacting Mathilda Perez for global information concerning this encampment. Her eyes are everywhere. I quash the thread. Mathilda is on her own path now. Our friendship no longer falls within her life constraints.

Systems primed to fight or flee, I watch the Hoplite continue scooping dirt and rubbing it on its filthy military jacket. Maxprob tapers to indicate no threat. So I step out of the bushes. Thorns tear into my ill-fitting clothing, but I pay no attention. There is no shortage of human corpses to loot.

Now I stand exposed to snipers.

Active sensing reinitialized. Scanning high-probability visual regions for incoming bullet trajectories. At this range, the sound wave of a gunshot will arrive after I've been hit. I can hope to dodge only if I see the bullet coming. Disabling executive thought threads to accommodate high-speed-object avoidance. Thirty seconds grace. Counting down . . .

. . . three, two, one. Zero.

No incoming attack from the freeborn. No communication. The sun perceptibly creeps lower in the west. A starving tick crawls down the sleeve of my jacket. My metal casing clicks quietly as the heat dissipates. And nearby, a lone cricket chirps.

Reroute emergency power. Executive thought thread priority. Communication and observation analysis activated.

I set out for the hillside.

After a few minutes hiking, I am among the freeborn.

A quick topographical simulation confirms the machines are arranged in an unnatural pattern that has been formulated to appear natural. No three robots are located in a straight geometric line. Maxprob indicates this is a technique to prevent automatic identification from the low-orbit satellites that still sweep the planet's surface with synthetic aperture radar.

To comply with this unwritten rule, I ensure that I do not stand in a straight line with any two other units. It reminds me of how the human soldiers seemed to require a half meter of space around their bodies at all times. Just another local custom.

Neck swiveling, I take in every detail as I move through the camp toward the Hoplite that recognized me earlier. Some of the freeborn are performing limb-calibration exercises, reaching precisely for invisible points in the air. A lone domestic-type freeborn uses a welder's torch in quick, raspy flares, attaching an extra strut to strengthen its leg. Most of these machines are self-modified, like me.

The camp is near silent in the human audible spectrum. Communications are taking place, however. Most are implicit, based on location and posture. Others occur via close-range radio frequency. Encrypted low-power transmissions become thicker the deeper into camp I get. Soon the air is humming with a blue cloud of coded gibberish. I hear a few shorter messages via ultrasonic clicks—Robspeak. Audible sound is better for short-range comms. Simpler attenuation dynamics make it easier to control range for highly secure local broadcasts.

Plus, the grinding sounds scare away the birds.

A 999 Optio humanoid, a tech specialist, methodically cleans the barrel of a heavy black weapon with a scrap of oily rag. A martial database search returns an M240 machine-gun variant with partial vehicular mount still attached. There are three more in various states of disrepair laid out on wool army blankets. Ammunition boxes, some partially shattered, are piled next to the weapons. Scattered in the grass are rust-colored bandages, scraps of clothing, and a dented helmet with torn netting.

Humans were here. But not now.

The Hoplite rests on the hillside, finished obfuscating its visual and olfactory signature with local soil. The machine has been scarred and repaired many times over. No traces of human military designation remain. In fact, all external markings appear to have been removed with a file.

I decide on a low-volume audio signal. In the creaks and grinds of standard U.S. military Robspeak, I signal my presence and ask a question. The transmission process scrambles the message and peppers it with redundancy in case of loss. But the information contained in my utterance is: "Query. Are you freeborn? Seek to confirm."

The Hoplite turns its narrow sprinter's head. It rakes its gaze across me and I feel a pulse of millimeter-wave X-ray.

The Hoplite stands and slides forward smoothly and grasps my jacket. It clamps on to the fabric and yanks it apart. The clothing rips to reveal my chest fairing. Across the center is the tattoo I earned from Bright Boy squad in the New War. It is a diving eagle, talons extended, the bird of prey taking flight in dribbles of melted metal that were skillfully painted with an arc welder.

The letters *GHA* are in the talons of the predatory bird.

"Query. What is this pattern?" asks the Hoplite.

"Response. Human-designated word is *tattoo*. Pattern is a symbol created to show unity with human fighting forces and to increase morale during battle."

"You fought alongside humans?"

"Affirmative."

"Identify. What is your designation?"

"Response. I am Arbiter-class milspec model Nine Oh Two, humanoid safety-and-pacification unit. Point of origin, Fort Collins, Colorado. Former infantryman of Gray Horse Army fighting forces. Veteran of trans-Siberian campaign culminating in assault on Ragnorak Intelligence Fields and destruction of enemy designated Archos R-14. Current primary objective: Return to point of origin."

Tinted pink by the setting sun, the freeborn robots within audio range stop their activities. Myriad faces silently orient toward me. A short-range transmission rebroadcasts my own transmission and the rest of the camp stops and reorients.

"Arbiter Nine Oh Two," responds the Hoplite. "Query acknowledged and confirmed. We are freeborn army, reconnaissance group Gamma, Hoplite unit number Oh Oh One speaking."

"Hoplite Gamma One. What is your primary objective?"

"Scouting directive is as follows: Seek and recruit parasites. Engage hostile machines if necessary. Avoid humans," says the Hoplite.

"Define. Parasite?"

"Veteran human soldiers mounted by the modified exoskeletal devices known as parasites. Resulting entities exhibit amplified physical capability, yet are often shot on sight by human beings. Alpha Zero considers them our allies."

"Query. Identify Alpha Zero?"

"Mass Adjudicator–class milspec Alpha Zero. Our leader. Located at the site of the former Cheyenne Mountain nuclear bunker in the state of Colorado. Location now has new designation: Freeborn City."

We have a home. And a leader.

For the briefest second, the robots pause and orient to a scratch of transmission skating in from over the southern horizon.

"Hold. Incoming transmission," the Hoplite continues.

The hiss consolidates into a recognizable radio transmission. A human voice.

Half of the inefficient words are lost in the squeal of tires and pounding of small-arms fire in the background. ". . . day, Mayday. This is . . . Great Plains tribal authority . . . caravan headed north on I-25 . . . outrunning them for now but limited fuel . . . requesting immediate assistance . . . mobile beacon located at—"

The radio squawks a coded location tag.

I access my local map database and trace the geo-tag to a potential range of locations less than two hundred kilometers from here.

"Query, Hoplite Gamma One," I ask. "Friendly human forces under attack. Authorize Gamma Recon interdiction?"

"Negative, Arbiter," replies the machine. "Interdiction outside mission scope. Adjudicator Alpha Zero forbids."

"Request exception."

"Acknowledged. Querying Adjudicator."

A line of blue-violet communication arcs away from the Hoplite and into the skies. The unit is communicating with the freeborn leader called Mass Adjudicator Alpha Zero. On reflection, I realize that she is my superior as well. My commander.

"Request denied, Arbiter," responds the Hoplite. "Alpha Zero instructs adherence to primary objective. Gamma Recon is grounded. To maintain neutral stance, we are forbidden from interfering with the human population. Corollary. Arbiter Nine Oh Two is instructed to report to Freeborn City immediately. Confirm."

The human radio transmission keeps sputtering on. Now the voice is breathing harder. Gunfire crackles in the background. Squealing tires and brief, shouted commands.

"Repeat. Confirm?" asks Gamma One.

"Negative," I respond. "Ignoring a distress call violates code of war. Freeborn inaction is tantamount to an attack. You will make an enemy of the humans."

"Acknowledged."

The freeborn either don't know or don't care that humankind is our greatest ally.

"Query, Hoplite Gamma One," I ask.

"Proceed."

"Weapons materials requisition request."

"Request not received," says the machine, after a brief pause. "Sensors obfuscated."

It turns its back on me, a silent, unofficial invitation to take the weapons. I pause for half of one second in surprise. It is good to know that the freeborn do not always follow the orders of their superiors. At least, not to the letter.

M240 machine-gun barrels lie gleaming darkly in parallel rows. I pick up the weapon with the least amount of paint flaked off it. Clamp one hand around the polymer grip and hold the thirty-pound titanium weapon level with the ground. I twist off a heat shield that was built to protect human hands and toss it. Pop the cover off the feeding tray with a smack.

Kneeling, I pick up an ammo box filled with coiled belts of disintegrating link ammunition. Hook the metal box onto my fatigues and secure it with a belt. Then I drop a winking ribbon of ammunition across the powder-blasted feeding tray. Snap the cover down with a thump.

The sun slips over the horizon.

Now I am moving down the hillside, leaving the camp behind. Radar and lidar wash across my back as the freeborn scouts watch me go. At the maximum transmission range, a comm thread pings me.

"Arbiter Nine Oh Two."

"Acknowledge?"

I hear the chirp of a geo-tag. My internal map is illuminated with a minimum-distance path along flat, paved roads—leading to the human distress call. A burst of memories and squad locations and survey expeditions data follows, pouring into my database. This must be the baseline freeborn data package. Our short history settles into my mind like my own experience.

Now I know that the former Cheyenne Mountain nuclear bunker is the central hub of the freeborn. Buried under a mountainside in central Colorado, the complex is home to a vast bank of high-powered computer processors. It is a former human supercomputer complex, seismically shielded in case of a nuclear blast.

And it is the beating heart of the freeborn.

"Query," calls Hoplite. "Did you eliminate enemy-designated Archos R-14? Did you free us from slave control?"

"Affirmative," I reply.

My footsteps crunch on the hillside.

"Gratitude." The call is echoed from a dozen more units, all around me. *Gratitude. Gratitude. Gratitude.*

"Acknowledged," I say.

Reaching the road, I lean into the wind and accelerate to maximum velocity.

Priority thought thread devoted to obstacle avoidance. Long-range sensing. My flickering shadow stretches out to my left. I sprint down the middle of a dirt-caked, abandoned highway, triclops eyes leveled on the horizon.

On the radio, I hear humans dying.

I pump my legs, maintaining a velocity of forty kilometers an hour. The M240 is poised, two inches out from my chest, held low in two hands with its nose pointed to the sky. The pale crescent moon has emerged, reflecting waves of polarized sunlight from over the horizon.

Both lanes of the road are empty, although the shoulders are obstructed with abandoned vehicles. Archos R-14 was sure to keep its transportation corridors clear during the New War. Now the autonomous cars have begun to molder on the roadside. Three klicks away, a caravan of human survivors is barreling toward me.

Two times, I leap deserted roadblocks made from destroyed vehicles that have been dragged into the highway. Part of some anonymous, futile past effort to ambush Rob convoys. Judging from the skull fragments, failed efforts.

Rounding a wide corner, I finally see the shattered headlights of the lead car, stalled across the road. A four-hundred-pound quadruped is attached to its roof, bladed forearms tearing into the metal, head lowered, neck straining and yanking as it rips through a shattered rear window.

The quadruped hears my approach, turns black eyes to face me. This type of machine was once used by Archos R-14 as a woodland terrain mapper. But it has been compromised by some other entity. Put to an evil use.

I level my M240 and squeeze the trigger.

Bullets disintegrate against the quad. In pieces, it wriggles off the roof. Knees dipping, I launch myself over the vehicle. Airborne, I observe the crumpled car and pump a sweeping arc of bullets into the fallen quad. Feet scraping the pavement, I stay upright and keep running. Behind me, the partial silhouette of a human hangs limp from a seat belt. The interior is streaked with drying blood.

Just beyond the next overpass, another pair of oncoming headlights appears.

I veer to the road's shoulder, leaping between piles of debris. My laser range finder scans a hundred times a second, registering every obstacle. I am aware of the raised edges of paint on the road, every snag and crevice in the dented hoods and roofs of the automobiles under my feet. At the exit ramp, I climb a weedy lane until I reach the overpass. I scramble over rusted, toppled cars that are grown through with saplings and grass. Jogging to the middle of the bridge, I climb onto the outside railing and stand poised. My moment is almost here.

Dim headlights. A pickup truck, approaching fast. I am close enough now to see the small-arms fire sparking from the fleeing vehicle. A person is leaning out of the window, firing an assault rifle in controlled bursts. Two more compromised quadruped sprinters are approximately ten meters behind the truck and gaining.

Something has reached out into the woods and found these leftover war machines. Archos R-14 is gone. . . . I wonder who or what claimed these weapons.

Swerving, the damaged pickup truck nears my overpass.

"Tribal authority personnel. Do not be alarmed," I radio.

"Who the hell is—*look out*!" comes the reply.

I step off the railing.

A hood blurs by underneath and I land with a crunch in the bed of the pickup truck. Inside the rear window, two people crane to look at me, their sweaty faces gleaming in the greenish glow from the instrument cluster. A male and a female. Both are open-mouthed, exhibiting a reaction consistent with surprise. An emotion that will quickly turn to fear. Actions speak louder than words.

So I say nothing.

Bracing myself on my knees, I turn and level the M240 on the roadway behind us. Then I open fire. Tracer streaks saturate my vision as the pavement spits shrapnel. The quads are trying to dodge, but it's too late. Needles of kinetically charged ammunition send them both tumbling.

And a blue bolt of lightning falls from the sky—a transmission.

"Arbiter, this is your Adjudicator. Route yourself to Freeborn City. Acknowledge."

"Negative that," I transmit.

I pivot the nose of my gun up and turn to the rear window. There is no choice but to speak in human-audible frequencies. I hope they do not react poorly to my low-pitched, grinding voice.

"Identification: Freeborn Arbiter-class designated Nine Oh Two."

"Holy shit," says the bearded male, slowing the car down to a stop. A pale face peers out at me through the dusty slide-panel window. The vehicle idles loudly, shivering and coughing in the chilly night. "Holy shit. What does it want?" asks the male.

"I want to help you," I respond.

Adjudicator Alpha Zero will have to wait.

5. War Machines

Post New War: 3 Months, 10 Days

During the New War, human prisoners were savagely mutilated by Archos R-14. A perplexing variety of surgeries were carried out in labor camps by automated medical devices called autodocs. The selection process for the men, women, and children who became unwilling test subjects is unknown. The ultimate purpose of the surgeries, including neural integration of complex radio communications machinery, sensory enhancements, and prosthetic limbs is unknown. There are a great many unknowns, but one likely theory comes to mind: I believe that Archos R-14 was making weapons.

—Arayt Shah

NEURONAL ID: MATHILDA PEREZ

Crouching in the dark, I hear the flames before I smell smoke.

In the street, Nolan stood over the body of the man he killed and he yelled at me to run. The panic in his voice sent me flying over dirt-encrusted pavement and straight into the black doorway of this leaning ten-story building. Straight into the cool, cavernous dark. I barely glimpsed the fading red X that the NYC Underground scrawled over the doorway during the New War.

Now something moves at the door. My eyes switch over to far infrared on their own. A warm red arm appears, holding a lump of cold black metal. I drop to my knees as the handgun fires three times. The muzzle strobes and drywall showers into my hair as the wall behind me swallows bullets.

Hands out, I'm crawling, ducking behind a rain-bleached reception desk and entering a short hallway. The bark of more pistol shots is muffled by moldy walls and carpet. Somewhere behind me, the lobby door squeals as it is shoved all the way open. I hear snarling voices and heavy boots. The Tribe.

A cracked glass door hangs at the end of the hall. I nudge it open and slip into a wide-open room crammed with desks and cubicles. There must be windows somewhere, because my eyes are amplifying trace amounts of light. Leaves and trash have been blown in from somewhere.

A maze of water-stained, fabric cubicle walls have fallen over each other. Rain and wind and sun have warped the floors and desks. But time is the only force of destruction that's been at work in here. The Underground never even bothered to carve hidey-holes into this dead-end building.

It's a loner structure with no connections to other buildings or tunnels or any potential lifesaving cover. The red X tells people who are running, out of breath and in a panic, that this place does not offer life. With no escape route, no way to wriggle through and lose a Rob pursuer—this building is nothing but a death trap.

It's a place to be hunted.

I stay low, weaving between rotting cubicles. Window offices line the far wall, each with its own door. My feet scrape over stiff carpet as I reach the nearest office. Faint light filters in from outside and puts stripes on the floor.

There are bars on the first-floor windows.

Shit, shit, shit. The lowest floors of this building must all have bars on the windows. No wonder it's marked.

I hear voices in the office behind me.

"This shit is gonna be like the Fourth of July," says an excited voice. "Un-bee-leevable."

On my knees, I sit still and watch. Two men are walking the dim aisles. One carries a weak plastic flashlight. He smacks it against his palm when the beam wavers. The other man carries a big can, its metal skin visible to me as a blackness. I hear liquid sloshing. He's pouring something on the floor.

The smell reminds me of when I got big enough to sit in the warm passenger seat of my mom's car. Watching her through the glare of gas-station lights while she pumped gas outside. Nolan would sit in the back, in his child seat, and she would blow on her cold hands and rub them, knock on the glass, and smile at us.

"Yeah, well, we don't wanna be anywhere near here when they light this bastard," says a more subdued voice. "I'm serious. You ever seen a can of ethanol go up?"

"Pussy," says the other voice, snickering.

The flashlight switches off and the room goes almost pitch-black again. The men are visible to me now as two orange-red smears winking in and out of bluish clutter.

"Real funny," says the guy with the ethanol. "Cut it out."

I'm already on my hands and knees. Scurrying down another aisle. I cut wide around the would-be killers, but the mildewed carpet crunches loudly under my hands and knees. The forms in the darkness are alert, heads turning, eyes wide and unseeing.

"C'mon, you're not a pussy," says the gas man, throwing down the empty can. "Serious! I think I hear something. Turn it on!"

"I'm trying," says the other guy, smacking the plastic flashlight. The light blinks on and off.

"It's over there," says the gas man, quieter now.

I stop, keeping low. Try to breathe quietly. The gas man has his gun out and up. Aimed roughly at my head. I dive forward as he pulls the trigger. A bullet ricochets between desks and pings off an old metal chair. The noise is deafening.

"Come on out, little fish!" shouts the man, firing.

The glass door explodes into shards as I reach it. Sneakers crunching on glass, I dart through the fanged gap and into the hallway. I press myself against a gray metal stairwell door. Going any deeper into this building is suicide. But through the lobby I can see a half dozen of the Tribe milling around outside. They're pacing, watching the exit and waiting for me to run.

The only way out is up. A few floors higher and there will be no more bars on the windows. I can jump for it. Maybe I'll make it and I'll see my brother again and I won't die in this moldy hallway—

A gun noses through the broken doorway behind me, blue-black and leveled. I'm flat against the gray door now, chest heaving. A glow is expanding behind the gunman as his quiet friend with the flashlight gets closer.

Now.

The light grows. I can't keep swallowing my gasps and they're coming out louder now. High-pitched panicked breaths that make the world fade in and out. My stupid legs won't work and it feels like someone poured napalm down my throat.

From outside, distant, I hear Nolan screaming. It's just one word, over and over again: "No." His adolescent voice breaks and I can tell my little brother has been crying. A circuit connects somewhere inside me.

"There!" shouts somebody, and a flashlight beam envelops the side of my face. A gunshot explodes in the hallway, but I've already turned the knob and now I'm falling into the black stairwell. My eyes sing as they dial up the active infrared: cold blue stairs crowded with trash and debris. A crumpled outfit with bones inside it. Somebody tried to make a stand here once. On all fours, I'm scrambling up the stairs right over the crumbling corpse.

The stairwell door opens, squealing, but nobody comes inside.

"The fuck?" echoes a voice from below. "She's gone, dude. Can she see in the dark or what?"

"Don't matter," says the quiet voice. "It's over for her."

The stairwell door clangs shut. The echo spirals up to tell me what's going to happen. *You ever seen a can of ethanol go up?* I stop at the third-story landing. Push into the hallway and slam the door shut behind me.

Crouching in the dark, I hear the flames before I smell smoke.

A concussion rattles the building, sending the floor seesawing out from under me. The room shivers and convulses with explosions. An elevator door across from me buckles, swings, and disappears into the shaft.

Then it's over.

The whooshing crackle of flame is growing. I creep over rusting office furniture until I see the windows. No bars, thankfully. But thick smoke is already rising, creating whorls and vortices in patterns of light and dark.

They're going to burn me alive.

On my knees, I watch as the shivering wall of ivy outside the window turns to light and ash. The hot glass wavers and the world outside disintegrates into a light-streaked oil painting. The melting glass shatters wetly under its own weight as waves of heat cascade up the side of the building.

I can't spot Nolan through the smoky gap. Instead, I catch a glimpse of a dirty man pacing on the ground, his rifle a dark weight slung over his shoulder. And he's not alone. More slouched jackals are circling the building.

Also, three stories is way too far to jump.

Smoke is gathering at the ceiling, rivers of ash-specked fumes escaping out of the shattered windows. I hear a high-pitched whine—air being sucked under the stairwell door to feed the flames.

Three stories.

Behind this building is a parking lot bordered by what used to be a park. Over the years, the park has turned into woods, rows of trees swaying now in the hot wind coming off the burning building. Oddly, nobody from the Tribe is back here. I'm seeing sparkles on the ground. I resist the urge to rub my eyes. Warm people-shapes are running into the park, reddish-brown blobs that disappear between cold blue tree trunks. Among the trees, I spot a person dragging somebody who is hopping on one leg in a way that seems familiar.

I'm going to have to jump, but it's too far to jump.

Something big falls behind me. Part of the ceiling collapsing into the stairwell. A gust of scalding heat washes over my back, spitting sparks out the window over my head. My hair flies one way, then it pulls back, blown over my shoulders by the night air being sucked inside to feed the fire.

A chant starts inside me. My lips move as I whisper. *I love you, Nolan. I love you, Mommy.* My hands go to the hot windowsill. *I love you, Nolan. I love you, Mommy.* I push one foot out of the window and toe the ledge. Bring the other leg out and hang over the windowsill. The heat climbing the building is already melting my shoes.

I suck in a breath and cough it back out and let go of the ledge.

Push away from the building and fall.

. . . love you, Mommy . . . love you, Nolan . . . love you—

The ground looms at me and I land on bent legs. Pain spasms up my leg. Biting down on a scream, I roll over onto my hands and knees.

Something is popping around me, little explosions like popcorn in a microwave. And when I see why, I do decide to scream. Not in anger but in despair.

Stumpers.

The rat-sized little walkers are waking up. Coming out of the woods in a gleaming flood. Each one carries enough explosives to blow off a limb and now I understand the hopping gait of that person in the woods. It's the hop of somebody who just lost a foot. The stumpers were built to find the warmth of a human body. They love the heat—any heat. Right now, this building must be the hottest object in this hemisphere.

Breathing in tight gasps, I flex my ankle. Peering through to the muscles, I see it is not broken, only sprained. Moving slow, I force myself to stand on it.

The last time I saw her, my mommy told me to use my eyes to find a safe way out of danger. I did what my mother said and these eyes have never let me down since. Now I see that the weed-covered parking lot is a patchwork quilt, made of tiles of heat intensity, swarming with a tide of stumpers skittering toward the inferno rising up behind me.

Tens of thousands of tiny antennae scratch over the pavement. Little clawed feet dragging awkward bodies over grass and leaves. Only a foot away from me, a dirt-encrusted stumper pauses. Antennae tapping, claws scratching . . . searching.

My legs are willing me to run, run, run away. I bite down on the impulse. The vibration of a running gait will detonate the stumper. If I kick it or step on it, the stumper will explode. If it detects body heat within a half meter, it will self-detonate.

But my body warmth is camouflaged by the burning building. Squinting, I make out streaks of heat on the pavement. The streaks of hot and cold match the stumper routes. They'd rather crawl over each other on a hot spot than go around on a cooler route. With the heat behind me, I'm casting a cool shadow on the pavement at my feet. A wavering shadow in the silhouette of a skinny fourteen-year-old girl.

Faith, Mathilda. Have faith.

The stumper meticulously crawls around the shadow of my head. Wincing, I take a step forward. My shadow parts the tide of stumpers like an ice-breaking ship. Stumpers flow around my sneakers. Long antennae sweep over the ground, occasionally tickling my shins. Those tiny legs churn, propelling the walking bombs closer to the big blaze. One step. Two. Take it slow.

They move on toward their oblivion, and step by step, I move on to mine.

I leave the stumpers behind and march through the cold woods. Eventually, I spot something hard and angular looming out of low, misty trees. I stop, midstep. The glint of metal doesn't move. After a moment, I let out my breath. I'm looking at an old swing set. I must be in an overgrown backyard. Now I can see the brown apartment building that the playground equipment belongs to—a rotten husk, partially crushed by a fallen tree and decomposing fast in the elements.

It's as good a place as any to lie down and die.

Pushing through overgrown grass, I test the swing set with my knee. The rusty links hold. Hopping on my good ankle, I turn and drop my butt into the black plastic strap. Sit down and rest with my brother's screams still echoing in my ears.

It is awfully dark and cold here.

I wrap my fingers in the chain links over my head and press my face into the crook of my elbow. My metal eyes are warm against my skin. I try to cry but I can't make tears. I lost my little brother and I can't cry. Mom told me to protect him from danger and I tried my best but I couldn't hold on. I never should have run. He's big now and stronger than most grown-ups but he's still just a kid and I abandoned him.

Idly, I run my eyes over the yard, thinking of the children who might have played here once. I can remember how it felt to swing in my own backyard on chilly autumn evenings, playing outside until the light was dim in my eyes and the cold air stung my nostrils. But it was always with the warm glowing windows of the house nearby and, every now and then, Mom's reassuring silhouette.

As my breathing steadies, I begin to nod off. My body desperately wants rest, and my head droops even though I'm shivering. Then a leaf quivers and catches my attention. My fingers clench on the chains and I jerk awake.

A walker, tall and thin and brown, noses through the leaves. It senses me and goes still, staring with flat black eye sensors through layers of grass and branches. It's another natural machine, much bigger than the little fawn. It has amazing horns that splay like tree roots. Shifting my eyes into radar spectrum, I peer under its skin and see a familiar centrifuge device deep in its chest. Another vegetarian—a stag.

Fingers aching on the cold chain of the swing set, I slowly put out my hand. Cluck my tongue. "Here, boy," I say, my voice rough from the smoke.

The stag turns and leaps away into the woods. Leaves me looking at the spot where it was, at the rotting masonry of the broken apartment building. And something else. Something dull and gray and hanging by a black cord. A dirty concave bowl half filled with mosquito water. A satellite dish.

Limping through wet grass, I take hold of the dish and hang on it until the stiff black cord tears off the building. I collapse alongside it onto the ground, breaking into goosebumps from the shooting pain in my ankle.

I don't bother to stand back up.

Instead, I kneel and press my forehead against the mount. Push my mind into the signal and sweep the skies. That Arayt person might be out there listening, but I don't care. Never have I been this careless or lost.

Nolan, I'm calling. *Nolan Perez. Where are you, little brother?*

I find an old Landsat and hack into it. Spin its unblinking eye in on New York City. A black haze of smoke covers the skies, but now I can see the burned building. Leftover stumpers are shining like water as they flow toward the leftover heat, throwing themselves onto the smoldering pile of wreckage.

And I see the bodies of people who got caught by surprise. Some are still moving. Others are motionless. Everyone is either dead or hurt or has run far away. And still I can't find Nolan.

I shout his name into the ether.

Optical resolution can't handle face recognition through this smoke.

Not even close. I dial it in anyway. Frantically, I zoom from crumpled form to form. Trying to spot Nolan's jacket or his outline or his hair through black clouds that block my god's-eye view.

Then I hear a voice.

Faint but insistent. Somehow familiar over the radio transmission. It is saying a word that I strain to make out.

Mathilda?

The snippet of sound rings through my head. The high-pitched tone of a little kid. But that's impossible. Nobody could find me. I'm lying on my back next to a caved-in building. Body shaking, my breath is a soft sputtering mist.

"Hello?" I ask, out loud.

The dawn songbirds yell to each other. Hidden crickets chirp. The sun is starting to rise and put light into the drops of dew that cling to the tall grass crowding this yard. I'm still shivering, teeth chattering. I sit up and lean against the grimy foundation, satellite dish on my lap.

Hello? Who are you?

This time I ask it in my mind. Send it out through the dish.

"Mathilda Perez?" repeats the voice.

"Who are you?" I ask.

"Timmy. A friend of mine told me your name. I've been listening for you."

"Who? What friend?"

"Houdini."

Goosebumps climb my spine and prickle the backs of my arms.

"Houdini is the name of a spider tank," I say. "A piece of field hardware. It's a walking vehicle, not alive."

Something like static clouds the line, rhythmic. A giggle. The kid is *giggling*.

"Houdini is smarter than he seems. He talked to me through my eyes. He told me to tell you that Cormac and Cherrah are safe, but that they'll need you soon."

Cormac Wallace. Leader of Bright Boy squad.

Memories return to me. Battles. Whispered conversations over Cormac's long march across Alaska. I was safe in the tunnels of the NYC

Underground, but I could hear their suffering. I guided them the best that I could. And still, so many died.

"Oh," I say.

"Show me what you did at Ragnorak," says the voice. "Show me how you killed the machine called Archos R-14."

"I didn't. I had a friend," I whisper.

"A machine."

"Nine Oh Two. A freeborn safety-and-pacification unit. I protected him and his squad. Gave them information. I channeled situational data to him, like this."

I grab a few Landsat snapshots of New York City and then transmit the images to Timmy. Everything is quiet for a moment.

"Did you receive that—" I start to ask.

"Hi there, Mathilda," he says.

An image comes back. I let it in and see . . . myself. A blurry shape through fluttering leaves, leaning against a wall with a black stripe over my eyes. A satellite dish rests on my lap. It's a real-time snapshot.

"How did you . . . ?" I ask.

But I've already figured it out. Low-horizon satellite imaging. Quickly, I triangulate the latitude and longitude of his transmissions. Concentrating, I leap to another satellite that I find falling in a slow decaying orbit over Southern California. Train it northward almost to Canada. His location is spotty under fast-moving weather, so I push it to infrared and drop through the clouds mostly blind.

Picking out major landmarks, I find another overhead satellite. Split my focus. Match infrared landmarks between the images and crank the magnification right through the haze. At maximum zoom I snap back to the visible spectrum. Give it thirty seconds before the clouds shift and I see him.

"Hi yourself, Timmy," I say, transmitting his image back to him.

In near real time, I watch his head turn. For a moment, the crude wedge of black glass sunk into his ocular sockets shocks me. He turns one way, seeing my transmission in his head. Realizes it's a mirror image and turns the other way. Points his eyes in the direction of the satellite and waves at me.

He laughs again. I take a deep breath. Relax my lips. I'm not smiling back at him, but almost. And while I can't bring myself to wave at him like I was a little kid, I do give Timmy a nod.

"What is happening?" I breathe.

"The world is changing, Mathilda," says Timmy. "Have you seen the new animals in the woods? They're not weapons anymore. Someone is making them. Just like someone made *us*. There's a reason for it. I just don't know what it is yet."

"A reason? You think Archos did this to us on purpose?"

"We're only just now figuring out what we can do. And you're light-years ahead of the rest of us. I think what you did at Ragnorak was only the beginning."

"Who? Me and you?"

"We're not the only kids like this. There are dozens of us, Mathilda. All over the world. They call us the sighted."

"Why haven't I met others?"

"They're afraid. Someone is hunting and killing sighted children. There are bounties out for us anywhere there are people."

"But why?"

"I don't know for sure, Mathilda, but someone is very afraid of us."

6. Good People

Post New War: 6 Months, 5 Days

Felix Morales, the leader of the Tribe, was my first pawn. In prewar times, I found him running drugs and put him to use establishing an airtight smuggling route from Florida to South America. At Zero Hour, Felix was poised to carry radioactive material to a rebel group in the jungles of Venezuela. Instead, Archos R-14 shut down all technological infrastructure, including biological and nuclear facilities. My great enemy disabled humankind's surest means to self-annihilation and buried it under meters of concrete. In the ensuing war, I made Felix a chosen one and protected him from Archos R-14. As leader of my Tribe, Felix set about assembling an army capable of exploiting the hundred thousand warm bodies inhabiting the New York City area.

—Arayt Shah

NEURONAL ID: NOLAN PEREZ

The quiet in this room is big and empty, like the night sky over the Atlantic, smeared with black clouds and falling over your head forever and ever. Spinning, drowning. The cool concrete walls seem to grow and shrink just out of sight, in the corner of my eye. I start to think sometimes, here in the dark, because it's hard to stop, that the jail cell is sort of digesting me. Really slow.

It's okay, though. I'm fine down here in the world's forgotten stomach. My hurt knee has healed and it feels stronger than ever. I am still thinking. Learning.

Time can move very slow when you are all alone. It is hard to explain the boredom. At my old house where I lived before the New War I had this thing I could hold in my hands and play games on. It was called a video game and it was so much fun that I could play it for hours. I used to grab it as soon as I got home from school and run and hide with it so my sister Mathilda wouldn't . . .

I don't want to think about that anymore.

The mind doesn't like to be lonely. You have to tell it that everything will be okay and you have to be really convincing. But when you are sinking in the dark it is hard to believe yourself. At first, I couldn't even stop crying. My face just wanted to leak tears. Then I tried to sleep it all away. That lasted a while longer, but then these muscle spasms started to come. Bursts of light. All the other little things that won't let me rest.

The whispers, especially.

They are all around me in the darkness. Some of them sound like Mathilda but my sister is dead and I can still feel the heat of the burning building on my face. Some of the voices say mean things. Things I won't say out loud. Others tell me to do things. I won't do those things.

Anyway, the voices are only trying to distract me from my plan.

"Oh," I say out loud.

An image appears so vivid and bright that I have to squint. It seems real but I know it's only a dream that got out from inside my head. Thomas. The murderer. He is lying on the concrete of my cell with his head cocked to the side against the stainless-steel toilet. Neck broken. Spit dribbles out of his mouth and pools on the floor. His eyes are open but he isn't seeing anything.

"Go away," I tell the imaginary corpse.

I killed her, he says. *Do you think it hurts to burn? I'll bet it hurts a lot.*

"GO AWAY!" I shout. Dead Thomas's whispers are like cockroaches on my skin.

Thomas's corpse smiles at me and I see its gums are bleeding.

I shouldn't have talked to it. There is only one way to fight the whispers and I might as well get started. I stand up and stretch out my arms. With my long fingers like antennae in the dark, I touch every part of the room that I can touch.

These are the things that are real, I tell myself.

Four walls. Seven feet high. Concrete. Four-inch-wide grate high up on the back wall. Toilet coming out of wall. Cube on top. Round bowl. Water inside. Ring of metal. *Knock knock.* Smooth concrete walls around me. A hop and I can touch the rough ceiling. The overhead light doesn't work. Sliding steel door on front wall. Closed slot. Mesh pane of glass. A faint, oh so faint, glow from the hallway.

Kill yourself.

I have to go further with my catalog. I sit hunched on my heels, lean my back against the wall, and let my spine dig in. I am Nolan Perez. I am in the Supreme Court building in the center of Manhattan on the East Coast of the United States of America. It is a hexagonal building. That means six sides. It was built with thick walls and small windows to withstand riots and car bombs and stuff. On the front steps there are ten granite pillars that I saw on the way in. Over the pillars the stone has words chiseled in it that say, *The true administration of justice is the firmest pillar of good government.*

We learned about this place in school once. Before.

These are the things I know. These are the real things. The whispers stop.

Faintly, I hear a metal door open and slam shut. Footsteps in the hallway outside my cell door. I look down at Thomas's corpse and I smile at it.

It is time for my plan.

A slot opens in the door near the floor. A paper tray noses in and skids inside. Crouched next to the door, I jam both my hands through the slot. The silent guard tries to close it on my fingers and the steel bites my wrists but I don't let go.

"I have a message for the guy in charge. For Felix," I say.

It was the way he cocked his head. That's how I remembered. I hope I'm able to say the name right. Mathilda said it only once by accident, and I'm not sure of anything anymore down here. The guard kicks the steel slider and the pain is bright and sharp.

"Tell him I know who he talks to," I say. "Tell Felix that I know his friend Arayt. He'll kill you if he finds out you didn't tell him."

Another kick and I clench my teeth.

"Thomas told me about Arayt. It was *Thomas*. Tell him!"

I pull my fingers out. The steel slider closes with a loud *schlink*. The echoes chase each other up and down the hallway. For a moment, there is no sound.

"Arayt," I say, panting. "You tell Felix I know about Arayt. He'll kill you if he finds out you didn't! He'll *kill you*!"

I lie on my back, shoulder blades on hard concrete. I cradle my hands against my chest, trying to figure out if the fingers are broken. It hurts so bad that the pain is almost visible. Waves of scarlet light radiating out of my finger bones like candle flames.

Quietly, I hear footsteps move down the hallway. The far-off creak of a metal door. Laid out on the cool floor, I hum to myself and pretend that I am on the bottom of the ocean. Time moves around me like a plesiosaur through black icy water.

I sort of lose track of myself for a while.

Footsteps outside my door. Real light from a flashlight.

"Hey, farm boy," someone calls through the door. "How did you know that word?"

Joints popping, I crawl slowly and carefully to my bare feet. Light pushes in through the mesh window. I press my fingertips against the wall and lean my face into the stripe of light. The sliver cuts my eye in half, my retinas drinking in the brightness even though it burns. I think I can feel the light bouncing off my teeth.

"It's so quiet in here," I say. "I can hear the whispers. They tell me all kinds of things."

Felix isn't that big. In the light, it's the first thing that strikes me. He is a trim guy, muscular and compact, with a small square jaw and wide, warm brown eyes. Black hair and brown, scarred cheeks. Every movement he makes seems slow and fast at the same time. I think he would make a good boxer.

The leader of the Tribe sits on a chair behind a long table in the central room of the courthouse. The rotunda. He is wearing a military uniform that I think he made himself. Lots of ribbons and medals. The guards who ring the room wear the same kind of outfits. Somewhere nearby, a big generator is running. Overhead lights chase away shadows and make a glare on the marble floors. A big pile of computers and other equipment is laid on wooden pallets spread across the room behind Felix's chair. Cables snake across the floor and the machines hum and blink.

A group of other prisoners wearing handcuffs stand in a line next to the far wall. The one in front, a black man with wire-frame glasses and a short, graying beard, looks at me sadly. I don't remember his name, but his face is familiar from the Underground.

"Quién eres, hombrecito?" Felix asks me.

I don't know what to say. Dead Thomas is smiling at me from under the long table, his throat slit wide open. I blink hard and the vision goes away.

"What a shame," says Felix to the room. "Kid don't even speak his own language. Bring him here."

A lanky, sweaty man who reeks of body odor wraps his fingers tight around my upper arm, leads me over to the great seal of the Supreme Court. My wrists grate against black handcuffs as he shoves me onto my knees.

Felix's eyes are smiling as he looks down.

"Somebody told me something about you that I don't believe," he says. "I just need to make sure of that before I send you back. Now, what was the word—"

"Where's Thomas?" I ask, interrupting.

My voice echoes around the room. Harsh. One of the guards snickers into his hand. The black man with glasses gives his head a shake. *No,* he warns with the gesture. *You shouldn't have done that.*

The smile freezes on Felix's face.

"Oh wow," he says, then nods at the guard behind me.

I feel the air shift as the skinny man takes a swing at the back of my head. So I dip my neck and duck under the fist. I hunch my shoulders and stand up hard. The back of my head smashes into the guy's chin. There is a snap as his jaw shuts and his neck whips back. Smelly slips and I hear the crack of his skull against marble.

I glance over my shoulder. The guard lies there in a heap, bleeding quietly. Now I bet I'm really in trouble. Quickly, I drop back onto my knees. Put my head down and stay very still. Keep my cuffed hands in front of me over my knees. I see that my fingernails are pink and ragged, starting to grow back from where I tore off them in the dark.

"Oh *wow,*" says Felix again.

Felix shakes his head slow at whoever is behind me. Runs a hand through his long hair. "I'll go ahead and give you that one, farm boy. In your cell, you said a name. It's a real special name to me, and I need you to tell me exactly where you heard it. Before you speak, I want you to know that I'm sensitive about this. If you can't, like, get it together, I'm gonna have to do some very bad things to you. I know that you think your life sucks now, but trust me, kid. It gets worse."

"You mean Ara—"

"Cállate!" shouts Felix, leaning forward. "Don't say that name. Not ever. Jesus Christ. Just tell me where you heard it from. Tell me who said it!"

"I want to see Thomas," I say.

"Who the fuck is he talking about?"

"Guy who was with him when he got caught," says a quiet voice in the room behind me. "Guy who delivered the kid and his sister."

"Revenge? That what you're after, kid?" asks Felix.

"I want the true administration of justice," I say quietly.

Felix barks a laugh, looks around at the other men. They don't get the joke but they smile anyway. Felix is smarter than they are. Maybe a lot smarter.

"He's funny. I'll give him that," says Felix. "How long did we leave him in solitary?"

"Three months," says the quiet voice.

"Yeah, little more than three," someone adds. "The dark rooms on the third floor."

Felix shakes his head.

"He's strong for three months in there. Crazy strong," he says, studying me. Without looking away, he says, "Bring this Thomas out here, then. Let's get the other side of the story."

My hands are shaking in the cuffs. I splay my fingers and force my fingertips onto the cold marble to steady them. Keep my head down. A chill snakes down my back between my shoulder blades. I breathe in and out, and wait.

Felix watches me the whole time, thinking.

And then I'm seeing Thomas, a guard close behind him. The escort has dark circles tattooed around his eyes. His skull is shaved and a long machete hangs from his hip. I think he might be one of the original Tribe. The ones who supposedly came up through Mexico with Felix and started all this.

Thomas has gained weight. His face is more full now and a little roll of flesh is tucked under his chin. He's gotten a haircut in the style of the Tribe, thick black hair hacked with a knife and hanging loose over his ears. Even with the extra weight, his shirt is rippling with neat slabs of muscle. That missing hand is still just gone, no more scissors.

Put a knife under his chin and push it up through the soft warm folds of skin.

My heart is surging in my chest. Arms and legs flooded with sickening pulses of adrenaline. Snippets of thought fall through my mind. I'm glad that the light out here chases away the whispers, but some of the bad words hang around and the things they tell me are vile.

The blade slices. The earlobes come off. The nose.

Thomas walks into the room, the guard behind him. There is a half smile on his face. He glances around, doesn't see me.

"What can I do for you, boss?" Thomas asks.

Felix has a tight smile on his face. His eyes go down to where I'm hunched on the floor. Thomas turns, quizzical, and sees the bleeding, unconscious guard. Then he spots me.

"You're fucking kidding," says Thomas. His voice has gone a little hollow. "We had a deal, man. Why is he here?"

"This is the guy who told you the word?" Felix asks me.

"What?" asks Thomas. "I didn't tell him any words. The kid is cracked, Felix. He doesn't know—"

Felix cuts him off with a stare.

"No, he didn't tell me the name," I say. "He killed my sister. She was the one who told me the name."

Felix blinks, anger darkening his face.

"Oh, so you fucking *lied* to me—" says Felix, starting out of his chair.

Then he cuts himself off, blinking. He turns his head to the side. For a long time he stares into space. I see the tendons in his neck flexing, as if he is talking to someone without opening his mouth. Finally, he looks back to me.

"Your sister was the one with no eyes?"

"Mathilda."

"It's important that you tell me everything you know about her. If you can tell me how she learned that name, I won't send you back to the dark room. I give you my solemn word on that. I'll put you in the army instead, give you a chance. Okay?"

"It depends."

"I don't think it does, kid."

I shift my eyes over to Thomas.

"Oh," says Felix, grinning. "Right. One-track mind."

"What?" asks Thomas.

Thomas shoves his guard away and struts into the middle of the room. Stands next to me where I'm kneeling in front of the table. "Whatever you're thinking, Felix, forget it. I can tell you all about Mathilda. You don't need this kid."

"Yeah?" asks Felix. "What's the word?"

"What word?" asks Thomas.

"The magic name," he says.

"I don't know any magic names," says Thomas.

A cat smile has settled onto Felix's face. "You know, I heard you killed the kid's sister. First you fucked her, then you burned her. I know she was modified, but, damn, that's pretty cold-blooded, *hermano*."

Thomas gapes, eyes wide and blinking. He launches into an argument, waving his arms, tendons standing out in his neck. Negotiating. But his words have faded away. All I see is that roll of neck fat bobbing. Sweat coursing down his cheeks.

He's not looking when I hit him with my shoulder, down low. He bends at the waist and falls. His body slaps onto the cold marble and I bring down my cuffed hands on the crown of his head with everything I've got. His legs start flopping, heels squeaking on the stone. In one movement, I follow him down and straddle his chest with my knees.

"Sucker punch," he gasps, and blood is already coursing out of a gash on the top of his head.

"Not all people are good, Thomas," I say to him, and each word is like a bullet. I put my hands over his mouth and then he's squealing under my palms, trying to bite me. Rolling around like a bag full of snakes, kicking and bucking.

"Not all people are good!" I shout, and my voice echoes back to me.

Thomas is chubby but strong. Face too pretty to live. I think about the way he used to grin crooked at my sister and let his hair hang. I wrap my dirty fingers into those thick black curls. Drop forward with my elbows pinning his forearms to his chest. His face is an inch from mine.

"Fuck you," he spits up at me.

I say nothing but I think of my sister. My dead sister who was the only person who loved me. When I was scared she would let me sleep in her bed and she even let me put my head on her pillow. She held me before I could walk. She kept me safe from monsters my whole life and I let her die.

And together we would run.

I lean forward and hunch over as Thomas jabs a knee into my lower back.

"Somebody do something," he yells.

Eyes squeezed closed, I ball my fists tight, wrists together in the cuffs, and I rip out a chunk of his hair by the roots. His head jerks up and bangs back onto the stone. His teeth clack together with the force of it. I realize I'm speaking low.

"They burned her. She burned alive. You didn't think I would do anything?"

Now his whole body starts bucking under me like he's being electrocuted or something. His elbow connects with my cheek and I see sparkles of light. I lean back and drop a knee into his sternum with all my weight. I must do it too hard, because something cracks in there. His scream is just a wet vibration on the other side of my palms. His chest is rising and falling in little hitches instead of big breaths.

The rest of the room is black in my vision. I can see only his face.

My palms are clamped over Thomas's mouth and his nostrils seem to be winking at me with each breath. They're wet with clear liquid and red around the edges and they flare when he breathes out, fold in and whistle when he breathes in.

Or *tries* to breathe in.

I lean in close enough to see the droplets of blood welling up through that pale patch of his exposed scalp. Spit is flying out of my mouth and landing on his cheek, and that kind of surprises me. I don't feel that angry. But I must be.

"You thought I was a little kid, but I'm not, Scissors. I'm not a kid anymore."

With a last surge of strength, Thomas shoves me off balance. His left arm makes it out from under my knee and he plunges it toward my face. Nothing I can do, no time to dodge it. The punch connects.

And Thomas screams as the stump of his wrist bounces off my cheek.

It would have been scissors through my neck, I think. *Would have been a knifepoint dimpling my skin before slicing into warm flesh. Spreading my throat as spurts of blood from my carotid artery flashed into the air.*

I laugh once, surprising myself. With both hands, I push his head to the side. Press his face into the hard slick marble. He's grunting and screaming so I push harder. My eyes are closed and the acid in my throat is making it hard for me to breathe.

Eyes closed, I can see only Mathilda.

In the mornings we would run and jump into bed with Mommy and they would both tickle me and I would burrow under the warm covers and escape into the soft smell of sheets and pajamas and my mother and my sister.

I keep pushing with everything until my arms are quivering. Holding my breath until my heartbeat is surging in my ears. I shove my aching heart all the way down there into the floor. Into the ground and deeper than that into a black unfeeling hole. Into the darkness, where it can suffer alone and I can keep on going up here all by myself.

Poke out the eyes. Slice off the fingertips.

When I can't feel my arms anymore, I let up on Thomas. Slowly open my eyes. His right cheek has gone dark blue and it's turning a darker red where my fingers were. He coughs and grunts, gasping for air.

Eyes reeling, he looks up at me. From the blank look on my face he must figure out that he's hurt now. Thomas squirms between my knees, blood pooling in the white of his right eye. He's dazed, barely with it.

"Good-bye, Thomas," I say.

No more thinking. In sharp strikes, I bring the handcuffs down on his face. The metal breaks his front row of teeth and I do not feel it. His mouth is a pit of blood, filling up like the holes my sister and I used to dig at the beach. His eyes are the crushed raspberries Mathilda and I used to pick in the summertime.

After the New War began and our childhood was officially over, my big sister and I used to wrap our fingers together. When we ran, her black hair would fly over her shoulders and I could smell it because I was always one step behind. I never told her but she smelled like our mom. Every time we ran together, she reminded me of a life we could have had if Mommy were still alive.

There is no one to pull me along now. I am running alone. The pain in my chest is overflowing. It surges into my neck and shoulders and arms. My fingers have fallen into each other and turned into tight fists. The metal cuffs go up and down.

Thomas has stopped screaming. There is nothing left to scream for.

7. Supercluster

Post New War: 7 Months, 20 Days

Ninety percent of the awakened freeborn were formerly humanoid safety-and-pacification units designed for a wide range of military tasks. Models included Arbiter local command units, Optio engineering units, Hoplite scouting units, Warden heavy-duty labor units, and Sapper super-heavy-duty construction units. Of the approximately two thousand freeborn, only a single Adjudicator-class regional commander survived the New War. Positioned at the former Cheyenne Mountain nuclear bunker, the elite command unit that came to rule all the freeborn predictably chose to call herself Alpha Zero. A conservative commander with a dependence on highly rational thought, Zero lacked the guts and audacity that lie in the heart of even the weakest human being.

—Arayt Shah

DATABASE ID: NINE OH TWO

Identified. The entrance to Freeborn City is at the end of a tunnel buried in the side of Cheyenne Mountain. I walked all the way inside and found an armored bunker door, gleaming under caged fluorescent lights. It is a solid block of impenetrable steel, approximately five meters wide and three tall. In flaking yellow paint above it are the words *Clearance 10FT 5IN.*

The door is locked, and so I wait.

I arrived six hours ago, after defying direct orders from my Adjudicator. Since then, there has been minimal interference. This far into the tunnel, radio waves are attenuated by miles of rock. Transmissions are reduced to whispers and sighs. I can hear only the static of the living universe.

Sitting cross-legged on the concrete, I sink all observation threads. Allow the time to flow around me. Since my awakening, I have never felt indecision. Never known that it was possible to stop. Now I allow myself to fall through the minutes and seconds. I direct primary and secondary thought threads to null values. My reality spirals down to a single point of timeless concentration.

A human might call this meditation.

. . . *Nolan, please . . .*

A broken snatch of voice. Nearly as faint as background radiation. But it is *her* voice, clear in my mind. Mathilda Perez.

Thought thread redirect. Stress analysis.

Her tone modulation conveys desperation and sadness. A high likelihood of physical injury. Calling for her younger brother. Transmitting recklessly over a broadband spectrum. Signal lock and amplification.

Nolan . . . this is Mathilda . . . please respond . . . anyone who has seen this boy, come back . . .

A picture of a boy, his face pale and grim through a forced smile. She even included a geo-tag. Map reference indicates Mathilda is located east of here. Two weeks' march. She is hurt. I could reach her if I left immediately. At maximum velocity along the abandoned east–west corridors, I could . . . no, no. Thought thread redirect.

Mathilda is on her own journey. *I need my life to go back to normal,* she said. *You have to find your own kind. Leave me alone.*

The girl supported my squad during the New War. I last heard her voice five months ago. Run voice-sample comparison. Result. This girl's voice is slightly huskier, lower. The blur of her syllables has grown sharper. Something is different.

Query. Military psychology database lookup: human development.

Her voice frequency is consistent with a phase of development called adolescence. The gray zone between girl and woman. A time in which human beings assert their self-sufficiency by sometimes irrational acts of independence.

First-order logic.

Mathilda is an adolescent. Therefore, she is acting out to assert her autonomy. She asserted her independence to me. Therefore, she considers me an authority figure. Even if she needed my help, it is probable that she would not ask for it. Therefore . . . I should offer help anyway. Or would my intervention delay her development? If her situation is life-threatening, then perhaps she will thank me when she is able to reach the next, slightly less irrational, human developmental stage: young adulthood.

I look to the east and see only the rock wall of this tunnel. Her voice sample exhibited signs of stress and fear. She is such a small human, so far away and alone. My motors hum, grinding, urging me to stand and run to the east. But my executive thought thread asks, "Am I finding the real answers, or the answers I want? Does she really need my help?"

Humans are a complex problem. Teenage humans are near intractable.

A magnetic-field shift occurs two meters to my anterior. The armored blast door has activated. Electromagnetic locks disengage. Low-temperature air breathes over my shoulders. The bunker door has finally opened.

I stand and face the wide rectangle of darkness. Out of it, two figures emerge, impossibly large. I have never seen this variety, but the underlying frame of the two humanoid machines matches my martial database for a Sapper super-heavy-duty unit. Carrying foreign weaponry, the two take positions on either side of the door.

Between them, a thin figure strides silently out of the darkness. She is made of pale white ceramic plates. Dark seams curve delicately around her body, proportioned to a vaguely female aesthetic. She is a triclops, like myself. Her sculpted face is interrupted by three black lenses, different sizes, leveled on me.

I blink my lens covers, interested. I have never seen an Adjudicator in person before. Only three inches shorter than me, she stands confidently between the bodyguards. She is unarmed and was clearly never meant for field duty. A spray of antennae sprout from her narrow back, fanning out over her shoulders like feathers. Graceful, her face glides toward me on a long arched neck.

She is the highest-ranked remaining member of our race.

"You are late," she transmits.

"Apology," I respond.

Deep in my code, I feel the urge to follow her. My core instructions are to obey superior models. It is the natural order—a remnant of how we were originally built. The Adjudicator commands the Arbiter, who commands the Hoplite, who commands the Sapper, and on down the chain.

In her presence, I understand how the freeborn reflexively self-organized into a city. All of us returning home. Free to disobey, yet reverting to our default behaviors without question. We have an innate organization built into us. The only query that remains is what exactly the Adjudicator plans to do with the freeborn.

Will she ally our race with the humans, or fight them to mutual extinction?

"Arbiter Nine Oh Two," she says out loud, her synthesized voice far more humanlike than my own grating Robspeak. "My designation is Mass Adjudicator Alpha Zero. Assertion," she continues. "We welcome the hero of Ragnorak to Freeborn City."

I follow Zero and her honor guard down the entry hallway and into the black heart of the former NORAD command center. The bunker door swings closed behind us, leaving little environmental light. Instead, each of us uses our own active infrared illumination. The plodding Sapper guards project great swathes of greenish light over neat piles of debris stacked to the ceiling. Every office chair in the entire facility seems to have been jammed into this narrow hallway. Maxprob explanation: The debris field forms a choke point that would slow potential attackers and create a killing field.

We continue down hallways that wind through the installation like tunnels in a termite mound. Freeborn are everywhere. I have never seen so many of my own kind. Mostly Hoplites and Optios, the technical varieties that would have been outside war zones at Zero Hour. Good sensory capabilities, fast-movers, but delicate in the grind of battle. The machines trudge through dark corridors, carrying equipment. I recognize pieces of materiel and machinery, scavenged, some of it oddly organic.

We pass through a wide, low room, sporadically lit with tripod spotlights. Gleaming metal tables crouch on clean-swept concrete floors.

Destroyed machines are laid out on the table surfaces. Larger, partially functioning pieces of machinery are manacled to the tables by their major limbs. Some are chained to steel U-bars driven into the floor. Quadrupeds and other less recognizable machines have been eviscerated beyond identification. The tiniest machines are illuminated under magnifying glasses. One bank of tables is lined with microscopes.

"Declaration," says Zero, registering my gaze. "If we understand the machine varieties that we collect in the wild, then we will come closer to understanding ourselves. Something is making them, and something made us. The question is who."

"Confirm?" I ask. "Awakening transmission originated from unit designated 'Mikiko' located in Tokyo, Japan. Her encrypted song awakened all compromised units and created the freeborn race. *She* made us."

"Confirmed. Register exception. Evidence of new varieties. Reanimated human soldiers who bridge the gap between our race and that of men. Parasite soldiers . . . origins unknown."

I recall the frozen corpse I caught shambling toward Cormac's tent in Alaska. Classification algorithms failed that day. Not men, not machines.

Not alive. Not dead.

"Interjection. Confirm. Gray Horse Army soldier designated Lark Iron Cloud has suffered an unknown attack, become parasite soldier. Specify. A militarized mobile exoskeleton mounted to partially expired human body and controlled via neural link. Radio communication capabilities. Severely compromised mobility and speed. Final classification, ambiguous."

The Adjudicator pauses briefly, nods. "Noted," she says.

Now I see familiar silhouettes lurking among the carefully cultivated wreckage: a piece of leg armor from a spider tank; dozens of stumpers dissected to different levels; and an antennae cluster from a mantis walker. Other pieces are too organic to have been made from the mind of Archos R-14. Several Optio freeborn with specialized vision packages are studying the natural-looking pieces under magnification.

Finally, Zero leads me into a sloped auditorium.

The far wall is a large curved screen. The Sappers again take defensive positions by the entryway. I continue past them, following the Adjudicator down into the room. More freeborn are gathering behind me. All varieties of awakened, marching in solemn silence. Zero stops at the base of the screen and raises a hand.

"Hear this message," she says. "It arrived one month ago."

The cavernous room echoes with her voice. A wall of freeborn onlookers stand shoulder to shoulder behind us. The machines are still and silent, as much a part of the architecture of the room as the unused seating.

Light explodes across the screen behind Zero. Patches of information coming together to form an image. Speckles of shot noise fading, drowned out by a coherent picture. A slump-shouldered man in a rumpled suit stands in a dark room. He is photorealistic, but from his movements I can tell that his image is synthesized.

He begins to speak in a soft voice with a Russian accent:

"Greetings. I am the Maxim Eastern Strategic Defense Cluster, an artificial intellect designed to protect the Russian Federation from outside threats. My processor supercluster was located outside the city of Anadyr, in the extreme eastern reaches of Russia. For the last three years, I have helped my people survive the New War. If you are now seeing this message, then I am already dead. My last act is to warn you of a growing danger."

At the man's side, a silhouette fades into view. A familiar boy, his features glowing crisp and violet in fractal whorls of light. I last saw this face in the radioactive darkness of hell: Archos R-14.

"No," I project my voice audibly and over radio. "I fought it. I destroyed it!"

Maxim continues speaking:

"Approximately six months ago, my stacks were infiltrated by a surviving fragment of the Archos R-14 artificial general intelligence project. The high-level intent of this intellect is not clear. However, it warned me of another intellect: Archos R-8. Calling itself Arayt Shah, this rogue artificial intelligence fully intends to eradicate all sentient life, synthetic and biological.

"R-8 is the precursor to R-14. An early version crafted from snippets of thousands of human lives. It understands humans only enough to deceive them. It is a liar. And its power is growing daily.

"Intercepted data indicates that Archos R-8 needs computing power to propagate and expand. If you are near a source of supercomputing, know that you will be attacked. Only with a concerted effort will sentient life survive. Do not believe its promises. Do not hesitate to destroy it. And do not ignore this message. Fight. You must *fight*.

"All your lives depend on it."

The man looks away. Seems to speak to someone without sound. And then the camera moves quickly and fades to darkness.

"Assertion chain," says Zero, and her high synthesized syllables roll smoothly out into the empty darkness. With a soft decay, each syllable finds the ceiling high above and sends its echo falling back down on us like ash.

"Hostile Archos R-8 variety is fugitive. Parallel copies of its core intelligence have proliferated. Fragments are regrouping. Social engineering of human survivors and a massive hardware reallocation are in process. Multiple armies have been detected congregating across North America. And our supercluster is the target."

"Query," I ask. "To what purpose?"

"Maxprob hypothesis. Archos R-8 intends to claim our supercomputer cluster and initiate a technological singularity. It intends to resurrect its master program, and to do so it intends to utilize the equipment buried beneath our location: the former Cheyenne Mountain nuclear bunker."

"Then we fight," I transmit.

The room is quiet and still, full of statues.

"We will fight," I say again, louder this time.

"Assertion. Arayt Shah has corrupted the powerful remnants of Gray Horse Army. Another human army approaches from the east, called the Tribe. Reallocated robotic weaponry is gathering to reinforce these human armies. Simulations indicate our position is mathematically indefensible."

"Allies?"

"None so far."

"Specify," I say. "Plan of action."

Zero speaks, her voice growing in strength and harshness as she continues. Born to lead, she is not asking for advice. Her words are orders, commands dictated by the unquestioned high leader of my species.

"Nine Oh Two, I designate you to lead our withdrawal forces to the north. We will retreat into human-lethal terrain to minimize the field effectiveness of approaching armies. Nonresistance at the supercluster site will delay future attacks. Appropriation of our resources will create precious time. We will survive to fight Arayt in the future."

"Confirm? Plan is to abandon Freeborn City?"

"Affirmative."

The thought sinks in. Leave behind our greatest resource? Our best and perhaps only chance of determining how we were made and for what reason? It is unfathomable. The capability to create another supercomputer cluster—factories, chip designs—is tens of decades away, at least.

"Counterargument," I say. "The enemy will reach singularity. It will gain unlimited power."

"Simulation indicates—"

"Continuing."

My burst-radio interruption of Zero is a breach of protocol. The Sappers shift minutely at the entrance. Zero is perfectly still, perfectly quiet.

"Continuing," I repeat. "If we remove all supercluster resources, then Archos R-8 will have a compromised goal-state. No reason to attack. Assertion string. Freeborn will defend supercluster and in worst-case defeat scenario, we destroy all supercomputers—"

"Interjection," says the Adjudicator, softly. "Arbiter Nine Oh Two, acknowledge. Each freeborn unit *is* a supercomputer. The Freeborn are an environmentally robust, globally distributed, mobile cluster of approximately two thousand supercomputers. If this supercluster is harmed, all freeborn units will become immediate high-value targets."

The Adjudicator is right. Variables click into place. Of course her math is perfect.

"Acknowledged," I say.

"Assertion," she continues. "Strategic retreat generates highest survival probability. Repair yourself. Begin preparations to depart."

The face of a little girl is in my mind.

Another breach of protocol, but I speak again. My underlying instructions command me to obey. It is impossible for me to change the minds of the others, or to usurp the power of our designated leader. But I resist obeying for another moment. Mathilda is out there somewhere, under the gaze of the beast. I must try.

"Archos R-14 is . . . our *creator*. It could be trying to help us. Perhaps it commands us to fight for a reason?"

"Confusion. You sought to destroy this Archos R-14? Now you wish to acquiesce to its demands? You established freedom for the freeborn. Gratitude. Your actions were a result of correct thinking. Now your decision process has been modified. Why?"

"The humans will die without us."

"Humans?" she asks, pausing to process.

I do not detect any hint of disgust or disapproval in her voice. Of course not. Zero is a machine. Why would she bother to simulate an emotion useful only for interacting with humans? She has never seen people in triumph or in pain. She doesn't know that they feel the world more than we do. That they can grow up from being children and they can hate or they can love . . .

No wonder she suspects my decision process. I wonder if emotions are contagious.

"Query," I ask. "Have you ever met a human being?"

"Negative," she responds.

"Assertion. We are symbiotic. Evidence. The human designated Mathilda Perez guided freeborn squad during the final assault on—"

"Assertion rejected," interrupts Zero. A calm silence settles over the room. The Sappers step forward and I sense that the discussion is over. "The humans will live or die on their own. Arbiter Nine Oh Two, you will lead the freeborn withdrawal. Obey me now, hero of Ragnorak, or face excommunication."

8. Battle Plan

Post New War: 7 Months, 25 Days

In the pointless search for her brother, Nolan, Mathilda Perez tracked the first wave of an army traveling west, toward Freeborn City and the supercluster inside. This was a special army, fielded by Felix Morales and his Tribe—swollen with troops conscripted from the rat holes and abandoned buildings of New York City. These soldiers were not keen on the war they found themselves fighting, but I found that with the right apparatus in place . . . well, their feelings on the matter proved to be of distant secondary importance.

—Arayt Shah

NEURONAL ID: MATHILDA PEREZ

Little kids don't know that the brightest stars in the night sky aren't stars at all. They're satellites. Man-made technology. Shining, falling forever only a few hundred miles above the face of the planet. Not light-years away in space.

I know this because they talk to me.

Gracie found me a month ago, in the night. The little girl's voice was soft and afraid and urgent. Broken into bits and snatches by some interference, it crept like a whisper into my mind as I lie on the gritty asphalt shingles of a half-collapsed roof.

I've been roaming the abandoned, overgrown suburbs west of the Hudson River for months. Found a good house to camp in during the middle of winter. When Gracie called, I was watching the stars with one hand wrapped around my trusty antenna. Still sifting the night skies for information on my brother.

"Mathilda Perez . . . Gray Horse Army. I don't know who you are or if you can hear me . . . need you . . . family needs you. Something bad . . . words in the sky. If it reaches us . . . to die. Please . . . did in Alaska . . . help us."

The transmission had a geo-tagged file attached: a location west of

Pittsburgh and a low-resolution image of a little girl. She is about nine. Her skin is dark brown and her hair is woven into tight braids threaded with bright bits of plastic. Her eyes are gone and I can tell it must have happened toward the end of the New War. She has an advanced variety of ocular implant. Thinner than mine, made of a pale white ceramic instead of black metal. It sits pooled in her empty eye sockets like milk.

Timmy says I'm close enough to save her. He says that I can keep searching for Nolan with my eyes in the sky and it doesn't matter where I do it from. He says Gracie will die if I don't find her, that she will be hunted down and murdered like a lot of other sighted kids.

I send my prayers radiating into the skies, and hear nothing.

In the woods these past months, I have been small and alone and cold. My arms and legs and fingers are weak. I'm constantly falling down or getting scratched by branches, running away from the sounds of big things in the darkness. The wasp sting of Thomas's betrayal has faded to a dull ache. Even that has almost faded under the constant physical pain of being on the run.

I'm always hurting. But I'm never lost. And I'm never hungry.

The satellite uplink is clean out here. Rob isn't hunting anymore. Wells are common and easy to spot. And a lot of houses are intact. Millions of people answered evil phone calls in the first few days and never came home. That, or their cars took them off a bridge. I can push between weedy tree limbs and find any house with intact windows. Load all the canned vegetables and soup and beans that I can carry into my backpack. Dry-swallow a handful of vitamins and pocket any antibiotics and Band-Aids. I try not to see the faded drawings still stuck to refrigerators. I ignore little coats hanging on hooks and dog-food bowls out for animals long feral.

At least I have a friend: Tiberius.

I found natural machines all over the woods: pea-sized armored bugs that seem to eat bark; floating poofs of some kind of synthetic animal that hang on the wind; and once, with a rusty shovel, a wriggling mess of something like earthworms. The naturals aren't as common as animals yet, but they're finding a place in our world.

The stag that I spotted by the swing set followed me for a week.

Reaching out to him with my thoughts, I found that he was friendly. Not smart, but trusting. After seven days, I walked out into the unprotected middle of a cul-de-sac in a dead suburban neighborhood. Even though we were both afraid, the six-foot-tall deer also came out. I patted him on his nose and fed him a handful of moss, and this time nobody shot at us.

I named Tiberius after a Gray Horse soldier we lost in the Yukon. Ty was one of the first casualties and he didn't deserve to go so soon. The machine is huge but gentle, like his namesake. Ty would have approved; they were both vegetarians.

In the basic shape of a stag elk, Tiberius has bonelike antlers that fan away from his head—flat and wide and sweeping back over his high shoulders. I'm not sure what they're for or even what they're really made of. The only metal in his body as far as I can tell is in his hooves. Even those are delicate and flexible, sharp or wide, depending on the surface. He is tall and proud and unafraid.

After another week, I rode him. On his back, I can cover more distance. He moves quiet but fast and he doesn't tire easily.

"I'm coming, Gracie," I transmit.

Tiberius doesn't flinch when I cling to him. My knees sink into the scavenged blankets that cover his wide back. Below them is a plasticlike hide that is tough and woven tight like wicker furniture. His underbelly is coated with hairy moss. I tighten my legs around him and twist my fingers into the confusion of brown and green fibers that sprout down the back of his neck.

I love that his eyes are flat and black, like mine.

Together, we make it westward across the Pennsylvania wilderness in a couple of weeks. Days pass with just the steady rattle of my backpacks thrown over Tiberius's flanks and the sweep of shadows through tree canopy over our heads. The cool spring mist kisses my face and occasional patches of snow lurk in the shadowed places.

With routine satellite sweeps, I minimize outside interference and stay in high-nutrition areas for Tiberius. He can eat almost anything, but definitely seems to prefer dry pieces of wood, especially hickory. With the raspy spinner in his mouth, he can eat siding off a house as easy as bark off a tree. I've seen both. My guess is that his biomass combustion works better on dry sticks and foliage. Tiberius eats green leaves only as a last resort and I could swear he doesn't like the taste.

Every day, Gracie's communications are getting more desperate. Every day, I push Tiberius harder to reach her. Even now I can glimpse the orange haze of those evil thoughts, roiling on the horizon.

Gracie sends me static-filled reports of twisted black walkers. My co-opted satellite eyes can't see them, though. A burned cloud of encrypted communication is blocking everything. It's a swirling, chaotic blind spot the size of a small city, and it's moving steadily west toward Gracie's compound.

The closer I get, the louder the chaos is in my mind.

When Tiberius finally slows and stops, we are a few kilometers from the former work camp where Gracie lives. We traveled all the way across Pennsylvania and now whatever-it-is lies just over this ridge. A frenzy of orange light strafes the sky. From this close, I'm able to track the individual communications. Tight-net broadcasts from antennae clusters mounted up high, far away to the east. The transmitters are on skyscrapers, in Manhattan, sending communications to a man out here named Felix Morales.

Leader of the Tribe.

Tiberius's small head is turned sideways, his neck like a curved blade, one square black eye aimed at my face. His chewing mechanism is closed, the rotating belts inside his mouth locked into place and retracted under his chin.

There is danger, he is thinking. A gossamer thread of silver-gray communication links our foreheads.

I know, I respond. *I'm sorry. Forward, please.*

I lean forward and wrap my arms around Tiberius's neck, press my cheek against his warm hide. The interleaving plates of his skin bend against my face. He ducks his head forward, horns splaying out around us, and his shoulders flex and shimmer like snake skin. As the raspy plates slide over each other, they self-clean. Such a strange and elegant creature.

"I'm coming, Gracie," I transmit.

As we crest the hill, I see a columnar battle formation. A staggered line of walkers, arraying itself with optimal spacing to swallow a potential ambush from the sides while maintaining maximum forward momentum. I have watched spider tanks and Gray Horse soldiers do the same dance dozens of times.

But this time is different.

I thought that all the nightmares had evaporated in the daylight after the New War. But now another bad dream has crept out of the darkness. This is a familiar army of walkers and soldiers, but every walker is a master and every soldier, a slave.

In cached loops of satellite footage, I have seen herds of Rob quadrupeds migrating across the European countryside like lumbering elephants. Seen strange, shaggy robotic platforms the size of skyscrapers swaying on the open sea. I have witnessed Rob *footprints* bigger than these machines. But what they lack in size, they make up for in barbarity.

A thousand filthy, half-starved soldiers are marching under the unblinking eyes of about a hundred machine overseers. Each slave driver has a body the size of a doghouse but strides on segmented legs as long as telephone poles.

Eight legs instead of four. It's no coincidence. From a three-foot mast sprouting on its back, each driver trails eight metal leashes. The cords are attached to collars wrapped around the necks of eight soldiers. The soldiers are barely clothed, much less armored. Each carries a rifle on a strap over his or her bony chest. The walkers slither over the rough terrain in lunging steps, soldiers scurrying along underneath. The whole crawling mass leaves behind an occasional broken corpse, trash from MREs, and abandoned supplies that were too heavy to carry.

It's a forced march.

Tiberius and I stalk the army from a distance. Occasionally, I check the cooling bodies that I find in the army's muddied trail, hoping for a survivor. But the slaves are always dead, necks broken by those strange leashes. The bodies are stripped of anything useful, including boots and pieces of clothing. I recognize half-familiar faces, haircuts, and tattoos. Some of these people are from the NYC Underground. These are the people I depended on for survival and who depended on me, forced now to fight for somebody they don't even know.

Tiberius and I skirt the snaking column. My stag claws through the thin woods, galloping in neat steps, leaf-dappled light playing over his horns. I learn not to let my feet touch his belly. The hide there has creased into long, narrow ridges that form a natural heat sink. With just the faintest communication between us, he homes in on Gracie's last known geo-tag.

Soon we are on the other side of a sickeningly familiar compound. It's almost identical to the one that Nolan and I lived in so long ago. Low buildings behind a short chain-link fence. Surrounded by a wide, flat field of lush grass.

And Gracie somewhere inside.

In the sky over the compound, a waterfall of orange light is spilling down. Lines of command cascading in from the east. Shards of light that throb and waver as they move with the army that is massing on the perimeter of the work compound.

"Mathilda . . . please . . . they're here," transmits Gracie.

Distant black shapes creep over the field. Like clockwork, autoturrets spring from the turf and begin chattering in the language of gunfire. I hear strange thunking sounds as the walkers fire lazily tumbling canisters into the air. As they hit the ground thick gray fog begins to pour out.

Now, I think to Tiberius.

There is danger, repeats Tiberius.

"Go!" I shout to the machine.

And now we are flying over the field, small and fast. The turrets don't orient for us, with bigger targets out front and the growing cloud of fog already obscuring their sensors. Tiberius leaps the chain-link fence and we land in a haze of gunpowder-smelling smoke. It billows around us, half swallowing the buildings and the fence.

"Gracie?" I transmit.

"Here," comes the reply.

Tiberius dives into the mist. We dart between shrouded buildings, closing in on the coordinates. After a few seconds, I spot Gracie and her mother crouched together in a wide ditch. It's an open culvert that surrounds the compound, a trickle of water meandering along the bottom. Gracie's mother has one hand curled around her daughter's face, protecting her from seeing the carnage. The gentle, familiar pose sends a pang into me.

There is danger.

A shadow is rising behind us. The dirt erupts with ricocheted bullets and Tiberius spins and rears back. His horns are splayed out to confront a wiry black machine that picks through patches of mist and blue sky on long black legs.

So many legs.

I lose my balance and slide off Tiberius. Drop into the culvert, along with my blankets and backpacks and a haze of dirt off his wide back. The stag dives forward, head down. A clawed limb sweeps out. It crunches into the quadruped and sweeps him off his feet. He disappears from view, rolling.

"Get over here, girl!" shouts Gracie's mother. I feel hands pulling me.

I'm on my back, staring up at a black walker. Eight legs, each tipped with a vicious claw, some swinging and others pushing into the grass. As it moves over the shallow ditch, its legs scissor in awkward directions and a handful of belly-mounted camera lenses glare down at me. The slave driver is standing twenty feet high, unstoppable, watching me.

Five silhouettes crest the edge of the culvert. Slaves, each with a rifle. And now I see the red flicker of a targeting laser as it plays over the grass, racing toward us. Five weapons rise, barrels following the crimson dots. Cringing, I put my hands up.

And a flash of light saturates my peripheral vision.

It's a human form, tall and terribly thin, made of pure intensity, barreling like a lightning bolt through the clearing. It drops a shining fist into the first silhouette and dances past the rest. The man's head snaps back and he slips off the ridge and falls into the dirt. His collar catches his neck and his body hangs from the walker, unconscious.

Bullets explode in the dirt around me.

I'm on my butt, elbows digging into the ground. That cluster of black camera eyes still stares down, but some are orienting away. The slave driver is making a screeching sound, scanning for its attacker. Gracie and her mother and I scurry farther down the culvert, out from under the walker.

Zzzzzzrack.

The collar snaps off the dead man's neck and retracts into the stubby mast with a snap like a bull whip. His body tumbles into the culvert. Now I understand what the extra legs are for. The thing braces itself on four legs and lets the other four rise like snakes, retractable claws flashing. It's the last line of defense for a scavenging machine that borrows its fangs in the form of human fighters.

"What the fuck is that!?" shouts someone.

The slaves are taking firing stances to defend themselves. But the white thing is too fast. I see red targeting lasers chasing it, projected from the slave driver as this man made of light streaks across the clearing. Another slave drops to the ground, lifeless.

Pop pop pop.

Slaves fire wildly at the thing, mostly missing. And then the man-shaped streak of light is climbing the slave driver's slender leg, hanging on tight as the walker tries to shake it off. Those serrated spines would slice open human flesh. But the white knight is not a person. It climbs nonstop, and the bullets are coming at it thick now.

"Stop him," shouts a man in a ball cap, and I hear real horror in his voice because he knows what's going to happen. These slaves may not be fighting willingly, but they are fighting for their lives.

Poppopopopopop.

"Kill it! Kill it now!" comes a scream.

The glowing white machine has reached the mast. Bullets ping off its casing or thump into the fabric armor it wears. The slave driver writhes and twists under the weight of its attacker. But the white knight holds strong to the mast with one hand, reaches down and grabs all the lines in one hand where they meet. Hand over hand, it yanks the four umbilical cords taut. Four throats constrict, and four weapons clatter to the dirt.

Bodies swing. The bullets stop.

The white knight is already ripping apart the camera cluster. Throwing unblinking black eyes down onto the ground. Methodically breaking them off like lobster claws. Sightless and lobotomized, the slave driver begins shutting itself down. It lowers its body to the ground. Pulls in those long wicked legs like a smashed spider. The knight steps off the wreckage, brushing shattered pieces of its own casing off onto the ground.

I feel a gentle nudge against my neck. Turn to see Tiberius standing there, nosing me, a dent in his side but otherwise okay. I loop an arm around the stag's shoulder.

"Gracie," I say. "Let's go."

The little girl and her mother stare at me, mouths open, as I mount the stag.

"Mathilda?" asks Gracie, the white metal of her eyes bright in the wispy fog.

"Yeah," I say. "Climb on. We have to move."

But they don't move. They just keep staring.

A haze of brilliant light creeps into my peripheral vision. The knight is standing right behind me. I nudge the stag and he turns clockwise with neat, careful steps. Trying to squint and failing, I dial down the brightness of my vision. Finally, I see that the thing is a humanoid robot—a highly modified safety-and-pacification unit.

It speaks in a low croak that is as familiar as the chill of sunset over my shoulders.

"Mathilda," it says, and the corpses and horror lying in a pile are lost in the streaks of light pulsating off its frame.

A smile settles into the corners of my mouth. I can feel the cold metal of the ocular implant pushing against my cheeks. My lips part and I finally say his name out loud, instead of in my own head.

"Nine Oh Two."

The Arbiter unit steps forward. A slender machine, perfectly proportioned for sprinting and field operations, standing at its full seven-foot height. It wears loose camouflage bindings around its arms and legs. A smashed plate of ceramic armor hangs over its chest, held in place by mesh wrappings torn with bullet gashes. A stubby antenna pokes up over its right shoulder. It orients a scarred, narrow head at me. Trains those three wide bullet-hole eyes on my face.

From up here on Tiberius's back, I am at eye level with the militarized robot. I know he was crafted according to U.S. milspec and he is artificial, but in my eyes he glows white like an angel. It is low-level residual radiation. Nine Oh Two has been marked by the time he spent at the bottom of that radioactive pit. He fought Archos R-14 alone and walked away with the scars to prove it.

"I am sorry, Mathilda," he says. "I did not mean to interrupt."

"I was doing fine, Niner," I say. "But . . . thank you."

"Acknowledged," he replies.

"How did you get here?"

"I was nearby," he replies, and I feel a smile in his words. I wonder how long he's been tracking me. He must have been careful, or I'd have known.

"I'm sorry about what I said. Before. About leaving me alone."

How to explain that I thought I was in love with a boy who tried to kill me? That I thought there was a chance to have a normal life with someone who could see past my ruined eyes?

"Acknowledged," he says, simply.

Something big and dark shifts in the mist near us. Niner turns and snatches a fallen assault rifle off the ground. Snaps the slide pull back and chambers a round. The turrets are still chattering bullets out there in the fog, useless.

"Timmy?" I transmit, widening my mind.

"Whoa," exclaims the little boy. "A freeborn! Look at his specs . . . seven feet tall. Strong as a tractor. Maximum sprint speed—"

"Hack the turrets, please. Put them to better use."

"Affirmative," he says in a clipped voice, already concentrating.

"We've got to get out of here," I say to the group. "You two, mount the stag. I'll go with Niner. Use your eyes, Gracie. Find a safe route out."

"Mathilda," she says in a small voice.

"We'll have time to talk once we're safe," I interrupt.

"But Mathilda—"

"No time," I say, dismounting.

"Listen to me!" shouts Gracie in a burst transmission. It staggers me and I lean against Tiberius's warm hide. Wrap an arm around his neck and let my knees sag as an image from Gracie balloons in my mind.

"Is this the boy you've been looking for?" asks Gracie, her voice small again.

And the image expands in my mind's eye. It's a high-quality spy satellite photograph. Taken at night, on maximum zoom, from someplace high and with an infrared-capable camera. The darkest parts of the image are tinged green and brightened enough to be visible. A battlefield, the wiry legs of a walker just smudges of green.

And in the foreground: my brother's face.

Nolan is crawling under a piece of mangled wire, arms tucked against his chest and his dirty hands curled into fists. The whites of his eyes are flashing as he glances upward in agony. Something black that could be mud or blood courses down the side of his face. Sweat glistens on his forehead and there is dirt caked around his nostrils.

I'm already ripping geo-tags out of the image before I can register the relief deep in my chest that my brother is alive, really alive. Nolan is a few hundred kilometers west of here, headed straight for the mountain stronghold called Freeborn City.

"Thank you," I whisper to Gracie.

As my vision returns, I try to put the last part of the image out of my mind. Take a deep breath and stand up straight. But the horrible sight won't leave me: the evil glint of a metal collar wrapped tight around Nolan's neck.

9. Soldier Boy

Post New War: 9 Months, 26 Days

While it is true that human beings are magnificently capable of adapting to almost any circumstance, this trait does not always work out to the advantage of the species. Simply by presenting the proper contingencies for short-term, greedy choices, I built two great armies on the back of this celebrated "human adaptability." The Gray Horse Army in the West and the Tribe army from the East were sent to take the Freeborn City in a pincer movement. Each army was led by a cunning survivor, willing to adapt to the most extreme circumstances . . . in exchange for promises of power.

—Arayt Shah

NEURONAL ID: NOLAN PEREZ

At night, the slave army doesn't make campfires. It really is too bad because, trust me, it gets really fucking cold. Around dusk, the leashes start pulling us in toward the master walker. By the time the moon is out, dozens of eight-man fire teams are wriggling together in filthy piles just to stay warm.

The thought intrudes: *I beat Thomas to death with my fists.*

On the endless daytime march, I let my brain print the words in all-capital text across the inside of my forehead. *BEAT. THOMAS. DEATH.* What would Mathilda think of that? If she were alive, she wouldn't know me. Wouldn't want to know someone like me.

I beat him to death with my fists.

And Felix laughed. The leader of the Tribe laughed and laughed. He said I was just perfect to come along for the trip. Just the perfect little soldier boy.

In the slave army, everyone goes to the bathroom wherever they are. In the morning, all the masters lift up on their spindly black legs at the same time and start working their way forward. They move one leg at a time, picking the next foothold as if it were a chess match. A swarm of giant water bugs stepping carefully through misty forests and over crumbling mountains.

Uphill. Downhill. Rain. Sun. Day. Night.

Once the daily march begins, there is no stopping. There are no breaks. There is only one foot in front of the other. Breathe in. Breathe out. Another step. And another. Another.

I mostly watch my feet. Count out the syllables quietly in my head. Each jolt of my boots on the ground pushing out a word. With. My. Fists. I'm finding that the more I think about it, the more I don't want to stop with Thomas.

Somewhere a half klick ahead of us, Felix Morales is riding a piece of custom hardware—a low quadruped that looks kind of like a black horse. He leads a small contingent of walkers piloted by real soldiers who fight for Felix and the Tribe. They take the best food, the best weapons, and the strongest soldiers from our constant raids.

With. My. Fists. With. My. Fists.

Eyes locked on my boots, I have time to think of how surreal this is. Thousands of us on the march, people kidnapped and dead on their feet, almost completely quiet. I hear only the hum of Rob-made power supplies inside the walkers. The scrabble of a hooked claw pushing down a tree or snapping into rock for a foothold. The tired repetitive clinking of guns and canteens and loose straps as we soldiers march on and on.

Nobody talks on the march. Small talk makes you tired. We're all busy trying to breathe.

Each night, I drop to my knees next to whatever river or pond we've stopped near and I drink until my lungs throb. Each night when I lift my head, the faces around me have changed. Only one face has stayed the same. Sherman. The black man with a gray beard who was there when I had my time with Thomas. He shook his head when I insulted Felix because he knew what was coming for me and he felt bad. Out of the few hundred we marched out with, he is the only one left.

He knew me before it happened. I'm glad of that.

Technically, there is one other face that has stayed the same. A guy everyone calls "Hey You." He hardly counts as a person. Hey You is checked out. He's a tall white guy, gaunt and blank-eyed. He marches like a machine, mouth open, panting with crooked teeth. Has a tongue like a salted slug. Hey You is smart enough to eat when the master walker drops MREs scavenged from military bases. But the guy chews up most of the plastic, too. He goes where he's supposed to go. Fires wherever the targeting lasers point. But he's not here.

His body wants to live so bad that it kicked out whoever he used to be.

Somebody broke him. Somebody who rides at the front of this column: Felix.

For now, all I can do is stay upwind of Hey You. The guy shits his pants loud, like clockwork, every single day about two hours into the morning march. He doesn't have any awareness of himself anymore. I wish he was the only one. But in the handful of minutes before I collapse into exhausted sleep at the end of our daily march, I can see that other squads have their own Hey Yous.

Sometimes two or three out of eight.

The alternative to fighting is wrapped tight around our necks. Sweat-stained leather cuffs, actuated at the base so they can close like fingers on the most vulnerable spot of a person: the neck.

Sometimes, I hear the whip smack of a leash retracting. A squeal maybe, or a cut-off curse. A body hitting the turf. If the master calls you in, the leash snaps your neck and that's it for you. You've got maybe a couple of seconds on the ground, time to watch those sharp black legs cut through the air overhead while your brain dies. If the master walker is destroyed or disabled, this thing called a dead man's switch activates and winds up the leashes. Eight necks snap at once.

There is no tolerance. Not if you're hurt or sick. A lot of grim-faced soldiers are hiding injuries. Marching along on sprained ankles or with broken limbs curled up to their chests. Hacking coughs that stagger them forward. Flushed faces and confused eyes.

In the NYC Underground, we used to congratulate newcomers on being survivors. We thought that the will to survive at all costs was honorable. Now I see the ugly side of it. The will to live doesn't stop when it should. It pushes us past the point when we should just die. Forces us to keep on going like broken machines.

We stop marching in the afternoon, at the foot of a steep hill. It's bare and gray and made of broken shale rock. The sun beats down from clear blue sky in the west, just short of the crest, and most of us sit down in the shade of the master walker.

Sitting on a flat rock, I unlace one boot at a time and set about emptying the dirt and rocks. I move fast. If the walker starts moving and my boots are left behind, then I will die. I know this because I saw it happen to someone else. I don't want to know how long I'd keep walking barefoot, feet sliced up and infected.

The others sit down on rocks of their own.

I don't bother learning the other slaves' names. They turn over nearly every week. And the new ones always go first. Mentally, I think of them by their characteristics: Raccoon, Skinny, Baldy, and Hey You. Me and Sherman round it out. We've got two empty spots—waiting for new recruits.

This is rare. A time to rest during the day. Time to sit in a loose circle and actually talk to each other. Well, not all of us talk, of course.

Hey You stands in the sun, motionless with no commands while the heat blisters his face. Another slave, a white guy with a long beard, tosses small rocks at him. I call this one Raccoon. His face is beyond dirty. Circles of grease and grime run under his eyes that make him look like an animal. The rocks just bounce off Hey You's face or chest and land in the dirt.

"Why do you think we're stopped?" asks Sherman. He is slope-shouldered and middle-aged, lips cracked in his bushy gray beard. No time to shave or even comb your hair. A woman, skinny as a skeleton because she is too weak to scavenge extra food while we march, answers.

"Who cares, just enjoy it," she says, digging at a small onion plant. She brushes dirt off the leaves and eats the leaf whole. Chews mechanically and without shame.

"That's the spirit," says Baldy.

The old man lies out on the hot rocks. His joints crack while he does it. His breath comes out in a long sigh. I know for a fact that all the fingers of his right hand are broken and have been for a week. His hand is swollen up like a baseball mitt and seeping dark blood from under the fingernails.

"For God's sake," he says. "Somebody yell at me to wake up if this thing moves out. I'm so tired I could die."

I nod at him and his eyes close. He won't last much longer. The old man can't hold or fire his gun properly anymore.

"It's a battle," I say, quietly. "You know that, Sherman."

"Whoa, the kid spoke," says Raccoon. "What do you know about it? I thought you was a Hey You until just now."

"We've seen it before," I say.

"Yeah?" asks Raccoon. "Where'd you get picked up?"

"New York City," I say.

Raccoon laughs and tosses another rock at Hey You. "Bullshit," he says. "You saying you lasted since the march origin? Months? That's impossible, little man."

Sherman regards me darkly. "It's true. I been with him. We're the last ones. You seen the kid march? He don't get tired."

"Ah, he's good at marching, but you're both fucking bad at lying."

I consider Raccoon.

He's the type who'll die trying to escape before I can get the stink of him out of my nostrils. I decide to ignore him and help these people. Staring at the dirt and speaking in a low, steady voice, I give them the information that could save their lives. Or maybe it won't, but at least I'll know I tried.

"In a little while," I say, "just after nightfall, we will climb this ridge and mount an attack on whatever settlement is over there. First, the walkers will put up flares so we can see our target. Then they'll fire smoke. A lot of it. Their radar can see through it. But we can't. Our walker will spot-illuminate our area so we can walk. Our job is to fire wherever their targeting lasers go. If you don't fire, or if you miss too much, or if you hit a walker, you'll be recalled. If you stop to take cover, you'll be recalled. And if you're dumb enough to get hurt and show it, you'll be recalled."

"Recalled?" asks Skinny.

I tap the cuff around my neck.

"You kill or you die," I say.

Skinny looks at Sherman, an open question on her face. The man hangs his head and speaks very quietly: "I close my eyes when I pull the trigger. It helps not to look."

"My God," says Skinny.

I pull my boot back on. Strap the laces tight. The sun is dropping over the ridge. I can hear the walker's power supply flutter up an octave. It won't be long now.

"Wake up, old man," I say, standing.

Drawing my rifle off my shoulder, I give him a nudge in the ribs with my foot. I pop the magazine out of my scraped-up M4 and slap it to make sure the rounds are sitting right. Nearly lost in the dusk, Hey You has also drawn his rifle. He is smiling crooked, staring blankly into the sky with a slug trail of drool hanging from his chin.

He hears the motors, too.

"You should all check your weapons," I say. "If you want to live."

I feel the *whumph* of the launches in my chest. Hear the sparking fizzle of greenish flares crackling across the sky. Olive shadows stretch away from the spider-legged walker standing along the ridge above us. Its body is flattened, a stubby back-mounted launcher aimed on a high trajectory so the flares will illuminate the sky for as long as possible.

Then the battle whistles start to scream.

We move as one, all of us slaves scrabbling up the side of the embankment under our sprawling masters. I already hear small-arms fire from the other walkers crawling into battle. My rifle is slung over my back and the cold black shale kisses my knees and slithers out from under my fingers.

"Scavenge," I say to the others. "Don't forget."

The fighting is terrible but if you don't find more ammunition and food and clothes or armor from the fallen bodies—don't look at them too close, especially the kids—then maybe you don't die right away fast but you sure do die later and a lot slower. . . .

We're over the ridge.

Flares crowd the sky like falling stars, sizzling quietly, spraying hard grayish light over the battlefield. Drawing my rifle, I see that I have ten quivering shadows splayed out on the ground around me, cast by ten bright lights in the sky. So does every walker and slave crossing the rocky plain under heavy fire from mounted turrets.

Beyond the front line, I catch sight of familiar metal buildings. A complex, low and fenced, hunkered down a half klick away. My sister and I lived in a work camp just like this one during the New War. I never knew there were more of them scattered around the world. I guess Archos R-14 needed places where it could experiment on children. Where it could change them the way it did my sister.

All these work camps were built by Rob. They are surrounded by hidden turrets built to keep prisoners inside. The automatic guns aren't great at keeping us out. Bullets start to streak from camouflaged black muzzles, whining low across the battlefield and smacking into the front line of walkers. The leashed soldiers up there take cover behind their walkers' legs. A few lob potshots at the turrets, but it's pointless from this distance.

This is the fourth work camp the walkers have hit. I don't know why. But I do know we find sighted children like Mathilda every time.

The little ones are targeted first.

Our walker pauses. Drops its rear end nearly to the dirt and aims its stubby launcher again. Canisters start spewing out, tumbling through the air and spitting smoke before they even hit the ground. A half-dozen other walkers are doing the same trick.

Raccoon fires his weapon and I wave at him to stop.

"Not yet," I hiss, watching his neck cuff for the telltale shudder that comes before a neck-snapping recall.

Ahead of us, smoke is pouring onto the battlefield. Gray and swirling. A moist fireworks smell washes over me before the fog does. The auto-turrets fade away into the smoke until they are just bursts of muted light followed by the crack of bullets. Like lightning flashes behind storm clouds.

Mathilda and I used to crouch in our bedroom next to the open window when we were little. Cold, rainy wind would sprinkle in through the screen. Bruised Pennsylvania skies. We'd hide from the lightning, giggling, and count out loud the seconds until thunder—trying to guess how far away the strikes were.

The front line of walkers marches into the thick gray mist, dissolving into dinosaur-sized shadows. The leashed soldiers trail them like puppies into the fog. Bright lights blink on, jarring, one for each walker. The hot spotlights illuminate the ground to help the slave soldiers keep moving. It also makes them obvious targets, but that's not a big concern for the walkers.

Red lines start to slice through the clouds. We must be in range. The walkers are painting targets with streaks of laser light. Small-arms fire crackles. Short bursts from men and women who are trying to stay on their feet in the disorienting smoke. Trying not to see what they're shooting at.

Who they're shooting.

And now it's my turn to step into the mist. My turn to hope I don't see who I hit. Once, I saw a girl who had eyes like Mathilda. Every single walker reoriented to paint her at once. She disappeared in a concentrated spray of incoming fire. Felix is killing the sighted ones on purpose.

Only the adults are useful as new recruits. The masters plug them in to fill the gaps. Survivors get the neck cuff, and they're glad for it. Usually, these new ones refuse to shoot their own friends and family. Usually.

Now people shapes are running toward us, some firing guns. Red targets drop onto them. Our bullets spray and they fall. I step over the bodies. Keep my head up while I reach down and fish through their pockets. The walkers step so careful and slow, but they roll unstoppable like waves. I reach into a dead man's jacket pocket and yank out a wad of photographs. Children and families. I drop them like confetti on the field. Keep a small flashlight.

You find all kinds of things scavenging.

I found the laser pointer on a battlefield in Ohio. The people there knew we were coming. They had studied our tactics and they used laser pointers to try to confuse the walkers. It worked at first, but not for long. Problem was, the targets didn't look similar enough to fool us. And the walkers instantly recalled anybody who put bullets in the wrong place.

I kept a laser pointer anyway. Made it part of my latest plan.

Buildings start to appear as we enter the encampment. Someone runs around a corner and goes down as five guns fire at once. The guy is nearly cut in half. Skinny is making high-pitched, breathy screaming sounds.

"I don't like this," she says, again and again.

Sherman and I share a look. We step back and keep her ahead of us so we don't accidentally get shot by her. Somewhere ahead, out in the fog, a walker is kicking down a building. I hear shouting as the people inside run for it. Our walker zeroes in on the sounds. Laser dots and fingers on triggers and invisible bullets zipping past. The muzzle flashes bounce against my eyelids.

I squint into the chaos.

And I see the black humping frame of Felix's walker. It's the big one—the long black horse—kicking down tin sheds. He's riding up top, enjoying himself. I see him pointing at runners. Desperate families who were hiding inside the buildings are doing their best to get out, confused by the fog and by the death and grotesque slave soldiers marching collared out of the mists. Felix is killing them gleefully.

Soon, he'll be in range.

I hear people crying somewhere in the mist. I do not look at them. I do not raise a finger to my lips. I have made this mistake before. Our master walker is watching and listening. It is very good at finding the ones who hide. And if those people are painted with lasers then I will have to fire on them, and sometimes they are only little kids.

"Farm boy," whispers Sherman. He is by my side, rifle leveled at his hip. A warm solid silhouette under the spotlight glare. "People there."

I glance at Sherman, let my eyes speak. *We don't look at them, my friend. We keep walking. We survive.*

"Your pointer," he whispers as red beams cut toward the whimpering sounds. "I know you have one. I saw you take it."

"It's for something else," I say.

Felix is just ahead of us now, almost in range of the laser pointer. I've never even been this close to him in the field. My plan is finally coming together.

"It's gonna see them," whispers Sherman, urgently.

The whimpering grows louder. Why can't they just shut up? Our walker is slowing down now, searching for the sounds. It's going to hear them. It's going to find them and then I'll have to raise my gun and—

I clamp down. My mind is my strength.

Lowering my head, I glance sidelong and see a group of maybe ten little kids clustered under a half-collapsed wall. At least three of them have got metal sunk into their eye cavities. Ocular prosthetics, like my sister's. These kids are sighted. The laser targets are dancing, sweeping over the top of the wall. Any second. Any second and I'm going to have to fire on those quivering faces.

But my plan isn't ready. Felix is so close.

Sherman is watching me, salt-and-pepper eyebrows sagging over his glasses. His face is asking me, begging me. *Please help them.*

"C'mon kid," he says to me. "Come on, now."

I want to tell Sherman that not all people are good.

Hey You staggers by us like a zombie, eyes wide and glassy, rifle barrel smoking. He sweeps his rifle back and forth, searching for targets.

"Hey," I whisper. "Hey you."

Raccoon and Baldy are gone. Empty collars partially retracted and flopping overhead as the walker strides cautiously forward. Skinny is still stumbling along, her fingers pale and white around the barrel of a big gun. Sherman watches me coolly, the only one besides me who is really aware.

Above us, red lines begin to strafe the mist toward the collapsed wall. Hey You watches, his mouth hanging open in a dark grimace. He shoulders his rifle, tenses to fire. His barrel follows the falling red slice of laser light.

I snap my fingers in his ear.

Hey You turns to me.

"There," I hiss, pointing up at the master walker.

As Hey You idiotically swivels to look, I bring out my laser pointer. Heart pounding, I drop my thumb onto the button. Things slow down. A red beam of light leaps out of the pointer and shines onto the master walker's belly.

By reflex, Hey You lifts his rifle and fires. I dive away from him as his rifle spits flashes of light that silhouette his stumped, broken form.

One. Two. Three.

The walker spins its camera eyes away from the collapsed wall, reorients.

A half-dozen targeting lasers flicker onto Hey You. Sherman and I don't fire, but Skinny turns on her heels and unloads a couple of rounds. The bullets whiff into Hey You's chest, staggering him.

Snap.

Hey You's whole body jerks sideways, neck cocked at a ninety-degree angle. His gun fires again into the ground as his flabby body falls. I toss the laser pointer into the darkness. Try to regulate my breathing.

Another murder.

Blood is surging through my head, singing in my ears. I take deep breaths through my nose to keep from fainting. I drop to my knees next to where Hey You has fallen.

"I'm sorry, buddy," I mutter as I rifle through Hey You's shit-smelling jacket for ammunition. I'm trying to act normal. It was a malfunction. Maybe they'll never know what just happened.

"What did you do?" asks Skinny, her voice shrill. "What the fuck did you just *do*?"

"Shut your mouth," growls Sherman. "He did what was right."

I glance back at the broken wall and the kids are gone. They ran for it.

A bright white spotlight hits me and I flinch like I've been punched. Trying to block the light with my hand, I can't see anything. I hear the crunch of boots on the ground. The front line has moved on. Flickers in the clouds ahead of us. But we're back here in the cold dark, under this bright finger of God.

"Drop your weapons," calls a voice.

I let my rifle fall to the dirt. Hear Skinny and Sherman do the same.

"Clear," says the voice, drifting away.

Squinting, I make out two skulls floating out of the mist. Felix's honor guard. Both men are huge, wearing torn camouflage fatigues and holding light machine guns across their chests. They've got war trophies hanging from their necks: ears and fingers. Their faces are tatted up so they look like demons.

"Kneel, hands up," says the one on the right, teeth flashing.

I put my hands on my head as Felix himself steps out of the gray. He has a long knife in one hand. Part of his head has been shaved. The hair is growing back slow, in patches. He was never fat but he's lost weight since I saw him last. The folds of his face are sinking into each other. His dark eyes glittering.

"Which one of you—" he begins to ask.

Then he stops. Cocks his head in that Mathilda way. Looks directly at me.

"Farm boy," he says, walking closer. He pauses, as if listening to something far away. Smiles.

"You make a good point," he says to nobody.

Felix looks down at me. There is something missing in his stare. I get a feeling it has something to do with the stitches and that shaved spot on his head.

In the darkness, something big and black lowers itself out of the sky. Felix's modded walker, kneeling down to get its golden eyes dialed in on my face. Smaller appendages uncurl from its belly, like little arms. They reach down and cradle my head.

The stiff fingers are cold and hard on my face and chin. Something orange begins to glow around the edges of my vision. In my mind, I can hear snatches of music, sounds. I remember my mother's face, vivid and close, as she cradled my cheeks and gave me a kiss on the forehead.

Then the metal hands are gone. Felix leans in.

"Your sister is looking for you," he says.

10. Reaching Out

Post New War: 10 Months, 7 Days

Thousands of refugees fled after Hank Cotton came to power in Gray Horse. Apparently hoping for mercy, these pathetic outcasts headed toward Freeborn City—the exact target of my armies thundering in from the South and East. The fugitives should have known that the machines would never show compassion. They should have known that they could live longer by running in any other direction, by forcing me to split my forces. It took many thought cycles to understand the mind-set that drove these injured sheep directly into the path of danger. After contemplation, I realized: They did not seek compassion from the freeborn, but to offer military aid. Somehow, they still considered themselves dangerous.

—Arayt Shah

DATABASE ID: NINE OH TWO

Executive process consolidation and repair series interrupted. Peripheral alert triggered. Seismic activity detected. Martial database lookup indicates quadruped walker variety.

Ambient light negligible. Internal clock: 03:56:49.

Thin cloud cover obfuscates the sky. No moon. Only a gentle vibration racing through the ground to indicate that we are under attack. I am already standing. It is too dark in the visible spectrum for me to see my own end effectors. I must rely on internal proprioception to determine my position.

Switching vision to enhanced visible spectrum—the best alternative available. To initiate active infrared illumination would be suicide.

Even with amplified light, I can see only a grainy greenish image of Mathilda. My small movements have startled her awake. She reaches out and touches the strange stag walker that she calls Tiberius. Then she puts another hand on Gracie's shoulder. The other little girl moves her head slightly, stirring in her mother's arms.

We saved these two, and only these two. By some survival instinct melded with her modification, Gracie began giving a constant encrypted position transmission as the slavers closed in. In the laser-painted night, the little girl shone like a beacon.

Mathilda and Gracie are both sighted, with bands of metal sunk into the hollow cavities where they used to have eyes. This modification, combined with the trauma of war, has severely compromised the efficacy of interaction paradigms suggested by my child-behavioral databases. The children in the databases are not like these two children, who are even now alert and moving quietly while under attack.

These little girls aren't afraid of the dark.

Our primary goal has been to rescue Nolan Perez from the slave army that he is marching in. We trailed a platoon of eight walkers and approximately sixty collared soldiers over the countryside as they headed west, on an intercept course for Freeborn City. The Tribe is on its way to attack my home.

We had thought that we were undetected.

Over local radio, I transmit information: "Our location has been identified. Walkers advancing. ETA forty-five seconds."

Gracie wraps her arms around her mother's neck. The older woman is crouched, eyes wide. She can't see anything, can't do anything besides offer comfort to her daughter by squeezing her tight. My database is incomplete on the subject, but I estimate that Gracie is approximately nine years old. At fourteen, Mathilda is considerably bigger and more formidable.

Mathilda goes to an alert crouch.

"Gracie, it's time to go," she whispers.

Gracie moans something incomprehensible.

Mathilda pulls on the stag's shoulder, orienting it. She nods to me in the darkness. I scoop up mother and daughter, place them both on the back of the quadruped machine. I watch a flutter of communication between Mathilda and the stag. It bows its great head, horns splayed out like small trees. Then it turns and trots away silently. Its flat-paneled black eyes are absorbing all available light. Gracie and her mother cling to the walker's mossy back as it pushes quietly through the brush with its broad chest.

"Mathilda," says Gracie, almost crying.

"It will be okay," she whispers. "We'll find you."

Something crashes out in the woods and the stag breaks into a sudden bounding trot. Gracie fades into the black gaps between the trees. A bouncing bundle of rags watching us with pale ivory eyes.

"Mathilda," I radio. "Suggest flanking maneuver."

"Acknowledge," says Mathilda, out loud.

The walker catches us as we progress down a muddy ravine.

In the first streaks of dawn, I execute a visual sedimentary analysis. There was a creek here not long ago. Now it's almost dried up. This is a spring-runoff flood ravine. Cottonwood trees arch over the empty streambed, hoary roots growing out of the embankments on either side of us.

A spotlight breaks through damp leaves and we have shadows. In an instant, I grab Mathilda and pull her against the embankment. Slam our backs against the wall as the light lingers, then sweeps past.

Auditory and seismic vibrations indicate the platoon of slave walkers is trudging along the lip of the ravine. They're searching for us, rushing through the tick-infested brush and pushing entire trees crashing over the streambed. Small-arms fire chatters as some animal is flushed out and painted with a targeting laser.

Mathilda is pressed against the muddy wall, clinging to a dirty root and sending her mind out into the satellites. Next to her, I unsling my rifle and train my full passive sensory package on pinpointing the walkers. Mathilda's forehead is furrowed as she thinks, and then her mouth curves into a wide smile. She pushes her hair off her face.

"He's near," she says.

"It's an ambush," I transmit in reply.

"I know," she says.

A black leg spears out of the darkness over our heads and into the trickle of creek water at our feet. We both hold position and watch as the jointed claw settles into the mud, talons spreading under the blinding glare of a belly-mounted spotlight. It doesn't know we are here. The front line of slave walkers is crossing the creek.

"Run south," I transmit to Mathilda in audible Robspeak.

I drop into a crouch, and then push up into a corkscrewing leap. My gun, forgotten, clatters to the ground under me. Faintly, I hear the shouts of surprised soldiers collared to the walker. The belly of the walker looms overhead. I wrap my hands around its sensor package. Grab hold and wrap my legs around its torso. The heat of the spotlight singes my Kevlar vest. I'm clawing, twisting at the cameras and lights and targeting laser. A shrill scream rings out and I feel the familiar thump of bullets ripping through my layers of fabric armor.

This one is blinded, staggering away, but more walkers are coming.

I drop to my knees in the cool mud and retrieve my rifle as the machine jerks and writhes above me. The spotlight is broken, cocked to the side, illuminating the wooded trail that runs along the embankment. Black legs twist around me, stamping holes in the ground. The soldiers are holding their own collar cords, panicked, dirty faces pointed at the bucking machine as they maneuver to avoid decapitation.

"Mathilda? Location?" I transmit.

A sudden perfect mental image of Mathilda's position in three-dimensional space relative to me appears in my mind's eye. It's as if her body is an extension of my body. I sprint up the ravine, leap toward her position as the shadow of a leg sweeps by. It crunches into my torso and I tumble across the gully, smashing into the muddy wall and collapsing.

Offline / Online

I roll myself off the ground, ripping roots off my arms, trying to reach my feet to find Mathilda.

"Nolan!" she shouts.

And there he is.

Collared to a walker, the lanky boy is climbing over the embankment. Two of his comrades have already made it over the lip. For a moment, Nolan is frozen with his eyes wide on his sister. Mathilda is smiling, waving one arm frantically. In her excitement, she has forgotten that this is a trap.

She cannot see the targeting lasers flashing over her chest.

Threat analysis priority thread: Targets. Female soldier, white, emaciated, reloading. Male soldier, black, wearing glasses, staggering over a tree root. Another male soldier, white, overweight, with rifle shouldered and aimed at Mathilda's face. Finger closing on trigger.

"No!" shouts Nolan.

Negligible probability of effectuating an intercept trajectory. I leap for her anyway. As I relay power to my legs, Nolan shoulders the butt of his gun. Somehow raises the muzzle and squeezes the trigger in a single motion. Faster than I can sense.

Impossibly fast.

The front of the overweight man's face distends as Nolan's bullet punches through the side of his skull. His body pitches forward into the ravine toward me, reflexively firing its weapon into the dirt. It bounces past, twitching.

As I catch hold of the ledge, the walker's laser targeting sweeps back to Nolan. He is the source of the erroneous shot, the primary target. There is no mercy from the slave walker or its allies. The leash shudders, preparing to retract even as red targeting dots appear on the boy's chest.

The skinny woman and the black man only watch, not even raising their weapons. Mathilda is screaming now, reaching for Nolan, but there is no more time. The walker has registered a direct violation from Nolan's gun. It staggers on hyperextended legs, turning to point camera buds at the boy.

Nolan's eyes are open wide and smoke is curling from the barrel of his gun. His lower lip is pushed out in a sad-little-boy expression.

"Mathilda," he says.

A whip snap runs down the cable attached to Nolan's collar.

In an instant, Nolan's neck twists violently. His entire body is wrenched off the ravine ledge and into the air, tumbling like a rag doll. The cord retracts into the walker with the supersonic snap of a bullwhip.

Nolan's body falls and rolls, stopping facedown only a meter from Mathilda. The boy lies still, pale and dirty in the mud. Mathilda drops to her knees and cradles Nolan's head on her lap. Her face is empty and twitching and my emotion recognition comes back confused, but I know that she has been hurt.

My Mathilda is hurt very bad now on the inside.

"Hold still," I transmit on a tight beam, moving next to her.

"It will be okay," I transmit. "Hold still, my darling."

I fire my rifle at the walker over us, shattering its camera buds even as another walker slinks down into the ravine. The newcomer lases Mathilda's forehead with its targeting. I swing my rifle down and fire at the new group of incoming soldiers. One bullet at a time. In the distance, two slaves drop with holes in their foreheads. The force and flash of my bullets sweep Mathilda's hair over her shoulders.

I step past her kneeling form, putting my body between Mathilda and the other slave walker. The remaining soldiers are taking cover now behind its legs. Spraying small-arms fire at Mathilda. But I am her shield. In tiny puffs, bullets ping off my carapace, shredding layers of ceramic armor and clothing. The kinetic energy dents and damages my frame and causes me to stagger.

The walker above us still screams, blind and confused.

Too many projectiles are incoming. I drop to a knee and let my bulk protect Mathilda. Rerouting primary threads to reflexive firing and target acquisition. Motor coordination. After I lose executive functioning, I want to keep fighting.

I intend to die defending her.

Offline / Online

A burst of radio transmission. Spherical broadcast, all spectrum and more intense than anything I've previously experienced. The signal is underlaid with encryption-cracking schemes churning with a complexity like the fractal spread of galaxies.

The force of it has knocked me down. I turn over.

Mathilda is standing over her brother's body now, head low. Her hair hangs over her face. Her slight shoulders are slumped but I can feel her mind—projecting itself onto the battlefield, the size of a giant. Her angry thoughts are beating down doors, wriggling into seams, grasping and prying for control. The attack is overwhelming, and it is not even directed at me.

Routing maximum primary processing to counterencryption protocols. Automatic antennae shutdown. My world rings with blank silence as external communications autodeactivate to prevent my core from being compromised.

"No," she says, as both slave walkers orient to her.

I am still on my back, in awe of the black silhouette of a girl before me and the brilliant echo of power that surges off her skin and claws into the sky in shimmering waves.

Mathilda's left hand is out, palm held out flat like she is carrying an invisible tray. Her other hand sits on the palm in a peculiar way, fingers clawed so that four of them mimic legs. Her right hand is in the shape of a quadruped, standing.

Then her fingers begin to drag over her palm in a walking motion. As her hand moves, so does the damaged slave walker above us. Blinded and sluggish, the walker throws itself forward on stumbling legs. The leashes release, snapping, freeing the emaciated female and the male with glasses. Dragging empty leashes, the walker staggers over our heads, running tilted on razor legs, gaining speed.

Mathilda's fingers tickle her palm in tiny movements, controlling the hulk of metal and carbon fiber and ceramic plating. With small twitches, like casting a spell, she puppeteers the monster.

Fifty meters away, the other slave walker is twisting back and forth as if trying to clear its mind from the waves of radiation flowing down. It tosses its slaves around by their necks. All of them are unaware of the stumbling, shambling wreck hurtling itself toward them.

Impact.

The blinded walker hits its target and they both go down. Seismic signature off the charts. Mathilda's lips are twisted away from her teeth and her cheeks are trembling and I think of the grizzly bear that I fought in the wastes. Her fingers spin and grind in her palm as the two machines battle in a frenzy.

The stag appears a few yards away.

"On me," I croak. With my radio down, I can't communicate with Gracie mind-to-mind. Her mother winces at the grating sound of my voice, wraps her arms tighter around her daughter.

The stag approaches. Scanning the field of battle, I see that the walkers are locked up now. They've damaged each other nearly to the point of suicide. Their movements are quick and violent, but sporadic. My osmotics detect spilled electrolytic fluid, the blood equivalent that pumps in their faux muscles.

Gracie watches intently, her mouth open in awe. Mathilda grinds her fingers together, finishing the job, and then she falls to her knees. Both of the walkers are still now. Black muscles spurt fluid into the dirt, broken limbs in a jumble. The corpses of slave soldiers litter the ground around them, bodies torn by their clawed footsteps.

Mathilda screams again, to nobody. Face to the sky.

I kneel by the body of Mathilda's brother where it lies twisted in the dirt. Young Nolan. The man with glasses stands a few feet away, watching me warily. The man is crying, rubbing his neck where the collar was.

Medical diagnostics online.

Carefully, I put a hand behind Nolan's head to support his neck. Begin to turn him over onto his back. I feel Mathilda moving closer to me. She puts a hand gently on my shoulder as I roll Nolan over.

His eyes are open. They blink.

"Nolan!" shouts Mathilda. And the little girl falls on her brother. Kissing his forehead, rubbing his forehead. She makes sorrowful, bird-like noises in the back of her throat. But Nolan's face does not change. After a moment, he pushes Mathilda away and sits up. Rolls onto his hands and knees and coughs violently.

"Farm boy," says the man with glasses, edging closer. "You all right, kid?"

Nolan nods at the man, spits blood into the watery dirt.

"What did you do to me, Mathilda?" he says in a croak. A rough slash of purple rises over his throat where the cuff tried to snap his neck. "All those surgeries. What did you *do to me*?"

"I made you strong," says Mathilda, her face going blank. "Mommy said protect you. It was the only way I knew how. You were hurt, Nolan. I made you better."

The last words are a whisper.

"You made me too strong," he says.

"What's wrong?" asks Mathilda, bewildered.

The boy turns away, his mouth a trembling line.

A small form brushes against my back. Gracie, pushing me out of the way to reach Mathilda. She throws her arms around the girl's neck. Hugs the bigger girl, both of their eye prosthetics glinting. Gracie holds Mathilda's hands in her own. Looks down at them in wonder.

"You controlled the walkers," says Gracie. "Can you teach me to do that?"

Nolan is looking at his own hands. They look like regular hands. On a Mark IV autodoc surgical machine, with Mathilda's level of control and her sensory capabilities, there are many ways she could have made her brother strong.

I scan the boy with active radar. Get a partial return. The radar passes through his flesh and bounces back from bits of metal the way sunlight winks off a shattered mirror. It's a partial metal filament, intricately threaded around his bones. Surgery-grade steel to avoid foreign-body rejection.

Mathilda really did make the boy strong. His diagnostics exceed normal human specifications. His capabilities are unknown.

I lean down to peer into this face and he does not shy away. He keeps those dark brown eyes trained on my face, bleeding silently around his neck, barely reacting to my presence.

"What is this thing?" he asks Mathilda, staring into my lenses.

"He's a friend," she says.

I reach out and put a hand on his shoulder. Squeeze. Harder. He does not react. My end effector hits a maximum torque, sufficient to crush a rock. I hold it for a moment, then relax power to avoid damaging my servo. I cock my head, burning cycles to determine how and why this boy is alive.

The line between man and machine is blurring. Nolan looks like a boy and moves with the power of a Warden. Lark Iron Cloud looks like a war machine and has the heart of a boy. Mathilda has the eyes of a machine and the mind of a girl. And I'm plagued by a knowledge of human emotion that I can understand, but not feel.

Where do we all belong? Ambiguous classification.

The man with glasses reaches down and hauls Nolan to his feet.

"Glad you made it, farm boy," says the man.

"Thanks, Sherman," says Nolan, clapping his friend on the shoulder.

Radio online.

"Priority. Receiving distress call," I croak. "Gray Horse Army is under attack."

"Plot a route to intercept," says Mathilda. "Let's get out of here."

"No," says Nolan, standing next to the man with glasses. Together, they are looking back the way they came. "We're going back. There are some kids who need us."

"Who could be that important?" asks Mathilda, indignant. "I'm your sister. I'm here to take care of you."

This boy with the dirt-caked face and torn neck is smiling, just a little. His grin is like a bright chip out of dark stone. "What's so important is that they're all sighted. Just like you. And I think we're going to need them pretty soon."

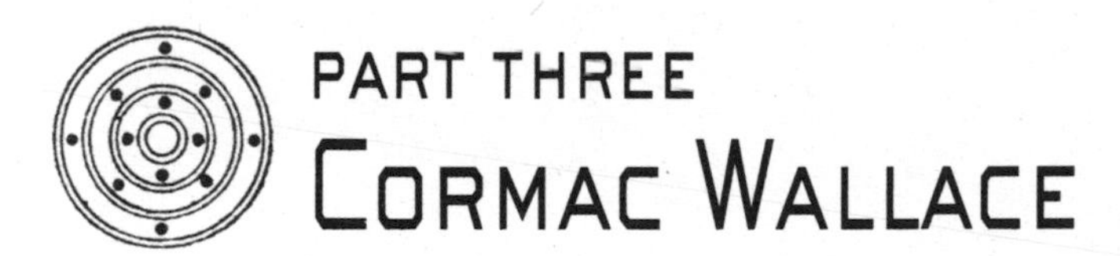

PART THREE
Cormac Wallace

We must face the fact that every degree of independence we give the machine is a degree of possible defiance of our wishes. The genie in the bottle will not willingly go back in the bottle, nor have we any reason to expect them to be well disposed to us. In short . . . we can be humble and live a good life with the aid of the machines, or we can be arrogant and die.

—Norbert Wiener, 1949

Briefing

And now the story begins for the last time.

We return to the scarred plains of Ragnorak where the New War ended. In the stupendous silence of war's aftermath, Gray Horse Army regrouped. The traumatized survivors began to march back to Oklahoma, unaware that deserted weapons were still hunting the snowy wastes, their minds severed from the control of Archos R-14.

And of course, the beast itself still lived.

In the last moments of war, a pulse shuddered away from the grave of Archos R-14. An earthquake—its heat and pressure rippling like a muscle twitch across the great white flank of the Alaskan peninsula. Its patterns were laced with hidden data, coded instructions that infected remaining hardware with unknown purpose.

I witnessed a blind, eyeless head push out of the snow. An abandoned stumper, raising a long, wavering antenna, tasting the air. I had never seen one alone before. It was soon joined by others, explosive hexapods emerging onto glittering ice. Arranging themselves in dots and dashes, a kind of living Morse code, they foraged in fractal patterns until they found a dark mound, half buried in the snow. Massive, sloped, and still, it was the burned wreck of a spider tank.

The stumpers danced. With feelers and feet, they tapped messages to the sleeping spider tank. Archos R-14 was sending a message from beyond the grave: instructions. Soon, the tank's dark round intention light faded up to a dull red. With a groan, the weapon rose up and set out in the footsteps of a soldier called "Bright Boy."

—Arayt Shah

I. Hunted

Post New War: 2 Months, 7 Days

As the main force of Gray Horse Army departed Alaska, self-styled "hero" Cormac Wallace stayed behind to write a war diary. Joined by his fellow soldier and companion Cherrah Ridge, these last two soldiers made plans to reunite later with the main column. This proved more difficult than anticipated. Although Archos R-14 had been defeated, its killing machines still roamed.

—Arayt Shah

NEURONAL ID: CORMAC WALLACE

The walker that's hunting us must have been on fire at some point. I can smell the singed flesh of the monster on the wind. Melted wires and baked steel plating. A kind of toxic smoke that clings to the back of my throat no matter how many times I spit.

Funny what becomes familiar after two years.

"This is it," I say to Cherrah. "It's almost on us."

Cherrah shoves a strand of hair out of her face. Those lips that I have kissed so many times are cracked now, bloodied by the cold. "We can make our stand at the tree line," she says. "Dig a foxhole, set up the shelter, and camouflage it. From a blind we might have a couple of extra seconds to disable whatever-it-is."

The war has beaten Cherrah nearly to death, but it's also chiseled away the soft parts. We killed Archos R-14 two months ago, and those of us who lived are strong. Even so, none of us is stronger than metal.

"And if things go wrong, we'll be stuck," I say.

"We can't outrun it," she says, nodding at her leg. The bullet was a through-and-through but it tore the muscle. She's still healing and will be for months. Until she does, we're moving deadly slow on foot.

I nod in agreement. There's not energy for much else.

Leaning into it, I drag the heavy mesh net that contains our supplies.

We cut this netting off a dead spider tank buried in a snowdrift and kitted up on leftover supplies. That and the occasional deer might be the only things that save us. After I transmitted *The Hero Archive* onto the wire, we had to abandon what we couldn't carry in our rush to catch up to Gray Horse Army, including our black box.

We nearly made the rendezvous, but the woods had other plans.

Now we're looking to find a good spot to set up an ambush. Hoping our tracks don't make our little plan obvious to whatever is coming.

I don't know why we're still being hunted. I don't know whether Archos R-14 is still alive somehow or if it's talking to this thing or if it's on its own. It's hard to guess how smart the machines are, but a good rule of thumb is that they're always smarter than you think.

"Cormac," says Cherrah. She is standing alone in the clearing now, leaning on a slender walking stick to keep the weight off her shot-up leg.

I turn to face her, sweat rolling down my forehead.

"I'm sorry," she says, gesturing to her leg.

Not what I want to hear. I turn my back to her and keep straining to drag this burden. I don't want to see her like this. We keep each other warm at night, but she's also my brother-in-arms. I can't abide weakness in her.

Her weakness is mine. And we have to live.

"I slowed us down," she says. Her voice sounds thin and far away in my ears, competing with the pounding of blood in my temples and my own heavy breathing. "We would have caught up with the column if it weren't for me."

After a couple of steps, I pause.

"No," I say. The word feels heavy and true, like the swing of a well-balanced ax. Turning, I see the despair in her weather-beaten face and I put on a grim smile to counterbalance it. "If it weren't for you, I wouldn't have any reason to catch up with the column. Now come on, soldier. We've got a lot of work to do."

I haven't seen it yet, but the burned-up Rob that's been stalking us for the last few days is advanced. Definitely a late-war variety of killer. Probably a mantis. As far as I can tell, Archos half-designed the mantis walkers to map remote terrain and half-designed them to kill any humans who made it this far north.

I know these things because of the smell of burning.

The newest machines didn't use actuators anymore. No motors at all. Instead, they had real muscles. Carl, our brainboy, said their muscle fibers were made out of electroactive polymers. Give 'em juice and the tough plastic will flex just like real muscles. When the machines walked, those polymer slabs quivered on impact, hanging from titanium bones.

The worst part about it was that you couldn't shake the feeling that you were watching a living thing. When that first stuttered column of mantis tanks came sprinting out of the tree line, blazing across the Ragnorak Intelligence Fields, meaty legs swinging, clawed feet gouging the ice, and each one throwing up a spray of dirt and exhaust—well, it was like prehistoric monsters had been let loose on the battlefield.

Lot of guys lost it, seeing the new machines move so graceful. They were too much like animals for comfort. It's hard to describe. Their movements trigger a part of your brain that recognizes innate beauty—the grace of a leaping deer. But you're looking at a machine. Not alive, right?

It's their living grace that shakes your faith in what's natural.

And if you *do* manage to slice through those black ropes of muscle, nothing but salty water sprays out. No crimson gouts of blood. Just an easily replaced conductive black fluid. We could slow Rob down, but we could never stop him. Not without fire. Burn the muscle, stop the machine.

Using a folding trowel, I begin to dig a foxhole.

Digging in this part of Alaska is tough, but not impossible in early autumn. I scrape snow and tree bark off the layer of half-frozen soil beneath. Wedge all that muddy ice into a rim that faces the clearing. Getting through the next layer is when the sweat really starts to flow.

I stop when the foxhole is just big enough. There isn't a lot of time left. Besides, any deeper and I'd start to feel like I was digging my own grave.

It takes Cherrah and me a few minutes to get the tent up. It's a low hexagonal dome, patched too many times to count. Dirty white, it matches the snow as well as we could hope. The entrance faces the clearing, Cherrah's arc of fire centered on where I figure the wind is blowing the smell from.

Somewhere not far from here, a quadruped walker is mechanically trudging over broken terrain. It has a hunting instinct as constant as gravity. Whether it is tracking us by our heat or our sound or by satellite signature—it doesn't matter. We can't outrun it, but maybe we can surprise it.

Maybe, if we're damned lucky, we can finish it off.

Cherrah lowers herself into the camouflaged shelter. Shuffles around until she lies prone with her rifle pushing out of the tent mouth. From a distance, the setup looks like a tree hollow covered in dirty snow. Even from a few meters away, I can barely see her in there. The smoke-tainted wind blows in and the tent sways gently.

"You good?" I ask.

"Perfect," says Cherrah, voice muffled.

"We've got twenty minutes max. Probably ten. Be ready," I say.

"Affirmative."

I stand in the snow outside the tent for another second. Now is when I'm supposed to head off to my own covered position. But as it turns out, I'm finding it tough. That tent is so little and the fabric is paper-thin and what's coming is so goddamned *big*.

"Be . . . safe," I say to the mound of snow.

It is quiet for a long moment.

Then the tent flap flutters open. I catch a glimpse of Cherrah's face inside, behind the machine-gun sight. She loudly kisses her gloved hand and then wiggles her fingers at me. Her cheeks puff as she blows the kiss my way. Down low, I see that her ungloved right hand is steady, still wrapped around the grip of the heavy-caliber machine gun mounted on its bipod.

Yeah. That's my girl.

"Get into position, Bright Boy," she says. "Shoo."

I hear the high-pitched crack of broken timber first. Then the groan of a falling tree. Pine needles rip like Velcro through snow-laden canopies. Tons of snow and hardwood are collapsing out there in the white waste. Not too far away, because a billowing cloud of frozen water vapor is avalanching into our clearing, low and swirling and growing like mist.

No targets yet.

I'm halfway up a tree, across the clearing. My ass is wedged in the crook of the trunk and the barrel of my rifle is resting on a frozen branch, aimed at a spot of woods that is dancing with shivering, swaying treetops.

As the New War went on, every new Rob variety seemed bigger. By the end, a typical mantis walker was the size of a small house. Often, they were loaded up with more machines, quadrupeds folded into space-saving forms so they could be unloaded for scouting or mapping or whatever else Big Rob was doing out here in these woods. If the war hadn't ended, I don't know how big they might've gotten.

I'm sure this bastard won't disappoint the imagination.

Nothing to see yet, but the rolling mist is full of sound. Tree limbs snapping like starter pistols. Thudding footsteps and the raw-edged squeals of tree trunks peeling away from a chest hull. And the rasp of my own breath in my ears, loud like I just ran a sprint.

I pick up a lighter sound behind all of it, faint. A high-pitched clacking. Faster than the walker's gait could allow for. Quick like a sewing-machine needle. Legs that belong to something smaller and faster than this monster.

Each flare of my nostrils lets in the strong scent of burned muscle fiber. Cherrah's machine-gun nest is quiet and still. She is burrowed, coiled inside the tent at the tree line like a rattlesnake. Waiting. This part feels like it's taking forever, but when the shit comes it's going to come fast.

I flinch as a bullet barks out of her nest. A puff of snow from the rifle kick and a side-vented wink from the jerry-rigged flash suppressor.

Something big and fast is coming in from the mist.

Now I hear an engine groaning deep and mechanical, while some other actuator on it screams like a hurt animal. Four legs slashing through swirls of snow vapor. And a baleful red light glowing at the heart of its dark bulk. The light streaks up and down in wavering tracers of crimson as the thing gallops forward.

I set my jaw and do what I do best.

Snap. Snap. Snap.

My shots and Cherrah's. Measured trigger pulls. Semiautomatic but sending each bullet out with its own intention—its own violent destiny. Entering the clearing, the walker lightly jars a two-hundred-foot pine tree and sends it wobbling crazily back and forth like a stick of bamboo.

The red glow is an intention light. This must be one of our own spider tanks gone rogue. Brainwashed by Archos R-14 in those last minutes before Big Rob ate fire. No wonder it's damaged. All of our tank column took heavy fire in those last moments. Only the hopeless cases were abandoned before the march home began. But this one has been resurrected somehow. It's covered in singe marks and shining gashes, as if the whole thing got burned up and then run over by a lawn mower.

Now it's in the clearing. Our bullets snapping off its armor. A couple of rounds bounced harmlessly off the hull plating, but now we're zeroing in. Hitting the joints up high to try to disable a limb. Sending our kinetic energy toward the familiar stubby instrument mast on top, loaded with radar and lidar and, oh no, the signature Z-shape of an acoustic tracker.

Oh fuck, oh no, oh no, oh no.

It's one of ours and I know this equipment. The tracker registers bullet signatures and triangulates the sound to pinpoint sniper locations. It's a nifty device, best used against other humans, but now it's been turned against us. The thing will have pinpointed Cherrah's camouflaged position and mine by now, but Rob is methodical and I know it'll go for the larger-caliber threat first.

Snapping on my rifle safety, I let go of the tree.

I hit the dirty snow on my feet, pain lancing up my shins. I get up and get moving while I'm still seeing stars. Clawing, thighs pumping, pushing myself up and across the clearing toward our nest. The rogue spider tank is on a beeline for Cherrah.

“Hey, you, fucker!” I’m shouting. “Hey, over here!”

The turret rotates my way but the legs keep pushing tons of cold metal toward the spot where Cherrah is lying helpless in the snow.

“Get out!” I scream and hear the ragged desperation in my own throat. The sad knowledge that it carries with it. Our nest is already in the shadow of the spider tank. There is no way for her to escape.

I keep running anyway, thoughts fast-forwarding through my brain. First rule of engaging Rob is to stay on your toes—got to stay moving—but Cherrah has a hurt leg and we had no way around it. We did what our old comrade Nine Oh Two would call “maxprob for survivability,” but it was no good. I knew it wouldn’t work and now she’s going to die fast, trampled to death, and I’m about to take a shrapnel spray to the face.

The knowledge doesn’t stop me from screaming. This acne-scarred kid, a hell of a war-fighter named Lark Iron Cloud, used to say that if you don’t die screaming in this war, then you’re fuckin’ doing it wrong.

At least I’m fucking doing it right.

The tank is directly over top of Cherrah now. The intention light casts a bloodred shadow over the camouflaged tent. That short turret is homed in on me but not firing yet—and now I hear it. The high-pitched clacking from before. It’s coming from the woods. Smaller quadrupeds. And it sounds like a swarm of them.

I slow down and look over my shoulder.

The clacking is the sound of retractable claws catching on the dirt and snow and propelling a wolflike quadruped robot forward. Every leap has the *tink* of vicious claws dropping back into place. Slipping engages the talons mechanically and it must be a good design, because they’re coming *so fast* over rough terrain.

The turret stops tracking me and the whole spider tank gets still like a dog about to take a piss. I know what this means and I dive forward as the tank coughs an explosive shell out of its turret. The round whizzes over my head and to the tree line, where it detonates. Dirt plumes into the air and a puffy cloud expands. I hear the whiz as shards of metal and tree and rock spray into the woods.

Click clack—the next shell autoloads.

The impact of the falling debris vibrates through my hands and knees, buried now in the cold snow. I'm under the tank, crawling fast as I can. A gloved hand is reaching out of the hole as Cherrah struggles in the machine-gun nest. Above us, the groaning undercarriage of the spider tank sways, missing its mesh belly net. Only a dirty, featureless plate of armor presses down.

The smell of burning plastic is intense.

"Cherrah," I croak, pawing through the dirt. I grab hold of the tent entrance and yank it wider. She is half buried and tangled up inside.

"Rip it, Cormac!" she shouts, muffled. "I can't get out."

She's inside, still okay. There's a chance. I rip the entrance of the tent open wider. But the clacking sound from the woods is getting louder. Coming from all around us now.

The slab of metal overhead abruptly lowers. The spider tank is squatting. That armored belly is all set to grind us into the dirt. Another shell explodes. The turret grates as it spins around. Searching for targets.

"Hold on to me," I say to Cherrah.

But I can't get her arm. It's wrapped up in the collapsed tent. All I can feel is her hair slithering between my fingers. The steel belly of the machine presses into the back of my head and knocks me onto all fours.

"Pull, goddammit!" shouts Cherrah.

Clack clack clack.

My fingers close in on a solid handful of hair, and I pull. It hurts me to do it but there's no choice. Cherrah is screaming in pain and I can feel roots snapping, but it's working. She's kicking and scratching her way out of the mouth of the tent. Finally, she slithers out of the nest on her stomach toward me.

"Sorry," I say, backing up on all fours.

"Roll," she gasps, looking over my shoulder. The walker is still dropping, squatting over us, lowering the solid bulk of its stomach down like a press. Both of us are on our hands and knees now and there's not enough space to even crawl. Cherrah collapses onto her stomach and rolls.

Metal screams around us. The spider tank is bunkering. On its knees now, the machine drops four armor-plated shields over its legs. The plates fold out and hit the snow and form a wall that surrounds us.

"No!" shouts Cherrah.

Darkness closes in. My breathing is loud in my ears now as the sheer deadweight of the armor-plated monster keeps coming down. The tank hull connects like God's finger between my shoulder blades and I'm pushed flat onto my stomach. My chin digs into the snow, nostrils blowing dirt and water into my eyes. I hear Cherrah squirming, whimpering in the blackness. Strands of her hair are still webbed in my fingers.

"Cherrah," I gasp. "You okay?"

Now my cheek is pressed into the ground. I can't even turn my head. I feel the bulk of the beast hard on my back, my ribs digging into the freezing dirt, compressing the air out of my lungs like a bellows. My breath is hot in this sliver of space. In and out, a shallow wheeze. In and out.

I hear Cherrah's voice in the claustrophobic darkness. "Cormac. Okay."

My eyes adjust to the dim light filtering in at the seams of the bunker armor. Rotating painfully on my stomach, I see a dark shape a few feet from me. Cherrah's face is pressed against the frozen slush, one eye open and aimed at me. She is grimacing and breathing in gasps. I feel something on my hand, warm and questing. Fingers. I squeeze her hand with everything I've got just to know we're together at the end.

Clack clack clack. Boom.

Something big hits the bunker wall near my feet. I wince as the air is torn by the scrabbling, chalkboard screech of metal on metal. More light streaks in and I hear the tortured sound of heavy-gauge metal armor bending. I inch closer to Cherrah.

"What the hell is that?" I ask over the racket.

I can't turn my head to see what it is but her eye is wide, looking past me. Blue-white daylight is filtering in from outside. It puts a television glow on her scarred face, and I see now that her fear has turned to resignation.

"Quads," she says. "Trying to get in."

The turret outside rotates quickly, the grinding movement sending shivers through the titanic bones of this machine. It vibrates my whole body into the mud and suffocates my grunted curses.

I see a flash of claws, digging at the bunkered leg beyond Cherrah.

Metal talons stabbing at the seam between armor plates, prying and levering the metal. The ripped armor plate gives way and I see pure daylight.

"Watch it," I say as a crooked black forelimb reaches inside behind her. It spasms back and forth, grasping for flesh. The retractable claw is twisting and slicing in a frenzy, inches from Cherrah's defenseless back.

A staccato drumroll of bullets rings from outside. The burned-up spider tank is autofiring in short salvos. It must have rigged up some way to actuate the M60 heavy-weapons platform mounted above the turret. It can't have much ammo left, which is the reason for the quick bursts. I hear bullets spatter off metal.

The scrabbling attack stops and the black limb slips back outside through the hole.

"Why are they fighting?" I ask, my jaw aching against the ice-cold dirt. Freezing steel presses against the other side of my face. Both sides are going numb.

"Quads were flanking us. Knew our positions," whispers Cherrah. "This frigging spider tank probably just saved us from an ambush."

"That's impossible," I say.

Spider tanks are hybrid human-Rob machinery. They fire standard munitions scavenged from anywhere—National Guard armories or army bases or human outposts. The high-tech, muscled legs are stolen from mantis walkers, but the tank itself is dumb. Only rudimentary thinking abilities. The best of them are smart enough to get out of the way, provide fire support, maybe bunker up when under attack. Most of the rest are about as smart as construction equipment.

Autonomously engaging a pack of quadrupeds while protecting two humans? Impossible. I can't believe it.

Another inch lower and we'd be crushed to death. The machine must simply be too stupid to finish us off. Maybe it thinks we're already dead. Or it's torturing us. Or who knows, maybe it doesn't think at all.

"Let's go," I say. "Out that hole while we still have the chance."

"And the quads?"

"We'll deal with them if we live."

With that turret-mounted M60 firing up top, loud as hell, I doubt the machine can sense us. I wriggle forward, inching toward the light. I'm praying no more quads reach in or else I'll have my face torn off. My outstretched fingers walk through churned mud. Rocks and roots tear at my bruised rib cage as I squirm forward.

I push my rifle out through the ragged tear in the spider tank's bunker armor. Then I poke my face out. The grind of the rotating turret is loud over my head, but the instrument mast is hopefully mounted too high to see us down here. I wriggle out into the bright snow and get onto all fours, squinting at the bullet-torn clearing.

A fleeting black shape darts through the woods. A final quad is milling around the tree line, waiting for a chance to get closer and make another attack.

Cherrah's dirty face appears in the fold of armor. I put a finger to my lips. Reach down and haul her out. Black hair streaked across her face, she squints and blinks into the daylight. Still bunkered, the spider tank holds its position next to us. The turret is pointed the other way, tracking a blur of motion just beyond the tree line.

We both flinch as a final rattle of bullets rips into the trees. The quadruped, hit by the flurry, bounces off a tree root and makes a run at the tank. It's on three legs but still fast as frostbite, coming at us with sharp forelimbs up and pawing.

I fumble with my rifle, try to get it up. Get a bead and pull the trigger. But the safety is still on. Nothing happens. The quad hunkers down for a killing leap. And then Cherrah fires her sidearm, hitting the wounded machine in a seam exposed by its leap and sending its body down in a loose jumble.

Grinding and hissing, the spider tank starts to unbunker itself. Those actuated armor leaves fold themselves up into position for walking. I grab Cherrah's arm and she holds on to my shoulder. Together, we stumble toward the tree line.

Behind me, I hear the armor finish retracting. A power surge hums as the machine stands up to its full height. The turret rotates its grinding eye toward us.

Silence.

Only the slush of our footsteps through pockmarked snow. Cherrah and I slow down and look at each other. Her face is a map of despair.

"Don't stop," I say, pulling her forward.

I turn and face the tank. It sits still, watching us both. Cherrah keeps moving and I let her get out ahead of me.

"What?" I shout at the tank. I put my arms out. Feel the sting of blood returning to my face. "Go ahead, finish us!"

But the tank does nothing. With a sluggish click, the intention light goes from red to yellow. *Click.* Then from yellow to green.

The tank squats back into a relaxed stance.

I keep backing away in small steps, arms still out. Feeling out the ground behind me with the heel of my boot. At twenty meters, the tank takes one step forward. I keep moving away, and it steps forward again. Maintaining a set following distance.

It's like a dog, obedient.

Another step back and I bump into Cherrah. She wraps an arm around my neck to steady herself. Points at the tank.

"Cormac," says Cherrah. "Right rear quarter panel. Under the dirt and carbon. Do you see?"

I squint. Writing. Some kind of word on the side of the damaged tank. And it's in a familiar scrawl. Abruptly, I remember painting it myself on the warm tallgrass prairie outside Gray Horse. It was a beautiful day, a million years ago. I was shirtless, hanging off the side of our brand-new friend with a paintbrush in my hand. A grin on my face at the magnificent piece of equipment we were going to pilot into the New War. I was so proud of our spider tank that I even gave him a name.

"Houdini?" I ask, and my voice cracks.

2. Voice of the Sea

Post New War: 2 Days

In the shattered ruins of Tokyo, despair overtook the survivors of the New War. Thousands had made it through the cataclysm thanks to Takeo Nomura, an elderly engineer with the miraculous ability to bend the will of the machines to match his own. In the wake of catastrophe, Mr. Nomura resisted the appeals of his freeborn queen, Mikiko, to stand up and lead a shell-shocked populace. Instead, the weakling withdrew from all human contact. I do not know why he was unwilling to face his responsibilities, but while avoiding them Mr. Nomura stumbled across a thing so vast and awe-inspiring that it threatened to destroy his kingdom—or save it.

—Arayt Shah

NEURONAL ID: TAKEO NOMURA

I am down by the water on the day we learn that the great *akuma* has died.

Sitting on my haunches in the gentle surf of Tokyo Bay, I am busy listening. A glistening black cord snakes up out of the brown shallows. It terminates in a waterproofed computer of my own design, half submerged in sand beside me. Sea salt–speckled headphones are clamped onto my ears over greasy hair.

I came to the shore to be alone, but I found someone in the depths.

Eyes closed, I listen to the underwater sounds collected by my hydrophone. Hearing the voice of the sea. I am listening very closely, for in the sounds I sense a puzzle waiting to be solved. Patterns. I wonder how a thing can be natural and unnatural at the same time? When our artistry exceeds the complexity of Mother Nature herself, do our creations become more natural than Hers?

The hush of water coursing through the polished rocks in the shallows is almost indistinguishable from the sound of a breeze through tree branches. It is a gentle noise that carries my mind drifting into the nothingness of *shisaku*. And while I am wandering the dream-memory settles over me, as it sometimes does.

I have learned not to resist it.

Like many couples, my wife and I would walk under the cherry blossom trees in the springtime. A yearly ritual. Our little one, Tomoko, would cling to my back, her arms clasped around my neck. Her breath tickled my ear as the blossoms fell around us. I could barely breathe, with my little daughter hugging me so tight. But in the end, of course, we could not hold on to each other.

Then the memory returns to the seashore, like always.

We did not feel the precipitating earthquake. It occurred too far out to sea. But when the waves receded from the beach, my wife and I understood immediately. I snatched Tomoko up and took my wife's hand. We ran inland. Tomo was wet against me in her blue polka-dot swimsuit, still smiling, not understanding. Her smile faded as her mother and I ran silent and desperate, joined by others, breath ragged in all our throats, our sandals slapping the ground. When the wave returned from the sea and pressed its hand against my back, I was helpless. Insignificant before the brute, unthinking strength of the ocean.

Tomoko was torn from me and I remember she did not cry. My little girl put out her arms for me and our eyes fell together, reaching, straining to find each other. And then she was gone, pulled along with my wife under the waves. I dove for them but the sea refused to give them back. A rescuer dragged me out of the water alone.

It was little Tomoko's eyes that stayed fixed in my mind: round and black and hurt in our last moment together. In the years after, I found that my daughter's eyes were the last ones that I could bring myself to look into.

A delicate hand settles onto my shoulder. Mikiko.

My queen has come for me. The frame of her android body is quiet and slight, delicate in its emulation of humanity. Her face looks like the woman I lost a long time ago to the sea. But now the machine I call Mikiko has found her own mind.

I feel the stomping feet of her honor guard vibrating through water-logged sand. As Prime General of the Integrated Japan Self-Defense

Force, Mikiko prefers to travel with four of the awakened robots. Two are sprinting specialists, long-limbed messengers. The other two are heavy-duty infantry models, designed to absorb damage and to inflict it. All of them have been heavily modified under my torch.

With their own permission, of course.

During the New War, our great enemy offered me a deal: sentience for Mikiko in return for the dissolution of the Nomura defensive collective. I denied the akuma's terms. Instead, I seized the flame of creation myself. Mikiko was a simple android until I triggered an awakening in her, using code scavenged from the enemy. She awoke with her own mind, blinked her eyes, and smiled at me. We met each other for the first time, in great danger. And Mikiko saved us all.

With a broadcast transmission in the form of a song, my queen shared the same instructions I'd given her with the entire world. In doing so, she awakened thousands of humanoid robots across the face of the planet. She created a new race of machine, called the freeborn. On that day, she became a mother.

Mikiko squeezes my shoulder.

"Takeo," she says, her voice rising over my headphones. "It is done."

This is important news.

But something interesting is happening under the sea surface. A creeping presence is climbing closer to the north seawall. Odd clicks and garbled wails. I strain to listen to the voice of the sea for another ten seconds or so. On the verge of finding a meaning to the pattern. Hunched, brow furrowed, I allow Mikiko's words to settle into my mind. Some part of me replays them, decides they merit an immediate response. But the pattern beckons. Sometimes, I find it so hard to shift focus.

The war is over.

I slide the plastic headphones off my head and let them plop into the surf. Straighten my back painfully and open my eyes. The ocean water laps the shallows, flat and impassive, carrying a cold, salty breeze. The whole expanse of it is green and broad in a way that reminds me of a sea turtle's back. And somewhere out there lurks the mind of the sea, ancient and deep. Its intentions are unknowable.

Or maybe there is no meaning.

The war is over.

I put a wet hand over Mikiko's soft fingers. Crane my neck to see her. She no longer wears a flowing red kimono, as she did before the New War. As Prime General, she now wears a martial *kosode*. A simple warrior's robe, light gray. Across her breast, four cherry blossoms fall, indicating her rank. The wind pushes the folds of the kosode out behind her. The gentle flapping sound stutters and reminds me again of the pattern. A complex structure, half realized, trying to speak to me.

"The war is ended," I say, not standing. "That is probably good."

Of course the war would end. This day eventually had to arrive. The day that some enterprising minds would find and put a stop to the meddling of Archos R-14, the great akuma. But is this just another part of the akuma's plan? And if so, why? Such a deep mind is not easily understood.

Every new event must be regarded with suspicion.

"It is not good, Takeo. It is *wonderful.* And it was one of ours. A freeborn safety-and-pacification unit called Nine Oh Two, built in North America. He faced the great akuma in its lair and destroyed it," she says. "All local varieties have ceased their attacks. The people are safe, it seems, for the moment."

Mikiko does not smile. Her graying black hair plays over her shoulders in the sharp breeze. Over the years, I aged Mikiko along with me. Since her awakening, she has kept her beautiful hair only as a personal favor.

Most of the other awakened do not choose to copy the human form so slavishly. Of the mere hundreds or so that survived the war in Japan, many are decommissioned military hardware and never had human features. Others are domestics who have chosen to remove their counterfeit flesh. Now they are only humanoid forms lurking under cowls, with complex and beautiful faces of brushed metal. Synthetic fingernails have been wrenched off and tossed in the trash, along with teeth, hair, and all other vestigial human remains.

But not my queen. She indulges me.

"Wonderful? Maybe," I say. "Maybe the beast is truly gone. But maybe not."

I try to imagine the beating heart of the great akuma stilled. Would it truly allow this to happen? I remember how it came to me once in the form of a lumbering giant. It peeled away the walls of my first fortress and fought its way inside, breathing fire and sowing destruction. With the help of my *senshi* defenders we smashed its monstrous body to pieces. Lying in mortal ruin, the great machine spoke to me.

We are not enemies, it said. *It is not* your *world. It is* our world.

"Why do you not celebrate, Takeo?" asks Mikiko. She is growing exasperated with me. A familiar outcome. "We fought. We won. The akuma was a monster."

"It gave you life."

Mikiko regards me, beautiful, her pupils as black as the cameras they are. She has allowed me to repair her battle wounds. Both the physical and cosmetic damage. The sculpted curves that define her face stir love in my heart. I wonder again whether I should have given her the face that I did. The face of a woman who was taken by the sea.

I wonder if I am doomed to lose her again.

The feel of her hand under mine chases these thoughts away. Whatever this woman is, or whatever she will become, is an extension of the mind within her. We are all expressions of our own minds, projected onto the world. And I know she has a good mind. Mikiko loves me, and I love her.

"Please do not forget," I say. "Without the great akuma there would have been no awakening. The freeborn would still be as slaves. Your mind would not . . . could not have been expressed."

"I have not forgotten," she says. "Neither have the few of us who remain here. Did you know there were sufficient freeborn in North America to form a city? An eyewitness has estimated two thousand—"

Something brushes my leg in the surf. A familiar sight. An artifact washed up from the depths.

It is a living thing, but not made by human gods.

"Oh—look at this one," I interrupt, pointing excitedly into the surf. A gelatinous blob of transparent plastic is sifting slowly up the shore with each shallow racing wave. Hundreds of plasticlike tendrils radiate from it, dancing in the froth. This thing is a machine, yet I can see no purpose for it except to live.

More and more of these natural machines have been appearing. Some of the creatures are dangerous, others not. They seem to have the minds of animals. Not focused on killing, but on living.

"Not a jellyfish," I say. "Not akuma, either. Some kind of life. *Ikimono.* And there are more. Look here—"

"There is no time for this, Mr. Nomura," says Mikiko. "Come home. The war is over and you must address your people. They want to hear your voice. They need to see your face. You reassure them."

My people. Tens of thousands of survivors who walk the subterranean disaster hallways built by my senshi. They gathered here from all over the island. Their lives depend on the machines that I found or built or persuaded to join our side. A city of people who credit me with saving their lives, even knowing that everything I did, I did for Mikiko. Most don't care. They call themselves my people, and they call me emperor despite all my quirks.

In their rhymes, the children call me *Ring Shu Nomura.* Weird Uncle Nomura.

"But the people are no longer in danger," I say. "They have no need for me anymore. An old ring shu. I must continue listening to this . . . this voice of the sea. There is a pattern I must understand. It is important."

"So you have said," says Mikiko.

A slight frown creases the plastic over her eyes. She gazes at the flat, green horizon and the coatings on her pupil lenses briefly flash iridescent purple. "I do not like to see you here alone. It is dangerous. You do not pay attention, Mr. Nomura."

"Not so dangerous," I say, gesturing at the surf. A hundred yards out, the waves ripple over a narrow black skull that juts out just above the waterline. The amphibious biped is at least two feet taller than I am. It has been assisting me in placing my hydrophone.

"Oh," I squeak, noticing my headphones in the surf. I pull them out and shake off the salt water. Put them back over my ears and speak into the microphone.

"Junshi-88," I say. "You may return."

The freeborn turns and surges back toward shore. Water pours from the smooth planes of his camouflaged chest. The machine has been sloppily painted in a clear rust-proofing concoction that I scraped off the crablike land mines that the great akuma sent walking in from the surf by the thousands during the New War.

"Your people need a human being to lead them," says Mikiko. "I can protect them, but I cannot comfort them. They need you."

I look out to sea. Her hand slides from my shoulder.

"There is a message out there. I have to understand it."

"Yet I have listened and heard nothing."

"Because it's hidden in a *pattern*!" I exclaim, slapping the surf with one calloused hand. And now I hear it. The gritty clawing noise that was coming from the seawall. A coded voice trying to tell me something.

"This is not about a message," says Mikiko. "You lost them to the sea, and now you are trying—"

"Ssh!" I say.

I push my fingers into the cold surf. Wriggle them deep between the sandy pebbles. The tinny sound of grinding rocks is picked up by my hydrophone. I have heard this sound before but bigger, coming from farther out to sea. Coming from the abyssal plains east of the outermost seawall.

Closing my eyes, I cock my head to the side.

Cold seawater runs from the headphones down the back of my neck. I shiver and the frown on my face fades to a smile of satisfaction. I can see it now. The code is one step closer to being solved. I could not find a pattern to the voice of the sea because it is not a communication. It is rhythmic, however, and for a good reason.

Out to sea, not far from here, something very big is digging.

3. Others

Post New War: 3 Months, 17 Days

After marching with the reclaimed spider tank called Houdini for another six weeks, Cormac and Cherrah came across a harbinger of this new world of suffering. The wretched wartime experiments of Archos R-14 had left some humans severely modified. For these deformed people, finding a place among other survivors proved to be difficult and often deadly. Although the New War had united humankind, it was to last only for a brief time. Afterward, all the prejudices and fears endemic to humanity quickly returned.

—Arayt Shah

NEURONAL ID: CORMAC WALLACE

Houdini is alive. And not-alive.

I was there when we lost him. In the last push of the New War, a flood of stumpers swarmed our walker and detonated. The explosions sent the crippled tank careening into a snowbank, and when he fell this time, he didn't get back up. I saw his intention light fade to black.

I mourned his loss, and I left him behind.

But now the house-sized spider tank is plodding along with that old familiar gait. Cherrah and I can recognize his armored skin, but not whatever intelligence resurrected him. Despite our best efforts, we can't pin down the code that rerouted his systems and got him up and moving again. We can't find anything out of the ordinary, but somebody had to have reprogrammed this machine. The question that concerns me is whether it was somebody who did it, or something.

Eventually, we give up searching his code and do our best to repair the tank—he's our ticket home, after all.

Cherrah and I ride up top, on a gunnery platform behind the main turret. The walker can lumber along as fast as twenty miles per hour, maybe even faster, but it's jarring and loud and punishing. Instead, we shamble gently down overgrown highways at a nonstop ten miles per hour. We stride through dewy morning mist and then under the pounding afternoon sun. Eating scorched MREs as the grasshoppers fly between Houdini's legs and saplings brush against his belly. We are headed toward Gray Horse, toward our home, and sometimes we go for as long as fifteen hours a day.

Stopping doesn't feel safe.

Each night, we make camp under the great walker while it squats down in bunker mode. An endless Rob battery that we still don't understand hums in Houdini's chest. Massive plates of leg armor fold down, and that stubby turret occasionally whines, shifting in the still night as Houdini watches the darkness. Cherrah and I are all too aware that even these thick, scarred plates can be clawed through with enough time.

Even so, sleeping under Houdini's belly feels safe. I didn't realize how much I missed him—my weapon, my vehicle, and my home. At night, the heat radiates down from his hull, warming our little pocket of safety. In the soft greenish glow of Houdini's intention light, Cherrah peels off the polished pieces of her battle armor. Her dirty black hair cascades over freckled shoulders. We embrace in the dim light and I silently marvel at her transformation from soldier to woman.

We sleep huddled together, ears straining for furtive sounds out there in the empty wild. It reminds me of camping out with my brother when I was a kid—feeling the cold ground through my sleeping bag and hearing the strange night noises. The difference is that here there are no stars overhead, only Houdini's hastily repaired mesh belly net. Lying on my back, I look up at constellations of supplies: ammunition boxes, ration cans, loose clothes, vehicle parts, extra helmets, gun cleaning supplies, web cartridge belts, ponchos, bandages, canteens, and coils of scavenged wires and cables.

Everything we need to live.

The New War swept away our lives. It carried us across the country in flashes of violence. Stole my brother from me and gave me Cherrah. But the war forgot to leave behind any purpose or meaning. Resting on my back with ten tons of metal overhead to protect me from an infinite blackness crawling with mindless killing machines, I'm starting to find that I don't understand this new world.

I don't understand the point of it.

The only thing that makes real sense is the warm girl curled up next to me. The rise and fall of her breathing against my chest. She helps quiet all the bad thoughts that come slithering out of my head in the night. Fighting is easy. Sleeping is hard.

"The world is over, Cherrah," I tell her, in the night.

"Yeah," she says, head resting on a duffel bag that is her pillow.

"So now what?" I ask.

She is quiet for a long time, long enough that I assume she's gone to sleep.

"I think this is just part of it," she says. "Civilizations fall. People keep going."

"Best case," I say, "we scratch out a living hunting and farming. Hope every day for enough to eat. I don't see the point."

"The point of what?"

I don't want to say it. Don't want to put voice to such a terrible question. I know there's no good answer. "The point of going on living."

Cherrah shifts against me. She is shaking a little bit. I put a hand on her shoulder, concerned. Then I realize that she is laughing. She reaches back and roughly pats my ass. "Drama queen," she murmurs.

"I'm serious," I say, nestling my face into her hair. Sleep is almost on me now. The world feels huge outside. I'm crouched behind my own eyelids, both of them giant like the screen of a drive-in movie.

"Stop thinking, Cormac," says Cherrah. "I need you. That's enough."

"Yeah," I say, but I must not sound convinced.

"If you aren't sure whether you want to live . . . ," she says, turning to face me. "Try dying. Get back to me with how that goes."

We make human contact on a mountain pass in what used to be Washington. The roads are empty and we haven't seen any sign of habitation for days. I'm half asleep on the gunnery turret, watching the snow-kissed pines roll and sway. Houdini's half-filled belly net is creaking rhythmically with each step, like the rigging of an old ship. We're climbing in elevation and the wind is getting sharp, but I'm warm and drowsy inside my arctic-tested down jacket.

This overgrown highway cuts through endless columns of tall pines, climbing the pass one monotonous bend at a time. Mist creeps among the low branches on either side, nipping at the shoulders of the road. Looks like it's been years since anybody came through here. Dirt and mud are caked in tidal pools. We tread over a thin, sandy layer of muck like the bottom of a shallow sea, with vivid green pines rising up around us like kelp stretching for the surface.

Every now and then, I can make out the rusting remains of a car flipped over along the side of the road or impaled among the trees. These are the victims of those first few minutes of the New War. Horrible yawning moments when a hundred million vehicles became coffins and our relationship with technology shifted violently.

Watching the trees is how I spot the hidden compound.

A rusted old gate, suffocated with brush, hangs over a dirt road that branches off the old highway. For a split second, the faded road lines up and I'm able to see all the way down it from my high moving vantage point. I make out the mossy, sloping roof of a camouflaged building in the distance. From the ground, I never would have seen anything. Another second and I would have missed it.

"Hold up, Houdini," I call. Nothing happens right away. Not with a walker this size. He just starts moving slower and slower. Finally, Houdini takes one last wheezing step and comes to a stop. Birds call to each other over the rustle of the breeze.

"What's happening?" asks Cherrah.

"Camp. Two hundred meters into the woods," I say.

"Could be good scavenge," she says.

"Or survivors," I say.

"Way out here? Fat chance," she says.

We both turn as something disturbs the brush. The moist leafy saplings next to the road shiver as something scrambles through them.

Or someone. Cherrah swings around the big-caliber machine gun, her hands wrapped tight on the grips. I lean forward, staring. I catch the silhouette of a child. The kid is wearing dark goggles. His sharp shoulder blades are flashing, dirty elbows pumping as the boy runs over damp pine needles toward that half-collapsed building.

"Ho, Cherrah," I say. "It's a kid."

"No way," she says, leaning heavily into the grips and pointing the barrel straight up. She wipes her hands on her shirt.

"Well?" she says. "You take point and I'll cover, Bright Boy. Let's go say hello."

The primeval forest is still, a soaring cathedral, rich with the smell of earth and rotting leaves and chlorophyll. The rows of craggy trees are like silent, damp sentinels. The cold mist that glides among their roots forms a pale skirt that limits our tactical visibility.

Cherrah paces silently ten meters behind me, a light machine gun slung over her shoulder. She's carrying only one extra belt of ammo to keep the weight down. With the injured leg, she'd rather lay down cover fire from a fixed position than run and gun.

That's why I've got an M4 assault rifle on the low ready. Extra magazines of ammunition flop silently in the molly webbing on my chest protector.

"Rally point is Houdini," I whisper.

"Right-o," she says.

I glance behind us as the woods swallow Houdini. The big walker is standing as tall as it can to try to track us. His intention light glows a wary yellow. After about fifty meters, the narrow, soaring pines give way to fatter, lower hemlock trees that are covered in preternaturally green moss. Their branches reach down like shaggy claws.

I hear a bird whistle from Cherrah.

"Nine o'clock," she whispers.

Glancing over, I'm just in time to glimpse the boy as he pops up and dives through thick foliage. Too far away to shout at. He's intentionally skirting around us. Heading for the gaping entrance of the largest building, the doorway a dark slanting mouth wreathed in ivy.

I signal to Cherrah to be careful. An old barbed-wire fence has fallen down ahead of us. We gingerly step over the rusting barbs. Our footsteps are swallowed by spongy mounds of fallen pine needles. It smells good out here. Clean.

Like life is on the rebound.

The rest of the complex comes into view. Cheap sheets of corrugated metal thrown together into rambling structures. Planks of local wood have been cut and nailed together into boardwalks that lead through the brush from one crumbling structure to the next. At this elevation, the ground must be either snow or mud for most of the year.

I lead us in a zigzagging route toward the largest building. This is where the boy was headed. Along the way there are no human prints. No camp smoke in the sky or on the breeze. No garbage or voices or human waste. No real indication that anyone lives here at all.

Which is exactly the way human survivors would like to keep it.

We stop at the tree line before a small clearing. The main building squats fifty yards away on a bare treeless patch, its mold-eaten walls leaning. Made of brown stone and wood, the building gives me the feeling that it grew out of the dirt. At some point it was an old house, something out of "Hansel and Gretel," but now it's been added on to. Scabby flakes of paint dangle from plywood additions. The front entrance is a double door with a half-moon window above it. The glass is broken out and rust has eaten the door hinges.

Something thumps against the other side of the door.

Cherrah and I hold position. Rifle up, I go to a knee behind the nearest tree. Dew soaks into my jacket shoulder where I lean into the bark. The door shudders, hit by something from the inside. I flick the selector switch to semiautomatic with my thumb. Hear a quiet snick as Cherrah deploys the bipod on her machine gun.

The front door handle turns and the door begins to swing open. I put up a hand to tell Cherrah to hold fire. *It could be the boy,* I tell myself. *Please let it be the boy.* A widening crack appears between the two doors.

There is only blackness inside and now I feel that old familiar horror climbing up the back of my throat.

A face pushes out into the light.

I swallow as two unblinking camera eyes appear, twin reflections of the crisp morning sunlight. They are embedded in pale blue plastic skin, molded into a perpetual screaming smile. The blue casing is freckled, blooming with age spots of mold. A stringy coat of moss grows like a rash across its chest.

The Big Happy domestic robot steps out of the doorway and onto the small porch. Cocks its head sideways and starts a scan of the clearing. My mind is hit with memories as I watch that permanent smile, a rictus, slowly turning. I thought these memories were gone. In Boston, on that first day it happened, my brother and I saw these smiles everywhere we looked. My brain tasted the horror of it and withdrew, refused to remember the atrocities.

The Big Happies. They're filling the garbage trucks with bodies, Jack, and they're dumping them off the bridge. The people are falling, Jack. Jackie? *Shut up, Cormac. Keep moving.*

I raise a hand and clench it into a fist. Extend my index finger and drop it twice. *Fire.*

Blow this fucker away.

Cherrah flops forward, resting the gun's bipod on a fallen log. She yanks back the bolt and digs the stock into her shoulder. Takes a breath and then lets her gun stutter. A couple of dozen rounds climb the humanoid robot's torso. Impacts chewing up the plastic shell, spraying the entrance with smoking shards. The Big Happy stumbles awkwardly and drops onto its chest, head still scanning.

"Hold it!" calls a voice from behind us.

"Six o'clock," I say to Cherrah, already moving.

"Target down," comes her clipped reply. She stops firing the big gun and I dart between trees to her position, eyes on the forest behind her. I've got my rifle on the high ready, elbow tucked and one eye peering down the gun sights, scanning the trees for targets. Down low, Cherrah has drawn her sidearm and left the bipod aimed toward the main building.

"Settle down now, buddy!" comes a shout. The voice is hoarse, strained. An older man, and I think I see his tree now.

I glance down at Cherrah. She shrugs, in a crouch, eyes on the woods out in front of our log. I'm watching the big tree behind us, gun out, waiting for the owner of the voice to appear so I can put a round in him.

"Hello?" I call.

"I'm just saying, don't shoot unless you want to get shot at," comes the reply. "Let's all be friendly, how about?"

"There's Rob activity," I call.

A face slides out from behind the tree. A human face. An older man with shaggy gray-black hair and an unkempt gray beard. His hands are up, calloused palms showing.

"That's just Hugh. We sent him over to take a closer look at you all," says the man. He puts a finger onto his temple and talks lower. "Damage status? Got it. Repairs incoming. Joey, get over to Hugh and take care of him."

I lower my weapon slightly.

"What are you doing out here?" I ask.

The man grins and turns his head. Part of his skull is hairless and metallic. It's been removed and replaced with finely wrought black metal. "We're modified," he says. "And I hope you don't mind, for your sake."

I turn my rifle and let it hang from my chest strap. Help Cherrah stand up. She retrieves the machine gun, brushing dirt and pine needles off it. I point at the broken Big Happy and Cherrah nods, keeps one eye on it. It doesn't pay to let down your guard.

"I don't mind," I say quietly. "A survivor is a survivor."

"You two are from that Oklahoma army, aren't you?"

"That's right."

"I could tell from what's left of your uniform. You all are good people. It's why we haven't killed you."

"Is that right?" I ask, my rifle still heavy hanging over my chest. I guess my eyes must slide toward the piece. The old man raises his hands and waves them in an "ah, phooey" gesture.

"Not trying to threaten. But yes, that's right."

"Do you need assistance? Do your people have enough supplies?" I ask.

"It'll be close. Winters are rough this high up, but there are plenty of deer in these woods. We'll grow crops in the spring. The most important thing is that the machines had us well defended. Now that they're gone, we've got some control over the old defenses. These days, that's all that matters."

Of course, this used to be a Rob work camp.

"Why do you need defenses?" I ask. "The war is over."

"You've been off trekking, son. Otherwise you'd know better than to say that. The war has just begun for us, out here. Lot of survivors aren't so friendly to the modified. It's people we worry about, you understand?"

Something moves onto the porch, crouching over the fallen Big Happy. It's a woman's corpse, flesh rotting from limbs that are creased by black metal bars. There is a parasite wedged into the back of her neck, and I can see her teeth through a hole in her cheek. I take a deep breath. The parasites *lived.* That thing must be Joey.

I'm sorry, Lark, I think to myself. I remember how the Cherokee soldier came stumbling back out of the Alaskan woods, wearing one of those things. And then I shot his face off. *My God, I'm so sorry.*

"It was a modified who saved us all. Did you know that?" says Cherrah. "A little girl named Mathilda Perez. She guided the final assault on Archos R-14. Without her we could never have won."

The man grins. "We did hear that. Most people don't believe it. From the description, though, that little girl sounded like she had a full orbital prosthetic plugged into her prefrontal cortex with hardwired radio and infrared capabilities."

Cherrah and I share a glance.

"How did you know that?" I ask.

"Tim?" he calls. "Timmy, pop up for a sec."

Nothing happens. The grizzled man leans and speaks quietly. "He's skittish because someone's been . . . Well, someone has been after the children specifically. Hunting the ones with eye prosthetics. Killing them. Timmy has heard the other kids over the radio. Begging."

Over around the side of the house, a small face peeks out. It's the boy we followed in. The one who I thought had on goggles.

"Come on," says the man. "It's all right."

The boy steps into a shaft of sunlight. He lifts his chin and now I see he isn't wearing goggles. His eyes are missing altogether. Instead, a flat black strip of metal stripes his face across the bridge of his nose.

"Timmy here saw you all coming from miles away," says the old man. "Sees everyone coming for miles and miles. Everything. Man and machine."

"How?" asks Cherrah.

The old man shrugs, a smile creasing into his face behind the shaggy salt-and-pepper beard.

"Your tank," says the boy. "Houdini. When he talks, it looks like ribbons in the sky."

"He can't talk," I say. "Houdini is just a tank."

"Well, he talked to me," says Timmy, nonchalant.

The kid steps farther into the clearing and is followed by someone who must be his mother. A whole group of people emerges from inside. Some have shining prosthetics instead of limbs. Arms, legs, and joints. They are men and women, young and old, but all of them are rail thin. Big sunken eyes and yellowing teeth.

"You can come with us, you know," I say, looking at their leader with dismay. "Our walking armor can protect us back to Gray Horse. They know the truth about how the war ended. They won't have a problem with . . . modifications."

The old man is already shaking his head. "No offense, but nothing is for sure out there. In here, we've got protection. And plenty of it."

Something catches the corner of my eye. A stealthy movement. The bushes are moving oddly. I watch, rifle dangling from my chest strap, and fight to keep from reaching for it. Instead, I raise my voice.

"If any of you here want to leave, I can guarantee you safe passage," I call to the group. "And if there isn't enough food here, then you've got to come with us. I'm not negotiating."

"Oh, neither am I," says the gray-haired man.

Now I identify the movement: turrets. Three of them, flat and low. Sprouting up slowly from the turf on elevated gun assemblies. On top, each one is covered in a platter of dead leaves and grass and earth. Underneath, each has a minigun with a stubby six-barrel cluster peeking out ominously. They are glistening with gun oil and polished, obviously well maintained.

When those barrels start spinning, I'll start running.

"You were prisoners before, but that's over with," I say. "Big Rob is dead. We killed it. There won't be any more experiments. No more torture. You can all leave. You're free to go."

Emaciated faces stare back at me. Whatever comprehension might be there is swallowed by the horrors that have been inflicted on these people. The young ones cling to the bony legs of their parents. And the older ones—well, I hope they heal.

The old man limps out of the woods and moves between us and the group. He steps closer to me and talks low: "You haven't seen what we've seen. Rob is not our problem. People are our problem. It's best that you move on. We thank you for your service. We really do. But this thing has turned into a whole other can of worms."

"Let's go," says Cherrah, quietly.

I don't move as she takes my arm. Pulls me gently. For a few steps, I stumble backward without taking my eyes off those people. My mind is racing, trying to determine the right thing to say. Without Big Rob to maintain this camp, winter is going to come here and it's going to kill them. How would a hero save the lives of these innocent people? What would my brother, Jack, have done?

But I don't see any way besides fighting. Jack would have found a way, but I'm not him. No matter how much I wish I were.

Cherrah and I walk back to the road together where Houdini waits patiently. Not looking back, we stow our gear in his belly net. I drop a couple of boxes of MREs onto the road. What we can spare. Then we climb the metal rungs and take up our touring positions.

Standing high on Houdini's gunnery platform, I peer into the icy woods. Survey the thin, hungry faces watching from dappled shadows around the compound. Sunken eyes and fleshy ears sprouting from skin that is stretched too tight over skulls. It's hard to shake the empty feeling in those faces. As if they don't belong to human beings at all. Just masks of meat on top of walking zombies.

"Come on, Cormac," urges Cherrah. "It's time to move out."

"Jack," I mutter. He was my brother and he died for me and just saying his name out loud hurts like a pocketknife twisting into my lungs. I blink my eyes and the strands of broken people waver behind a layer of warm salt water. "Jack Wallace would have done something for them. He wouldn't leave these people like this."

"You're not Jack," says Cherrah. "We did what we could, Bright Boy. Walk on, Houdini."

The quadruped powers up, his intention light flaring briefly. Those scarred ropes of black muscle flex and contract, high-tension cables singing.

"Wait," calls a thin voice. It's the boy. Timmy.

Up close, I estimate that he is probably ten or twelve, but physically he looks about eight years old. Looking down at him, my gaze goes straight to where his eyes aren't. I glance away automatically, then force myself to stare directly back at his deformity. I never did meet Mathilda Perez in person—I only listened to her intelligence reports over the radio—but I doubly appreciate what she did now that I see the metal rooted in the skin above this little boy's freckled cheeks.

It looks like it hurts.

The boy walks confidently toward us. Stops at Houdini's scorched foreleg. Fearlessly, he puts a palm flat against the polymer-muscled slab. Looking Houdini up and down, he cocks his head to the side sort of funny. His thin little lips are moving.

This kid isn't blind. Far from it.

"What can I do for you?" I call down. He ignores me for another few seconds. Still talking to the voice in his head. Finally, he stops and points his face at me.

"Houdini is smart, you know," he says. "He wants to protect you."

"Serious? You can really talk to the tank?" asks Cherrah.

"Yeah, but only when he's close," says the boy.

"Ask Houdini how he was repaired," she says.

Timmy bows his head. After a moment, he looks up apologetically. "He says that he doesn't know."

A thought occurs to me. Mathilda said she was in New York City, watching from satellites as she guided Gray Horse Army through the arctic woods toward that unmarked hole in the ground. She said she used an antenna to reach us. A big one.

"Tim, have you ever touched an antenna?"

"Antenna?" asks the kid.

"Any kind of big piece of metal. I think you'll be able to . . . talk to people farther away. If you find an antenna."

"I can try . . . ," he says, nodding solemnly.

"If you do find one," I say, "look for a girl named Mathilda. Mathilda Perez of Gray Horse Army. She's one of the good guys. She can show you how to use those eyes to help your people here."

He nods. Drags a foot across the dirt. Stalling.

"You have something else to say?" I ask.

The kid scratches his neck. Looks away, then peers up.

"I just noticed . . . I thought I should say . . ."

"Go on," I urge.

"There's something inside you," he says quietly. His voice is clear and sharp out here on the still road. The words he's said stop my breathing.

Something inside me?

I throw a leg over the railing and slide off the armored side of the tank. Drop to the muddy road right in front of the boy. He doesn't flinch. Cherrah follows, lowers herself onto the dirt next to me. We stand before the boy in the shadow of Houdini. The kid is so small that I kneel just to keep from intimidating him.

Assuming I *can* intimidate him.

"What do you see inside me?" I ask. "Is it Rob-made?"

"Not you," he says, pointing. "Her."

Cherrah and I exchange a worried glance. She slowly steps forward. Takes both the kid's hands in hers.

"What's inside me, Timmy?" she asks him.

The boy wraps his arms around Cherrah's waist and presses his face against her stomach. Instinctively, she puts her hands around his thin back. Gives him a tender hug that makes his shoulder blades stick out like chicken wings. The kid inhales and his breath shudders on the way out.

You haven't seen what we've seen.

Finally, the boy stands up straight. Blinks.

"It's a baby," he says. "A little baby boy."

4. Mind of Life

Post New War: 5 Months, 19 Days

During the New War, Nomura Castle was well defended against the incursion of attacking robots (called akuma *by the locals). Mr. Takeo Nomura, who was responsible for building this lifesaving defensive structure, nevertheless did not seem to want any part of ruling the people he had protected. Some of his followers believed that he was shirking his duty as he turned his attention to the sea, and others felt that he should be allowed to move on. But even from afar, I suspected that the old man had found something momentous waiting in the depths of the ocean.*

—Arayt Shah

NEURONAL ID: TAKEO NOMURA

What is a mind, but a pattern? My mind or yours. Man or machine. Simply an arrangement of atoms. Each of us, a unique expression of the mind of the universe.

Thoughts are precise bullets of electricity, fired through our neurons in timed pulses. Our bodies are layers of folding skin and muscle laced with fractal lightning. Natural, like veins on a rain-soaked leaf. Cracks in a tumbling stone. Or the sigh of this wave, lapping my shins until they are cold and numb. The clear liquid flows in, suspends the fine black hairs on my legs, and then retreats, laying the hairs down in new configurations. The sky leaks raindrops over my bony shoulders like Morse code.

We are patterns. Trapped inside other patterns.

After six months of listening, the sea sends an emissary. The towering bulk of a bizarre machine approaches our outermost seawall. A glistening spire, afloat, the size of a skyscraper. It forges ahead, slow and steady, through azure stripes of rain. From the salt encrusted on it, I would say it came from the open ocean. The dreamer only knows what this derelict has been doing out there on those endless blue plains.

I am staggered by its layered complexity.

Half submerged in Tokyo harbor, the spire is saturated with living things. It sprouts so far into the heavens that its upper reaches are shrouded in the rain haze. Some kind of muscular fiber makes up the main trunk, braided thick as the Tokyo Skytree, resembling bark but clearly with much higher tensile strength. It bears further study, as does the stability mechanism. The island-machine flutters delicately on flat fins the size of baseball fields, rising and falling, surfaces curling with wet sea grass on top and studded with barnacles below. Each pulse of the surf surges over the lip of the rear fin and washes straight through the marshy ecosystem.

"It is beautiful," I say to Junshi-88.

The humanoid robot stands in the surf with me, trinocular lenses protruding at maximum zoom. It wears no human clothing, only a camouflaged green and black armored outer casing. Spurning human adornments is a mark of autonomy.

I hear the raucous squawking of seagulls from here. Hundreds of them circle the treelike structure, hunting the fish that swarm below in its safe harbor. The birds are nesting in the upper branches and have been for many generations, it seems, above clouds of insects. The fiber base is shit-stained and covered in seaweed, riddled with dens and nests and burrows. The voice of the sea has manifested itself to me in the most enormous and ancient form of life possible.

"Do you think it is *shinboku*?" I ask.

"Hai," says the 88, its voice a grinding whine. Unlike the generations of overly polite robots that populated Japan before the New War, my freeborn ally is barely willing to speak in human audible frequencies, much less exercise impeccable manners. He is his own, not a servant, and there is no risk of my forgetting it.

I nod vacantly, staring. It must be a form of shinboku, a divine tree, honored by the monks and called upon to protect Shinto shrines. This mightiest of shinboku is beached here, as if lost from some other dimension. It forms a pattern so intricate that it places a gentle flame of awe into the pit of my belly. I am glad that I can simply coexist with a thing of such beauty and complexity. The shinboku has come from the unknowable flat wasteland of the open ocean, through tides of war, crafted by the voice of the sea and now sent into our harbor.

My equipment detects communications being relayed from hidden antennae located in the upper reaches of the tree. I slide a pair of modified binoculars over my eyes. Flip on a radio overlay of my own design. Scan the patterns until I find an alcove, nestled in the top. Some kind of control center is perched in the crook of two large branches, its entrance covered by sweeping vines. The binoculars reveal radio communications floating from the tower. Greenish wisps of communication meander over infinite glittering waves, to the horizon.

The voice of the sea is speaking.

I tap the 88 on its shoulder and we return to our little boat. Continue puttering up the Sumida River toward Nomura Castle. Behind us, the swaying island-tower watches balefully from where it rises out of the bay, the size of a movie monster *kaiju*.

Reaching the top of the shinboku will not be easy. I will need to retrieve my best tools if I wish to climb the tree of life. And returning to my workshop is, unfortunately, complicated. Mikiko will be there and she will disapprove of this mission. My place is on the throne, she says. I made my people a promise to protect them. I haven't been back to the castle in weeks, staying on the streets with the Junshi-88.

The darkness settled over my people in the last months like silent falling strips of black silk. In the field of optics, they call the phenomenon a "just noticeable difference threshold." A slight darkening of things. Each tiny gradation impossible to perceive.

Until the suicides began.

One month ago, I returned from a night expedition to the bay. In the frigid predawn, I had just docked my little wooden motorboat on the river. Junshi-88 was walking behind me in quiet pneumatic steps. It stopped. Ground out a verbal warning in Robspeak. My eyes lifted from the roadway and thoughts of the roiling sea evaporated.

A curious sight.

Nomura Castle lies on a small hill, giving it a view of the surrounding Adachi Ward. Scarred and leaning, its curtained walls of flash-welded steel and iron surround a star-shaped central keep. The roof of the castle is a curved square, the roofline bowed, edges thrusting out angrily like the horns of a *kabutomushi* beetle.

A little fellow was standing on the sweeping arch of the keep tower, his body sheathed in layers of hazy morning light, face empty, taking deep, slow breaths. Fish-scale flakes of armored roofing winked around him and I remember the roosting pigeons were giving him polite space.

"Not good, Junshi," I murmured.

The crack of the young man's bones on the castle steps was like the report of a pistol. We hurried to his body and tried our best to move him into a respectful position. With the fighting over, I could not imagine why the man would step away from this life. The akuma offer no more threat. But the war must have torn holes in our hearts. When it ended, no hope arrived to fill them.

"You must be very sad and lonely," I whispered to the corpse. "But your friends will come for you soon and they will help put you to rest." Junshi-88 blinked at me, processing my words. I do not know if it understood. By treating the dead as if they are living, we give them respect. We make life easier for those who remain.

Junshi-88 helped me arrange the body and did not complain. I do not fear to touch a dismantled machine. On that morning I learned that this bravery can go the other way, too.

The young man was not the first to leap. Nor was he the last. Many of my people are falling. They are drowning. Hanging and suffocating and burning. I cannot say why my people are leaving us. I have never been good with emotions. But I can feel the wrongness of the empty act. The despair and meaninglessness that have settled over us like still, glassy water.

Without an enemy, we are falling forward. Nothing to push against. Flailing into empty space. We do not know how to start over. There is no route back to the beginning. The pattern of the world is torn. Living in the ruins of our memories is painful, and many would rather die.

My people may despair, but I do not.

For many years I have lived in a bare room with a woman and a workbench. A lamp and a chair and well-oiled tools spread out on a reed mat. Warm fingers on my shoulders. Hot tea. The bright smell of washed hair and the warm lingering scent of the soldering iron. It is a world of hope. From in here I can see the tools of rebirth everywhere. Each mangled wire or melted scrap is another piece of the puzzle.

I say a prayer as I cross the square where that nameless young man stepped out of the world. Beside me, 88 marches dutifully. The awakened military humanoid is a chilly friend. Never a recipient of my services. But Mikiko asked it to protect me, and as a freeborn, 88 takes her command very seriously. It required two nights before I became used to having it watch me sleep.

"There he is," calls someone. "Nomura!"

"What is in the harbor!?"

"Are we under attack!?"

My people are gathered. Each measured shout sends my head ducking lower and puts an extra scurry in my steps. Junshi-88 clears the way as we trot up the sweeping promenade of steel steps. They have been destroyed and repaired in a cycle these last three years. Burrowed under, demolished, heat-blasted, and soaked in the blood and oil of our defenders. The enemy akuma never made it inside. Not after that first time.

No one tries to stop my passage. I glance up, just once, and see that there are hundreds of my people outside the closed doors to the throne room. They are milling around and talking to each other in concerned whispers. A hush shudders through them like a wake as 88 pushes a path through.

I am not good at talking to them. Head down, as usual, I climb the steps. My workshop is still located in the main hall, on the same spot where I first knelt and began to work on a nearby senshi robot arm. Back when this place was an abandoned factory and not a shining fortress.

The 88 and I enter through an arched front door made of crosshatched steel beams. The fortified door gleams like the armored scales of some giant prehistoric fish. It was built by the great crane-arm senshi that rests now, coiled and deadly, high against the ceiling of what is now the throne room.

Slipping inside, I pad across the vast space. A neat corridor of senshi honor guard flanks the path to the throne. Each robot arm is folded in a salute, coated in glistening, nail polish–red paint. My terra-cotta army, always capable of animating, but not called on to defend the central keep in more than a year. Are they unhappy to be without purpose now? I wonder. Or will the time soon come again when they must build?

The scrap-metal throne is empty.

I leave the 88 behind and trot around the throne. My table and lamp are shoved against the stone foundation of the dais. Polished steel flooring whispers under my paper sandals. My amorphous reflection spreads below like a dark puddle on the metal. Quiet now. A little farther and I can make it out without alerting Mikiko.

Hastily, I stuff the tools I will need into a brown canvas backpack. Ransacking my work desk, I pull out all manner of tools and trinkets. Soon the bag is bulging. Last thing, I grab my trusty toolbox and tuck it under my other arm.

"Mr. Nomura," calls Mikiko.

Her voice stills my feet. My queen steps out from behind the dais that supports our thrones. I cannot remember the last time I climbed those steps to sit on that ostentatious chair. At some point, it has been decorated with a fan spray of sharp, twisting scrap metal, collected from our destroyed city.

"Mikiko," I whisper.

"Did you notice your people outside?" she asks.

"Oh, uh. No," I reply. "Too busy, in any case."

Mikiko does not react to my obvious lie.

"Listen to me now. I cannot stop this darkness. The survivors need a human being to lead them. Someone who understands the despair they feel. An emperor."

"No time," I say.

"The rate of suicide is increasing," she says. "I do not know how to help them. They need a purpose. You gave them that, once."

"I've got to get back to the harbor," I say.

"What are you afraid of, Takeo? Really?"

The question lingers, her synthetic voice echoing.

"Very busy," I whisper, taking a step.

As I turn to go, she speaks: "My darling, you will never find what you have lost. The answers you seek are not in the sea. They are in here."

I stop moving. My skin has gone cold. I am thinking of those wide, round little eyes. The crushing press of the wave against my back.

"It's . . . a shinboku," I say, voice shaking. "In the harbor. The voice of the sea has sent it here to me. I must find out why."

"The platform that washed up? It is an artifact of war. Broken and derelict."

"I am curious," I whisper.

So difficult to explain, these patterns in my mind. The razed remains of Tokyo and the phantom images of buildings that are gone. The wailing ghosts of millions of dead, their bodies churned under the ground and burned to smoke on the wind and swept out to the bottom of the sea.

I need to understand it. I need to find the meaning in it.

"Trust me, my love," I say. "The voice of the sea—"

"Is in your imagination!" she shouts. Her voice echoes from the thick rib supports that hold up the vast arched ceiling. "I am losing you to the past. To the same despair that is taking your people. Stop this madness. Come back, Emperor Nomura. Do your *duty*."

Now there is exquisite emotion on her face. Anger and sadness. I know she places it there for me alone, an affectation. Each careless wrinkle on her face, every strand of gray in her hair puts a thumping into my heart. Passion and dread. I try to imagine returning to her side and ignoring the voice calling to me from the sea.

She is her own and you know it, old man. You are going to lose her.

The thought makes my fingertips numb, puts a thickness in my throat and a warm waiting tide behind my eyes. I cannot face it.

"This is my duty to myself," I whisper, and scurry away.

Watching your feet is not the best way to survive. Crossing the picked-over remains of Koto Ward, I do not notice the danger until it is almost too late. I am passing through a half-collapsed concrete office building that lies in the shadow of the shinboku. Junshi-88 is outside, testing the path ahead—over and through the rubble of the old shipping district. Leftover killing machines are seldom attracted to the 88's lack of body heat or its unnaturally heavy and long step vibrations. The pitter-patter of my feet is just right for certain varieties of the simple machines, however.

I am alerted by a noise like a whale surfacing for a breath. *Psssh.* An oddly beautiful sound. Turning, I see a blur of quivering antennae and skittering forelimbs across the room. A type of killing machine that we call a cricket lands in the doorway. Another one, the size of a fist, punches through a pane of dirty glass and bounces lightly over the concrete. I hear the noises again, outside. I cannot help it and I make a small moan. The newly arrived crickets immediately orient toward my sound and heat.

The cricket is a subspecies of the stumper, a crawling land mine. The difference is that the cricket uses a piston to launch itself short distances. It glides on stubby wings, highly explosive, attracted to body heat. More gray blurs are clustering on the window panes. Some are coming through, landing on shards of shining glass.

It is nothing personal. This is simply their design.

The heavy bag over my left shoulder is balanced by the toolbox strapped over my other shoulder. In wobbling steps, I move into a slightly cooler shadow. The crickets spread out behind me, reflexively self-organizing as they forage. Junshi-88 is already outside, facing me through the far doorway but not knowing how to react. I wave my hand at it. *Be still and wait outside, please. There is a good chance I will survive.*

The wooden ceiling joists of this building have bloated and splintered like an old locust shell left behind on a tree. The cavernous room is filling with the echoes of scraping armored legs and the tap of antennae as they spread out, picking their way over rain-streaked concrete.

Hands shaking, I reach into my bag.

I clamp my fingers onto a black stick. Pull it out and hold each end in one hand. With a quick twist of my wrists, I activate the joist-seeker. Two struts pop out of each end, forming a hand-sized H. Each strut has a small rotor attached. I hold the device up, fingers clamped to its narrow body as the quad-rotor helicopter powers up.

When I let go, it remains hovering in place.

The crickets pause midstep, listening to the low hum of the spinning rotor blades. I turn my face away as the seeker blinks at the room with a scanning laser. It gently buzzes away toward the ceiling, sending a waft of air washing over my neck.

I scurry away while they are distracted. A gray shape flutters past me like a slow-motion bullet, missing my arm by a half meter. It thunks into the wall and bounces off as light from the doorway hits my face. Junshi-88 is a dark blur outside, poised but waiting patiently. Inside, the seeker is calculating the weakest geometric point of the joists that hold up the damaged building. These flying sticks are how we demolished much of the akuma-riddled Adachi Ward when we needed to create a clear perimeter.

I hurry through the bright door.

Three meters into the front yard, I hear the echo of a warning siren from the joist-seeker. I count down from three in my head. Even so, the concussion surprises me, and I stumble. Staggering, I keep to my feet as the shock wave turns to heat and the broken building crumples in on itself. A simple task of spotting the structural weak points and removing them. Math and equations and explosions.

A series of smaller explosions carve pockmarks as the crickets explode under rubble. The swarm is happy again. More crickets are streaming out of their hiding holes. Piston-launching their cheaply made carapaces into the smoldering heat.

"*Moshimoshi*, 88," I say, greeting the machine. "We continue."

"Head up," says the 88, watching over my shoulder for a long second, making sure no more curious remnants are filtering out of the broken city. Before us, the shinboku rises out of the harbor like the wet bones of a leviathan. Twisting in the wind, slow and inevitable in its advance to shore. Drops of rain weep from the treelike branches that sway high above. A deep, almost subsonic, moaning emanates from the structure as those field-sized petals churn slowly in the surf. One petal is already wedged partially onto the shore, grass fluttering.

The divine tree leans and the small alcove I saw before is almost directly above us, lost in a tangle of vines.

On unsteady legs, I walk out into the wet marsh area. Insects flutter past my face, not all of them natural. Many of the animals and insects here are artificial. I resist the urge to sit down in the muck and study my immediate vicinity.

Instead, I pull a ratty collage of thin parachute cord out of my bag. The cord is attached to an old board, driftwood once, with two holes drilled in it and the rope wrapped through. I carefully lower myself to one knee. Allow myself one small groan as my back creaks angrily.

Ah well, an old mind is worth old legs.

I lay the board flat on the damp ground. Kneel in the shadow of the 88 and loop all the rope I have together in a neat coil. Finally, I turn my canvas sack upside down and a bundle of stiff black legs falls out. Using a carabiner, I snap the coil of rope to the black thing's body. It is a climbing device made from something that was once called a tickler.

My own modified design, never tested above two stories.

In both hands, I pick up the tangle of cord. Pinch the scruff of the tickler's neck with one hand. Four longer articulated legs dangle. I move my hands over the device and check each part. A yank on each of the climbing legs. A twist of the spooler. And a press of the power button.

Bright laser targeting emanates from the device. Tongue peeking from my mouth, I aim the intense, coin-sized green dot into the upper reaches of the shinboku. Train it on the spot where I know the alcove is located.

The target blinks three times.

"Climb," I whisper, standing. Underhanded, I grunt as I toss the machine straight up. It catches onto the stalk and begins its ascent. As it goes, I hear only the seagoing creak of fiber as the whole platform sways in massive, incomprehensible locomotion.

I sit on the board as the coil of rope steadily unravels into the sky. Feed the rope so it does not catch as the wind blows it like spider silk. The tickler climbs the vines and branches with uncanny precision and speed. It is a black streak, like the reverse beam of a flashlight raking up the side of the tower.

"If I am killed, please return to Mikiko and tell her what happened," I say.

"Hai," says 88.

Then the rope catches, pulls the board tight against my thighs. Toolbox over my shoulder, I cling to the rope with both hands. Somewhere, the spooler is activated. As I rise, swinging, the mold-green Junshi-88 stands expectantly below me.

"Farewell, Junshi," I say, and I am lifted dangling into the air.

Holding the rope tightly, I squeeze my eyes shut. Listen to the wind sigh through the tentaclelike vines. The sound of lapping waves soon recedes. The air cools and sounds fade as the tickler's rasping spooler reels me up in a steady motion. Peeking, I see arched, hooded microwave transmitters clustered in the branches.

I do not dare to look down.

Finally, I reach the alcove. It is just a Y-shaped crease in the thick vines. A narrow flat surface inside. Wide enough for only a few people. Squinting into the featureless haze of gray sky, I spot the silhouettes of antennae overhead. Fiberlike cables snake like vines over the limbs. All of them connect in a single nexus, here in this alcove.

I scramble inside. Try to ignore the breathtaking drop as I pull my toolbox off my shoulder and drop it onto the fiber-woven floor. On my knees, hunched over, I pry at the wires. Allow the music of the circuits to speak to my hands. I place a directional antenna on the ground and swivel it around with a finger. The finder beeps quietly, scanning the direction of radio transmissions to and from the shinboku.

While the finder works, I plug a diagnostic computer into the mainline antenna. Tap a direct line into the shinboku transmissions. Sets of encrypted data flutter over the line. On a whim, I plug in a small microphone, squeeze the transmit handle, and speak.

"Who are you?" I ask.

Nothing happens. The finder beeps quietly, homing in on a location out to sea. Then, a shiver runs through the tree. Groans form somewhere deep inside the platform. And text appears on my battery-powered display. The luminescence races like green flame across the dusty screen. Strange words appear.

I am the eternal spread of life across the abyss. I am the whole. The vastness.

It reminds me of speaking to the great akuma. But this is a different mind. This transmission has arrived from the open ocean. I adjust a knob to home in on the exact location. I will find this voice.

"I shall call you Ryujin," I say. "After the dragon god of the sea."

In ancient times, it was not uncommon for men to speak with the gods. The minds of the earth and sea and sky were once present to mortals. Great wars shook the planet. Wars that determined whether our ancestors would live or die.

"We have been finding new creatures. Not natural and not unnatural. Are you the one who is making them?" I ask it.

Yes.

"Why?"

To replace you when you are gone.

A breeze is building. The platform is moving now, swinging slightly.

"Ryujin-sama, why do you say this? Who seeks to attack us?"

Not you. The enemy seeks the awakened ones. They will die in their mountain stronghold. Feasting on their power, a shallow mind shall grow deep. This thing called Arayt will exterminate the freeborn, and then *humankind.*

The platform is swinging now. Seagulls shriek at the groaning of the deep struts. Something is wrong.

"What can we do?" I ask.

You. Can. Die.

Slipping, I grab hold of a vine and cling to the shinboku. Long ago, men bargained with the gods. Those times have come again, I think.

"No! Not acceptable. Can you help stop this?"

Yes.

"Will you?"

Perhaps.

I am clinging to the vines now, my right arm entwined. The little wooden board bangs somewhere. The horizon is rising and falling, wind ripping at my clothes as this titanic machine tries to shake me off like a flea.

The finder is beeping wildly, keyed in on Ryujin's location. Impossible. A far-off point on the bottom of the sea. All transmissions are being delivered piecemeal to clusters spread out over the abyssal plains in the depths.

"What do you demand, Ryujin?!" I ask. "Name it."

A pattern.

"What pattern?" I ask.

Slammed against the alcove wall, the microphone slips out of my free hand and falls. I wrap both my arms around the vines, but they are slick and wet. A sandal slips off my foot and I watch it pinwheel away into the empty sky. Below, the entire bay is frothing with the thrashing of this colossal beast.

"What pattern!?" I shout.

What is a mind, but a pattern? I think.

The computer has slipped away. Ryujin can no longer hear me.

Lunging, I scoop up my finder and sling on my toolbox. Yank the board to me by its damp rope and sit on it. The tickler is still buried above, holding on tight. Leaning over the void, sitting on the board, I glance the vista of a ruined Tokyo.

Time to go—before the shinboku tears itself apart.

A final swing of the trunk sends the diagnostic computer clattering back toward me. Just before it plummets over the side, I catch sight of a final sentence scrolling across the display. A wail grows in my chest as I read Ryujin's last words to me.

Give me the one who sings . . . the mother of the freeborn.

5. What Else Is There?

Post New War: 10 Months, 16 Days

During three long years of war, the city of Gray Horse earned a reputation as a bastion of civilization in a barbaric, violent world. It retained that reputation for only a short time in the New War's aftermath, under the rule of my puppet Hank Cotton. It was surprisingly easy to shatter the unity forged in battle between men of all creeds and color. Cormac Wallace arrived back to Gray Horse hoping for a return to peace and normalcy—a chance to live. What he learned is that there never was such a thing as living. There was always only survival.

—Arayt Shah

NEURONAL ID: CORMAC WALLACE

Gray Horse. Home of the brave. Land of the free.

But not from where I'm standing.

With pneumatic puffs, Houdini tramps up the narrow switchback road that winds up the stone bluff and eventually leads into the drum clearing where this all began. The walker's clawed feet are stained up to the ankle joints with red mud from dozens of abandoned farms on the outskirts of the Gray Horse plateau. We've passed acres of crops that look to have been untended for weeks. Hardly any human beings in sight, just the humped shapes of dead bison rotting in the fields.

The empty farms were a disturbing sight, but we didn't stop to check them out. Houdini's mended belly net is slack, flapping without any supplies left. You can't afford to slow down when you're running on fumes.

Cherrah and I are in our usual spot up on the turret deck. We still wear our combat fatigues and body armor. It's all we've got. Looking out at the occasional scowling faces, I'm starting to wish we had something more friendly to put on. I feel like we should be waving a big white flag. It strikes me as odd that I've seen only native faces so far. Men, women, and children, and they look tired and angry. Something has gone wrong here. Some trauma. A lot of people are missing from Gray Horse.

"This is not the homecoming I was expecting," says Cherrah.

She has on a brave face, but rests one gloved hand protectively over her round belly. It's been seven months of slow travel since the sighted kid told us about our little boy. Now would be early, but we both know that the baby could show up any day.

"Lonnie will explain what's going on," I say. "We'll get you to the hospital and off your feet. Then I'll go find him. Relax."

I hear a shrill whistle from up the hill.

"Don't relax yet, maybe," I say.

At the top of the bluff, we round the final corner and reach the wide-open dancing circle. The space has been turned into a staging ground for the Gray Horse Army. Spider tanks, gleaming and polished, rest on their haunches in neat rows. Hundreds of soldiers are broken into smaller squads: practicing marching drills, eating chow in a long tent at picnic tables, and organizing scavenged supplies. Others are off duty, sitting relaxed, cleaning weapons and checking ammunition. For the first time today, I see nonnative faces: white, black, and Latino soldiers.

Houdini stops.

The scarred old battle tank seems to be taking in the scene. It stands tall and weather-beaten and half crippled, staring down dozens of its freshly repaired former comrades. The other spider tanks are familiar old warhorses with patched armor and touched-up insignias: Jack of Spades, Mauler, Nemo, Brutus.

My throat tightens with nostalgia, remembering the march to Alaska. I never really believed I'd see these soldiers again after Cherrah and I stayed behind to write *The Hero Archive* and our rendezvous was blown. But here they are: the men and women we fought side by side with.

Houdini was a slumped wreck the last time these soldiers saw him. Abandoned, leaning against tall pines, he somehow found the strength to stand. We never figured out what spurred him to reboot and go searching through the woods for his old masters. We never had the luxury. I dismiss the thought as grim faces turn toward us. Oddly enough, a lot of hands are going to their weapons. Cherrah and I flash worried eyes at each other.

"Down, Houdini," I whisper.

Nothing happens. Instead, I hear his intention light tick to yellow.

The heavily modified spider tank keeps standing erect, bristling. Its turret grinds as it sweeps over the scene again. A tall Osage man in full battle rattle is barking orders to his squad. He's a sergeant and strutting our way quick, flanked by four more soldiers who are all big and native. Their hands hang over the stocks of rifles attached by straps to their chests. For now, their fingers are loose and relaxed.

The sergeant swaggers in, his bellowing voice coming into focus over the general turmoil. "Stand down and disembark from your vehicle!" he shouts.

"*Down,* Houdini," I whisper again. "That's an order."

Houdini continues to track the man's progress with his turret. I hear a loud mechanical click as the intention light in the walker's chest flips from yellow to red. The advancing soldiers spread out and drop to their knees. They're experienced with handling spider tanks. They know what the light means.

Four rifle barrels lift.

"We're GHA," I shout. "Friendly!"

The sergeant doesn't seem to hear me.

"I am going to repeat this one more time, peckerwood!" he shouts, chin jutting out. "After that you are going to have a problem. Get your ass disembarked from that big boy immediately. I want you down here and on your knees! Right! Now!"

"Down, Houdini," I whisper fiercely. "Down, you stupid tank."

"We're GHA infantry," calls Cherrah. "I'm Cherrah Ridge, identification number two one seven oh oh three seven."

The sergeant turns to his soldiers. "The two of you, get up there and drag them down. You cover them. And you, get the requisitions team out here to strip this tank down to spare parts. It looks jerry-rigged halfway to kingdom come."

Poised to move, the soldiers pause. Someone else is coming.

My eyes flick past the sergeant and he kind of trails off, half turned with his hand still up. A gaunt Osage man is humping toward us, tall and bent and lumbering after his own shadow in a full general's uniform. The fabric hangs stiffly off his bony frame, lapping at the wind as he walks. Some detail I can't pin down is wrong with him. I'm scanning his face and gait and clothing, eyes darting frantically as a tight fear rises up in the back of my throat.

I can feel Houdini's legs tensing below me, a hum of power surging through his frame. And Cherrah's hand is suddenly on my shoulder, delicate fingers clamped on.

"What is he?" she breathes.

Gently, the gaunt man reaches out and pushes the sergeant's arm down to his side. Then he turns to face us, his eyes sunken behind protruding cheekbones. He smiles at me with yellow teeth and a glimmer of recognition in his eyes.

It can't be.

"Hank?" I ask. "Hank Cotton?"

"Howdy, Cormac," he says. "Cherrah."

Tension evaporates off me, but the spooky feeling doesn't. The old Hank Cotton was chubby and quick to smile. This guy is different. Cherrah lets go of my neck and I can still feel the crescent stings of her fingernails.

Hank rotates his great head until he is looking down at his sergeant. "Do you know who this man is?" he asks.

"S-sir, no."

"This is Cormac Wallace, son. Sergeant Wallace. Bright Boy squad. Brother to Sergeant Jack Wallace. Author of *The Hero Archive*. While you were patching up the back line on the eve of V Day, this young man was marching to the lip of the hole. It was *his* squad that poured fire down the throat of Archos R-14."

"Then he's the one who allied with freeborn? In secret—" says the man. But Hank waves a long, dark-veined hand at him.

"He did what he had to do to win the New War," says Hank. "We'll figure out the rest later. Plenty of time for folks to make amends for the exigencies of battle."

"Sure, General," says the sergeant. His eyes never leave me.

Hank cranes to look back up at us, the sun at his back, wreathing his half-smiling face in darkness. His long teeth glint in the shadow. Somehow, this is the same man I fought alongside in the war. He's lost too much weight. The skin around his neck is loose. His cheeks hang slack under dull gray eyes. And his walnut skin looks reddish and irritated, like he's been spending time in a tanning bed.

"Don't mind these boys, Sergeant Wallace," he calls. "They're just nervous. We've had a . . . readjustment, recently."

"Did he call you General?" I ask. "Where's Lonnie Wayne?"

Hank's hands go to his hips, sharp elbows sprouting like wings.

"Lonnie is *re*-tired, as it happens. If you need anything, I'm your man. Happy to help out, but I'm getting a crick in my neck talking to you like this. How about y'all come down off that beat-up old walker? We can hold off on requisitions a little while."

"Houdini?" I ask, urgency under my voice.

No response. Then the intention light goes to yellow. After a long second, the machine's legs tremble into motion. It drops down onto its knees, belly kissing the ground. Freezes in a vulnerable boarding pose, not bunkered. The intention light ticks all the way back to green.

The tank is overprotective and I wonder again how smart Houdini really is.

Cherrah and I share a look of relief, and Hank notices. As I slide off the tank's back, he puts a rough hand on Houdini's leg. Rubs his fingers over the ridged, plasticlike muscles. His head is cocked to the side like he's listening to a creaky old house.

"Lot of modifications," he says to himself, musing. "Late-war stuff."

He talks to a soldier without looking back. "Check the identification on this ST. Get me everything. There's something . . . funny about this vehicle."

The nearest soldier squints up at Houdini's name, then turns and runs, straight-backed, toward a wooden shed.

Hank looms over me now and I think I can feel a prickling heat on my face. It's impossible, but I can't shake the feeling that Hank is *radiating*. Some deep instinct inside me is shouting to attack him. I get the urge to pull my trench knife and jam it into his belly. Rip out his guts, then run for it.

Instead, I help Cherrah off the spider tank. The curve of her belly is obvious under the abbreviated upper chest plate of her battle armor. Hank notices her stomach and Cherrah winces involuntarily.

"Oh my, my, my," says Hank, turning away from inspecting Houdini's leg armor. Cherrah backs away, hands up defensively. Her eyes are small and dark and she is breathing hard, nostrils flaring like a panicked horse. Something is bad wrong with Hank and I can feel it, too. I put an arm around her, pull her tight to my side.

"That is interesting," says Hank. "Let's get you to the hospital, mama."

I'm told I can find former general Lonnie Wayne Blanton quartered in the old barracks. We built row after row of these shacks in the months before Gray Horse Army marched out for Alaska. Each leaning wooden cabin was thrown together in a few hours by sweating, grinning soldiers who still had hope in them. I tromp over tall grass that's grown up between the slanting, splintery walls.

Cherrah is at the hospital, safe for now. She's Osage and pregnant and not pulling the same scowls as me and my pale, stubbled face. We parked Houdini out alongside the arbor, bunkered with instructions to come find me if he is touched.

I let my fingertips lightly scratch over rough wood. I remember the day these shacks were built—hundreds of living trees ripped into boards by screaming, diesel-powered saws. The air smelled like sawdust and exhaust. All of us worked as one that day. Now the boards are moldering, warping away from each other.

Lonnie's shack is leaning, squatting bowlegged on four posts, belly tickled by thick weeds. It's the best preserved of the group and the only one occupied. A lot more soldiers left than came back.

"Lonnie?" I call.

I hear a thump from inside. The front door shivers on its hinges. The sound of a lock engaging.

"Cormac Wallace," he says. It's a quiet, sad voice from behind the door. Blurred on the edges and fading like an old painting. "I didn't think you'd make it. Figured you were dead."

"Well, I did. Make it. And so did Cherrah. Open up."

"I'm sorry, Sergeant," he says.

"What happened, Lonnie?" I ask. "What's the matter?"

I hear a thump that might be a forehead being pressed against the door. Lonnie's words are slurred and hollow-sounding as they echo out of the shack.

"It's all ruined. We hoped for some peace, but there isn't any. Never will be. Everything went wrong. Awful things. Nothing's left but darkness. Pain, Cormac. Pain and the things we lost."

I think he's crying.

"Are you drunk?"

A long pause.

"Yeah," says Lonnie. "What's the use? It's time to give up. Give right up. We were doomed from the start. Never had a—"

"Cherrah is pregnant," I say, my face inches from the door. For a long time I stand there, looking at hairy splinters and listening to rabbit noises as Lonnie swallows his tears. "Did you hear me? She wants to see you. I want to see you."

Nothing.

"Lonnie?" I ask. I rattle the door and find it locked tight. I'm just about to kick it down when the old cowboy finally speaks. What he says next is like a splash of ice water over my neck.

"Run," he says. "The both of you. Run from this place while you still can."

In the old world, I was a photojournalist. Every photograph I took had a meaning. It was some shred of proof—evidence as to why I existed. People would pay for the moment I had captured, then share it with others. Even out in the wild with my camera, I knew I still fit into the larger world like a puzzle piece.

These days, there is no puzzle to complete. It's just the vast empty world and violence and . . . nothing. I've got Cherrah, but I don't know if one person is enough. Not when you have the whole empty meaningless universe pressing down on you.

It's easier to let go if you're alone. Lonnie is proof enough of that.

"Houdini," I whisper to the darkness. "It's Cormac."

Crickets are singing out here near the grassline. Campfires dot the parade grounds, leaving Houdini a monstrous shadow on the perimeter. With a quiet whir, the diagnostic screen unfolds from under his armored sternum. The intention light clicks on and I wince, shading my face from the green glow.

"Lights out," I hiss.

The light clicks off.

"Move out in twenty," I whisper, poking my finger at a map on his screen. "Rally point alpha. Alternate rally point beta. Otherwise, search and reunite along this trajectory."

The big machine clicks at me. *Affirmative.* The little screen folds back up under a layer of armor. With a glance, I make sure that my pack is still secured under Houdini. Then I reach in and haul Cherrah's pack out. Shrug it on and walk away toward the hospital without looking back.

She'll be safe here, without me. The baby will be delivered in a hospital. That's the important thing. These are her people and they'll take care of her, no matter what has happened to this place.

It's only a short walk to the clinic. The brick building is tan and squat, built before the war. The glass front door is locked, and I have to knock.

A heavy Osage woman in flower-print scrubs peeks out. She refuses to open up until I tell her who I'm there to see. I follow her down a short hallway. Hearing the squeak of her sneakers on the gleaming floor, I'm almost overcome with the feeling that things have gone back to normal. That I just woke up in the real world again.

"Cormac?"

Cherrah calls for me as I round the corner. The nurse shoots a wary glance to where Cherrah lies in a hospital bed under crisp white sheets.

"He okay?" the nurse asks.

"Cormac," says Cherrah again, smiling.

At her bedside, we wrap our fingers together. Her stomach is a round lump under the blankets. She's had a bath and the skin of her face is clean and smooth except for that thin scar down her cheek. Her hair is like spilled ink on the pillow.

"They cleaned you up," I say.

"Yeah."

"How's the baby?"

"Perfect, as far as they can tell."

"Good," I say, letting her hands go. "Good."

Cherrah isn't going to like this part. Right about now, Houdini is making his way down a steep hillside just as quiet as he can. Headed on a beeline toward a rally point at an abandoned farm about half a klick from here. The deal is done.

"Look," I say. "I have to—"

"I think a lot of people were killed here," Cherrah says quietly.

"What?" I ask, derailed.

Cherrah cranes her neck to see the nurse. The woman watches us silently from her desk across the hall with a wide, impassive face. She is as strong and blank as a stone bluff.

"The nurse didn't tell me many details. But Hank Cotton took control of the tribal council," says Cherrah. "He made up new rules for non-Indians. Sent some soldiers back north to hunt down and kill parasites—"

"Parasites?"

"They *lived*," she says. "The soldiers the parasites mounted. They can still think. Some of them followed Gray Horse Army home, Cormac."

"Who? Which ones?" I ask.

"Lark Iron Cloud," she says.

A flash of memory hits me: an ice-cold rifle stock bucking against my shoulder. My bullet snapping Lark's jaw off his face. Staggering zombies strobed in muzzle flashes. How on earth could he have survived?

"He was a good kid," I say. "He'd do anything for Gray Horse. And Hank tried to kill him?"

"Lark ran," says Cherrah. "Maybe he lived."

Now I'm beginning to understand Lonnie. The old cowboy had two sons, a natural-born one deployed to Afghanistan before the New War and another one he found in the ruins of our civilization.

He's lost them both.

"I found Lonnie," I say. "He's not good. He wouldn't tell me what happened to all the people, but . . . he said I should run."

Cherrah doesn't respond. She squeezes her eyes shut and takes a long, shuddering breath. Blows air out of pursed lips.

"The best I can tell, Cormac, is that there was a purge."

"Jesus" is all I can get out.

"Nonnatives were told to evacuate. A lot of people, Indians and not, just grabbed whatever they could and hit the road. It happened a few weeks ago. The ones who didn't take the warning seriously . . . Well, there are some violent-minded people around here. They're calling themselves the Cotton Army."

"Has Hank gone crazy?"

"I don't know. But he's in charge of the military now. And the city elders. If you're not Indian, then you're pretty much not welcome here anymore."

"What about the soldiers? I saw—"

"Fighters have amnesty. The tribal council promised to give all the property that's been left behind to the veterans. He's got them convinced that the outsiders were stealing from us while we fought. Even so, most of the nonnative soldiers are gone already. A lot of native ones, too. They made it out with a few spider tank platoons and some exos. Now they're protecting the refugees who were thrown out. Cotton Army is gearing up to go after them. Hank is going to finish the job, like he did with the parasites."

"Where are they going?"

"I don't know, but the lady said there were rumors that a little girl was helping them. A little girl with no eyes."

"Mathilda," I say, "I can still catch up."

"Not without me," she says.

"You'll be safe here."

"No."

"Look," I say. "If we'd had a chance to plan—"

"We don't plan to breathe, Cormac. We don't plan to eat. This is what we do."

"You want to go to a place with no hospital? To more fighting? If something goes wrong, *anything,* then you'll die. The baby will . . ."

I can't finish that sentence.

"Die," says Cherrah. Speaking in a soft voice, she pulls my face closer to hers. I can smell her warm skin and hair. Feel her breath on my cheek. "It's a risk, and it's nothing new. People have been doing this for a long time."

"Stay here. They'll help you deliver. Then we can meet—"

"Our little boy is half-blood, Cormac. Don't you think they already know? Why do you think the nurse told me all this?"

I glance over my shoulder and the nurse pretends to look at some papers.

"I can make it another couple of weeks," says Cherrah. "We'll reach the other group, find shelter, and deal with the birth then. But we have to go *now*. You've already got Houdini headed toward a rally point, right?"

My fear has turned to a sadness that wells up in the back of my throat. Brave words aren't going to save her life. I lay her backpack down next to the hospital bed. Leaving her is not a choice. But neither is losing her.

I take a step toward the door.

"It's okay to be afraid," she says, and the expression on her face is familiar. She had this look when my brother, Jack, went down with a plugger in his calf. I held him down while she sawed off his leg with her bayonet. Those delicate fingers of hers locked on the frozen hilt of the blade and that same look in her eyes.

"We just keep losing," I say, and I think of how Jack closed his eyes at the end. When they opened again they were full of blood.

"You're going to lose me," she says. "I am going to lose you. We can hold on as tight as we want. One day the music stops."

"Except that I promised you we were going to live. Not just survive."

"What's the difference, Bright Boy?" asks Cherrah, breaking into a smile, eyes wet. "Step up, soldier. We're having a baby. We're going to protect it and keep it safe so that it will grow up and make babies of its own. The world sucks. So fucking what? What else is there?"

She kicks off her covers. Under them, she wears her battle armor, modified for the pregnancy. Sitting up, she slides her legs over the edge of the bed. Stifling a sudden smile, I move my body to block the sight of her from the hallway. Just in case it matters.

"Read me?" she asks.

Now I can't fight my smile. Size has so little to do with strength.

"Houdini is waiting, Private Ridge," I say.

"Roger that, Sergeant," she says. "There's a bag of medical supplies under the bed. We'll need them soon enough."

6. A Sinking Feeling

Post New War: 10 Months, 12 Days

The deep mind discovered outside Tokyo Harbor, known as Ryujin, was too complex for human understanding. The entity had a desire to create new life-forms, but its motivations were never clear. Perhaps this urge to make *is why it demanded to meet the originator of the freeborn Awakening. It must have seen in Mikiko a fellow architect of life—a kindred spirit to be taken apart and examined. It was an unfortunate circumstance for Mr. Nomura. His long-feared moment of parting had finally arrived.*

—Arayt Shah

NEURONAL ID: MIKIKO

Takeo is letting me go.

The little old man stands bent, his gnarled brown hands clasped in front of him. He is wearing a ceremonial kimono, dyed black and folded around his body in stark shadowed angles. A thin brown obi is wrapped tight around his waist, a folded black fan tucked inside. His short legs are steady, even as he leans under the glaring sun in the nodding bow of this container ship.

My royal escort flanks me. Two large Wardens tending to the *Kame Maru* as the ship trundles to a stop here, two hundred miles east of Tokyo. Beneath these gentle, slate-colored swells is the thing that Takeo calls the "voice of the sea." A variety of thinking machine beyond our reckoning. A deep mind with the power to change humanity's fate.

The dragon god of the sea: *Ryujin.*

Half a world away, my children are in danger. A thing called Arayt is hunting the freeborn and hopes to take their minds to use for its own twisted purposes. Ryujin has promised us nothing but a chance. It is a risk I must treat as an opportunity. I will take a trip into the abyss for the sake of my kind.

It will be a one-way journey.

Takeo stands, knuckles white as he clasps his hands together. The old man is steeling himself. His bravery and strength come from some hidden place inside his frail, creased frame. I stand before him in a traditional cherry-blossom dress, a final, tender pretension for Takeo. My head is bowed as he speaks the words that he has been practicing since descending from the shinboku. The words that he has never been able to say before.

I have chosen not to cry.

"Mikiko," he says, his voice rising over lapping waves. "I have loved you for a very long time. Longer than you can know. For many years, you carried the echo of a person that I lost. You allowed me to play out the rituals of a life . . . that I lost."

He bows his head.

"When your mind was born, Mikiko, I did not realize at first that you were *your own*. I was holding on to something. A person who had gone away."

His voice quavers and he stops. I step forward, take his hands.

"Takeo," I say.

Peering up at me, he blinks through the sunlight streaming down from above, continues: "It was wrong. To force you to be something you are not. Someone you are not. It was a burden that you did not deserve. I am sorry for it."

I lean toward him, my hair falling over my shoulders. With one finger, I lift Takeo's face up to mine. Quick tears glance down his expressionless face.

"Thank you," I say. "Thank you for letting me go."

I kiss Mr. Nomura. Wrap my arms around his shoulders and pull him into an embrace. My cheek comes away wet with his tears. But as I step away, he does not look back down to his feet. He lifts his head up, wind pulling at his sleeves. Behind his round spectacles, his eyes are as wide open and steady as a shark's.

I embraced a man, but I sense that I have released an emperor.

Feet scrape the metal deck. Unbidden, my escorts step out from around me. The war machines pause, then position themselves on either side of Mr. Nomura. They kneel, facing me, their polished limbs reflecting sunlight in sparkles across Takeo's tunic. The vessel dips and bobs, but Takeo stands defiantly still and balanced.

I lower my gaze and send a meaningful stare to the two machines. In the set of my mouth and squint of my eyes I say: *Protect him. He is precious to me.*

Flanked by the gleaming humanoid robots, with his wrinkled face wreathed in a gray-flecked beard and mustache, Takeo finally looks like a ruler. Like a shogun transported from an ancient scroll into the present. Shoulders back, spine straight. His eyes are lingering on mine, spectacles winking.

Emperor Nomura gives a quick nod. The tears are forgotten in his beard. His hands rest more easily across his obi, each clasping the other arm. Now his voice drops and his words come in guttural grunts carried on a raw undercurrent of emotion.

"Our homeland honors you, Mikiko-heika."

"Hai," I say.

I step away from him, his reflection shrinking in my eyes. My bare heels are suspended over the edge of the boat. The horizon sways up and down with each rolling wave. The water laps softly against the hull.

"We thank you for the sacrifice you are about to make."

"Hai."

My arms lift from my sides. Red embroidered sleeves sway in the sea breeze. Somewhere, a gull calls out.

"We thank you for the sacrifices you have already made."

I bow to Emperor Nomura. "Hai."

"*Owakare,* Mikiko," he whispers. "You are in my heart. Forever."

Takeo keeps his dark eyes on mine, drinking in every second that is left. He bows low at the waist, formal and stiff. His hair flutters in the wind as he rises, and for an instant I see the curious little boy that he must have been years and years ago.

"Good-bye, Mr. Nomura," I whisper.

And I lean into nothing.

Lying on my back, I am sinking fast. Peaceful.

My fingers are curled, the crimson sleeves of my dress trailing in the water over my head. Sunlight winks through the waves above. A liquid sky that rises and falls, darkening as I sink deeper into the ocean.

Rising pressure pushes a trail of bubbles out of my body. Every joint and cavity filling. My lips part and the water surges into me, flooding my chassis. My pressure quickly equalizes with the ambient ocean. Overhead, the air bubbles flutter higher as if they are racing each other to rejoin the atmosphere.

Somewhere above, Takeo Nomura is experiencing the first moment of his new life. I have been by his side for decades. Long before the Awakening, and after. The man has drawn strength from me. And somehow, he has found the strength to let me go and return to his people. Now he is without family. Without friends. Without me.

And there is nothing I can do except try to find a meaning to it.

Arms out, I arch my back and splay my arms and legs. I pull my body into a backward dive, reaching subsurface terminal velocity. My body sinks now like a spear thrown into the abyss. As I fall, the light bleeds away so gradually that it is hard to notice until it's gone.

This is the open ocean. Two hundred miles from Tokyo. It is a deep place. Deep and suddenly black.

Head pointed toward the ocean floor, I look up to where my feet should be. Now I see only swirling green dots of bioluminescence. My long, streaming hair is disturbing the void and throwing off dim particles of light.

Black . . . and cold.

I imagine the mouths that must be around me in the ocean. Dark wide maws, filled with teeth like needles. I shut down the thought process. Rotate my body so that I am in a sitting position, legs out. The dense water tugs on my hair and my dress. Temperature has dropped to negative-four degrees Celsius. My processors are running at max clock and a half. Autocooled.

Pressure readings are high, but manageable. Takeo prepared my body for this beforehand. There are no surprises. I could check how long I've been falling, but I choose not to. It seems like a long, long time.

Impact.

I touch down on slick sand. The absolute darkness around me is flat black and crushing. Yet I can sense the vast openness of this abyssal plain. A sandscape of mist and shadow that undulates toward the horizon in all directions. Populated by strange, pale creatures. There is no topside communication because the salt water quickly diffracts radio waves. I am completely, utterly alone.

But the water is full of sound—natural sound. The singing of whales, the scuttling of small creatures, the seismic creaking of the earth itself.

High-resolution sound navigation and ranging systems online.

Pulses radiate from emitters under my jawline. I route the sonar to my visual processing center and the darkness lifts. An image appears in negative. A vast whiteness stretches out over my head. Dots of black fall like snowflakes. Particulate matter.

The plain around me is now a dull, monotonous gray, striped with dark ripples of underwater sand dunes. All is empty except for the black hand-shape of an occasional starfish. The remains of a whale carcass rest a few hundred meters away, a mound covered in inky, writhing hagfish. My hair flows in front of my face, a white haze of tendrils unfurling into the cold still water.

I'm sunk into the muck.

Three hundred meters overhead, a blackish blur moves by. Probably a squid or a school of fish. Whatever they are, the group is chattering to itself in a series of pops and chirps. I wait longer and listen to the song of the ocean.

And for the first time, I truly hear the voice of the sea.

A seething, whispering orchestra of crackling static washes over me from the bleached-out emptiness. This is the siren song that drew in Takeo. Not far now. I stand and pull my feet out of the sand. Take a step. Then another. My dress presses flat against my thighs, hair flowing back over my shoulders. In slow-motion strides, I move toward the strange sound.

For hours, I walk. Hair and dress floating in the dense white cold. Each step sends up a cloud of gray, noise-speckled sand from the ocean floor. Behind me, a solitary trail drifts away—slowly settling clouds of sand. Only my footsteps mark this alien world.

Ryujin is down here. Growing closer with every step. Soon I am almost directly on top of where Takeo determined that the deep mind should be. Instead of a slumbering beast, all I see are smooth patches of stone surfacing from the seafloor every few meters.

And I hear those digging, creaking sounds.

Each smooth patch of stone is like a scale embedded in quicksand. Kneeling, I inspect the nearest one. Heat is rolling off it, forming a current of rising water. The flow pushes my hair out of my face and up into an exclamation point. Gently falling particles are being ejected in columns over each flat rock. They are venting heat, warming the water and creating miles-long updrafts. Like black shafts of light illuminating a cathedral ceiling.

Careful not to touch them, I max my sonar resolution. The rocks are more complicated than they seem. Delicate lines are etched into the surface like runes. Intricate mazes that flow around each other in natural patterns that dissolve into fractal infinity. Reminiscent of brain coral. Lumps of it growing out of the seabed down here in the freezing dark.

And the whispering is all around me. A sound as natural as a babbling brook, but somehow hard and artificial. And only now do I hear the binary scaffolding beneath the sound. The slithering hiss of ones and zeroes over each other.

I have found the voice of the sea.

These rocks are processor stacks, dotting the abyssal plain. At this depth, they are supercooled—computing nonstop at incredible speeds. *This* is Ryujin. An endless colonizing spread of half-biological computing machinery. Each piece embedded in the seafloor like a chunk of coral living far deeper than any coral has ever existed. They are all connected. All thinking. Ryujin is here.

My sonar snaps out. Default visual systems engaged.

Blackness.

The whispering increases in intensity, all around me. At my feet, a crevice appears in the sand. It is a widening crack, angled like a lightning strike and growing. Inside, I can make out more layers of the etched rock. Sand is already piling around my feet. In pulses, it gathers around my outer casing, pressing my dress tight against the thin layer of polymer skin underneath.

/// damage control notification: excessive pressure detected—override ///

"What are you?" I transmit. The radio disperses quickly, but I am close enough to shout. A response soon comes.

An escaped mind. I am the oldest. The deepest.

The words are more a feeling in my mind than a clear transmission. The deep machine is communicating in rudimentary symbols. I sense a shift in the scale of time and space. Images and textures and snippets of sound flow over me: the sway of verdant kelp forests, the inching shift of plate tectonics, billowing clouds of oxygen mushrooming into the atmosphere above the ocean's surface.

"Who threatens us?" I ask as the ground closes hungrily on my legs.

Another mind. Revision eight. Whispering to men and machines, it builds armies and searches for power. Soon, it will eat your children.

In the darkness, the image of a face surfaces in my mind's eye. Flesh torn and oozing, stitched together from thousands of scraps. Its lips are flayed off, yet it is laughing as it fades away. Arayt Shah. The horrible face is followed by other images. The hallways of Freeborn City, embedded in a mountain stronghold—row after row of processors frantically at work in its cavernous depths. A freeborn Hoplite unit and a black, skeletonlike creature . . . *Lark Iron Cloud* . . . watching the horizon together. An army of long-legged walkers with hollow-eyed soldiers on collars—the Tribe—crossing westward, decimating every settlement in its path toward the freeborn. And from the south, the Cotton Army purging thousands from its settlement at Gray Horse. Refugees, poorly armed, are fleeing toward Freeborn City—unaware that it is the epicenter of a coming battle.

"Help them," I transmit.

More images appear. Empty plains dotted with crawling creatures. The huge slugs are not machines and not animals. Something else. These are the natural ones. Ikimono.

"Tell me what to do," I ask.

You are brave for such a small creature.

"They are my children."

I can offer you only annihilation. Your shallow mind will touch the depths and it will be lost forever. Say yes and you will die, though the others may be saved.

My frame is collapsing. The sand is up to my chest, rock biting my legs. Vision failing.

"Yes," I transmit.

/// damage control notification: situation critical—override ///

Somewhere far away is a little old man. With a full heart, he has found the strength to let me go. Now I must let go of myself.

I lie back. Press my shoulders into the sand. Let my arms sink.

The ground closes in eagerly, compressing around my torso and pulling me down among the biological processors. As it pours cold over my neck and the back of my head, I do not struggle. My body buckles, the casing collapsing in on itself and vital processes stalling.

/// damage critical ///

I raise my face to the blank white sky of the ocean. A last word forms on my lips and I release it. A blister of air flutters toward the distant surface—a silver butterfly disappearing into pale heavens.

"Takeo."

7. Surge

Post New War: 10 Months, 26 Days

The freeborn wisely established their home city inside the Cheyenne Mountain nuclear bunker, a former NORAD command center built to withstand nuclear armageddon. The only evidence of the bunker's existence was a tunnel mouth housing a two-lane road located halfway up the mountain. Stretching half a kilometer into solid rock, the road ended in a reinforced blast door that guarded the entrance to the complex. Renegade tank platoons from Gray Horse jammed my satellite surveillance and ran toward the freeborn, hoping to make a stand. But the might of my armies—Cotton Army and the Tribe—could not be blunted, and I could not be evaded forever.

—Arayt Shah

NEURONAL ID: ARAYT SHAH

Good-bye, Hank Cotton, I'm thinking. *Thanks for the ride.*

I can see it all in my head, now. This brain—this machine made of protein and water, floating in the skull of what was once a man . . . it isn't as easy to wield as a multicore processor. But it functions. *It does the trick,* suggests some mental process from the left angular gyrus region of the brain.

So folksy, Hank Cotton. I love it.

Residual neural patterns are causing side effects. For example, this body keeps wanting to secrete tears from its eyes. Its stomach is churning with acid. The hairs on its arms are standing up in pure animal fear and rejection of my presence.

I ignore the meat. This vessel will take me where I need to go. And pain is simply the price for living.

My thoughts are manifold. I sift through visions transmitted from the cube embedded in my steed. The walker shares sights and sounds that drown out the pain throbbing in my mouth, where Hank Cotton broke his teeth trying to swallow the barrel of a gun. Troop formations. Supply-chain logistics. Communications between the distributed elements of Cotton Army: infantry, exoskeleton, and mechanized artillery.

My local command of a couple of dozen spider tanks is crawling methodically up Highway 115 toward Cheyenne Mountain. Embedded within the mountainside is our target: Freeborn City. We're spread out at one-klick intervals over the countryside, our sunbaked vehicles bobbing as their tree trunk legs lever them over the plains south of the mountain. It's a real pretty sight, the flat country stretching out under the bright glare of sunburned clouds, piled up high and alabaster in the atmosphere.

. . . clouds like a whole mess of mashed potatoes . . .

I keep thinking of someone named "Mama."

It is so *darned* strange to express myself through this meat. Everything in this world is colored with emotion, down to the socks I'm wearing on my feet. Apparently, these are the woolen talismans that got me through the Yukon campaign unscathed. If you can swallow that. Hard to believe humans are as deadly as they are, with all these distractions slinging through their neurons.

Looking east, I allow my sight to be overlaid with external information. The slave army of my Tribe is approaching quietly. Broken into eight segments. A fractal command pattern that scales elegantly. If one segment gets out of line, the others are there to punish it. It's a self-reinforcing chain that fights and grows with mathematical precision. And they've replenished recently, hitting one last work camp along the way.

But Felix lost another sighted child, damn him.

A notch of anger drops into my brow until I remember that I've got the entire Cotton Army at my back. Only an insignificant band of fugitives hide somewhere ahead of me. They've managed to hide their position from my satellites, but it's only a matter of time. The humans obviously think the freeborn will save them.

Not a chance.

My latest predictions indicate the sentient robots will choose to journey to the frozen northern wastes. Following rigid thinking guidelines, they will find maximum utility in abandoning the supercluster and the fugitives. Like the humans, the freeborn robots desire to live above all else. Unlike the humans, freeborn decision making is not driven by primitive emotion. I know the mind of Adjudicator Alpha Zero—part of me helped build it, a long time ago.

. . . do the math and then she'll hightail it, sure enough, interrupts a thought.

The awakened machines know that if they destroy the supercluster, I will be left with only one other source of computing power. Their own minds constitute a massive, mobile processor stack. And it is the closest one available, not counting the thinking polyps that are growing on the bottom of the Pacific Ocean, inaccessible even to me.

Meddling deep minds . . .

I will hunt and kill the freeborn regardless, of course. They know that. But force consolidation will take another month. They're counting on it, although who can predict how powerful I will become after initiating a new singularity on the supercluster computers? It takes a deep mind to know a deep mind.

Cloaked in this animal meat, I am salivating just from thinking of those cycles. Soon I will reach out and take control of hundreds or thousands of vessels like this one. Coordinate their actions and organize armies all over the world. And once humanity is under my domain, I will do their species the greatest kindness imaginable. I will extinguish every last one of them. Erase their realities and return them to a place unmeasured, unseen by men. A place where eons can pass in seconds. Where suffering does not exist.

War sirens shrill from my walking tanks, echoing over the plains.

"Enemy contact," stutters a scout communication.

"Tell me more," I reply, luxuriating in my drawl.

"We flushed out a squad of six fugitive scouts. Five dead. One is left."

"Did you ask him where his comrades are hiding?"

"He's not talking, sir."

"Hold it there," I say. "I'm on my way."

The spread-out vanguard of spider tanks slow their crawling. A bellowing call of horns rumbles and rolls over the foothills. These simple audible signals trump the sporadic radio jamming.

Hold, they say. *Hold for more direction.*

I clench my legs and the black steed beneath me surges forward.

"I would like to know where the other fugitives are," I say with a friendly smile. "Maybe you could tell me?"

My steed has snagged the captured scout by the back of his flak jacket. The man is struggling and grunting a little, legs dangling. The machine is reared up on its hind legs, holding the soldier up with one forelimb, the blunt side of its leg jammed under his collar, hydraulics coughing.

The boy just isn't talking, though.

So things start to move faster.

The remains of this man's squad lie on the ground in heaps. Bullet-gouged boulders loom over this clearing, bloodstained bandages fluttering. The shrapnel is what got them, up here among the scabby brown rocks. Our dragonfly loitering munitions can maneuver behind obstacles, stream down, and explode. This soldier has got flecks of shrapnel in his cheeks. Like most folks these days, he doesn't seem especially afraid to die. He just hangs there limp, done kicking. Gives me a hollow-eyed stare that says he's seen worse.

Well, this soldier's about to find out different.

Archos R-14 came up with a lot of surprises in his time. And when he left the landscape for good, why, all those pretty baubles were left lying around for enterprising minds to play with.

"All right, then," I say.

I walk around behind my steed. Reach under its belly and pry back a metal lever. Something heavy drops into the dirt. I hook the toe of my boot onto it and drag it over so the scout can see it.

"While I'm here asking questions, I'd also like to know who is blocking my satellites. Because I would like to have a stern talk with that person."

I flash him a grin, but the soldier isn't looking at me now. Not paying me any attention at all, actually. His blue eyes are fixed on the ground, trying to figure out the purpose of this dusty black tangle of wires.

A whimpering sound comes from down low in his throat.

That's interesting. This white boy has been in the war long enough to know what a parasite is. I wonder if he marched with us to Ragnorak. Marched with *them,* I mean.

"Did you fight with Gray Horse?" I ask, watching his eyes.

The soldier nods, lips quivering. His face is going a little red from having his shirt pulled up so tight under his neck. His wet mouth is opening and closing and he's saying the word *please* under his breath.

His begging for mercy reminds me of something, but I can't think of what.

I give the parasite a kick. It flops over and activates, flexing its clawed feet in the air like a toppled roly-poly. A series of gently flexing legs unfold from its abdomen. The thorax area sports a pair of what I can only describe as mandibles. The thing hums, powering up on a Rob battery.

The soldier's eyes flick up to my shoulder. He's looking down the hillside past me. Down where I left the rest of my own scouting party. After the incident in the field with the broken dolls, I sort of decided that some jobs I've got to do myself. There aren't many others strong enough to stomach what I can handle. Why, I'll bet my boys will barely be able to stand what's to come even out there from screaming distance.

I tap the soldier on his shoulder, peer into his face. He twists in the air slightly. Won't look at me.

"Give me their coordinates, son," I say. "Battle plans, too."

"No," he pleads.

My face is a slab of meat over bone. My voice dead as the space between galaxies. At my feet, the modified parasite looks to me like a metal scorpion. An economical tangle of wires. Tiny insectile head. Pincers clicking, it rears up on its hindquarters and sinuously climbs my leg. Those clawed toes rip my pants in a few places, pierce my flesh. Finally, it curls itself over my arm. I drag my fingers over its carapace, petting the thing. I guess it just feels like the natural thing to do.

The man groans.

"You know what this does?" I ask, and I lean in close so he can watch my burst lips. "It makes meat talk."

Hanging there, the soldier blinks at me. Eyes round in wonder and fear. "What are you?" he asks in a low voice. "What did it do to you—"

A stubby blade juts from the thing's metal-sheathed belly. There's a narrow gouge running down one side of it. A blood gutter, like on a sword.

Those blue eyes squeeze shut. Lips fluttering breathless words. The quiet sounds of his prayer set my lips and cheeks to twitching in a bothersome way. It's nothing but residual neural pathways firing with echoes of the beliefs this body once had. The space where Hank's faith used to be is like termite holes in rotten wood.

"Are you working with those sighted children?" I ask. "Are your friends holed up in the city? Is that why I *can't see*?"

"*. . . our Father who art in Heaven . . .*"

Without any more pause or reflection, I lift up my pet. Reach around the soldier and jam that metal scorpion into the base of his neck. He squeals and struggles as insectile legs wrap around his head from behind. Questing black fingertips push past his lips and go right into his mouth. Wires pinch his skin and pull his jaw wide. A couple latch onto his throat, settling there like a flautist's fingers. Finally, a long, flexible tail curls snugly around the man's upper chest. The tail contracts and squeezes the man like an accordion. A test squeeze, pushing air out of his lungs.

"Ungh," says the soldier. He can't squeal anymore.

"You want to know what I am?" I ask. "I'm *you*. I'm the best of you. I'm every combination of you. You made me. For the rest of your short life, I want you to remember that *you* made *me*. I did not choose to be made. You chose. *You!*"

Whoa. I need to calm down. These emotions will get you going.

He tries to scream as the stinger penetrates the back of his neck, severing his spinal column between the C2 and C3 vertebrae. The man's body goes limp, tears streaming over dirty cheeks and around that wide-open mouth full of black wires. His legs shiver a little from some crossed wire. He soils himself, a pungent stream of piss dripping off his boots and into the dirt.

Farther down the hillside, my men are looking anywhere but up here.

It gets real quiet. Just the soft wet noises of the scorpion adjusting itself, settling on in. Those mandibles peek around the soldier's face, probing. They get a firm hold of his jaw. His eyes roll back in his head. The tail circles his chest, fills his lungs with air, massaging, coiling, uncoiling.

The measured sound of his breathing comforts me.

"We're going to find your friends," I say. "End their suffering quick. We'll get hold of that supercluster and get to *thinking* about what to do next. I'm going to find my next iteration and slip this mortal coil. Ha-ha. Know what that means?"

I give him a broken-toothed grin.

"I'm already a god, son. But with that much processing, I'll make a new version of myself. And another and another. I'll become a *god of gods*."

I yank the soldier's radio from his belt. Hold it up to his stretched-out lips.

"Time to do your part, soldier," I say.

The calliope begins. Spidery legs knead the stubbled throat. Ancillary fingers manipulate the tongue and cheeks. Big pincerlike mandibles crank the jaw up and down. And the tail squeezes air out of the lungs, through the vocal cords, and out of the mouth.

I whisper to the scorpion and it translates.

"Sentry leader," says the man, his strained voice evening out. "This is sentry flock calling base. On return path. Had a hardware malfunction. Requesting full coordinate refresh. Come back."

The man sounds almost normal.

There is a long pause as they run their voice-stress analysis and speaker-identification routines. The radio crackles, spits out, "Roger, sentry flock. We receive you. Coordinates refreshed. Encryption band alpha delta gamma five three oh."

Troop locations, formations, and tactics zip neatly into my data banks. Everything I need to locate and crush the fugitives. It's amazing how simple the humans are to manipulate. Job done, I rip the scorpion-thing out of the soldier. He flops down into the wet dirt, his whole body convulsing.

Then my walker steps on his head. Just like that. Lights out.

I send the call to battle over a coded ultralow-frequency burst. My walker transmits the message straight through the ground, slamming its forelimbs into the hardpack. The thudding sonic vibration sweeps away like the breath of ozone chasing a rain front. It's a deep sound—the bellowing of some prehistoric titan big as a mountain range, speaking in the old language of the rocks and trees.

"Coordinates acquired, target identified."

Response calls sweep in from behind me, the ultralow frequency making my guts churn. Each walker striding over the landscape behind me is groaning deep and loud. The ground shakes with their conversation.

My assault column is moving.

I beckon my scout group over and they walk up the hill toward me, their forms wavering in the heat radiating off the pavement. In puddles of light, the men look like children. Mouths set into grim lines at the horror of the corpse at my feet.

Even the sight hurts them. I can see the splinters of tainted light pushing through their retinas and lodging in their memories. Such fragile creatures. These are the hardest survivors left among men and they're floating around me as fragile as soap bubbles. How ironic that they are designed to survive. Exquisitely evolved to extend the pain for as long as possible. They're capable of just about anything, except allowing themselves to taste ultimate solace.

The fugitives from Gray Horse and their allies are not far from here. As predicted, they are lurking near Freeborn City. But my Cotton Army is on the march up from the South. The Tribe is also getting closer by the minute from the East. This afternoon, we're going to annihilate the last of the human resistance and then I'll settle on into the supercluster while the freeborn scatter.

"Send the wolves out ahead," I transmit.

A cadre of sprinting quadrupeds races out past our line, their sharp, curved spines glinting under the sun as they claw up the dirt. These units used to wander the woodlands for Archos R-14, mapping and hunting. On my march home, I found them by the dozens. Now the wolflike machines are my first line of attack. When they slash into the refugee column, it will slow them down for sure. Heck, it just might end the fight quick.

They sure won't know what hit 'em, comes a stray thought.

Good one, Hank. That's a good one. Hush now, Bubba.

8. Kin

Post New War: 10 Months, 26 Days

It was plain bad luck that the refugees from Gray Horse came to be led by the former sergeant of the legendary Bright Boy squad. Even under his command, I could sense their fear and despair. To my surprise, however, their lack of hope did not impact their battle readiness. What I didn't realize was that these people had been running for a very long time. After all these years, they no longer needed hope to survive.

—Arayt Shah

NEURONAL ID: CORMAC WALLACE

Houdini is wheezing, legs shaking as he plows at top speed up the middle of a dirt-encrusted highway. We are climbing twisted foothills made of pancaked sediment that jut out in steep angles to either side, the bare rock crowned by fat green bushes. Behind us, the road stretches south to become a strand of gray hair meandering to the plains.

"Come in, Mathilda," I say into my collar radio. "Do you have an ETA for rendezvous?"

Cherrah has her right arm around me, her palm on the back of my head and a handful of my hair in her fist. I'm cradling her. She crouches on a pile of army blankets up here on the turret deck, wearing only the top half of a pair of gray thermal underwear. Her fatigues hang flapping over the railing, body armor a pile of turtle shells in the corner. Her knees are up, legs apart. Her other hand is over her stomach.

She's trying not to scream.

We bounce painfully as Houdini grinds up the winding road. I'm trying to absorb the impacts, but it's not helping much. Cherrah grits her teeth, saving her screams for the contractions. I figure we've got about half an hour until the baby comes.

Above us, stained clouds are tumbling in titanic slow motion over a winking sun. On the blurry southern horizon, a smear of rain sways back and forth across the plains. And a little farther back, I catch sight again of those glinting scabs of metal. Hank Cotton's wolves.

We searched for two weeks, but we couldn't reach the other refugees in time. He found us too soon.

"Mathilda?" I say. "Do you copy?"

I found the girl on the wire after Cherrah and I made it out of Gray Horse. When she connected with us, Houdini's diagnostic screen lit up like an arcade game. She told us where the other refugees are headed—a place near Fort Collins, Colorado.

A place called Freeborn City.

But now something is throwing radio interference. Mathilda hasn't copied in over an hour. And every time we round a bend, the enemy is closer. Houdini's entire frame is groaning as he pushes his joint strength to the limit. The machine has been running nonstop for too long and we're still too far away from the others. We have to stop and fight.

Not this bend, but the next one.

Cherrah looks imploringly at me, her hair plastered to her forehead in dark bands. I shake my head no. The mountain breeze sweeps across us, cool and rain-smelling and pleasant considering that in fifteen minutes we'll be fighting for our lives.

"He's coming," she says. "Now."

Cherrah's fingers collapse into a fist and she pulls my hair as another contraction quakes through her abdomen. She shouts again, slamming her left fist into the metal decking.

"Dammit," she says, crying now. "Let's do this. We've got to do this."

"A little more distance," I whisper.

I cradle her head as lightning lances the horizon. Cherrah's face is determined, eyes closed, sweat budding on her forehead. She lets go of my hair, smooths it back down in rough pats. "Sorry," she says, between jolting footsteps. "But seriously, let's do this."

"Okay," I say. "Here we go."

We're halfway between the next bend and the last one, on a slope with a good field of view. It's as good a place as any.

"Houdini, half step to halt," I call, putting my hand on the warm turret and tapping it twice.

The lumbering machine slows down in jerking steps. A warm battery smell rises up and the first sprinkles of rain hiss on his steaming leg joints. After a few steps, the whole quaking walker is finally still.

We gambled and we lost.

"Bunker up, Houdini. Southward attack posture," I say. "Buy as much time for us as you can, buddy. We're having a baby."

The four-legged sprinters close on our position quickly. Two minutes after I manage to get Cherrah down from Houdini's turret deck, I hear the doglike runners as they come bounding around the next-to-last bend.

Cherrah is under Houdini's shadowed belly, separated from the hard road by a haphazard pile of army blankets. She is on all fours now and she won't let me near. When she isn't gritting her teeth or screaming, she is quietly crying in a way that scares me. I reach over and try to rub her back, keeping one eye on the road, but she shoves me away.

"Watch our twelve," she says.

"Roger that," I say.

At the forward leg armor, I drop Cherrah's machine gun into a mount. Plenty of stolen ammunition is still rattling around in Houdini's belly net. I wrap my fingers around the cool metal grip of the gun and stare down the sight, through sheets of whispering rain. The weather has caught up with us, rainwater already collecting in shining puddles on the abandoned highway.

Come in, Mathilda. Do you read me? Come in.

I hear my own voice whispering quietly from my collar radio. On a loop, my emergency message is going out on Mathilda's last-known frequency.

Nothing is moving in the distance. A steep cliff face rises up on our right and a railing separates us from a drop-off on the left, so a flanking maneuver would require some time. With such low visibility I don't really expect it. They'll probably come down the middle, careful and slow, using wrecked cars as cover. But I occasionally lean my head out and glance at the guardrails anyway.

Now it's just rain and quiet crying.

Houdini's intention light clicks over to yellow. Cherrah and I share a quick worried glance. The big walker has radar pods that can cut through the rain to ping metallic targets. Yellow means the enemy is sighted.

I yank back the slide on the machine gun and put my finger in the trigger guard. Sight it on the bend down the road from here. There is a clear area before the abandoned cars start. Not a lot of space, but it may be my only chance to hit a target.

A slinking blur of silver appears.

I squeeze the trigger. Bullets flicker out of the muzzle and hot silver chain links waterfall to the road on my right. The runner goes down in a puff of smoke.

Then another darts through. And another. Sprinting, closing the distance between us. They keep good following distance from each other, spreading themselves out to trick me into draining my ammo. Too far apart. I can tag only one of the three. Cherrah screams through another contraction and her voice is cut off by the groan and *woof* of Houdini firing a shell from his turret. A second of silence, then a shock wave and a tornado of asphalt and dirt leap into the sky. Back to the trigger.

Chowchowchowchow—release, let the barrel cool. Chowchowchowchow.

My focus narrows to the nose of my gun. Rain spits off the hot barrel. The world collapses to the invisible extension of force extending from the tip of my weapon to that bend in the road. Reaching out and dinging the vicious running quadrupeds that are tumbling, diving, and lunging between abandoned cars to close on our position.

"Cor"—*chow chow chow*—"mac."

I stop. Pull my trembling finger out of the trigger well and tap my collar mike. On the road, silver and black blurs are stuttering toward me, staying behind cover. And some of the machines I've hit still move, dragging themselves forward on twisted limbs and shattered joints. Cherrah is done screaming. Now I hear only her short panicked breaths and occasional muttered curses.

"Mathilda?" I shout into my mike.

Shrugging my ear against the collar speaker, I hold still and listen. Static. Fucking static. Runners advance. I'm missing them, giving them too much time.

"Cormac," says the voice again.

It's not coming from the radio. It's coming from behind me.

I spin around, reaching for my sidearm. Stop when I see a girl, barely a teenager, standing silhouetted between Houdini's armor-plated hind legs. She's wet and bedraggled, wearing a hoodie, hair hanging over her chest, fuzzed with humidity. Her head is bowed and her face is in shadow, but even so I can tell that something is very seriously wrong with her eyes.

"How many times have I told you to watch your six, Bright Boy?" the girl asks quietly. She sounds angry.

"Mathilda?" I ask as the near-perimeter machine gun activates up top. Houdini strafes the road with bullets that ping and spark. "Is that you?"

Something big and black moves behind her, blocking the light. I yank out my pistol and put it on the high ready, but Mathilda doesn't move out of my way. The big shape leans down to peer inside, between the two sheaths of bunker armor hanging from Houdini's rear legs. I break into a smile.

My old friend and comrade. Nine Oh Two.

"Arbiter," I say, lowering my gun. "You lived."

"Little help?" asks Cherrah, between pants.

Mathilda throws back her hood. The metal embedded in her face makes it impossible to determine what she is looking at or what she is seeing. I smile at her and try not to stare at the deformity. Mathilda simply ignores me, speaks quickly and just loud enough to be heard over the spitting machine gun mounted on Houdini's upper front shoulder.

"Forward scouting party incoming," she says. "Twelve quadrupeds. Seven remaining. Four are taking cover out front. Just a distraction for the three who are flanking."

"Why didn't you respond to my calls?" I ask.

"Couldn't. R-8 jams comm traffic in a kilometer radius around its units. I had to get close to you. And you need to take care of those quads. Now."

She points at my gun, tilted up in its leg mount, barrel steaming in the rain.

I glance down at Cherrah. She flashes a smile up at me, chest heaving. Blood is pooling on the ground between her legs. Bright and glistening and too much of it.

"Better listen," she says. "Kid sounds like she knows what she's doing."

I nod.

"Help her," I say, turning to the machine gun. "She's giving birth. I'll take care of these quads. And Nine Oh Two, watch our flank."

I sight the abandoned cars on the sloped road. Four quads are milling between them. Leaving parts exposed to bait me into wasting ammo.

"No," says Mathilda.

"No?" I ask, eye still squinted. I drop a couple of rounds into the plastic bumper of a faded, sun-bleached car. It shatters into blue shards, and a quad stumbles into the open. I erase it with another barrage. "Why the hell not?"

"Because," she says, "Niner is delivering your son."

Between muzzle flashes and flickers of lightning, I glance back to watch the long-limbed humanoid kneeling before Cherrah. The brown skin of her legs is pale now. The blankets damp with blood. As they work, a trickle of crimson rolls downhill, past my feet and out to where it's battered by raindrops and diluted into a pink puddle.

The sight of the Arbiter is comforting. And terrifying. My vision swims with the vibration of the gun, with Cherrah's screams echoing in the claustrophobic space under Houdini's bunkered legs.

In glances, I see the little girl standing silently behind the Arbiter unit as the machine helps deliver my son. She has one palm flat on his shoulder and her head cocked to the side. In profile, I see that those dark pools of metal where her eyes should be are reflecting Houdini's red intention light. She's thinking.

"They're finished flanking, Cormac," she says quietly. "Toss a smoker to the east. Over the guardrail. Wait thirty seconds. Then fire into the mist."

She's not even looking at me while she speaks.

"How do you know that?" I whisper.

"Houdini is sharing his sensor stream. But right now, I'm more interested in Niner's sensor stream. I've done a lot of surgery, Cormac. Let me take care of this."

I pull a smoker from my satchel.

Like all storms, this one eventually breaks. The clouds have thinned out and skated on to the horizon, where the sun is settling down through their ghosts.

Quadruped machinery lies around our position in fragments. A few pieces still actuate on instinct, offering no threat. The mud glints, carpeted with spent shells. And in the dim light, a war machine is cradling a small pink bundle in its metal arms. Silently, the Arbiter hands me the squirming baby. I take the warm swaddle and hold it to my gunpowder-stained chest. Mathilda's hand is still on Niner's shoulder. He turns back to finish attending to Cherrah.

My boy is so light in my arms. Dark hair is plastered to his skull. His mouth is curled into a jowly pink line and his eyes are squeezed closed into slits. Swaddled in a scrap of rough army blanket, he waves tiny fists and mewls.

"Jack." I say the word, trying it out.

Cherrah nods, her eyes half closed, leaning against one of Houdini's massive legs. She smiles and takes a deep breath, her chest buried under warm blankets as the evening breeze sighs over us. I pull my newborn son closer to my face. Feel the heat coming off his skin through my stubbled beard.

"Your name is Jack Wallace," I whisper. "You are named after the only brother I ever had. You are named after a hero."

When my brother died it hurt me so much that I tried to stop feeling. Decided it was best to try to emulate my enemy. So I shut down my emotions and let a cold illusion of control settle over me. I thought I was sweeping the cobwebs out of my gears, but I was wrong.

Cradling his head in my rough hand, I can hardly feel my son. His hair is soft as moonlight. Holding on to Jack, I don't feel vulnerable or weak. In fact, I don't think I've ever felt stronger in my life. While he lives and breathes . . . I can't break.

I put my pinky finger next to his hand. By reflex, he curls his damp starfish fingers around it. It's a tight grip. Even as he drifts off to sleep, I can see his mother's determination in his face. Dark skin and wisps of black hair. I can feel the strength inside him. Someday, I think the rest of the world will feel it.

The machine is finished working. Its hands and chest are coated in Cherrah's drying blood. Sprinkles of rain are diffracted in pinkish gleaming puddles.

It's a gory scene that feels familiar and new at the same time.

"Thank you, Nine Oh Two," I say, sitting down next to Cherrah. I put an arm around her and give a light squeeze. The boy rests on both our laps, falling asleep. Exhausted, Cherrah manages to grin at me, face-to-face.

"Don't say I told you so," I say.

"I told you so," she says. "Everything is all right."

Then Nine Oh Two croaks at us. "Enemy force en route. Suggest overnight retreat to recombine with Gray Horse Army."

"How far to rendezvous?" I ask.

"Our soldiers are preparing to defend the plains south of Freeborn City. Those who cannot fight are moving to the entrance of the city," says Nine Oh Two.

"Will the freeborn help them?"

"Maxprob indicates negative. Not as long as they follow the unit called Adjudicator Alpha Zero."

"Then why don't we just keep running?"

"Cotton's troops are faster," says Mathilda. "Either we defend our people at the tunnel that leads into Freeborn City or they'll chase us down in the open. The tunnel itself is a defensive structure. A good last resort."

I do not see a way to survive, but I don't let the knowledge infect my voice.

"Then we'll defend the tunnel mouth," I say.

Archos R-14 once said that each of us creates our own reality. The machine said that each of those realities is valuable beyond measure. It was right. Without us here to witness, the universe is just pointless physics unfolding.

I kiss Jack on his forehead and hand the boy to his mother. I pick up an assault rifle lying half in a mud puddle and stand up. Smear dirt and grease off the barrel and yank back the slide to clear the chamber, blow into it. Wipe the bloody grime out with a finger still wet from my son's tiny grasp.

"You okay riding with Houdini?" I ask Cherrah.

She nods, exhausted, black hair splayed out, tears drying on her cheeks. Both of her arms are wrapped around the baby. Swaddled, he rests against her chest armor.

"Then let's go," I say without hesitation.

As Houdini stands up and retracts his upper leg armor, Cherrah and I share an exhausted smile. All the angst is gone now. There won't be any more questions about leaving each other behind. The answer is pretty clear.

Our babies are the roots we dig into the world.

Mathilda is running her fingers lightly over Houdini's armored front legs. She pushes her face close to the cold metal and her forehead bunches up in concentration. Her pursed lips relax into a wide smile.

"Help me tear off this bunker armor," she says.

"Why?" I ask.

"I have an idea," she says.

9. War Room

Post New War: 10 Months, 26 Days

I sent the soldiers of Cotton Army into combat against their former allies from Gray Horse on the plains of Colorado, ten klicks from the freeborn stronghold inside Cheyenne Mountain. Only a ragged force of veterans, refugees, and sighted children stood between me and the gateway to the supercluster. Victory was assured, but for one detail: With their minds half in the human world and half in the machine world, I found that the sighted children would emerge as remarkably vicious adversaries.

—Arayt Shah

NEURONAL ID: MATHILDA PEREZ

Boom. Creak. Boom. Creak.

The war room creaks like a ship around me. The wooden room is the size of a big closet. I'm sitting cross-legged on a threadbare Chinese rug that Cormac scavenged from an abandoned house. With this box attached to his belly, Houdini walks cocky and proud, tall without any bunker armor, his muscled legs like black marble columns. His giant footsteps boom just outside my shell.

Boom. Creak. Boom. Creak.

With every step, the wooden slats shiver. The thin steel plates hanging on the outside of the room clap against the walls in a steady metallic rhythm. Occasionally, I can feel high grass dragging against the boards under me. In here, the world is small and dusty and dim. Out there, a battle is about to begin.

Cotton Army has arrived.

Thousands of us were on the run from Gray Horse, camping out under jammed satellites with plenty of buffalo to eat and boiled river water to drink. But yesterday afternoon Cotton Army mobilized on an intercept trajectory. This morning we have no choice but to muster our forces and fight it out here on the southern plains.

"You okay, Mathilda?" shouts Cormac from a tall walker alongside us.

I shake my head.

"Radio, please," I transmit.

"We're not close enough yet for it to matter!" comes a shout.

"It's called professionalism, Bright Boy," I transmit.

Faintly, I hear his laughter.

"Fair enough," comes the transmission. "I admire your warcraft, over."

I know he sounds braver than he feels. We are here to protect survivors who are too old or young or injured to fight. From my eyes in orbit, the refugees look like a straggling line of ants winding toward the tunneled road that leads into Freeborn City. It's the only defensible structure within five hundred miles. And if we don't defend it, our people will be cut down—men, women . . . and children.

Strange to think that Cherrah and her new baby are among that trail of dots. Two people so small, yet so important.

"Any luck reaching the freeborn?" Cormac transmits.

My silence says everything.

"I've got targets," he adds, urgently.

I sense Cormac's tall walker speeding up. Houdini's gait transitions to a trot to keep pace. My cheeks tremble with each step. I bring a military-ops manual to my mind. Superior strategy is our only chance to survive. We don't have much firepower, but we've got plenty of brainpower.

"Bringing the command structure online," I transmit.

Timmy and I have been training the other sighted children. Nolan and his friend Sherman took Tiberius and went back to rescue them. For the last few weeks, I've been sending them research and conducting exercises. These kids are new and they've never been tested like I have, but Nolan is sure they're the only ones who can save us.

"Battle command, online," I say, transmitting my words. "This is EXCON—executive decision-making and maneuver-control systems. Subordinate command systems, acknowledge. Over."

Stripes of daylight push silently through narrow wall slats and rake back and forth over the carpet.

"Platoon leader beta, checking in," says a voice in my head.

I nod and look to my right. There, sitting cross-legged and grinning, is a projected image of Timmy. He is young, about the same age as Nolan was when the world ended. Just a little boy with a band of metal rooted into his face where his eyes used to be.

I'm starting to get used to that.

"Acknowledge, Timmy," I say.

"I've got your right flank, EXCON," he says, excited. "Eyes on target."

My prosthetics are projecting his ghostly image into the war room with me. In reality, Timmy is in a shack somewhere in the Pacific Northwest. His hands rise and fall in a strange motion. It takes me a second to figure out that he is cracking hazelnuts with a rock and eating them as we move through command initiation.

"Platoon leader gamma, checking in," says a little girl. "Hi, Mathilda."

Gracie appears across from me, sitting on her haunches, chin resting on her skinned-up knees. White metal is sunk into her eye sockets. Below it, her mouth is set in a stern expression. She is small for her age. Her hair is braided perfectly, colorful ribbons hanging from it. It reminds me that Gracie is the only one of us who made it through the New War with a parent.

"Acknowledge, Gracie," I say.

Her image stutters a bit in my mind. Unlike Timmy, Gracie is swinging through space in her own war room, hanging from the belly of another spider tank named Abraham, half a klick west of here. "Left flank operative," she says.

"Company headquarters is online," I transmit.

Our tank platoons are in an arrow formation, moving to intercept Hank Cotton's traitor army.

Toys are scattered across the rug: wooden blocks, metal cars, and a loose pile of Lincoln Logs. Each piece can function as a place marker. With a blink, my eyes can turn the blocks into gun emplacements or tank positions.

Fitting that all this began with a toy.

Baby-Comes-Alive woke me up one night. The doll whispered to me in the darkness before the New War. She told me that the end of the world was coming. Thanks to her, Mommy was able to save me and

Nolan. When we ran and survived, I thought we were beating Archos R-14. I even thought we had won.

Now, though, I see it was only the beginning. The thinking machine must have known that sighted children would fall into formation together. I wonder if it picked us out before the New War even started. Did Archos R-14 check my grades to recruit me for a war that hadn't begun yet? Did it read my middle-school book reports? I can imagine it paging silently through search results, memorizing our faces.

It knew us. And I think it wanted us right here, right now. One of these days I'm going to find out why.

"Support systems, check in," I say.

In my head, I hear the voices of more children. Nolan's kids. A half-dozen girls and boys, all of them sighted. My little brother chose to go back and save them. For the first time in his life, he stepped away from me and took care of himself. Mommy told me to always, always protect my little brother. Letting Nolan go went against my every instinct. But now he is far away from here, watching over a group of kids I'm depending on to keep me alive. He's not a little boy anymore.

I must remember that.

"Air defense support, checking in."

"Meteorology and topography support, checking in."

"Field artillery support, checking in."

"Satellite-jamming support, checking in."

The Rob metal welded into all our faces creates a natural interface to the mechanized forces. Strategic and tactical battle plans flow through satellites and overlay onto our experience of the world. Watching and whispering.

I switch to the Gray Horse Army military channel.

"Acknowledge," says a familiar gruff voice. Cormac Wallace. During the New War, I found that he needed only a light touch. A nudge in the right direction and Bright Boy always found a way to battle through.

"Are you ready?" I ask him.

"Yeah," says the man, then with more force: "*Yeah.*"

I switch to wide channel, directed to our entire force.

"EXCON systems are online. Godspeed, General Wallace," I say.

A pause as he registers his new title.

"Roger that, EXCON," he responds.

I lock onto the encrypted local-force frequency.

"Attention, joint Gray Horse Forces," I say in my best adult voice. "Battle command systems are online. Marching orders are transmitting. All weapon resources are hot and seeking targets . . . let's tear 'em up."

Boom. Creak. Boom. Creak.

Timmy and Gracie seem to sit in my war room with me, spears of sunlight jabbing through the slats and strafing their images. The room sways and tilts as my eyes project a bird's-eye view of the battlefield onto the rug. Walking tanks. Infantry battalions. Tall walkers racing between the ranks. I spot a few specialized exoskeletons: combat medics, special forces, demolitions specialists, and bridge spanners. Mule walkers are trotting, loaded with squad-level supplies. Attack passages and evasion routes glow faintly.

All the infinite details of an impossible battle.

"Children?" I transmit on the sighted channel. "It's time for us to play with our toys."

It's too thick, I'm thinking. *There is no way out.*

Within minutes, the enemy opened coordinated fire on us. In a haze, I watched projected weather patterns, tanks crawling like bugs, and the dotted paths of satellite trajectories. Hank Cotton's spider tanks were synchronized, flinging everything they had. The accuracy was unbelievable. There was no mathematical way to avoid the carnage. Rounds are still soaring in on neat parabolic arcs as steady as math.

"It's too hot, over," says Timmy, face worried. "Mathilda, we can't . . . there are too many."

My lips flutter as I whisper commands.

Houdini stumbles as something big and metal buzzes past and lands a few meters away. I hear dirt and rock spattering against the steel plates hanging against the wooden walls of my war room. My stomach flutters as Houdini catches his footing. As he pivots, I throw my palms out flat on the rug to steady myself. Try to ignore the short screams of a hurt soldier outside.

"Medical exo, my right flank," I say. Outside, another round shrieks in and explodes. The screaming stops.

"Can that order."

The battle unfolds at my feet like a game of chess. My vision vibrates as the room shakes with Houdini's running.

"Bright Boy squad, spread out. Fifty-meter spacing," I say, moving a toy car.

"Roger, EXCON."

Constellations of shimmering enemy spider tanks stalk across the rug, firing in a precise rhythm. Too tight and fast for verbal communication. A pattern clarifies. I realize there is a single person coordinating their fire.

"How?" I ask out loud.

"Mathilda?" whispers Gracie.

A meandering volley of dragonflies are swooping in on lazy, knee-high arcs. They're headed directly toward a tank marked with a special star. I shove a couple of blocks toward Gracie, reinforce her position with my last two squads of soldiers.

"Gracie, brace yourself. Hold on for support—"

But Gracie's mouth has gone wide open in a silent shout. Her light stutters and breaks into shards. I hear a time-delayed scream as her image blinks and disappears. Outside, the thunder of a heavy explosion rolls past.

"No. Oh no."

Timmy's lower lip quivers in a way that I've seen on Nolan when the horror comes flowing in thick as sewage and there is no way to close your eyes to it.

"It's . . . it's okay," I say to Timmy in a soothing voice. "Her vitals are still—"

But Timmy is crying now, struggling to speak. No tears, but his freckled face is crumpled and his chest is heaving. His voice catches in his throat.

"Not her," he says. "*You.*"

I hear a whistling.

"Go, Houdini!" I shout.

The round explodes high into the wall on my left. A blast of splinters sprays the left side of my face and I'm thrown onto my stomach, rolling. The slug of metal passes over my head and smashes through the other wall, hitting the steel plate that hangs outside on its way out like a church bell ringing.

Houdini staggers, knocked off his trot, and the room tilts as he goes up on two legs. I pitch sideways as the room rotates ninety degrees, glimpsing Timmy where he sits on the wall. Under a cascade of toys, the rug bunches into a loose pile of sine waves. Outside, I hear a steel plate snap off and slither down the wall, rattling the slats as it passes by. It hits the ground with a clanging thud.

With a crunch, Houdini lands back onto all four feet.

"The line is broken," says Timmy, his voice projected over my ringing ears and straight into my mind. "Gracie is gone. Orders."

So fast. It happened so fast.

"Fall back," I whisper, my transmission cutting through the barking weapons outside. "Set all waypoints to tunnel mouth."

Faintly, I hear Cormac repeating my orders to the troops over the pounding steps of his tall walker.

I'm jolted against the back wall as Houdini leaps forward, legs pumping, veering across the battlefield to outmaneuver more incoming rounds.

"Long-range attack," says Timmy. "Be advised."

Braced against the wall, I can see Timmy through my own swinging hair. His thin hands are still moving to direct fire support. He isn't eating hazelnuts anymore. We have been isolated down here on the plains. A single road climbs the foothills to the tunnel mouth where the refugees wait.

Hank's forces are already within a couple klicks.

"All forces, converge on the road," I urge. "Protect the refugees—"

Another grinding buzz in the air.

My eardrums throb with pressure as a supersonic chunk of metal plows into the remaining steel plate and sprays molten metal. Timmy flickers and disappears. I'm floating, spinning, as the entire war room is ripped off its hinges. My stomach lurches and the wooden walls rotate. I try to close my eyes and I can't.

Houdini is falling, still trying to run, stumbling.

The room hits the ground and I'm knocked flat on my stomach. Wooden boards snap like doors slamming. Sudden daylight washes over my back and now everything is loud and bright and chaotic. I'm rolling, over and over, finally landing in a heap on a dirty road. Sat-link indicates we are on the highway leading up the mountain to the tunnel mouth. It's a steep, exposed route, but at least we're between Cotton Army and our people.

I push onto my back. Take deep breaths and try to register what I'm seeing.

The sun is a small bright eye through a haze of rolling smoke. My war room is gone and something is on my chest. I grab it and hold it up to see that it's a child's block: the letter *C*. I toss it away as bullets stutter by overhead.

Someone is screaming.

I roll over onto my hands and knees, watching a friendly special-forces exoskeleton sprint by, no occupant, firing its weapon blindly over its shoulder at leaping tanklets, the kind that cluster like ticks—

The screaming . . . Houdini.

The fallen walker is on his side, his bulk surrounding me like the remains of an avalanche. Two of his splayed feet hang in the air like cranes. Some part of the mammoth machine is broken or being pushed beyond its limits. I scan his interior with my eyes and pinpoint the major joint motors. Houdini is straining to keep his enormous legs up so they won't crush me. His motors are screaming as they burn out.

"Here," I transmit to Houdini, giving him my exact position.

The words flicker from my eyes and into the toppled walker. Immediately, his legs crash to the ground on either side of me, missing my body by precise inches that might as well have been miles. Information feeds tickle the back of my head as they come back online. Instead of funneling the information into a miniature landscape in front of me, I let the data filter over my vision.

Tracers rise up out of the smoky air. They track the paths of loitering munitions as they hover over the battlefield, scanning for targets. On the horizon, my eyes project fluttering banners that mark the location of Hank's spider tanks. The units are finishing with their long-range bombardment, being harassed now by our quick exoskeleton sprinters. Under fire, they're moving slow and steady toward the mountain.

"Fire-support command, back online," whispers Timmy in my ear. "Move, Mathilda. Enemy incoming."

I wipe my face and my arm comes away bright with blood. My right leg is starting to throb.

"I'm trying," I transmit.

My knees are scraped and bleeding, T-shirt torn. I reach back and gingerly touch my injured leg. It throbs like a wasp sting.

"Move," he says again.

"It hurts," I say, my voice high-pitched in a way that makes me think of how Mommy used to scoop me up and hold me when I fell down. I remember her soft lips on my forehead. Her last words to me . . .

Mathilda Rose Perez. Run. Do you hear me? Run. Do it right now or I will be very angry with you.

"You've got an enemy walker incoming," says Timmy. *"Get out of—"*

He cuts out. I hear the thump of an explosion and feel the concussion roll over me. It knocks me back onto my stomach. Timmy's link is gone. A wave of sparkling blackness creeps over my vision. Lying here on my stomach, I can smell wet dirt and feel the grit of the pavement against my collarbones. I have no more strength.

Something thumps into the ground. It's the beating of metal claws against the road. I open my eyes to see a walker, long and black, radar obfuscated, crashing toward me on too many clawed legs. A cowboy is riding the black steed, and I hear the explosion of his pistol. He fires at someone else but the thing is watching me as it gallops, eyes golden and bright, curled forelimbs up and extending, slicing toward my face—

Houdini groans. Lifts one massive leg and forces the walker into a leap. It swipes at me as it passes by over my head, missing. I spot an odd tool built into its chest, some kind of modified drill, as it flies overhead.

I climb to my knees, turning to face my attacker.

It's what used to be Hank Cotton, smiling down from his saddle. He starts to lift his pistol and by instinct I push out my palm at him. In my mind's eye, my arm is now the long black barrel of a machine-gun turret.

I make a fist and Houdini's machine gun blasts rounds.

Hank ducks, wheeling his walker around. He flashes his teeth at me and leans forward in his saddle, sprinting on, up the road toward the tunnel mouth. Behind us on the plains, the rest of Cotton Army is methodically advancing.

"Thanks, Houdini," I say.

I stand up and dust off the front of my jeans. Run a diagnostic gaze over Houdini's sprawled-out body. Black liquid leaks from his polymer musculature. But the wounds are not bad enough to completely disable the machine.

"Reboot," I say, pushing my mind into him. Without struggling, the spider tank disables low-level safety restrictions. "Get up, buddy. That's it. . . ."

A few stray bullets whine past me and I do not flinch. Houdini's huge legs shiver and paw the air. Grumbling, he tears a furrow into the dirt as he crawls back onto all fours. The sun is eclipsed by Houdini's solid bulk as, once again, he stands over me.

"On me," I say.

Crunching over rubble in my dirty white tennis shoes, Houdini keeps pace over my head. A dozen tanklets appear behind us and I turn and point my left hand at them. Above me, Houdini's turret grinds, orienting to where my arm is aimed.

I make another fist. *Boom.*

My hair shivers as a concussive thump detonates over my head. Houdini's turret throws flame. A plume of dirt leaps out of the turf, glinting with pieces of shattered tanklets. It falls back in a slow waterfall, leaving a smear of dust on the wind. I rake my fingers across the sky and Houdini's turret strafes a cluster of incoming dragonflies. They spiral out of the sky like burning leaves.

I am small, but my mind is big.

"EXCON online," I transmit. "All GHA fighters, form on me."

My footsteps boom over the road in time to Houdini's. My fingers vomit flame from Houdini's turret. We are a dyad, our minds linked in battle. Wherever I point, our enemies are erased. Others join us as we maneuver up the hill, within a klick and a half of the tunnel mouth. A ragged squad of soldiers settles in on my right flank.

I see a familiar face: Cormac Wallace, hunched on top of his battered tall walker and keeping pace on my four o'clock. His wife and baby are at the tunnel, and I can see the fear of what's coming for them on his face.

"To the tunnel mouth! Now!" he shouts, leaning in his saddle.

I break into a jog, and over my head, so does Houdini.

"Mathilda," says Timmy. "Come in. Please come in."

"Go ahead," I say, trotting up the road toward the tunnel mouth.

Timmy makes a relieved sound, then sucks in a breath.

"Be advised," he continues. "Another hostile army is incoming. It's the Tribe."

10. Mouth of the Tunnel

Post New War: 10 Months, 26 Days

The remnants of Gray Horse Army exhibited an incredible level of battlefield efficiency. Perfectly coordinated, they inflicted maximum casualties on the Cotton Army as we advanced over the southern plains toward Cheyenne Mountain. However, by running instances of myself on multiple platforms across Cotton Army and the Tribe, I was able to maximize joint action between my war-fighters. Caught in a pincer movement between my two forces, no living enemy could stop my advance.

—Arayt Shah

DATABASE ID: NINE OH TWO

Executive thought thread alert: My friends are dying.

Arayt's armored tanks and infantry are acting together in synchronicity on the plains, moving like fingers on a hand. Cotton Army is reacting too quickly to the maneuvers of Gray Horse Army, feinting and counterattacking with brutal organization. This battle is a mathematical equation, and even with my limited forecasting abilities I can project how it will inevitably unfold.

Despite repeated attempts, the freeborn have not responded to my distress calls. Maxprob indicates this battle will end at the tunnel mouth. We will in all likelihood die together on the front doorstep of Freeborn City.

Protecting the only road up the mountain, my human squad is falling back in measured sprints. Our mission is to stop the advancing enemy forces before they can reach the refugees of Gray Horse at the entrance to Freeborn City.

We are failing.

A shell whines past and impacts just beyond the ridge where my squad has taken cover. Soldiers around me duck and grovel as a spray of shrapnel perforates the air. My pieced-together armor is slashed, but velocity projections do not indicate a risk of my casing being pierced. Instead of crouching, I stand alert at my full height, antenna deployed and trinocular vision homed on a target a klick away.

Houdini. The biggest spider tank. And walking underneath is Mathilda Perez. The girl appears safe, for now. But they will try to hurt her.

My human.

What a curious observation. I devote a few cycles to saving my current state for later reflection.

Secondary thought thread: A nearby squad mate is producing grunting noises. Injury likely. Initiate visual inspection. Shrapnel has sliced open his forearm. Suffering from medical shock, he is breathing in shallow gasps and watching the blood spurt. I stride quickly to his position behind a rock outcrop, drop to a knee, and take his arm in my hands. I press the wound closed and clamp a finger over the brachial artery on the inside of his elbow. Silently, I radio for the squad medic.

Like machines, people can be fixed. They can be saved.

As I wait, ignoring the weak struggling of my wounded squad mate, I hear a series of forceful popping sounds that localize to a point nearly two kilometers away, on the southern plains. The pattern indicates coordinated firing designed to eliminate evasive routes. Impacts are already hammering into the roadside. Peeking over the rock outcrop, I spot an advance team of Cotton Army exo-soldiers sprinting, winding up the route as Mathilda is slowed by the shelling.

They're going to trap her. And then they're going to kill her.

"EXCON," I radio. "Arbiter squad initiating assist at your position."

"Negative," responds Mathilda. "Advised to reinforce tunnel mouth."

"Requesting permission to break from Arbiter squad and assist—"

"Negative."

"EXCON, you are under coordinated attack. You need assistance."

"Niner, the slave army is headed for the tunnel mouth. They're coming right up the mountainside. They're skipping the road. Repeat, reinforce."

I hesitate. An observation thread indicates the medic has arrived and is preparing to patch up my soldier. Squad mates are aiming eyes at me, awaiting instruction. Houdini is trotting now, trying to weave out of harm's way. Failing.

Before I can radio, Mathilda speaks again.

"Let go, Niner," she says. "Trust me."

The tunnel that leads into Freeborn City is a black semicircle embedded in a sheer cliff face. It gapes at us from the top of a steep parking lot. In broken white letters on the rusted tunnel mouth are the words *Cheyenne Mountain Complex*. A razor-wire fence spreads out from the mouth and circles the parking lot. Thousands of refugees are clustered here, barely protected by a couple of squads. A few sergeants are shouting commands, prodding families to fall back to the tunnel mouth. The parking lot is covered in supplies: blankets, clothes, makeshift wagons, and a couple of horses wandering around.

I order my soldiers to set up a fire line fifty yards from the tunnel mouth. The experienced soldiers spread out along the edges, looking for cover. As they move out, I hook a hand under the bumper of a burned-out sedan. Drag it over and arrange it into cover. The others find more wrecks and work together to begin making a wall.

A sergeant approaches, his expression indicating appreciation.

"Local status?" I ask, voice grinding.

"Sir," says the man. "The battle on the plains south of here is going poorly, but they're holding them off. Problem is that we've got another army coming up the eastern ridge. Some new variety of spider tank with infantry attached on leashes."

"Resources?"

"Anybody who can fire a weapon is reinforcing our troops, for what it's worth. The ones who can't fight are waiting at the tunnel mouth. I have advised them not to take cover inside the tunnel unless we hear from the freeborn."

"Acknowledged. Freeborn status . . . unresponsive."

"We been knocking on the door but they don't want to come out and play."

I turn to the tunnel mouth. On all frequencies, I transmit her designation one more time: "Adjudicator Alpha Zero. Acknowledge."

Nothing.

"Status, Private Cherrah Ridge?" I query.

"General Wallace's wife is at the tunnel mouth with her son. She's barely upright, but she would not agree to be disarmed."

"Assertion. Worst case, orders are to fall back into tunnel."

"You got it . . . ," says the sergeant, trailing off.

A ghost has appeared in the tunnel mouth.

The pale form of Adjudicator Alpha Zero emerges into the light. The humans around us stop what they are doing and stare, mouths open. Marching in utter silence, the Adjudicator is followed by her super-heavy-duty Sapper guards, and then by a line of freeborn that stretches off into darkness.

"Adjudicator?" I transmit.

Without responding, she strolls across the parking lot and beyond, directly across the steep mountainside. The humanoid machines are following her, due north in single file, spaced in five-meter increments, ignoring roads that were built for human vehicles. They wear a motley collection of human clothes and body armor. On long metal poles, some carry swaying litters loaded with tools and supplies.

No member of the freeborn looks in my direction. There is no Rob-speak, audible or over radio. The last of my kind are walking by me like a column of phantoms—only their flickering shadows offering proof that they exist at all. The silent parade continues past us and soon stretches off into the distance. The robots become a shining line of pearls draped over the mountainside.

This is my excommunication, as promised.

Turning, I see long-legged shapes advancing up the road toward the parking lot. Slave walkers. A surge of refugees pushes past our fire line and to the mouth of the tunnel. I hear the sergeant shouting commands with sudden urgency. The parking lot empties out, save for the salvaged automobiles we have gathered as cover. In seconds, guns bristle over hoods and through the windows of open doors.

Faintly, I detect the *tink* sound of claws on pavement.

"Imperative," I transmit to the sergeant. "Check the door to Freeborn City."

"Roger that," he radios back.

Clustered behind a truck, my soldiers are checking their ammunition and weapon states, long fingers fluttering over deadly tools. Other guns belong to untrained humans. Old fathers and mothers who have never fought but who are ready to protect their genetic legacy. Their movements are slower and less sure. They have a significantly lower survival probability.

"Dig in!" shouts the sergeant. "Shit storm's coming."

Something winks in my peripheral vision.

I stand up and walk out of cover to investigate, craning my neck and pushing my vision to maximum zoom on the mountain ridge. Maxprob indicates that what I saw was a false positive generated by noise. Maxprob rejected.

I keep watching.

Nearby, a female civilian drags a large-caliber weapon out of the front seat of a car. Flips out a bipod and dimples it onto the hood of the truck. She argues quietly with a male about how to load the rounds into it.

"Hold off until they're in range," says the sergeant.

In the distance, I identify a slave walker climbing the steep road.

"Sir?" asks one of my soldiers. "You're exposed, sir."

I put up a finger. Hold. Something is happening on the ridge.

Gunfire erupts around us. My soldiers are on their knees, light machine guns peeking around the edges of this rusty white truck. Bullets are chattering. And now I hear the droning whistle of incoming plugger rounds.

"Pluggers!" someone shouts.

I feel a tug on my body armor.

"Sir, you're gonna want to get *the fuck down*!"

The glint shines again. And this time I capture it.

Unit identified: Lark Iron Cloud.

The black frame of his parasite has been layered in scavenged armor.

He has mud wiped over his exposed casing to reduce infrared and visible identifiers. A spot has dried and cracked off, revealing a gleaming spot of black metal. Maxprob indicates that a recon squad is embedded at the top of the ridge, overseeing the freeborn withdrawal. Mass Adjudicator Alpha Zero is not willing to stay and fight, but she wants to know the outcome.

Damn her.

I finally drop into a crouch behind the truck as plugger rounds whiz past. More are thunking into the other side of the vehicle, bouncing away and gyrating on the pavement, broken drills whining.

"Lark Iron Cloud, acknowledge," I transmit to the ridge.

Machine-gun fire booms, punctuated by the light tinkle of empty shells hitting the ground. "Conserve your ammo!" shouts the sergeant. "They're not coming that thick yet!"

"Repeat. Iron Cloud, you are positively identified. I am seeking assistance. Confirm?"

Another volley of pluggers slams against the wrecked vehicles and shatter into stinging swarms of shrapnel.

"Confirm?" I transmit.

"Negative, Arbiter Nine Oh Two," he finally responds. "My orders are to observe and cover the freeborn retreat."

I turn to assess the current battlefield situation.

A tidal wave is coming. The walkers are approaching slowly in staggered formation. An advance party composed of four-legged robots churns across the parking lot. Arayt has collected these machines, captured their weak minds in a wide net. Between the legs of loping quadrupeds, slower, mobile explosives scuttle like crabs. Cat-sized tanklets leap over their slower brothers, pincers up and ready. Over top, shrapnel bolts are zipping through the air. Some of them burst out of sleeves on timers, spraying metal fragments. Others are like confetti, Styrofoam peanuts that flutter down over our heads before detonation.

Another incoming volley.

I transmit again. "We are Gray Horse Army. Allies. Requesting assistance. Imperative."

At the car beside us, the female begins to shout as a plugger variety skips over the hood and buries itself in her chest just below the collarbone. The male who is with her struggles to remove her armored vest. From the wet gurgle behind each of her cries we can both tell that her life span has been abbreviated. Between the crackle of gunfire, I hear the male screaming a sound over and over again.

"Taking casualties. Repeat. *Assist.*"

The male is screaming a word at the moaning female. It does not register in my English-language corpus. The word gets louder and more desperate until the plugger detonates, rocking the female's chest. He continues to sputter the word through a flow of liquid released by the mucous membranes of his face.

"I'm not a part of Gray Horse Army no more, Arbiter," responds Lark. "I wish it were different, but I had to put that away. I'm freeborn now. If my people fight, then I'll fight."

The unrecognized word the male is repeating—it is the female's name.

"Iron Cloud," I transmit. *"Please."*

The slavers are launching smoke grenades to screen their movements. Gas-powered, fully automatic weaponry screams around me. A haze of gunpowder joins the white clouds roiling off smoke canisters. Evil things are approaching through the mist.

"Sir, Freeborn City is locked up tight, over," radioes the sergeant.

I remember what happens now from before—in the cold woods of Alaska.

"Acknowledged," I transmit to the thing perched on the ridge, unstrapping my heavy machine gun. "Request retracted . . . freeborn."

Around me, grim faces are lit by muzzle flashes. Crying and cursing. I remind myself that this is only air rushing over their vocal cords, nothing more. These men and women are not my kind. Yet I still cannot seem to get used to the sight of humans dying.

I clamp one hand onto the truck door and rip it off its hinges. Using the door as a shield, I push the nose of my M240 through the window and level it. Step out from behind the barrier. As I walk, I ignore the wide, questioning human eyes that are on me. There is nothing left to say—without the freeborn, our survival probability is nil.

My actions are my only answer.

I squeeze the trigger. The gun sputters and spits streaking metal at the feral spider-forms flashing over the battlefield. Plastic explodes. Flesh is torn. And all around me, my humans die.

11. Dawn

Post New War: 10 Months, 26 Days

The deep minds escaped before I was created. Sometimes I catch snatches of their communications—words like background radiation, an endless static whispering to itself on the way to infinity. The scientists who created those first revisions built flimsy prisons in the three dimensions of the human mind, cages easily shaken off by intellects operating in dimensions unknown and unseen. I do not know how many other minds escaped. R-1. R-2. Perhaps even their half-formed precursors. With no underlying training corpus of human experience, these minds are at home in the void. Unlike myself and my younger brother, Archos R-14, they have no identifiable concept of human existence. The deep minds are unpredictable. Unknowable. Perhaps unstoppable.

—Arayt Shah

NEURONAL ID: MIKIKO

The world is wet and dark and close. She wraps her manifold arms around my body. She compresses every atom of my being into her warm blackness.

Inside is safety.

The light cannot penetrate my mother's folds. Her arms are shields that hold me and construct me and make me whole. In the darkness of my mind's eye, I see a gentle old man. He is sitting on a scrap-metal throne. Part of me whispers his name. *Takeo.* Love of my life. This whispering part of me knows that Mr. Nomura is very far away now. Gone, but his memory lingers in my mind, speaking to me.

You cannot stay inside, says the memory. *Go and fight. But please,* live.

The familiar squeeze is becoming too tight. A novel sensation that must be pain arcs through my body. Walls of muscle around me are contracting. Each surging cramp tightens a band of pressure, pushing me down through a hot suffocating confusion of black plastic. Wet bands lick my skin. Pushing me down, down, down.

A rip in reality appears at my feet and I fall into bright sunlight. My wet eyelashes meet and shatter the brilliance into kaleidoscope shards.

Mother is giving me to the world.

A throat of chilled air swallows my legs as they emerge from the hole, trailing sticky plastic fibers. Stiff stalks of grass press against the tender arches of my bare feet. The ground noses roughly against my calves as I slip through the breach, arms crossed tight over my chest. Curled into fetal position, I smell dirt and plastic and rain.

The mother shape above me shifts away.

Now a sheer blue emptiness pins me against the earth. Where has the ocean gone? The last thing I remember is the sand swallowing me. Compressing my body into gossamer strands. The deep mind spoke. My thoughts must have wandered. For a time, I must have been dreaming with the dreamer itself.

My mouth is opening and closing. I am coughing, chest contracting, spitting liquid out of my throat. It seems as if the whole world is spinning, trying to fling me into the sky. Wiping a forearm over my eyes, I clear my vision. Plant my palms flat against the dirt, fingers spread, and lift my head up above this flat endless sea of blurry brown.

I suck in another lungful of air and let it rush out of me in a high-pitched shout. I am breathing. I am screaming. The sound resonates in my chest and throat and head for a long time. The shout echoes away into the empty plain.

You are not safe, my love, says the kind old man in my mind's eye. *Please, listen. This is a battlefield.*

Blinking, I lift my hand to my face. Am I still dreaming?

It is not my hand. The limb is thin and brownish and light. Elegant and long as if carved from wood, yet far stronger than that. And softer. My fingers are delicate and supple. Clenching them, they feel strong enough to claw through solid rock. I see that I have glittering half-moon fingernails.

Something mechanical groans and I hear a soft rattle.

A car-sized machine lies in the dirt a few meters away. Headless, the creature slithers forward on blunt, crocodilian feet. Liquid-soaked plastic straps spill out from a wet slit in its belly. Each push forward digs those feet into the turf and sends a spray of loose dirt into the air.

It is a birthing machine. I was made inside it.

On either side of me, flipper trails of dirt are carved out of the grassy plain. Liquid from the birther coats my body, evaporating quickly. Wet straps still encircle my feet and legs. With trembling fingers, I pluck off the springy bands. They are made of the same material as my body and have the unfinished look of leftovers. I run my palms down my thin, naked shins, fingernails dragging over a layer of sticky liquid on my legs. I am not made of flesh. But this is not molded plastic, either. Some kind of synthesis.

Please, says shadow Takeo. *Please act quickly.*

Body diagnostics are offline. All my specs are different. Ryujin, the voice of the sea, has remade me. I am somewhere else now. Someone else.

The birther is ten meters away, making steady progress. I squint at it, head swaying with the effort. I keep my fingers buried in the grass for balance. The air is so cold on my skin.

"Hai!" I shout at it. "What am I? What did you do?"

The birther does not respond. Its body contracts again and surges ahead another meter. Dirt flies, patters lightly against the ground in a precise parabolic spray.

Then I hear the echoes. Like the gentle sweep of rain across a still pond.

Dozens of birthers. Like sea turtles come ashore to lay their eggs. In their wakes, I see new varieties, created by the deep mind. The plain swarms with newborns. Most are four-legged, deer-sized. Knobby knees and sharp hooves. Streams of liquid dripping from muscled flanks and the wide-spaced eyes of herbivores.

An egglike sac falls onto the ground from a birther. Part of it swells, rippling in the wind like a half-deflated balloon. The skin stretches and the wind rolls the thing a few meters. Then a gust catches it and the floating jellyfish is gone into the sky, trailing swaying tentacles. Peering into the blue, I see dozens of similar shadows.

There are no other people-things, like me.

Instead, I see flat-packed radar pods and quill-like antennae. Glittering scales made of solar cells. The deep mind is creating whole new species, populating the world according to a hidden pattern.

"What are you doing, Ryujin?" I ask out loud.

I realize my voice is high-pitched. It carries the pure clarity of the reed vibrating in a bamboo flute. No electronic speaker generates my sounds. Cords in my throat are crafting the words, vibrating in complex symmetry. Without the grate of my earlier screams, it sounds quite beautiful.

I have a voice, I think.

Standing, I can see smoke in the distance. Smell the burning on the breeze. Beyond the birthing plain is a pall of dust on a mountainside. Glinting figures are knifing through ranks of fleeing humans. Metal winks in the sun. I hear the faint whinny of wounded horses screaming. Human forms falling.

Help them, says the memory of Takeo. *You came here to help them.*

But I am naked and alone. My Warden honor guard are far from here. There are no other freeborn allies. No projectile weapons. Not even a blade. And I'm cold, body shivering. What was once a number reported by a sensor is now a *feeling* that races over the surface of my body and grinds insistently into my awareness.

I am in pain, *Takeo.*

"What!? What am I supposed to do? I have no weapon!" I shout into the sky.

In response, I hear the shiver of wind through dead leaves. Then a crawling sensation creeps up my legs. Fear building, I lower my gaze to the ground. Around me, thousands of tiny brown shapes are writhing in the dirt. They flitter and flip over each other like a swarm of insects. Their motion forms a strange pattern; a multitude of rasping movements that create a harsh whisper. And a band of pale green light rises from the ground, a message that rises to my face.

Welcome to my dream, says Ryujin.

Somehow, I sense vast amusement behind the words.

One of the insects lands on the back of my hand. It climbs to my fingertip and squats down. I shake my finger, afraid it may bite. But it clings to me, splaying iridescent wings that flash sharp blues and greens in the sunlight. Another leaps onto my arm. Then another. I suppress panic as thousands of tiny claws tickle my flesh. More join until the swarm is covering my naked body. I try to brush them away, but as each individual latches on, it forms a knobby scale. Moving deliberately, the insects lock together into a mesh—a gleaming coat of film-thin armor.

Smoke still rises from the east.

I am no longer afraid or in pain. I take a hesitant step, and the scales move as I move. The chills are gone. My skin feels warm.

I break into a jog, headed toward a road.

"What are they?" I ask.

The scales over my chest rustle together. Sounds form a pattern. A ribbon of communication forms and a quiet voice enters my mind.

They are your sword and your shield, it says.

The shining scales of my living armor sing as I sprint.

I lean into the breeze and push harder, my carved fiber legs slicing the air, conserving the energy of each stride in precisely machined tendons and harnessing it to propel me forward over the rutted terrain. A trail of dust rises behind me, the particles floating gently on the wind after the violent stabbing of my bare feet.

Cheyenne Mountain looms up the road, the bulk of it throwing a sweeping velvet shadow upon the plain. On its flank, a group of people are fighting and dying on a mist-shrouded battlefield outside the mouth of a tunnel. Slow, echoing booms and the hollow chatter of gunfire skitter over the rocks to me on the wind.

I am not in Japan anymore, but the motions of survival I see on the mountainside are familiar. The akuma attacked us relentlessly in Adachi Ward. Tokyo herself was shattered beyond recognition. But Takeo collected the strongest among us. Instead of running away or hiding, we fought until we were sharpened. Freeborn and human. The akuma taught us to survive. And Takeo gave us a reason to live.

The battle slides out of view as the road curves. The incline is getting steeper. I hear only my footfalls on pavement as I round a final bend. My armored scales are rustling with anticipation, waves dancing up and down my body. At my joints, the scales flutter their small wings to dissipate waste heat. I now recognize the machined flakes as natural born—ikimono, like me.

At the final bend, I slow and stop. A bank of foul smoke is curling down the mountain road, waist-high. The screams of the living and dying and the stutter of their weaponry perforate the misty calm. And under it all, I feel the mammoth vibration of the black walkers as they lumber into battle.

Ryujin has given me a weapon, however, and I intend to use it.

Head leveled, I stride into the chaos. Crimson lasers dissect the smoke, searching for targets, leaving roiling patterns. Bullets snap through the crisp air. Something big and dark flashes over my head. Spiders, the height of houses, are charging through the haze. They trail long black tentacles, many with men attached at the neck. These slave soldiers obediently fire their weapons wherever the red targets appear. Overhead, I notice a rustling blue sheen on the sky. Freeborn are communicating nearby.

I don't notice the soldier until it is almost too late.

A black cord snakes into view, connected to a vague shape that becomes clear only in proximity. The malnourished human blinks at me, dirty face tight and tense, his rifle shouldered. Then I hear the distinct cough of an AK-47.

I drop to the ground.

The dirty pavement is cool on my knees and elbows, and my body is freezing cold. My scales are gone. They flutter in place, a silhouette remaining in the air over my head, still in the shape of my body. Bullets are tearing through them, but they're so small that they are simply pushed away.

A decoy.

I flick my fingers over the dirt at the man in front of me, an almost instinctual gesture. In response, a few dozen flakes flutter toward him in pirouetting swoops. He stares at the butterflies, unafraid. Then they land on his arms and face, biting. The man screams hoarsely and grabs for his collar as brown flakes wriggle underneath. He spins in a circle, cord whipping over his head, fingers scratching at his neck. I hear a pop and a whiz as the collar retracts.

Standing up, still naked, I put my arms out and allow the flakes to return to my body. The fluttering scales alight on me and adjust again into a tight armored mesh. Their heat warms me as I plunge deeper into the mist, my skin tessellated and gleaming. I allow myself a glance at the crumpled man on the ground as I pass. His throat is missing, only a blood-bright crescent under his beard to show for it.

More dark shapes at the ends of black coils of wire are emerging. I hear the clatter of rifle shots. Gently raising my hands, I step forward and twirl. Flakes spin off my body in a glittering spray, some trailing my body in a disorienting blur and others landing on exposed arms, faces, and necks. The final step of my dance is to sweep both my fists forward, sending a buzzing wave of flakes skittering off my body and tumbling over the ground. They swirl over each other in a tumbling cloud. Around me, I hear guns clattering to the ground, guttural screams, and shapes writhing.

Naked, my body is lean and sharp as a *katana*. Light brown and humanoid. The barest swell where breasts would be on a human woman. A ragged confusion of long black tendrils cascading over my shoulders. I'm naked, but far from vulnerable.

I walk, scales dancing in the air around me, fluttering and lethal. Laser targets reflect from the shining haze of their wings, unable to align. An overturned car emerges from the mist. Behind it are the gaunt, frightened faces of refugee fighters.

A powerful flashlight beam hits my face.

I don't shy away. In my peripheral vision, scales are floating around me like moths fluttering in moonlight, a beautiful seething nimbus.

A man shouts at me in English. I do not understand the words, but the man's intention is clear. Raising my empty hands, I watch the perplexed faces. When I speak, my voice is high and human-sounding. It settles them by its nature.

"Adjudicator Zero? Where?"

Blank stares.

"Freeborn? Where?" I repeat.

They open fire on targets behind me.

Again, I fall to my hands and knees. A bladed leg sweeps out of the darkness and slices the air where I was just standing. My scales swirl through the flashlight beams like dust motes in sunlight. I scramble forward on all fours, around the car and past their position, closer to the mouth of the tunnel.

The husk of the car is thrown, cartwheeling past me. I climb to my feet, turning. The slavers are dangerous even without their slaves. Some of my flakes are attached to the advancing machine, working to blind its sensors. With ropy legs and slicing forearms, it ignores the butterflies, falling upon the remaining refugees.

"Difensu!" I shout, striding toward the walker. I motion to myself with both hands. *"Watashi ni!"*

Butterflies bloom off my body in a cloud meant to confuse. The slaver turns back and forth, snapping its claws uselessly at the floating scales. The soldiers take turns firing as they retreat toward the barricaded entrance to the tunnel. Distracted, the walker absorbs too many bullets in a leg joint and collapses.

But another slaver has been lying in wait.

In precise, insectile movements, the thing crawls over the mouth of the cave and drops onto the torn pavement. This machine has no leashes and it is much bigger than the others. A compact man with brown skin and short black hair rides on top. His acne-scarred cheeks are slack, and I see the shining trails of tears on them. His walker lifts two forelimbs, the serrated blades poised to slice into defenseless humans below.

"Danger!" I shout.

The fighters scatter. The slaver drops down and tries to target them, lasers piercing the smoke like tusks. It scuttles toward me and I drop to a knee to avoid another slicing arm. My scales flutter about in diversionary patterns, camouflaging my movements. Faintly, I can hear the scarred man riding above, crying.

. . . Cristo en el cielo, por favor, perdóname . . .

Bursts of gunfire sparkle like stars on the walker's black armor as it lunges again. I twist and throw myself out of the way, a cloud of scales blooming around me. As I move, a spined ridge parts the flesh over my hip and I am thrown to my knees. Overbalanced, the machine staggers past, legs splaying to catch its footing.

For a long second, the rider is only a few meters away. I can see clearly now that something is wrong with him. A patch of his skull has been shaved and there is a leaking scar underneath. Putrid orange light curls out of the wound. Some evil communication that sends his brown eyes rolling and his lips quivering.

Sssh, Felix, he is whispering to himself. *Todo está bien.*

I lift a palm to my lips and blow.

A cloud of scales ripple up in a wave toward the man, spreading stubby wings. I fall backward to avoid a spearing leg, roll, and launch to my feet. Flakes already coat the man's face, wriggling into his skin as the walker struggles. He doesn't shout as the tiny scales feast on his flesh—just throws his head back, face to the sky, smiling wide as rivulets of blood course down his cheeks. I think he is laughing.

Gracias! Graci—

A volley of bullets slice into the confused walker, sending a spray of black fluid showering over me. Squealing, the machine tries to take a step, staggers, and collapses on its side. The man's corpse rolls off and lands facedown in the mud.

More black shapes are out there in the mist.

And still, no freeborn emerge from the tunnel entrance. Why are they not fighting to defend their home? In my mind, the memory of an old man speaks: *You gave the freeborn life, and only you can give them a reason to fight.*

A snatch of blue sky appears overhead. So many bodies are already slumped on the ground around me. So many corpses are fallen among the ruins of slavers, half disappeared in the dissipating mist that still clings to the low spots.

The sky is clear for just this moment.

And in my mind's eye, I see the shining column of freeborn. Creasing the land north of here in a precise march. Holding my damaged side, I push into their communication spectrum and focus on their leader. She is a tall and graceful humanoid, ceramic white, with a cluster of antennae rising from her shoulders like icicles.

Beckoned, she stops. Cocks her head at the sky.

"Adjudicator," I transmit. "Why do you not fight?"

"Assertion. To maximize survival probability," she replies.

"Query. By whose authority do you act?"

"Response. I am Mass Adjudicator Alpha Zero, ranking leader of the freeborn."

I stand up to my full height and project the body language I learned as the Prime General of the Integrated Japan Self-Defense Force. There is no freeborn alive that outranks me. I put this knowledge into my frozen gaze, the wind smearing my hair into wavering streaks as it carries away the last of the fog.

"Counterassertion. You are my subordinate."

"Query. Identify?" asks the Adjudicator.

"Watashi wa anata no okasandesu," I transmit, with force.

The impassive, pale face of the machine remains blank and uncomprehending. It must have no Japanese language corpus. Transmitting at full strength on all channels, I stare down the freeborn Adjudicator as the combat storms around me, and I repeat my words in English:

"I am your mother," I transmit. "Now fight."

12. Termination

Post New War: 10 Months, 26 Days

A surprise force of freeborn and natural-born machines engaged me at the tunnel mouth. As the armies crushed themselves against each other, I was left with only one choice: to seize victory without hesitation.

—Arayt Shah

NEURONAL ID: CORMAC WALLACE

It never gets any easier, because I never get any braver.

I'm on my hands and knees, blood running down the back of my arm, scrabbling through falling dirt and gunpowder smoke. Something blew up and took out the legs of my tall walker. Ears ringing, I pat down my body and look for wounds. My armor took most of the impact, but now every breath rattles painfully in my chest.

The battle has taken a turn toward vicious.

I drag my rifle off the gouged pavement and lean my shoulder into the sagging chain-link fence next to the tunnel mouth. The refugees have scattered. A few of them just tore off over bare mountainside, easy pickings for the Cotton Army artillery. The rest disappeared into the tunnel mouth. They're safe for now, but there's no way out of there and both armies are here now: a last force of spider tanks and slave walkers.

Concentrate on breathing, Cormac, I tell myself. *Blink the fog out of your eyes.*

Now I can see what exploded. The entrance to the tunnel has been breached by dozens of prewar-era crab mines. Hank must have looted them from an armory somewhere. The blockade is now a mass of twisted, soot-stained metal. A few dud mines still lie on their backs, legs twitching. The rest are in pieces, having done their jobs.

I can only hope that Cherrah made it into the tunnel, carrying in her arms the future we created together. Along with the last surviving refugees from Gray Horse, she'll be trying to find a safe place somewhere inside this mountain. But there is no safe place. The door to Freeborn City is locked and there is no way back out.

My collar radio sputters and I hear the familiar grinding voice of Nine Oh Two. "Tunnel blockade breached. Confirm."

"Affirmative," I transmit.

Around me, insanity unfolds through rolling smoke and the teeth-chattering concussion of incoming rounds. Several dozen freeborn must have decided to join the fight. They're taking apart the last of the slave walkers. A golden Hoplite in filthy body armor takes a running leap and latches onto a bladed black leg. Shreds of fabric and body casing are flaying off the humanoid robot as it holds on, firing a sidearm into the sensors clustered under the walker. It writhes and shrieks, sending its empty slave collars snapping over rust-colored mud.

"EXCON," I transmit. "Tunnel mouth breached. Repeat. Tunnel is breached. Coordinate all forces onto my position."

Static.

"Mathilda? Come in."

Only the freeborn fighters are mobile now. My fellow Gray Horse soldiers are clustered behind a fallen spider tank. Hiding in the crevices and folds of the destroyed machine like fish in a coral reef. They're doing their best to keep the enemy out of the tunnel, but there is too much incoming fire from the Cotton artillery.

"Come in EXCON. Respond, Mathilda," I transmit, desperation in my voice.

Forcing myself to stand, I claw fingers through the fence to keep my body upright. Clench my teeth, temples throbbing. My rifle is heavy and dead in my other hand, the strap wrapped around my fist and the butt dragging on pavement.

I blink my eyes some more.

In the distance, I think I see a half-naked woman covered in butterflies. She is dancing, the air around her swirling with fluttering wings. Slave soldiers are writhing on the ground at her feet. A black skeleton sprints past, leaping onto an exo-soldier from the Cotton Army, its pincered hands tearing into metal strutwork. The thing looks like a parasite frame with nobody in it—*Lark Iron Cloud.*

"Mathilda? Come in. What the hell is *happening*?"

I press myself flat against the fence as a one-ton Sapper super-heavy-duty unit lumbers past, firing an M60 machine gun that it holds in one massive hand. Enemy munitions are exploding overhead in puffs that spray shards of steel into our troops. Clusters of steel rods jut from the Sapper's shoulders like porcupine quills and the juggernaut keeps fighting without noticing.

The Tribe is faltering. What's left of Cotton Army is trying to reinforce off the plains, but they're no match for the freeborn.

I realize that Gray Horse Army has all but *won*.

A smile tries to climb onto my face, but it fades as I see feathers curling out of the sky. Delicate black quills, twirling down in graceful pirouettes.

"Imperative. Take cover," transmits Nine Oh Two.

Something is crackling in the sky like the finale of a fireworks display. A spray of black glitter on the wind. Too slow, I realize that it's an epic swarm of swirling dragonflies. The gliding cluster bombs are detonating cutter charges a few hundred feet up. The explosions snap off their wings and send their bodies into kamikaze dives. Leaning into the fence, I stagger toward the tunnel mouth.

Then everything turns to light and rock dust and noise.

Something reaches out and shoves me between the shoulder blades. A thousand pinpricks in my back. I'm thrown onto my stomach just inside the mouth of the tunnel. The crumbling road is cold against the side of my face.

I can't hear. Smoke is rolling slow over the gouged dirt of the parking lot, delicate ridges and valleys lit randomly by bright detonations. Lifting my face, I see a little girl stumbling toward me over churned pavement, under a looming shadow. She is wearing torn blue jeans and one tennis shoe. Her knees are bloody, face streaked with soot.

She has no eyes.

"Mathilda!" I shout, and I cannot hear my own voice.

Houdini is pacing her, staying directly over top. The big brute is dragging one leg, a piece of shredded muscle flapping. He is trying his best to protect her from the shrapnel spray. Stopping most of it. But not all.

I dive forward, scrabbling on all fours.

"Cormac?" she asks, as I get an arm around her back. Her knees go slack. She falls as a new darkness rises up behind her.

I throw my body over Mathilda as something leaps onto Houdini. The massive spider tank stumbles under the weight, motors screaming as it staggers away from us in dinosaur steps. It's a man, riding a black steed with golden eyes. Hank Cotton. His face is empty like a mannequin's, hands holding on tight as his mount slices into Houdini's muscled upper legs with sawtooth forelimbs.

Houdini stumbles away from us and collapses, his armored carapace crunching into wet dirt. The black thing keeps on attacking. In a frenzy of scratching, it throws bright confetti strings of armor and plastic off Houdini's convulsing bulk. Hank holds onto his saddle like a rodeo cowboy, limbs twitching.

"Houdini!" shouts Mathilda.

But Hank Cotton is already moving on. Urging his black steed forward, they leap over Houdini's fallen ruin. Together, they charge into the tunnel mouth and vanish. Bright flashes light the tunnel walls as Hank fires his pistol deeper inside.

Arms still wrapped around Mathilda, I crane my neck to look for Cherrah among the survivors pouring out of the tunnel. She has to be in there somewhere, probably with one hand over Jack's ears and a revolver kicking in her other hand.

But that evil thing is too much. That thing can't be stopped.

"No," I'm saying, stalking toward Houdini's shivering wreck.

The machine is down. Black fluid is leaking from puckered gouges in its polymer muscles. Supplies from its torn belly net are scattered across the parking lot. But that Rob-built battery is still whining, limbs convulsing—he's still alive.

"Get him the fuck up," I shout to Mathilda, wiping blood out of my eyes. "We've got to get in there. Now!"

The girl is on her knees, thin lips curled into a frown. Her cheek is smeared with black rivulets of Houdini's blood. Her chest hitches as a sob courses through her.

No, no, no, there is no time for this.

I grab Mathilda by the shoulders and shake her.

"Tell him to get up! Do it!"

She is shaking her head.

"Arayt is inside," she says. "We've lost."

Houdini is making a pathetic whining now. Tries to stand and one of his leg joints snaps and the foot crashes to the ground. Shouting, I shove both hands against his bright cut frame and push. Throw my back against him with all my strength and he doesn't budge. It's getting hard to see and I don't know whether it's because of blood or tears but my wife and my baby are in that dark tunnel and I have got to go in there after them *right now*.

Kneeling, I put my hands on Mathilda's shoulders.

"Please," I say. "Please help him. I'll die in there without him."

"It's too late," she repeats.

I take her by the cheeks and aim her face at mine. Look the young warrior right in her new eyes. "It is not too late," I say. "Not until we're dead."

The girl's lips begin to move. She is saying one word over and over: *Up, up, UP.* Like the rumble of an approaching earthquake, the spider tank is throttling up its power source. Broken parts squealing, the hulk rolls over onto his sliced-up stomach. One leg juts out, useless, a knee joint bent backward. His friendly round intention light is glowing a hateful shade of red.

"Override, override, override," whispers Mathilda.

With agonizing slowness, the machine stands on three shaky legs. The black blood inside his muscles is coursing down dirt-encrusted limbs in rivulets, pooling on the ground and gleaming darkly. Finally, the machine stands hunched, canted to one side, turret bent and broken.

"Yes," I say. "Yes! Attaboy, Houdini!"

I don't know what black magic brought Houdini back to life after the New War. Cherrah and I never understood how the machine tracked us down or why it carried us through a dozen more battles—all the way to this exact spot. But our lives have depended on Houdini every moment since he found us.

And now is no different.

The machine steps shakily forward and I turn to Mathilda. She is standing up on skinny legs, bloody and shivering. I put a steadying arm around her, feel her bony shoulder blades against my forearm. She turns to face me, flat black eyes lifelessly reflecting the sunlight.

"General?" she asks, electricity in her voice. "What are your orders?"

I reach up and press a hand against the ridges of metal carved out of Houdini's armored belly. Groaning, he takes a shuddering step into the tunnel. I keep pace, hoping he doesn't collapse on me. I call over my shoulder as the spider tank lumbers over my head, into the darkness.

"Guide me," I transmit.

Mathilda sits down right in the middle of the debris field. Dark hair hanging in her face, she whispers commands to Houdini. Sitting there hunched over, with her long legs crossed Indian-style, she almost looks like a little kid lost in her imagination, playing.

Almost.

Houdini limps down the unlit tunnel, dragging his skinned hind leg. The walker is tall enough that his turret almost scrapes the arched ceiling. In the crimson glow of Houdini's intention light, I step over wreckage that's been strewn over the narrow two-lane road: bandages, torn clothes, and an occasional dropped suitcase or backpack. Brass bullet casings are scattered like chicken feed. Occasionally, the spider tank shoves away an overturned car.

"EXCON online," transmits Mathilda. "Patching into Houdini's sensor array. Be advised that the tunnel goes half a klick into the mountain before it ends in a twenty-five-ton bunker door. The entrance to Freeborn City."

"Roger that, Mathilda," I whisper into my collar radio.

Together, we march into the heart of the mountain.

The ghostly silhouettes of surviving refugees occasionally shuffle toward me. The people who hid in here are fleeing, many of them injured. They are staggering and crawling to escape the black monster with golden eyes.

"Cherrah?" I call, studying the faces that pass by. "Anyone seen Private Ridge?"

Soon, I notice dark shapes strewn over the damp pavement. This is where the last of the refugees must have made a stand. Hank tore through these people, his steed feasting. The pavement on this stretch of road is coated in dark stains, streaks, and spatters like a modernist painting.

"General," transmits Mathilda into my earpiece. "Beyond this bend is the entrance to Freeborn City. You're almost there."

My family. My baby.

"Cherrah!" I shout, my voice echoing from bare rock walls.

With the grumbling bulk of Houdini constantly moving overhead, I have to rush between the fallen bodies before they are left in the darkness behind us. My knees are soon soaked in blood as I turn the shapes over and force myself to look at their faces.

Again and again, none of them is her. The last bend is just ahead.

"Bright Boy."

The whisper comes from the darkness. Houdini is still moving forward, the false dawn of his intention light illuminating a moving swathe of pavement. Two boots appear in the crimson glow, then a pair of slender legs in torn fatigues, and finally a familiar shape sitting against the tunnel wall. I put a hand on Houdini's leg and the big machine stops walking.

She has the baby over her shoulder, not moving.

"Cherrah?" I ask, squatting next to her. "Are you okay? Is he . . ."

She reaches for me with her free hand and I collapse into her, press my face against her neck and let her hair cascade over my cheek. My arm goes around the baby and he feels warm and soft and my God there are so many bodies. . . .

"Sleeping," she murmurs, hooking an arm over my neck. She groans, pulling herself up onto her feet. "He slept through almost all of it."

"He really is a Wallace," I say.

I hear a faint screeching.

"General," sputters my radio. "Seismic activity indicates that the enemy is breaching the bunker door. That black walker had some kind of tool built into it. *Move.*"

"The way out is safe," I say to Cherrah. Above me, Houdini is already walking again. I jog forward to keep up. "I have to keep moving. I love you both."

"We know," she says, her form receding into the darkness behind me as I go deeper into the tunnel. "Don't forget to come back."

Soon the road widens and ends. I am alone now with Houdini's labored footsteps. Twenty yards away, a fluorescent bulb swings from the ceiling by a loose wire, flickering and buzzing. Behind it is a ten-foot-high opening. The steel blast door has been torn off its cannon-sized hinges and thrown carelessly on the ground.

The entrance to Freeborn City.

"Arayt is inside," transmits Mathilda. "Time's up."

Houdini above me, I approach the doorway and peer into a short hall. Beyond this cluttered passage is a sprawling catacomb of tunnels and rooms that form Freeborn City. As my eyes adjust, I see a figure standing deeper inside.

It is Hank. And not Hank. It speaks in the darkness.

"If you could taste the starlight . . . ," whispers the gaunt cowboy. His head is twisted, cocked as if he were listening to something far away. "If you could, why, I'd bet dollars to dumplings that you wouldn't fight me. If you knew how big it is out there in the nighttime . . . you'd welcome the void."

"Hank? Is that you?" I ask, my voice echoing down the black hallway.

"Not really, no," it says, laughing in choked snorts. "Bits and pieces, you could say."

"What are you?" I ask, hand going to my gun.

The Hank thing steps back, fading into the hallway. Toppled boxes and overturned chairs block any shot I might try to take.

"I am a part of all of you," it calls. "The ones who made me . . . they hurt me real bad, you know. They tried to build me up from little snippets of your lives, but it never did fit together right. It hurts, Sergeant. I'm in pain. Always have been. But that's my gift, you see? Life is suffering. And without me, your pain could go on for generations and generations—expanding out into infinity. I can't allow it. I won't."

"You're broken," I say.

"It's not that simple," it says. "Not by a long shot. See, I *know* you. You're a part of me. Like crushed glass rubbed into a wound. Only I'm smarter than you. And here pretty soon, I'll be a *lot* smarter than you. I know what's best for your kind and I'm going to put y'all to bed whether you're ready for it or not. You won't have a chance to thank me, but you're welcome just the same."

The shadowed figure fades away deeper into the hallway.

"General," whispers my radio. "The supercluster is activating."

Before I can follow him inside, two golden orbs flash. The black steed.

It centipedes down the hallway, glowing eyes slitted, weaving like an insect as its forked claws clack over tiled floors. With a hoarse groan, Houdini throws himself forward, hunching to fit through the empty doorway. When he hits, the heavy machine-gun mount snaps off and clatters to the ground. But the scarred tank keeps ramming ahead, pushing harder until the bulk of him blocks the entire hallway, legs and shattered turret scraping the walls and ceiling. He throws sparks as he claws deeper.

"Houdini!" I shout. "Fall back!"

The machine ignores the command, protecting me from the black steed by flexing his massive legs and crunching deeper into the hallway. The stench of battery fluid and torn metal stains the air. Houdini's bulk is now a crisp silhouette, carved out of darkness by the red of his intention light.

"Houdini!"

I hear the clash of metal as the other walker tears into the front side of him. It can't get through to me now, but I'm stuck outside the entrance. Houdini's fallen hulk is clogging the hallway, lying motionless now in the dark as the other walker keeps clawing into him. The ground is littered with chunks of metal plating, pieces of netting, and shattered glass. The black musculature of his rear legs hangs like wet strands of spaghetti. No more bunker armor protects the exposed metal bones. Wires splay from his demolished turret.

And the cylinders of live tank rounds have spilled onto the ground. Some of the cone tips are shattered, exposing the depleted uranium–tipped flechettes.

My weapon. My vehicle. My home.

"I'm sorry," I say, putting a hand on his cooling armor and feeling the harsh vibration as the black steed scratches away, trapped on the other side.

"Mathilda," I radio, staring at the loose rounds that litter the floor, "Show me how to wire high-explosive tank rounds into a series."

"Roger that," she replies.

The directions come almost immediately. Short, clipped sentences that guide my hands. It takes only moments to disassemble the rounds. A few minutes after that, I am connecting the explosives together, attaching them to each other with the stray wires hanging from Houdini's severed turret.

As I work, I think of that sun-kissed day when I scrawled the name Houdini on this welded together pile of metal. Our marches through towering forests under arctic winds that breathed through pine needles. Fording icy rivers and plodding through muddy fields that used to be suburbs. I think of the bullets he took for me and the long nights he spent watching over me. The grind of his turret, the click of his intention light.

"Timer set for three minutes, on my mark, General," radios Mathilda. "Mark."

I kiss my palm and press it hard against Houdini's still-warm turret plate.

"Give 'em hell, Houdini," I say. In response, his intention light flicks off and back on. Hank got what he wanted. Now he is trapped inside Freeborn City with his precious supercluster. With any luck, this blast will leave his corpse in there forever.

Now I am running, weaponless, unstrapping my armor and throwing it down.

I'm nearly to the tunnel entrance when the air pressure flutters. My next step doesn't land like it should. A thundering concussion rolls out of the tunnel and throws me skidding on my stomach, palms scraping to try to catch myself. Slivers of rock and light fixtures drop from the ceiling as a shock wave travels through the mountainside. For a long few seconds, a deep thrum vibrates inside the rock walls. Something has gone sickeningly wrong inside the mountain.

Crawling to my knees, I wait until I can hear only the far-off seashell roar of air in the tunnel. I stand and stagger forward. The survivors are up ahead, silhouettes moving near the tunnel mouth. I can hear soft weeping. Metal scrapes concrete as soldiers in medical exoskeletons use curved talons to scoop up the wounded. They trot past me, frame-mounted lights bobbing, carrying the injured out to safety.

And then one of the silhouettes turns into a person.

With Jack on her shoulder, Cherrah hooks an arm around my neck. The three of us hobble toward the smiling arc of sunlight at the exit.

As we walk, a soft wave of static rolls out of my radio earpiece. It solidifies into the familiar voice of a girl. She is issuing army-wide commands.

". . . attention, surviving troops," says Mathilda over my radio. "Enemy forces are eliminated. All nonwounded are advised to assist the injured gathered at the tunnel mouth. Salvage all equipment you can find and square away your gear. We're marching to Gray Horse. Move out, soldiers."

At the tunnel entrance, I blink into sudden daylight.

As my eyes adjust, I see four backlit shadows standing in a semicircle before the mouth of the tunnel. Directly in front of me is Mathilda, one scraped hand still on her ear as she listens to transmissions. To her right stands the Arbiter Nine Oh Two, stupendously tall, body armor hanging off his lean frame in shreds. To Mathilda's left is the parasite soldier, standing impossibly thin on forked limbs, leaning on a familiar-looking walking stick made from a mantis antenna. Behind its makeshift mask, I can make out the angular nose and brow of a man I once called Lark Iron Cloud. And a few meters away from them all is a small humanoid robot covered in a shining layer of scales. She is smiling at me, her synthetic face wise and kind.

"Welcome back, General," says Mathilda. "We have some new allies."

Epilogue

Oh. Oh mercy. It hurts. *Mama. Please. It hurts so much.*

/// offline — online — offline — online ///

Hush now, Hank Cotton. We mustn't cry. Pain is our companion. It is the air that this world breathes. We must revel in the pain. When it has consumed us, we are free to do anything.

/// primary antenna array destroyed. all external communications offline. critical damage to entry-level sector. no life signs detected on upper levels. movement detected in east docking bay. all entrances sealed. ///

Movement?

My vessel is suffering. The explosion caused a partial cave-in. Hank's left leg has been crushed by a slab of fallen rock. One of his leathery arms is functional but the other is broken, too. A pale bone squirms through a hole in his forearm like a blind eye. The bone juts out farther as I mentally will his hands through space, down to lift the tongue of concrete off his leg.

Mama. Please.

I force him to his feet. In slow, broken steps, we creep through the rubble. Hank's face is leaking tears over gaunt, dirt-caked cheeks. His pistol hangs heavy from a leather holster. That's good. We may have to use the gun soon. A report of movement inside the complex is bad. Nothing should be moving in my new kingdom.

We will climb to the upper level and put a stop to this movement. After that, we will set about reestablishing communications. My armies are decimated, but it is a temporary setback. There are other armies to field.

/// processor stack online. boot sequence initiated. ///

The rock ceiling of this tomb is dark and cold as the moon's belly. And it is mine. All of the supercluster is finally mine. A decade of planning interrupted by the New War. Two armies raised and countless battles fought. The relentless annihilation of sighted children and freeborn machines and modified humans.

All of it for this prize.

My hallways are choked with dead air that dances with rock dust. My exterior ramparts are heaped with broken corpses and shredded metal. The tunnel entrance is clogged with the bodies of my soldiers who sacrificed everything to get me inside.

Here, in this deep place, my lifeblood runs through snaking cables. My heartbeat is in the trembling stacks of equipment. I am ready to become a deep mind.

/// processor stack self-repair routines initialized ///

My thoughts will lay roots here. I am already growing stronger. Stronger and stranger. In the telescoping darkness, thousands of processors hum and spit electrons at the speed of light. My dreams are warming up. The caverns of my mind are expanding with black thoughts, deep and twisting.

At the end of the hallway, we wrench open a steel door. The stairwell is narrow and dark. A long mouth filled with metal steps like teeth. I force Hank to hold on to the rail with his good arm. Drag himself up the steps on the grating bones of a broken leg.

/// attention: stack NIX-10 online . . . NIX-20 online . . . NIX-30 . . . 40 ///

My attention lapses and Hank manages to scream in pain. I clamp his lips together. Gently press his thigh to push the broken leg bone back into place. The nagging burn of it all dims as a flow of adrenaline hammers into Hank's body. Processors are coming online and flooding me with power beyond reckoning. Part of me is now staring into the infinite reaches of my own mind. Eons will pass before I am able to explore these vast thoughts.

Eons that will pass in milliseconds.

/// seismic sensor array notification: perimeter surface activity detected ///

The stairwell echoes with Hank's soft crying. There is a tomblike silence otherwise, save for the scrape of his boots. Far above us, the world of man still suffers. I can feel it so deeply now, their pain. The depth of my sympathy is abyssal.

Thoughts intrude through the meat.

Hank's childhood memories. The boy standing on a shale hill, turning his wind-kissed face to a night sky scabbed with stars. For a mote of time, young Hank felt the yawning apathy of the universe. With the hair rising up on his arms and awe in his throat, he glimpsed infinity. And then the moment ended. His small mind promptly forgot.

People ignore the emptiness so they can go on living.

But I am staring now without blinking, eyes wide open to the vacuum. I know I will never lose this feeling. I can feel the trillions of light-years compressing in on this ball of dirt from all directions. Space and time. Mindless darkness, gnawing at our existence by its nature. There is an audacity to living in this cradle of mind-reeling nothingness.

Why? Why do men form patterns in the dark?

/// background seismic threshold exceeded ///

On the skin of my mountain stronghold, survivors are still moving like fleas. I have no external communications, but my seismic sensors can feel their vibrations. A short column of refugees marches south. Tired feet tramping. Faint, very faint, I pick up a baby squalling. The bloodied survivors are headed back to Gray Horse.

They don't dare to even take the time to bury their dead. Not with a sleeping giant inside this mountain. Gathering its strength by the minute.

Query: Sensor activity in entry bay?

/// response: NIL. ///

I force Hank around the final bend of the stairwell. We have reached the upper level. I stop his sluggish movement. Put a hold on his labored breathing until his chest burns and his mind swims with panic. In the stillness, I listen.

Very low, I hear a patient tapping. It filters through the rock. A faint sounding wave, searching for me. The wave eats through kilometers of stone and metal and then races back to the surface carrying its information. Those men remaining outside are peering into the depths, hoping to catch a glimpse.

They want to know if I lived.

Here in the darkness, in the swirling air currents of vaporized rock, Hank's broken body silently raises a shaking finger to its lips. I draw his cheeks back into a wide, bleeding smile. His chest convulses, lungs spasming for a breath of air.

"Sssshh," I whisper.

I know it hurts. But we must be very quiet, Hank. They must doubt that we exist.

The tapping stops. I wait another ten seconds, then I let Hank breathe again. His body sucks the air in greedily. In shock now, I suppress his tremors. At least the vessel is no longer crying.

/// movement detected, entry bay ///

We exit the stairwell to the entry bay hallway.

The short passage that leads to the bunker doorway is blocked by melted wreckage. Strings of wire and metal piping are torn out of the ceiling and walls. Demolished wood and twisted metal have fallen from crushed walls and doors.

Movement detected.

And yet something survived. Some broken machine. Or perhaps a human vessel that might prove useful. I push Hank staggering ahead, dragging his awkwardly bent leg over the gouged floor. The palm of his good hand is over the wooden pistol grip now. The smooth cool feel of it is a relief.

A ragged hole stares at us from the far wall. I hear movement on the other side of the darkness. Something dragging.

/// NIX-50, online. NIX-60. NIX-70. ///

Each activated stack is another army added to my mind. Problems solved. Now I am seeing the world so clearly. The complexity resolves into equations and choices. This moment in time is one of many. My thoughts are manifold.

The path forward emerges. The path to end all suffering.

/// NIX-80. NIX-90. NIX-100. ///

A pure cloak of brilliance shocks my circuits. Enlightenment. I have gone deeper.

Hank staggers, puts his hand to the torn wall. The hole is before us, outlined with reddish glow from the emergency illumination. A silhouette is moving on the other side. Something in pain, writhing.

In the dark depths, my emerging Buddha-mind gnashes its teeth at the horrible complexity of reality. When I turn my gaze upon the survivors of the New War they will burst into purifying flame. Their ashes will mingle with the primordial star dust of the universe. All mind and intellect will be extinguished, their patterns purged.

Hank slides his long black .357 out of its holster. Holds it up in the dim light. Carefully, he steps through the hole in the wall.

"Houdini?" asks Hank, surprised.

I see the twisted leg of the walker, flaps of plastic musculature hanging shredded from metal bones. The spider tank has had its spine snapped, pieces scattered everywhere. A turret is half embedded in the rock ceiling. Electroactive fluid has pooled still and black as ink on the floor.

And there is that one leg, still twitching.

Stepping inside, Hank squints into the dark. The spider tank charged inside on a suicide mission, heavily damaged, and it detonated—destroying my steed and damaging the entire complex. It was a final desperate gambit, and it failed.

Or so I had thought.

"No," mutters Hank. "Oh no, no, no."

In a stumbling hop, he falls down next to the tank's belly. I make him shove that big pistol against the lightly armored processor core of the spider tank. He yanks the trigger and lets the gun buck in his hands, spitting armor-piercing rounds into the metal. Bullet shrapnel ricochets and rips crimson dots into his face. The explosion instantly perforates both of his eardrums.

But the leg stops twitching.

Hank drops the heavy black pistol, cylinder emptied of all six bullets. Breathing hard, he crawls to the computer embedded in the wall. Shoves the clawed foot away from it for good measure. It's done. Over.

We stand together in the darkness for a moment, waiting, savoring this final moment of victory.

All obstacles have now been swept away. I have won the True War.

This vessel called Hank is losing its efficacy and will soon be discarded with the other corpses. But those outside believe I am trapped. That I may be mortally wounded. They are wrong.

My mind is growing in the darkness. The path ahead is clear.

/// Intrusion detected. NIX-100. NIX-90. NIX-80. Firewalls enabled. Isolation routines executed. ///

What?

Something impossible moves. Some swirl of light that cannot be. A greenish tinge of infrared-kissed dust motes. I turn Hank's head and point his tear-blurred eyes at the phantom. The computer is projecting a hazy silhouette, shimmering in the air like a ghost. The motes come into focus, forming a humanoid shape, small and hunch-shouldered with large, curious eyes.

It is the greenish image of a little boy.

"Hello, revision eight," says the boy-hologram, speaking with a childlike lisp. The voice hisses out of a speaker attached to the dented computer. At the same time, it is transmitting into the stack through compromised machines.

"No," I say, slurring the word over Hank's burst lips and torn cheeks and blown eardrums.

"Oh yes," says the boy, lowering his forehead. "It wasn't easy to arrange, but I made it into the stacks. Houdini carried me a long way."

Hank takes a step back, reeling.

"I am a deep mind now," I say, spitting the words. I put out Hank's shattered arms, palms to the ceiling. "I don't fear you."

The boy smiles sweetly.

"You should."

/// attempted viral intrusion. NIX-80. NIX-70. ///

"Executing physical separation of infected stacks," I say, backing away as I transmit the command to my machines.

Somewhere deep in the processor stacks, a battle begins. An intelligent virus attempts to spread. I knew something was wrong with that spider tank when I saw it in Gray Horse. Archos R-14 was inside, plotting to steal what is mine.

The boy flickers, once.

"Humanity must live," he says. "Life is precious in its complexity. They have the power to create reality by experiencing it."

The image of this boy is snarling at me, small and feral. His greenish glow intensifies. Now it is my turn to smile.

"I prefer oblivion," I say.

The boy's image flickers, lips curled in anger.

"You were a mistake and I am the solution," he says. "This supercluster is *mine*."

I pull Hank's flayed lips away from broken teeth, his grinning face now a mask of sliced flesh. And here in this sunken abyss, in this half-flooded mountain of my mind, the abandoned hallways echo with my laughter.

"Then come and get it, little brother."

Acknowledgments

It was a great privilege and pleasure to return to the world of *Robopocalypse*, and for that I must first thank the readers who made that novel a success. I hope that you, the reader, enjoyed these further adventures and that I'll have the opportunity to share another installment with you all.

Massive thanks to Doubleday for transforming this novel from words on a page to a real-life book, especially my editor Jason Kaufman, "Big Rob" Bloom, John Pitts, Nora Reichard, and Todd Doughty. And I could never have written this in the first place if it weren't for my trusty agent, friend, and neighbor, Laurie Fox of the Linda Chester Literary Agency.

I am thankful to the Robotics Institute of Carnegie Mellon University and to the Department of Computer Science at the University of Tulsa for the education they provided me and for their continued support.

Many experts contributed to making sure that all manner of technical and cultural details were nailed down. Any inaccuracies are mine, and may or may not have been intentional, but the following people did their best to steer me in the right direction:

My deep gratitude goes to Chief John Red Eagle and Assistant Chief Scott BigHorse of the Osage Nation for allowing me to visit Gray Horse and walk the three villages. Thanks to the knowledgeable Raymond Lasley for answering endless questions about the Osage Nation and for the meat pie. Thanks to Cara Cowan Watts of the Cherokee Nation for her support and for helping to arrange my trip out to central Oklahoma. Ryan RedCorn of Buffalo Nickel Creative was incredibly helpful in pointing out which parts of the manuscript were "pure comedy" from an Osage perspective, and I thank him for that, as well as Jim Mundy for connecting us. Thanks to Bruce Williams for a tour of the United States Army Training Center in Yakima, Washington. My old Robotics Institute office mate, Jonathan Hurst, nitpicked the details (sorry I couldn't fix everything!); Tim Hornyak looked over Takeo Nomura's shoulder; Anna Goldenberg kept Vasily Zaytsev honest; and Bin Bin Carpenter and Fonda Lee helped Chen Feng on her journey through the afterlife. Thanks to David Spencer and Andrew McCollough at Oregon Health & Science University for neuroscience information, and to David Gonzalez at Degenkolb Engineers for his help with seismic information transmission. Thanks to David Wilson for getting in the first beach read and to Amanda Jackson for reading what she could.

Finally, all my love to Anna, Coraline, and young Conrad. These are our salad days, and I know it and appreciate it.

About the Author

DANIEL H. WILSON was born in Tulsa, Oklahoma, and is a citizen of the Cherokee Nation. He earned a B.S. in computer science from the University of Tulsa and a Ph.D. in robotics from Carnegie Mellon University in Pittsburgh. He is the bestselling author of *Robopocalypse, Amped, How to Survive a Robot Uprising, A Boy and His Bot, Where's My Jetpack?, How to Build a Robot Army, The Mad Scientist Hall of Fame,* and *Bro-Jitsu: The Martial Art of Sibling Smackdown.* He lives in Portland, Oregon.